ROYAL STREET
REVEILLON

Reviewers Love the Scotty Bradley Series

Advance Praise for *Royal Street Reveillon*

"Herren's wit, ingenuity, and sharp social eye are a constant delight, and every time I read him I fall in love with New Orleans all over again. Scotty may have hung up his go-go boots, but I hope his adventures go on and on."—Alex Marwood, Edgar and Macavity Award–winning author of *The Wicked Girls* and *The Darkest Secret*

"A delicious, witty, deftly plotted mystery. Greg Herren offers up a compulsively readable tale."—Megan Abbott, Edgar-winning author of *Queenpin* and *Dare Me*

"[A] witty, engrossing slice of New Orleans life (and death)…delicious bits of gossip and hints of hushed-up scandal…wry observations about old money in the new New Orleans…a plot full of lively characters and satisfying twists."—Lia Matera, author of the Willa Jansson and Laura Di Palma series

Baton Rouge Bingo

"I very much enjoyed this book. I love the way Mr. Herren writes, and the humor that he pops into the story from time to time…It is a pure and simple mystery, and I loved it…I recommend this book to anyone liking a good mystery with gay MCs."—*Love Bytes: Same Sex Book Reviews*

Lambda Literary Award Finalist *Vieux Carré Voodoo*

"Herren's packed plot, as always in this imaginative series... revels in odd twists and comic turns; for example, the third man of the ménage returns, revealed as a James Bond type. It all makes for a roller-coaster caper."—Richard Labonte, *Book Marks*

"This novel confirms that out of the many New Orleans mystery writers, Greg Herren is indeed one to watch." — *Reviewing the Evidence*

"[T]his was well worth waiting for. Herren has a knack for developing colorful primary and supporting characters the reader actually cares about, and involving them in realistic, though extreme, situations that make his books riveting to the mystery purist. Bravo, and five gumbo-stained stars out of five."—*Echo Magazine*

"Herren's work is drenched in the essence of the Big Easy, the city's geography even playing a large part in the solution of a riddle at whose end lies the aforementioned Eye of Kali. But unlike the city, it is not languid. Herren hits the ground running and only lets up for two extremely interesting dream sequences, the latter of which is truly chilling. Is this a breezy beach read? Maybe, but it has far more substance than many. You can spend a few sunny, sandy afternoons with this resting on your chest and still feel as if you've read a book. But even if you're not at the beach, Herren's work makes great backyard or rooftop reading, and this one is a terrific place to start."—*Out In Print*

Praise for Greg Herren

Sleeping Angel "will probably be put on the young adult (YA) shelf, but the fact is that it's a cracking good mystery that general readers will enjoy as well. It just happens to be about teens...A unique viewpoint, a solid mystery and good characterization all conspire to make *Sleeping Angel* a welcome addition to any shelf, no matter where the bookstores stock it."—Jerry Wheeler, *Out in Print*

"This fast-paced mystery is skillfully crafted. Red herrings abound and will keep readers on their toes until the very end. Before the accident, few readers would care about Eric, but his loss of memory gives him a chance to experience dramatic growth, and the end result is a sympathetic character embroiled in a dangerous quest for truth."—*VOYA*

"Herren, a loyal New Orleans resident, paints a brilliant portrait of the recovering city, including insights into its tight-knit gay community. This latest installment in a powerful series is sure to delight old fans and attract new ones."—*Publishers Weekly*

"Fast-moving and entertaining, evoking the Quarter and its gay scene in a sweet, funny, action-packed way."—*New Orleans Times-Picayune*

"Herren does a fine job of moving the story along, deftly juggling the murder investigation and the intricate relationships while maintaining several running subjects."—*Echo Magazine*

"An entertaining read."—*OutSmart Magazine*

"A pleasant addition to your beach bag."—*Bay Windows*

"Greg Herren gives readers a tantalizing glimpse of New Orleans." —*The Midwest Book Review*

"Herren's characters, dialogue and setting make the book seem absolutely real."—*The Houston Voice*

"So much fun it should be thrown from Mardi Gras floats!"—*New Orleans Times-Picayune*

"Greg Herren just keeps getting better."—*Lambda Book Report*

By the Author

The Scotty Bradley Adventures

Bourbon Street Blues

Jackson Square Jazz

Mardi Gras Mambo

Vieux Carré Voodoo

Who Dat Whodunnit

Baton Rouge Bingo

Garden District Gothic

Royal Street Reveillon

The Chanse MacLeod Mysteries

Murder in the Rue Dauphine

Murder in the Rue St. Ann

Murder in the Rue Chartres

Murder in the Rue Ursulines

Murder in the Garden District

Murder in the Irish Channel

Murder in the Arts District

Young Adult

Sleeping Angel

Sara

Lake Thirteen

New Adult

Timothy

The Orion Mask

Dark Tide

Survivor's Guilt and Other Stories

Going Down for the Count
(Writing as Cage Thunder)

Wicked Frat Boy Ways
(Writing as Todd Gregory)

Edited with J.M. Redmann

Women of the Mean Streets: Lesbian Noir

Men of the Mean Streets: Gay Noir

Night Shadows: Queer Horror

Edited as Todd Gregory

Rough Trade

Sweat

Anything for a Dollar

Blood Sacraments

Visit us at www.boldstrokesbooks.com

ROYAL STREET REVEILLON

by
Greg Herren

2019

CREDITS
EDITOR: STACIA SEAMAN
PRODUCTION DESIGN: STACIA SEAMAN
COVER DESIGN BY TAMMY SEIDICK

Acknowledgments

As always, I have a ridiculous number of people to thank for a ridiculous number of things.

First off, I need to thank Jacob Rickoll for sharing with me his experience with actually getting shot. One of the kindest and most generous people I know, he took a bullet trying to stop a robbery in a bar in the wee hours of a New Orleans Saturday morning...and then came to work straight from the emergency room.

I need to thank Paul, for always being patient, understanding, and kind...and understanding the necessity of making me laugh at myself whenever I need to—which sometimes can be a daily lesson.

I have an amazing friend group who teach me about life and love and joy on a daily basis, so I can never thank Pat Brady, Michael Ledet, Jesse Ledet, Michael Carruth, John Angelico, Harriet Campbell Young, Mark Richards, Konstantin Smorodnikov, Jean Redmann, Gillian Rodger, Michele Karlsberg, Rob Byrnes, Becky Cochrane, Timothy J. Lambert, McKenna Jordan, John McDougall, Bev and Butch Marshall, Carsen Taite, Nell Stark, Trinity Tam, Steve Driscoll, Rob Tocci, Stuart Wamsley, Brian Lord, Susan Larson, Martin Strickland, Meghan Davidson, Robin Pierce, Cullen Hunter, Erin Mitchell, Mark Drake, Josh Fegley, Ryan McNeeley, Serena Mackesy, Richard and Laurie Stepanski, Janna Sill, Sally Anderson, Dawn Lobaugh Edwards, Karen Bengtsen, Mike Smid, and so many others I cannot even begin to remember them all.

At work, I need to thank Allison Dejan, Ashton George III, Leon Harrison, Fernando Cruz, Bryson Richard, Nick Payne, James Husband, Joey Olson, Katie Connor, and everyone else who is a part of the Crescent Care team.

Everyone at Bold Strokes, from Radclyffe to Sandy Lowe to Stacia Seaman to Ruth Sternglantz to Cindy Cresap for being so awesome at what they do.

The FL's—well, JOVANI. That's all I have to say to you bitches.

And of course, that bitch Michael Thomas Ford, for always being there to commiserate about this insane business we find ourselves in.

This is for all the librarians,
who cherish and protect the written word

"There are witches in the Garden District."
   Anne Rice, *The Witching Hour*

"The Medusas are spawned by the bitches. You want to know the truth behind this gossip? Or would you rather believe a pack of malicious inventions?"
   Tennessee Williams, *The Milk Train Doesn't Stop Here Anymore*

"Don't be all, like, uncool."
   Countess Luann De Lesseps, *Real Housewives of New York*

PROLOGUE

New Orleans, match to my flame, flame of my soul. My sin, my passion, my confession. New Or-lins: the tongue trampolining up to the roof of the mouth then down before bouncing back up again. New. Or. Lins.

She is just New Orleans in the mornings when the mist rises like ghosts from the river. She is the Big Easy to musicians, N'Awlins to tourists trying to go native, *home* to the locals. She was Nouvelle Orleans to the French, Nueva Orleans to the Spanish, Nuovi Orlini to the Italian immigrants, Nua Orleans to the Irish.

For many years film and television producers called her Hollywood South.

But in my heart, she is always simply New Orleans, my home. A magical place like no other, nestled in curves created by the wanderings of the father of waters. She is surrounded by water, connected to the mainland by bridges and a ferry across the river. A mystical island of sorts where what rules there are differ vastly from those elsewhere and are rarely enforced; where the words *last call* are never called out, where anything worth doing is also worth doing to excess, where Piety and Desire have been a block apart for hundreds of years.

She resists yet welcomes change, encourages people to be themselves, and never judges; celebrates and embraces eccentricity.

To know her is to love her, despite the daily frustrations of blinking traffic lights and deep potholes that can swallow cars whole, the herds of stray cats and the swarms of Formosan termites in the spring, where school board money disappears without a trace and frequent street flooding and snarled traffic from unexpected parades and second lines are all just a part of the fabric of life. Once you've lived in New Orleans, everywhere else seems tame, bland, colorless, the same as everywhere else.

New Orleans decays and crumbles and collapses, yet always rises to meet the latest challenge and will never surrender, will never bow because, as the song says, "we don't know how."

New Orleans shouldn't exist, yet somehow does, her head high and arms wide open to welcome visitors and tourists and explorers, bachelor parties and fraternity trips and conferences.

And newcomers, seduced by her charms and wiles.

After the Flood Caused By the Failure of the Federally Built and Maintained Levee System, written off for dead, she rose from the ashes, for if New Orleans didn't exist, someone would have to create her.

We need New Orleans, and always have.

The flood of newcomers after the flood waters receded was welcomed but watched with a raised eyebrow. The newcomers brought change in their wake, and New Orleans has always been slow to accommodate change. Working-class neighborhoods were rebuilt, only to become short-term rentals rather than homes. New construction went up everywhere—luxury condos here, a new University Medical Center complex there, grocery stores and restaurants and gas stations. There were concerns that the charm was being lost, but can one really complain about the Costco? The revitalization of the Carrollton corridor? The rebirth of the Central Business District, and the Marigny and Bywater neighborhoods?

But rents and property values rose.

Nothing says *gentrification* more than bathhouses being turned into luxury condos.

I do miss those bathhouses.

But the city was changing *before* that fateful flood. K&B had already been replaced by CVS, Maison Blanche bought out by Dillard's, and Starbucks had opened a couple of stores. But we were all so busy putting our lives and homes back together it seemed like one morning we woke up and the city wasn't quite the same place we remembered. The new Rampart streetcar line, new hotels on Canal and in the CBD, Sewell Cadillac became a Rouse's Grocery, Mary's Tru Value left Bourbon Street for the newly repaved Rampart.

So much has changed it's hard to remember what changed before the flood, and what changed after.

And…I'm not getting any younger, and my memory isn't what it used to be.

Although I've yet to find a gray pubic hair. The Goddess has thus far spared me that horror.

I am that rarest of rarities in the newest and latest iteration of our beloved city: an actual native. There was a time, not all that long ago, when someone who'd lived here for twenty years would be sniffed at, airily dismissed, waved away, as a *parvenu*. In those antediluvian times you could live here most of your life, but someone would surely say at your funeral, if you weren't born here, "I'll miss him, he was a great guy…for a *parvenu*."

My name is Milton Bradley, but everyone calls me Scotty. I suppose most people would say I lead a strange existence, which would be true if I were anything other than a born-and-bred New Orleanian. I lead a charmed life—money on both sides of the family, grew up in the French Quarter, and have been involved in a long-term relationship with not one but two incredibly great guys who are also incredibly hot and sexy. (For the record—and you know you were wondering—the sex is *amazing*.)

Although there are times when I question the *charmed* thing. I have a bad habit of stumbling over dead bodies and running afoul of criminal conspiracies, with a tendency to get kidnapped by bad guys now and then.

It's a long story, but I have a tendency to be in the wrong place at the wrong time a lot more regularly than most.

I don't think I was ever destined to have a normal life, to be honest. My mother's a Diderot, which means she was from Rex royalty and expected to be a nice Uptown lady who married into another old society family and lunched and did charity work. My father is a Bradley—not quite as blue-blooded as the Diderots, which Papa Diderot never lets Papa Bradley forget—which meant he was supposed to go to Vanderbilt and come home to either law or medical school at Loyola. Instead they fell in love as teenagers and turned their backs on everything their respective families have always stood for—and went to the University of New Orleans, becoming what I guess is now called sneeringly *social justice warriors* or *hippies* or *pinko commie bastards.* I never gave it much thought; they were always just Mom and Dad to me. They are very liberal—very much anti nuclear weapons and nuclear energy, very much in favor of equality for everyone—and are unrepentant stoners. They've been arrested numerous times at protests, and some of my earliest memories are of my parents chained to fences at nuclear power plants and marching in protests carrying signs.

I think my first words were "I want to speak to a lawyer."

Another way they rebelled against their parents was naming me Milton Bradley.

My grandmothers' maiden names were Milton and Scott; that's how Mom and Dad claim they came up with the name. The family legend is that both sets of grandparents insisted Mom and Dad give me a normal, family name—they named my older brother Storm and my sister Rain (she started going by Rhonda in junior high)—and that's what they came up with; a family name but also a middle finger to their parents.

The legend also holds they were going to name me either Ridge or River. Either would have been better than being named after a board game company. Other kids made my life miserable at school until Storm started calling me Scotty.

Having Milton Bradley as your legal name causes no small amount of hilarity when dealing with things like the Department of Motor Vehicles, or the passport office, or whenever you need to show legal ID, like at airports.

Trust me, I've heard every possible joke that can be made about my name, thank you very much.

Don't get me wrong, my parents are the *best.* No young kid grappling with his sexuality could have had better parents. Mom and Dad were thrilled when I came out in high school—they've marched in every gay pride parade in New Orleans since, hang rainbow flags on the house every Pride, Decadence, and Mardi Gras, and have worn out numerous *I'm proud of my gay son* T-shirts. They own and operate a tobacco shop on the corner of Royal and Dumaine in the Quarter, and I grew up in the spacious apartment directly above. I went to Jesuit High School, and like a good little Bradley went off to Vanderbilt after graduation. But I hated the school, missed New Orleans, and finally flunked out at twenty, returning to New

Orleans an abject failure. Dismayed at the dark stain on the family honor my flunking out had created, both grandfathers tied up my trust funds until I proved myself worthy of access to all that money and accruing interest.

Or turned thirty, whichever came first.

It probably goes without saying that the trust funds were released on my thirtieth birthday, doesn't it?

Then there's the psychic thing. I have what is known as a "gift," which means that I can sometimes see the past or the future, and sometimes I can commune with the Goddess in one of her incarnations. That usually happens when something big is going to go down, but she also speaks in maddening riddles that I often can't figure out until it's too late. Sometimes I can focus the gift using tarot cards, and sometimes the cards will answer my questions. It doesn't always work, and for some years after the Flood Caused By the Failure of the Federally Built and Maintained Levee System, it went away completely.

I don't really understand how it works, to be honest.

If I did, I suppose I could have made money doing it. But without a degree or work experience other than working in my parents' shop, I was kind of at loose ends.

So, I became a stripper. I was also a personal trainer, but no one ever mentions that. It's always "Back when you were a stripper..."

I was a personal trainer by day and a sometime go-go boy at night in gay bars. I originally worked with Southern Knights, a booking agency that sent me all over the country to dance. Sometimes I made great money, sometimes I didn't. But it required me to stay in shape. I was already in pretty good shape from being a wrestler in high school—Storm got me to go out for wrestling when I was in junior high, when kids were picking on me—and I was pretty good at it. I rented an apartment from a lesbian couple, old family friends that I call my aunts, on the last block of Decatur Street, across from the old Mint. Millie and Velma were awesome, and never minded if I was late sometimes with the rent.

The summer I turned twenty-nine, a porn star who was supposed to dance at the Pub for Southern Decadence weekend overdosed and went into rehab, and the manager asked me to fill in. I needed some quick and easy money, so I said yes. I wound up helping the FBI stop a crazed right-wing politician from destroying the French Quarter (it's a long story) and wound up with not one but *two* boyfriends. Frank Sobieski was the FBI agent I worked with, and Colin Cioni…well, he told me that weekend he was a cat burglar (it's a long story) but it turned out he's actually an international espionage agent, working for the Blackledge Agency.

His boss, Angela Blackledge, is who governments call when they need something handled but also need plausible deniability. Colin is gone for long stretches of time, on jobs we can't know anything about. Frank retired and moved to New Orleans, and eventually chased his dream of being a professional wrestler, signing with Gulf Coast Championship Wrestling and becoming one of their biggest stars and draws. He keeps saying he's going to retire but hasn't yet.

I joke that his farewell tour has lasted longer than Cher's.

I think both of them being gone so much helps keep our three-way relationship fresh and alive—we're never around each other long enough to get annoyed or bored.

The sex is also fantastic. Have I mentioned that?

Once the top floor of our building became vacant we rented it, too—so we have the third and fourth floors of our building.

But Millie retired from her law practice—Velma had retired years ago. Tired of living in the city, they wanted to live at their beach house in Florida. I bought the building from them—but haven't figured out what I want to do with it yet. There are four floors: The ground floor has always been leased to a business of some sort, but it's been vacant since the coffee shop closed a few years ago. Millie and Velma's apartment on the second floor has been vacant since they moved. Colin has always had his own bedroom up on the fourth floor, while Frank and I both have our own on the third—but we mostly all sleep together in my room. Frank's nephew, Taylor, also lives with us now. His parents disowned him and threw him out when he came out, and he's now attending Tulane University. He also has a bedroom on the fourth floor, and since Colin is often away, he pretty much has his own place.

Both Frank and Colin think I spoil Taylor.

Maybe I do. I have a soft spot for gay kids who grew up with homophobic parents, sue me. I was lucky, as I said, with my own parents, so I feel a bit of a karmic debt that needs repaying.

I keep thinking I should renovate the building and turn it into a four-story home for my little family, but I tend to procrastinate—and Frank and Colin aren't much help. My accountant, Bonnie, tells me I should actively look for a business tenant for the first floor, and I could make a fortune renting out Millie and Velma's apartment, too...but I don't know. Millie and Velma were family, and after the Duchesnays closed their little grocery store after Katrina, having other businesses in that space seemed weird to me. I never got used to the coffee shop being there—and it didn't last long anyway.

I'm also a private eye, licensed by the state of Louisiana. After that first experience with a criminal conspiracy and catching a killer, Frank convinced me to become a private eye. He retired from the FBI and we opened an agency together...but I don't use the license much, honestly; we might get an actual paying client once in a while. Most of the time, my detective work is limited to doing research for my brother Storm's law firm. But sometimes, a body will drop out of the sky, bullets start flying, and I'm right in the middle of the whole mess.

The New Orleans Police Department—particularly detectives Venus Casanova and Blaine Tujague—used to find me annoying. Over the years, they've come to a kind of grudging respect for my skills, such as they are.

At least I like to think they do, anyway.

I also have a deep dark secret: I love reality television.

Not all of it, of course. But when it first got started, I was obsessed with *The Real World*, and later, with *Project Runway*. I liked the competition shows, where people were required to have some sort of talent in order to participate, but I didn't care for the singing ones. I don't watch the ones about finding your true love or about families with more money than they need who are just terrible people or any of those. I stopped watching *Real World* when they stopped casting actual real people and instead starting casting wannabe models and actors with rage and/or drinking problems.

And then one of the cable networks launched a show called *Grande Dames of Marin County*. I didn't watch, but one Sunday when I was the only one home I turned on the television while cleaning, and it was on. I didn't change the channel right away because I'd turned it on just for background noise, and having seen preview commercials I immediately knew what it was…and so I paused, with my finger on the channel button, ready to flip to something else if it was as awful as I figured it would be.

But I couldn't stop staring at the television. Two women, their faces frozen rigid and expressionless with Botox and fillers, were screaming at each other about something. Curious, I kept watching as they screamed at each other, finally agreeing to disagree but now that They Had Had a Conversation and Made Their Feelings Known, they were happy they could Move Forward and start fresh with their friendship.

Everything about these shows annoyed me. They began, basically, as a rip-off of a hugely successful prime time soap starring actresses too old to play love interests for men two or three times their age and too young to play grandmothers yet. I hated that they catered to the lowest common denominator. I hated that all the women on the show were certifiably insane, encouraged to behave badly and make all women look bad, like a bunch of shrewish self-absorbed monsters—the absolute worst stereotypes of women: shallow, vain, petty, and unsupportive of other women, only concerned about their looks and money and things.

I suppose it goes without saying that I couldn't stop watching, nor could I stop hating myself for watching. Frank and Colin roundly mocked me for being so addicted, but I watched them all: *The Grande Dames of Marin County, Manhattan, Malibu, Palm Beach, Baltimore, Boston,* and *Houston.* The franchises spread across the country like bubonic plague in fourteenth-century Europe. The formula was the same, no matter which city served as the setting: women with money who had never progressed emotionally and intellectually beyond junior high school with too much time on their hands and way too much access to a plastic surgeon.

Narcissism and borderline personality disorders were also apparently a plus in getting cast.

It was only a matter of time, of course, before New Orleans got a franchise.

A previous attempt to launch a franchise in New Orleans had failed spectacularly when the producers couldn't find enough women interested in being on the show. The network had been getting complaints about racism and the lily-whiteness of its casts;

even the Houston show was all white women, with nary a Latina in sight. The producers' plan had been to make the New Orleans show the "black" one, but they couldn't find enough women of color with the requisite narcissism and mental problems to air their dirty laundry for the cameras. The New Orleans show plans were scrapped, and they'd moved on to Baltimore, where they'd had great success finding women of color to film—and the Baltimore show was wildly popular.

But one summer the news broke that the producers were, once again, trying to launch a New Orleans franchise. Naturally, it was a lot of fun trying to figure out who would say yes to being on such a show—casting it became a very popular parlor game around town. I couldn't imagine anyone who was actually old-line New Orleans society—Comus and Rex and the Boston Club—agreeing to go on television and look bad to the entire country.

When the cast was finalized and made public with a blazing fanfare and burst of publicity, no one was surprised they hadn't landed anyone from the upper echelons of New Orleans society— the kind of woman they wanted here would *never* do a television show. The women in the New Orleans cast were all successful in varying degrees, but no one who'd ever been any sort of Mardi Gras royalty. Chloe Valence was probably the closest out of them, but she wasn't from New Orleans and had married into an old Garden District family. Rebecca Barron was the widow of a *nouveau riche* restaurateur. Fidelis Vandiver had been a weather forecaster for one of the local news stations but had gotten her own local workout show, which led her to owning a string of health clubs scattered around the metropolitan area. Megan Dreher was married to a man who'd been a slumlord before Katrina and was now making a fortune in the building boom of the last decade—and becoming one of the most loathed men in the city. Margery Lautenschlaeger was the oldest member of the cast, with a family fortune from liquor. Her family name and money went back to the nineteenth century…but they were also Jewish, which meant no Boston Club or membership in Rex or Comus.

The final member of the cast was the one I knew the best, Serena Castlemaine, an oil heiress from Dallas who'd relocated to New Orleans several years earlier. I loved Serena, with her platinum blond hair and enormous breasts and her earthy sense of humor. Serena was a *Grande Dames* natural. But she has a great sense of humor, and her reason for doing the show was neither fame nor fortune, but simply because she thought it would be fun.

"And, darling," she said, rolling her enormous eyes at me with a wicked grin, "when it stops being fun, I'm done."

New Orleans being the small town it was, I had met all the women cast on the show in passing or knew who they were. New Orleans being New Orleans, I'd also heard plenty of gossip about all of them. And once filming began, their presence became hard to miss: restaurants and bars put up the *filming tonight coming inside indicates permission to be filmed* signs on their doors.

"I was going to go to that fundraiser/party/event, but those dreadful reality show people were going to be filming there" became a common refrain throughout that late summer and fall, always mentioned with sighs and eye rolls. I suspected that most people couldn't wait for the show to air but would never admit it— and would certainly never admit watching.

I managed to avoid filming, even though Serena kept asking me to film with her. I always declined—when one of your partners is an undercover operative working around the globe, the less attention you bring to yourself, the better. Besides, I didn't want to know how the cookies got made. I preferred to just continue being a fan, pretending that it was all unscripted and none of the women were putting on a show for the cameras, trying to be liked, trying to claw their way up the ladder and become a *brand*.

But...you hear things. New Orleans has always been about a block long and everyone is on a party line, as they used to say when people still remembered what a party line was.

And the weekend the show premiered, I got sucked into the drama against my will.

Like I said, I have a talent for being in the wrong place at the wrong time.

So, this is the story of how I sort of became a Grande Dame of New Orleans.

They didn't even have the decency to give me a fleur-de-lis to hold in the opening credits.

Bitches.

CHAPTER ONE

PAGE OF CUPS

A young man who is courageous when it is called for

I fished the last olive out of my almost empty glass and popped it into my mouth. I glanced at my watch as I chewed it, and moaned after swallowing. "There's nothing like a good martini," I said, glancing around the bar and getting our server's attention.

"Do we have time for another?" My nephew Taylor finished the rest of his sazerac and looked at me hopefully.

"I take it you liked it," I replied, not even trying to hide my smile. "But no time for another unless we want to be late."

This was Taylor's first time at the Sazerac Bar. He'd turned twenty-one just a few weeks before Thanksgiving, and since we were going to a party at the Joy Theater, I thought I'd treat him to a sazerac in the bar where they were invented. I personally don't care for the drink—give me gin or vodka any day of the week—but everyone in New Orleans is required to try a sazerac at least once.

And now I could rest easy, having done not only my civic duty but treated Taylor to a New Orleans rite of passage.

I'd also wanted him to see the Roosevelt Hotel's Christmas decorations. The Roosevelt is one of the grand old hotels of the city, and their lobby decorations are truly spectacular. Since we were going to a party at the Joy Theater—a mere block or so from the hotel—I thought, why not kill two birds with one stone? This was Taylor's second Christmas with us, and I wanted to do it right. We'd already done Celebration in the Oaks at City Park, and I'd loved seeing the beautifully decorated ancient live oak trees through a newbie's eyes.

I know it's corny, but I love Christmas.

I love everything about it. I love decorating my apartment. I love picking out a present that is 100 percent perfect for the person and carefully wrapping it up in beautiful paper, topping it with a bow, and twining ribbons around the box. I love picking out a tree, and the wonderful smell of pine that permeates everything inside once it's delivered. I love getting the boxes of ornaments down from the storage closet and adorning the branches with them. I love tinsel and opening a new box of icicles for the branches. I love Christmas cookies and cakes and pies and turkey and celebrating and spending time with people I love.

I even love carols—although I do think that September is a bit early to start playing them unless the intent is to drive people to homicide by December.

I love how New Orleans puts on her Christmas best every year, the houses and buildings festooned with lights and decorations and wreaths, massive trees sparkling and shining and blinking in picture windows. It's fun walking through the French Quarter after dark to see the decorations at Jackson Square and on the houses along the way. I love driving down St. Charles Avenue and through the Garden District. I love going out to City Park for Celebration in the Oaks. New Orleans takes decorating just as seriously as costuming. I even watch the movies and specials—I get a little bit misty with *A Charlie Brown Christmas* every year, and yes, I may cry every time Clarence gets his wings and George Bailey decides his life is wonderful after all.

Sue me.

My favorite thing about Christmas, though, is a New Orleans tradition known as *reveillon* dinners, a traditional dinner that originally followed midnight mass on Christmas. Local restaurants started offering these meals (not just after Christmas midnight mass, of course) in the weeks leading up to Christmas. New Orleans food is amazing, and a bad restaurant doesn't last long in this city. Reveillon is just really an excuse to get dressed up and go out for dinner at a nice place and feel festive for the holidays. Christmas was less than two weeks away, and we'd already been to several restaurants to enjoy a reveillon meal.

"Another round?" asked our waitress, a perky and friendly

young woman in her mid-twenties, as she walked up to our table. She'd been obviously flirting with my gorgeous sort-of-nephew ever since we arrived, but he was completely oblivious.

"No thank you, just the check, please," I replied, fishing out my wallet and my black American Express card.

Smiling at Taylor, she replied without looking at me, "I hope everything was good?"

"Fantastic." I smothered a grin. She still hadn't really done more than glance at me—she'd only had eyes for Taylor since we walked in.

Not that I blamed her, Taylor was a good-looking kid—*man*. It was hard for me to get used to thinking of him as anything other than a kid. Sure, he'd only been nineteen when he first came to live with us, and there's nothing like having a young person around to make you feel a little old. I realized that in my head I still thought of myself as twenty-nine, which is a hard pretense to maintain when your partner's nephew is living proof that you're not. Don't get me wrong—I don't mind getting older. I'm not one of those people who cling desperately to their youth. No face-lifts or Botox for me, thank you very much. I'm letting my sandy-blond hair go gray—and it's also starting to thin a little on the top. No, I earned my gray hair and my wrinkles, and I'll wear them proudly.

I'll cross the gray pubic hair bridge when it happens.

I do miss how easy it was to keep weight off...and not aching in the mornings when I get out of bed. But metabolisms slow down the older you get (how many times had I said that to a client back when I was a personal trainer?) and not only do I no longer teach seven aerobics classes a week, I haven't in *years*. It's hard for me to go to a class someone else is teaching, and I hate the stationary bike and the treadmill and the elliptical and all those other instruments of torture I used to make my clients use.

I know, I know. Excuses to fail, not reasons to succeed.

Frank and Colin, damn them, only gain muscle.

"Thanks for bringing me here," Taylor said, slipping on his jacket while we waited for her to bring the charge slip for me to sign. "The lobby is gorgeous."

It was an understatement. The lobby was filled with trees, all done in twinkling white lights and white ornaments. The polished marble floor and the dark wood lit up, reflecting the lights so it was almost like walking through the night sky, the heels on our shoes clicking with every step. The lobby was a bit warm and stuffy, and I could feel sweat forming along my scalp underneath my woolen stocking cap. We went down the stairs and out the doors on Roosevelt Way, shivering as the cold wet wind smacked us right in the face.

I slipped the shivering doorman a five for holding the door open for us, and we headed quickly to the corner at Canal Street.

A cold front had swept down from Canada the weekend after Thanksgiving, blanketing the Midwest with an early winter blizzard and freezing temperatures. Even in New Orleans the mercury took an enormous, unnatural dive. We'd had a couple of hard freeze alerts, with everyone being warned to run their taps to prevent pipes from bursting. Even after that front passed, the temperature hadn't risen much, hovering somewhere from the mid-thirties to the low forties. The sun hadn't been seen in weeks—and tonight's forecast was for cold rain ahead of yet another unnatural cold front. There was a chance of snow.

Snow!

It doesn't snow in New Orleans often—only a few times in my lifetime that I can recall—and the city comes to a screeching halt when it does.

It hadn't started raining yet, but we both had enormous umbrellas tucked under our arms.

Canal Street was practically a ghost town with tumbleweeds blowing down the neutral ground. One of the red Canal Street streetcars passed by on its way to the river, its windows twinkling with white lights and a gigantic green wreath on the front. The palm trees lining Canal's neutral ground were banded with white Christmas lights, and each one was festooned with a huge red velvet bow. I looked over at the Ritz Carlton Hotel and smiled a little ruefully. When I was a kid, that building had housed the Maison Blanche Department Store, and every year at Christmas an enormous Mr. Bingle—their Christmas snowman mascot—hung from the side of the building.

I still have my ratty old Mr. Bingle doll. He sits on my bed in my old bedroom at my parents'.

The wind was worse on Canal as we walked hurriedly away from the river to our destination, the Joy Theater.

Our friend Serena Castlemaine had scored us tickets for tonight's world premiere of the first episode of *The Grande Dames of New Orleans*. I'd met her through my sister Rain, and she lived in the old Metoyer house in the Garden District, where we'd solved a decades-old murder last year. We all really liked Serena—she had an enormous personality and a great sense of humor. She also knew she was over-the-top, and that self-awareness gave her the ability to also laugh at herself.

She was perfect for a show like *The Grande Dames*.

As Frank said, "She's always played to the cameras when they weren't there. Imagine what she'll be like actually on camera."

He had a point.

I had a slight buzz from my martini as we hurried across Rampart Street to get to the theater. The Joy was an old vintage theater that had been falling to pieces before Hurricane Katrina and was severely flood-damaged when the levees failed. I hadn't been inside since its multi-million-dollar overhaul and renovation was finished, so I was curious to get a look at it after its face-lift. The traffic was terrible. Limousines and town cars, cabs and Ubers and Lyfts swerved and lined up and honked their horns at each other as they tried to get close to the front doors to let their passengers out.

We managed to get across the street without getting killed and joined the group of people milling about outside the theater entrance, smoking and shivering and talking. We got into the line and I fished our invitations out of my trench coat pocket. I didn't recognize anyone in the line as we slowly shuffled forward toward the entrance. Opinion in the city about this new reality show was pretty divided. Old-line New Orleans rolled its eyes and dismissed it out of hand. Two seasons of MTV's *The Real World* had filmed here, and neither had been embraced by the locals. But the newer people, the *parvenus*, as my grandparents referred to them, were a little more open to the show and more excited about it. After all, it was a great way to showcase how far the city had come since the flood after the levees failed. Tourism is the engine that drives a significant portion of the city's economy, and a successful *Grande Dames* franchise could possibly rev that engine even higher.

We finally made it to the front of the line. A blast of hot air washed over us as the front door opened and closed behind the people who'd just been in front of us. I gave our invitations to an unsmiling young woman with cat's-eye glasses with rhinestones in the corners, skintight leopard print leggings, and a massively baggy black T-shirt with *Grande Dames of New Orleans* in gold lettering on the front. She checked our names off a list on a clipboard. "Right, then," she said in a British accent. "Go on in, then. There're bars and food tables set up both in the lobby and upstairs in the balcony. Enjoy the show."

As I looked around as we walked inside, I was impressed. I'd only been inside the theater once before—years ago, for a fundraiser—and the decay had been apparent. The building had great bones, though. The renovation had worked wonders. It had been 30s-style art deco before, and they'd kept much of the original style, yet added a modernistic flair. The color scheme was red, black, and white, and it looked very classy and elegant.

"I'm going to get some food," Taylor said, and vanished into the crowd near the food tables before I could respond.

It never ceases to amaze me how much that kid can eat.

"Scotty!"

I turned and grinned. I bent down so Paige Tourneur, the editor of *Crescent City* magazine, could give me a hug. Paige was cool. She had reddish hair with blond streaks in it, one blue eye and one green eye. She was barely over five feet tall, and she was wearing heels. She had a great sense of humor and could always make me laugh. She also tended to dress flamboyantly. A favorite look was something I thought of as *fortune teller chic*, which was what she'd chosen for tonight. Flowing brightly colored silks and lush dark velvets. I kissed her cheek. "Where's Ryan?"

Her fiancé, Ryan Tujague, was a lawyer who was a sometimes colleague of my older brother, Storm. Ryan's younger brother Blaine was a police detective whose path I crossed sometimes when on a case. The Tujague brothers were both handsome, with bluish-black hair and blue eyes and olive skin. I'd actually met Paige during the course of a case, and we hit it off. I was a little surprised to find out she was engaged to the older brother of one of my cop frenemies.

New Orleans is a *very* small town.

"Getting me some wine, like a good fiancé who wants to keep his hopes of getting some tonight alive." She grinned at me. "I thought I saw a tangle of arms and legs heading to the food table. Taylor?"

I nodded. "Always hungry."

"Where's Frank and Colin?"

"Frank's doing a show in Montgomery and Colin's out of the country, so it's just me and Taylor tonight."

She rolled her mismatched eyes. "You know, for someone in a throuple you never seem to have a date when you need one."

You're telling me, I thought.

"You know," she waved me to bend down, then whispered, "there's food and a bar upstairs in the balcony, and I bet no one's up there. When they get back, let's head up there." She shifted the blue-and-orange silk draped around her shoulders. "It's much too crowded and stuffy down here."

"Okay," I replied. "It's weird, as crowded as it is, I don't see many faces I recognize."

"Oh, none of the Old Guard is going to show up here." Paige laughed. "Even my boss isn't coming anywhere near here." Rachel Delesdernier Sheehan, publisher of *Crescent City*, was from an old political dynasty in Orleans Parish and had married into another one. "They asked her to do the show, you know. She told them she lived in Old Metairie, thank you very much, and hung up on them."

I laughed along with her, adding, "Well, if worse comes to worst, it can't be as bad as those seasons of *The Real World*."

"Have you watched any of these *Grande Dames* shows?" She raised her eyebrows and rolled her eyes. "Narcissists and sociopaths, all of them."

"I know. I hate myself for watching." I saw Ryan heading our way with two glasses of red wine. But he was stopped when a remarkably good-looking man grabbed him by the arm. I caught my breath. *Remarkably good-looking* was an understatement. "Who's that guy in the gray jacket?" I asked. He looked familiar to me in that way everyone in New Orleans looks familiar, but I couldn't place him. "There, with the blue shirt and gray tie." He was very sexy. His dress pants were tight in the back over a rather shapely bubble butt. His waist was narrow and his shoulders broad. He had a thick head of dark hair he wore long and pulled back into a ponytail. His skin was swarthy, darkly tanned, and he had a dimple in his chin and a strong nose.

"Him? That's Billy Barron." Paige shook her head. "He's been trying to get Ryan to rep him in his lawsuit against his stepmother."

Oh, yes, the Barron family drama was perfect for reality television. "So, he is going to sue her?"

The struggle over the Barron restaurant empire had tongues wagging all over the city since Billy's father, Steve Barron, had died suddenly from a heart attack just over a year earlier. Steve was a local boy made good, from a blue-collar Irish Channel family who'd borrowed money and opened his own fast food New Orleans style po-boy restaurant, NOLA Boys, when he was just twenty-two. NOLA Boys had been enormously successful, spreading across the country the way Starbucks would later and making Steve ridiculously wealthy in the process. He'd been a real New Orleans character, vain and arrogant and not ashamed to court controversy. He'd built a colossal home on the North Shore, right on the water, in a gated community and had publicly feuded with the homeowners' association over almost everything you can imagine—including his garish Christmas decorations that were so bright they could be seen by passing airplanes. When he was in his late forties he sold NOLA Boys for a fortune and started opening what he called "fine dining" restaurants with New Orleans–style food all over the country. The local Barron's restaurants primarily appealed to tourists. I'd never eaten in one.

He kept himself in top shape and, as he aged, dyed his hair shoe-polish black and had been prone to skintight shimmery shirts open to expose his chest. He'd been married numerous times, and his widow, Rebecca, had been cast on the show. She was about forty years younger than Steve, and there were rumors he'd been planning on divorcing her when he died suddenly. He'd cut all of his children out of his will shortly before he died, hence the ensuing battle between the grieving widow and his children. Billy had been a baseball star at LSU and had played several seasons for the St. Louis Cardinals before an injury ended his career.

As I watched him talking to Ryan, a woman tucked her arm into his and led him away. I didn't see her face. She was wearing a blue silk dress and had long, thick dark hair. They disappeared in the crowd. She also looked familiar, but I couldn't place her.

"Hey, Scotty, good to see you." Ryan smiled at me, giving Paige one of the glasses. "I would have gotten you something—"

"Oh, Taylor's in there somewhere supposedly getting me a drink." I frowned, trying to spot him. It's usually easy to do, given he's six four, but I couldn't pick him in the crowd. "I'll just text him." I pulled my cell phone out of my coat. *Going upstairs to the balcony with Paige and Ryan, meet us up there.*

"Let's go," I said over the dull roar of the crowd. The lobby was filling up, and more people were outside in line. I slipped off my coat, draping it over my arm.

It was much cooler and less crowded upstairs. There were maybe twenty or so people milling around the concession stand. It had been set up as a full bar with two tuxedoed bartenders, and two enormous tables groaning with food had been set up along the small wall separating the balcony from the concession area. Paige and Ryan headed over to the food tables while I got a glass of Chardonnay from a bartender who looked slightly familiar. I walked over to the food tables and made a sandwich with a roll and some slices of Cajun fried turkey, adding some roast asparagus and bacon-wrapped shrimp to my clear plastic plate before joining Ryan and Paige at a tall table set up off to the side. My phone buzzed.

It was Taylor. *Should I get more food before I come up?*

I rolled my eyes. *There's food and a bar up here and not nearly as many people.*

Less than a minute later I waved at Taylor when he reached the top of the stairs. He had a can of Coke and my wine glass in one hand while balancing enough food to feed a family of four on a plate with the other hand.

Taylor came over and placed his plate on the table, said hello, and headed back to the food again.

"I'm going to get another drink and then we should find seats," Paige said. "Anyone want anything?"

"I'll get some food," Ryan replied, "and meet you at the seats." I was finished with my plate by the time Paige came back—I'd been hungry and kind of scarfed it all down embarrassingly fast and chugged down the wine Taylor had brought so I wouldn't have to carry two glasses.

Classy. That's me. My grandparents would be so proud.

Taylor followed behind me, a plate buried in food in each hand with his Coke can tucked in his jacket pocket. We walked down the aisle and found seats in the front row of the balcony. I looked down. The seats on the main floor were filling up. There was an area at the foot of the stage where some women I recognized as the actual cast members were standing around sipping wine and idly chatting with well-dressed men I presumed to either be husbands, lovers, or network executives. I spotted Serena, who of course was wearing a shimmering gold satin dress with spaghetti straps screaming at the burden of holding up her enormous breasts ("They're mine, too," she told me once. "No implants for this girl!"), her platinum blond hair curling around her face in ringlets. A short, animated man in a tuxedo joined them as I watched. I recognized Eric Brewer, the creator and producer of the *Grande Dames* shows.

Eric Brewer was good looking, if you liked that type. As his creations took off in popularity, he wound up with his own talk show that aired every night after episodes of the shows. At first, his guests were just cast members of the various franchises, discussing what happened on the episode that just aired and giving a behind-the-scenes look at how the shows were made. As the shows continued to grow in popularity, so did his talk show and his own celebrity. Soon, major stars who were big fans of the shows began showing up on his show, and he began appearing in tabloids and on the gossip sites.

Personally, I didn't see the appeal. I thought he was annoying and never watched his show. He clearly believed he was clever and witty and funny. His short brown hair was going gray, but rather than embracing being a silver fox he acted like he was still a wide-eyed twenty-year-old twink. The gossip sites often ran photos of him with much younger men—he had a definite type: muscular young guys with dark tans, big white teeth, and no body hair that liked to wear skimpy bikinis. He always acted on his show like he really wanted a life partner, but I suspected that was an act. He was rich and famous and good looking and had a powerful job in television…if he couldn't find a life partner, who could?

Taylor had a huge crush on him, which I didn't understand.

Then again, I didn't have to, and it was none of my business.

The lights flickered, and Eric Brewer climbed up the steps to where a microphone had been set up on the stage. He said, "May I have everyone's attention, please?" The theater fell silent, and he flashed his what-I-am-sure-he-thinks-is-a-dazzling smile. "I want to thank you all for coming tonight to the premiere of Season One of *The Grande Dames of New Orleans.*" This was of course followed by a few whoops and hollers mixed in with mostly polite applause—golf claps. He started off saying some great things about New Orleans, but it wasn't long before he moved on to how brilliant he was.

"Yeah, yeah, yeah, you're wonderful, your shows are wonderful, blah blah blah, can we get on with it already?" I muttered under my breath.

Taylor, hanging on his every word, shushed me.

Finally, Eric said, "Enjoy the show."

The lights dimmed all the way and the network logo appeared on the big screen. I settled back in my seat as some unrecognizable music began and the opening credits rolled.

CHAPTER TWO

THE EMPRESS, REVERSED

A selfish and ruthless woman

The first episode was…boring, which is death for a reality show. We don't tune in to be bored. We watch for the *drama*.

But in fairness, even the first episode of each new season of a well-established *Grande Dames* franchise wasn't full of the drama and nastiness we gratefully loaded into our crack pipes every week to enjoy. Those first episodes were what I called "let's catch up with the girls" shows. Rarely, if ever, were any of what would be that season's dramatic storylines set up in those season premieres. Sometimes some unresolved drama from the previous season lingered—like the long-running feud between Helen and Wendy on *Marin County.* (Those two never resolved anything, and the rest of the cast simply spent their time switching allegiances from one to the other, with new girls added as others dropped out. But that was getting old, and the show's ratings were sagging accordingly.)

So, this first episode of our local franchise was just a "hey, get to know our cast" episode, with the women themselves barely even interacting with each other. Serena and Megan had a nice boozy lunch at some uptown restaurant I didn't recognize, but that was about it for interactions between the women. The rest of the episode was devoted to showing us snippets of each woman's life as they got ready to attend a party at Margery's castle on St. Charles Avenue. We saw Margery's enormous closet (shelves and shelves of shoes—more shoes than a Chinese Nike factory), the gigantic room full of books with its little decorative balcony overlooking the pool where Chloe wrote, and went to one of Fidelis's sessions with her trainer (mainly so we could see her fit, strong body in a leotard,

I think, as well as the inside of one of her health clubs). We saw Rebecca talking with the chef at Barron's, the flagship restaurant of the Barron food empire, on St. Charles Avenue just past the Garden District (he looked bored and like he was trying really hard not to roll his eyes at her; it was obvious she knew little to nothing about cooking and food).

But to give credit where credit is due, the show's visuals would have made a great ad for New Orleans tourism. Living here, it's easy for us to take the city for granted and stop noticing how breathtakingly beautiful it is. The show's cameras lingered lovingly on the canopy of live oaks over St. Charles Avenue, the streetcar as it clattered its way uptown, the ships going up and down the river, the majesty of Jackson Square, the Caribbean flavor to the architecture of the Quarter, the majestic houses uptown, and the lush green ripeness everywhere—it took my breath away.

Plus, the episode hinted at the party at Margery's, which would be shown in episode two. A hallmark of the shows was that every time all the women got together (*especially* at a party), lots of drama ensued. I'd always wanted to see what her castle looked like on the inside. It was one of my favorite houses on the Avenue, and I'd heard Margery's parties were always over-the-top events considered excessive—even by New Orleans standards.

Which was saying a lot.

As the credits rolled to polite applause from the audience in the theater, I heard champagne corks popping. The lights came up, and as we were getting up a woman came hurrying down the balcony aisle to where we were standing. It was Sloane Gaylord.

Sloane worked for the show—I was never clear as to whether she was a production assistant or an associate producer, but I did know she worked a lot with Serena. I'd met her when Serena had invited me to lunch back in September and tried picking my brain for gossip about her fellow castmates. I didn't blame her for trying—she'd only lived here a few years and so her castmates had her at a disadvantage with their shared histories—but I didn't want anything I said winding up on national television. Despite Serena's loading me up with watermelon margaritas I didn't let anything slip...at least I didn't think so.

I guess I'd have to watch to see.

Sloane was petite, probably barely topping five feet on a good day, and always wore her dark auburn hair pulled back in a severe ponytail. Her features were delicate, almost nondescript, and she wasn't wearing any makeup, which made her pale skin look washed out and her green eyes faded. She was wearing a pair of tight black jeans and one of those black *Grande Dames of New Orleans* T-shirts. She pushed her enormous glasses up her pert nose and smiled. "Oh, good, you're all together."

"I generally don't come apart in public," Paige replied.

Sloane's wan face flushed. "No, I, um, meant that you, and um, well, you"—she pointed at me with a long index finger with a chewed ragged nail at its tip—"are who I'm looking for." She mumbled something, shook her head, and smiled. "Let me start that again. Sorry." She took a deep breath. "Serena sent me looking for you two. There's an after-party at the Hotel Aquitaine in Eric's penthouse, and she wanted to make sure you were both invited." She reached into her shoulder bag and produced two key cards with the Hotel Aquitaine's logo on them. "You'll need these for the elevator, it's penthouse 1C."

Paige palmed hers, gesturing at Ryan. "I'm with my fiancé and Scotty's got his nephew with him. Can we bring them along?"

Sloane pushed her glasses up again. "Yes, of course, the more the merrier." She leaned in closer. "There's a town car waiting for you—you can ride over with Serena. If you'll come with me..." She gestured up the aisle.

"I don't know," I said. It was tempting, but Frank would be home tomorrow and we were going to start putting up our Christmas decorations.

Experience had taught me that hangovers made decorating a miserable experience.

"Oh, come on, Scotty, can we go? Please?" Taylor was bouncing up and down in excitement.

"Okay." I relented. "But we're not staying long. We can stop by for one drink."

Famous last words I'd uttered many times.

I shrugged on my trench coat, following Sloane up the aisle and through the small crowd in the concessions area. It was even more crowded downstairs, with mobs lined up for the bars while the food tables looked like they'd been ravaged by a plague of locusts. We somehow managed to navigate our way through the crowded, overheated lobby and out the front doors. The heavy rain had started falling while we were indoors, and the temperature had dropped a good twenty degrees or more. A big burly driver opened the back door to a Lincoln town car. Taylor opened his umbrella and I stepped underneath it, handing mine to a very grateful Paige and Ryan. I almost stepped into the full gutter but managed to avert that tragedy, sliding into the back seat with Serena.

"Darling Scotty!" she said, her Texas accent even more pronounced than usual. She air-kissed me on each cheek. She was wrapped up in a luxuriant mink coat. Diamonds sparkled at her throat, ears, fingers, and in the deep canyon of her cleavage. She smelt of cigarette smoke and expensive perfume. "And Taylor! And Paige! And Ryan!" The door shut behind Taylor as he tried to fold his long legs into the space between the two seats in the back of the car, without much luck.

"Isn't Sloane coming with us?" I asked, a little confused as I took a glass of champagne from Serena, who started filling another glass.

"Production staff are riding together, which always makes me nervous. I shudder to think what they say about the cast when we can't hear them." Serena managed to pour a second glass without spilling a drop when the car pulled suddenly away from the curb. "I'm so glad you're joining us for our private little get-together. What did you think of the show?"

"It was boring," Paige said flatly before I could think of something polite to say.

Serena erupted with her enormous laugh. "It *was*, wasn't it? But I promise you, it's going to get better." She grinned. "A lot better. I just pray I get the bitch edit!"

"You *want* the bitch edit?" Taylor stared at her. "Why?"

The so-called *bitch edit* had become a cliché amongst fans of the show. Every woman who came out of a season looking bad claimed production and editing had done it to them, giving them an edit to make them look like a bitch. Basically, they claimed things they said on film were shown out of their proper context deliberately to make them look bad. No one could argue that editing didn't have something to do with how the women were perceived by the audience...but as Dana on the *Boston* franchise once said, "They can't edit the words into your mouth."

"Darling, the bitches get all the press," Serena said, pulling out an electric cigarette from her little purse and switching it on. She took a deep tug on it, the little tip glowing bright blue. She still smoked regular cigarettes—as long as I'd known her, she claimed to be trying to quit—but smoked the electronic ones while in what she called "mixed" company—smokers and non-smokers.

"And become the biggest stars," Serena went on. "And some viewers—if you do it right—love you. And you can always reverse yourself and have a redemption season!"

"But you have to do it right," I said. "Or everyone will hate you."

Oline from *Palm Beach* had been so hated on the first season of that franchise she'd even appeared on the cover of *In Touch* magazine with the headline, "Most Hated Grande Dame." The following season had been her redemption season, and her transformation from hated to beloved was the blueprint other Grande Dames tried to follow.

On Eric's show, Oline had simply smiled when asked and said, "I just learned to be more tolerant."

The "bitches" were also primarily responsible for the storylines on the show—the ones that got people to watch, anyway.

"Who do you think everyone will be?" Paige asked. "I think Margery will be the one everyone likes, and I think it's probably a toss-up between you and Chloe for the bitch edit."

"Oh, that's right, you worked with her, didn't you?" Serena blew smoke out the window again and turned the e-cigarette off, dropping it back into her purse. "What was that like?"

"She was a prig," Paige replied with a dramatic eye roll. "And she slept her way into an editor's job. I don't know if that's true," she added quickly when she saw the gleam in Serena's eyes, "but it was the rumor around the paper. She certainly didn't get the job on her merits. *That is not for use on the show.*"

"Didn't she leave the paper when she got married?" Serena asked, leaning forward. The car was stuck trying to cross Bourbon

Street. Despite the heavy rain, Bourbon was full of partying tourists. "Someone told me that, I don't remember who."

"She married money." I came to Paige's rescue. I could tell she already regretted gossiping about Chloe. "Remy Valence, old Garden District money."

Serena turned her glittering blue eyes back to me. "He's the gay one, right?"

"Uh—I, I don't know." I lied, because I did know.

I'd slept with Remy Valence a long time ago, when I was in my twenties. I knew all about him and his marriage. Remy had grown up completely under the thumb of a domineering mother, and it wasn't a secret that Dierdre Valence—a racist, homophobic shrew of a woman—would not hear of her only child, her baby, living as an openly gay man. The story I'd heard was she threatened to cut him out of her will unless he married a woman, and so he had. Whether Chloe knew he sometimes slept with men and married him anyway was anyone's guess.

Gossip held that Dierdre had left her estate to Remy in a trust. If he got a divorce, it all went to charity. So, Remy remained chained to Chloe in their big old house on Third Street.

It made for great gossip, but how much of it was true nobody knew for sure.

Maybe he was bisexual. Maybe they had an arrangement.

It wasn't anyone's business, really.

The bottom line was I wasn't comfortable with talking about my one-nighter with Remy. I certainly didn't want it winding up on television.

The night I'd slept with Remy I didn't know who he was—he was just an attractive man who'd come into the Pub that Saturday night. Sure, he looked familiar, but in a town the size of New Orleans everyone does.

I was still in my early twenties, having just moved from my parents' house into my own apartment. I was enjoying my freedom, but freedom, of course, isn't free—I needed to buy groceries and pay the bills. My personal training business was starting to pick up, but I was still dancing for extra cash whenever I could. I got the call to dance at the Pub at the last minute that lazy summer weekend.

I had no food in the house and was dreading having to drop in to eat at Mom and Dad's until my clients were due to pay me again. The night had been slow—too hot and humid for most people to leave the air-conditioning. I'd only made about a hundred dollars all night, making it one of my worst nights dancing ever.

There was about an hour or so left in my shift that Friday night when a nice-looking guy parked himself at a barstool on my side of the bar. He looked up at me when he ordered a drink with a big smile on his face and winked. He held up a twenty-dollar bill and waved me over. I smiled and danced down the bar to where he was sitting. I squatted down with him in between my legs and rested my knees on the sticky bar. I gave him my most seductive smile. "Hey there, how ya doing?"

"Better now, sexy," he said, touching the bill to the hollow at the base of my throat and lightly stroking it down my torso to the waistband of my sweaty black underwear. He hooked his middle finger inside the elastic and tucked the bill inside, letting the elastic go so it lightly snapped my damp skin.

I put my hands on his shoulders and tilted my head flirtatiously. "Like what you see?"

"Very much." He leaned in closer, putting a big, well-manicured hand on each of my pecs.

He was uniquely handsome, his individual features not quite right, but somehow it all worked together. His dark hair was cut short, tucked behind smallish ears. His eyes were big and brown and expressive underneath a thick brow. His lips were a little thin and his mouth wide. He was tanned, his forearms thick and smooth. His tight white Polo shirt stretched over a strong chest and broad shoulders, the sleeves rolled up a bit to show off strong arms. His legs were a little thin for his upper body, and his khaki shorts hung loose. But there was something about him, an unexplainable charisma, that drew me to him. I winked back at him and stood up, dancing my way down the bar to someone else waving a bill at me.

He remained on his barstool, watching. I went back to him a couple of times over the course of the next hour or so. Every time I did, I got another twenty, and he would stroke my calves, my legs, or my chest. I kept an eye on him, watching as he kicked back a few more drinks and a couple of shots, trying to puzzle out where I'd seen him before or if I even did know him. One time as he stroked my shaved-smooth legs I noticed a white band on his otherwise tanned ring finger. *Married*, I thought, *bi or closeted.*

There are a lot more of those in New Orleans than you could possibly imagine.

Finally, two in the morning rolled around and I was finished for the night. He was responsible for almost half my take for the night, so when I climbed down from the bar I walked over to say thank you.

"You're off duty now?" He slid down from the barstool. He was about my height, maybe an inch or so taller. His left hand, the one with the telltale white band on the ring finger, lightly brushed against my crotch. Sweaty and tired as I was, I reacted.

Hey, I'm only human. I was also an unrepentant slut.

"You want to come back to my place?" I breathed in his ear, leaning against him so our chests touched.

"I'd like that. You nearby?"

"Close enough."

"Great."

"Let me get my stuff."

We held hands as we walked through the silence of the lower Quarter back to my place. When I got my keys out at the gate at my house, he hesitated. "Something wrong?" I asked as I unlocked the gate and pushed it open. A flirtatious smile, a raised eyebrow, a slight tilt of my head to the right.

He flushed. "It's just that—no, never mind. Nothing's wrong." He smiled back at me. "What are we waiting for?"

The sex wasn't particularly good. He wasn't a good kisser—too aggressive, which was a tip-off about the sex about to happen. But I've certainly had worse. At some point over the next few hours he told me his first name was Remy but never told me his last name. I didn't need to know it, and I didn't want his phone number. Once the sun was starting to come up, he got dressed and borrowed my phone to call a cab. I walked him down to the gate and waited with him. When the black-and-white United cab pulled over to the curb, I lightly kissed his cheek, said, "See you around," and went back to upstairs to bed.

And figured that was the end of that. I'd probably see him

around again, but there wouldn't be an encore. I didn't give him another thought until I ran into him again, about a year or so later, at a party at my Diderot grandparents' mansion in the Garden District.

It was a fundraiser for one of my grandmother's pet charities, the Tennessee Williams Literary Festival, and I was bored out of my mind. The big house was full of people. Some of them I knew, some were strangers, some I wished I didn't know. Papa Diderot was holding court in the library while Maman Diderot was rushing around making sure everyone had enough food or drink and making sure coasters were being used and nothing was getting spilled anywhere. I was standing at the buffet table, debating whether I should get some more of the shrimp creole when I felt a hand lightly brush against my ass. I turned around quickly, ready to slap a face and there he was, Remy whose-last-name-I-didn't-know. He just looked familiar at first, but after a moment it all came back to me—the white Polo shirt, the khakis, the way his breath tasted of tequila. "Hi, how are you?" I smiled and walked outside to the bar on the back veranda. The bartender was handing me a glass of champagne when I heard his voice behind me, the light touch on my ass again.

"I didn't expect to see you here."

I smiled my thanks to the bartender and turned around to face Remy. He was wearing a seersucker suit over a pale blue shirt and waving a hand fan with Tennessee Williams's face on it, drops of sweat beading up on his forehead. "Hello," I replied, wondering how I could politely get away again.

"Remy! There you are." A very pretty woman slipped her arm through his and pecked at his cheek, not getting any closer than a half inch. "You're such a bad boy. If I didn't know better I'd say you were trying to lose me." Her long chestnut hair was twisted into a French braid draped over her right shoulder. She was slightly taller than me and Remy, wearing what looked like a pale blue satin toga-style dress that matched his shirt perfectly. Diamonds glittered at her ears, on her fingers, and she was wearing a matching pale blue choker around her neck with a pink cameo of a woman's profile in the front.

Well, this couldn't get more awkward, I thought, hoping he was her brother but knowing better. I glanced down and saw that the wedding band was now there on his left hand.

I was raised to be polite, and the whole point of manners was, after all, to get people through social awkward situations. "Scotty Bradley," I said with a smile, holding out my hand to her. "I don't believe we've met?" She didn't look familiar at all.

"Chloe Valence." She smiled, her perfectly capped white teeth sparkling in the fading light of late afternoon. Her hand clutched his arm so tightly I could see her knuckles whiten. She clearly saw me as a threat. But she gave me her hand and I bent down to brush my lips against it.

"*Enchante*," I said in my most gallant voice.

"And I see you've already met my husband."

"Remy Valence," His grip was loose, his palm damp with sweat. He started fanning himself more vigorously. "Bradley?" He looked confused.

I smiled at him. "My mother is a Diderot." I gestured with the hand holding the champagne glass. "My grandparents' place."

He looked even more confused—probably wondering if he'd been mistaken and I wasn't the stripper he'd slept with after all.

People from society families in New Orleans generally don't make side money stripping in gay bars.

I like to think I was the first to break that glass ceiling.

"Now, honey, come along, there's someone I want you to meet," she said, still smiling at me as she tugged at him insistently. "If you'll excuse us...so lovely to have met you."

I nodded, watching as she maneuvered him back inside. I didn't see either of them again that night. After the guests were gone, alone with my sister and grandmother in the drawing room, relaxing and gossiping, I asked them about the Valences.

My grandmother was the one who told me the tawdry tale of Remy, his possessive domineering monster of a mother, and the woman he married to guarantee his inheritance. "She seems nice, but what a life." Maman clicked her tongue with a sad shake of her head. "She's from out west somewhere"—to my grandmother, "out west" could mean Baton Rouge—"I think, not anyone, really. She used to work for the *Times-Picayune*, I think. She has literary aspirations." She made a face. "I do hope she finds a use for her talents."

It's not the life I would have chosen for myself, but who was I to judge Remy Valence?

We all walk a different path.

"Oh, we're here," Paige said gratefully as the town car pulled up in front of the Royal Aquitaine. "I'm dying for a cigarette." She didn't wait for the driver to open the door.

As I started to slide out, Serena grabbed my arm. "Darling, I need to talk to you about Remy. Don't forget now."

Great, I thought as I got out into the cold. *Just great.*

CHAPTER THREE

NINE OF SWORDS

Suffering, doubt, suspicion

Ah, the Royal Aquitaine Hotel.

It claimed to be the oldest hotel in New Orleans, but so did any number of the other grand ladies of the city. Originally built in the mid-1830s so New Orleans would have a "European-style hotel" to impress foreign visitors and convey the impression that the city was a cosmopolitan mecca on a continent still mostly wilderness. Its name came from being on Royal Street; the hotel had been built above the Café Aquitaine. The café was long gone, but the name lived on. There was no trace of the old café in the hotel's grand lobby, decorated with the finest white marble and sparkling crystal chandeliers and red velvet armchairs. Independently owned and operated by its founding family, it had finally been sold to one of the big hotel chains during the Truman administration but had kept its historic name rather than tacking on the chain's name. It took up most of a city block—the property itself would be worth a ridiculous amount of money even without the four-star hotel sitting on it.

I'd tricked there more times than I could possibly remember when I was single.

And, of course, there was that one time I'd found a dead body in one of the rooms.

Wanting to avoid Serena and whatever her questions about Remy Valence might be, I stayed out on the sidewalk in the cold with Paige to keep her company while she smoked while the others went on ahead. The overhead gallery protected us from the rain.

"Ryan wants me to quit before we get married," Paige said, taking a deep inhale as an older couple dressed to the nines walked past us on their way to the front doors. "You're not going to out Remy to Serena, are you?"

"I don't want to, but I'm not a good liar," I replied, shivering as another blast of cold and damp wind from the river buffeted us. "And it's not anyone's business, anyway. I don't want to be responsible for people talking about Remy's sexuality on television. You regretted that crack about Chloe, didn't you?"

"I'm not used to having to watch what I say in my private life." Paige inhaled, shivering as a blast of cold wind came from the direction of the river. "It's true—she pretty much did fuck anyone at the paper she thought could get her ahead, but damned if I want to be the one who gets that information out there."

"And who cares about Remy's sexuality anyway?"

"Oh, God, you haven't heard." She shook her head.

"Heard?"

"You really need to listen more to gossip." She grinned at me. "There's been a whole brouhaha about Remy and Chloe's marriage in front of the cameras."

"Seriously?" My jaw dropped.

But why would anyone with something to hide go on a reality show? It's just asking for it, really.

"One of the main storylines is a feud between Margery and Chloe." She turned her back to the wind and took another drag on the cigarette.

"Really?" That struck me as strange. Margery didn't seem the type. I figured she was going to serve as the Voice of Reason character, the one who tries to make peace between the other women.

"The story I heard is that Margery told one of the other women she thought Chloe's book was reductive, poorly written, and borderline racist."

"Um, wasn't it?"

Paige held up her forefinger and thumb, about a quarter inch apart. "Little bit. And it's not like other people haven't said it. So, Chloe wasn't thrilled when someone told her what Margery had said. She never could take criticism back at the paper. I guess that hasn't changed." Paige exhaled smoke through her nose. "And she was drinking at a party and got pretty nasty with Margery—do you know her?"

I shook my head. "No, never met her."

"She's not someone whose bad side you want to be on. That woman can hold a grudge—and she's got a *lot* of money."

"So, what happened?"

Paige shook her head. "Stupid Chloe took a shot at how Margery dresses, and Margery was having none of it. She blew up and said, for the cameras, 'Oh shut up, everyone in town knows you married a homosexual so he could get his inheritance, and you're nothing but trailer trash from some backward parish no one of quality has ever come from.'"

"Ouch." Even for the *Grande Dames*, that was harsh. "I can't imagine they'd want that to air?"

"You really haven't been paying attention, have you?"

"No, I wanted to be surprised when I watched the show." It had been difficult, blocking out all the gossip about the show and what was going on between the cast members during the months of filming. I was proud I'd managed to succeed.

Well, I'd heard some things, but nothing like this.

"Yeah, well, Remy and Chloe got their lawyer to send her a cease-and-desist letter, and also sent one to Eric and the network." Paige tossed her cigarette out into the gutter. She took my arm and smiled up at me. "As you can imagine, the network is scrambling, trying to do damage control while trying to see if the contract she signed doesn't have some loophole the Valences could slip through in court, and make the show and the network liable for damages."

The doorman nodded and held the door open for us.

It was hot inside. I took off my coat and draped it over my arm, feeling sweat forming at my temples and underarms. We took in the Aquitaine's Christmas décor. The lobby, mostly white marble with some gilt trim, smelled of pine. There were three enormous Christmas trees placed strategically around the lobby, all decorated in white and gold. White lights were wrapped around banisters and railings, winking at us. The mahogany chairs with their red velvet upholstery were placed around white marble top tables with red Christmas candles centered on them, sprigs of holly and pine branches completing the décor. The marble floors were so polished the chandelier lights reflected on their surface.

"Wow," I said as we went up the short flight of stairs to the mezzanine level and over to the elevator banks. I pushed the up button and fished the room card Sloane had given me out of my coat pocket. "Why can't they just bleep out Margery saying it, or edit the scene so it's cut?" I asked while we watched the lights above the elevators move from PH down as the elevator descended. "They bleeped Gillian on *Malibu* when she brought up that Lori had used a surrogate for her two kids when Lori threatened to sue." That had been an ugly mess, and Lori's secret had come out in the tabloids anyway.

It all ended with Lori leaving the show and an out-of-court settlement—with a sealed record and a nondisclosure agreement.

The elevator doors opened. "Chloe doesn't want to leave the show," Paige replied. "It's a big mess. I'm glad I'm not Eric Brewer."

I stuck the card into the appropriate slot and pressed PH. "Then she's crazy. This won't end well for her. She's going to get fired, and everyone's going to find out about Remy anyway. It's not like it's this huge secret around town, no matter what they think. Everyone knows Remy has men on the side." I couldn't be the only man in New Orleans who'd slept with Remy. Someone was bound to come forward and sell the story to a tabloid—or ask for hush money from the Valences.

And at this point, who cared? His mother was dead. Why not just say he was bisexual and Chloe was okay with it and it was nobody else's fucking business what went on in their marriage?

As Gillian said at the *Malibu* reunion after Lori left the show, "Why go on a reality show when you have things you want to hide? Everyone is going to find out."

Paige made that very point as the elevator stopped at the penthouse level and the doors opened. "So, yeah, watch what you say around all these women and around everyone at this party. They may have finished filming the season already, but…they could always go back and reshoot scenes, you know."

And they haven't filmed the reunion yet, I thought.

I made a mental note to stop at one drink.

There were four penthouses on the top floor of the Aquitaine. They were basically enormous apartments, complete with kitchens, bedroom suites, and terraces with stunning views. Eric Brewer's suite was one of the two facing the river. Each suite's terrace was private; there was a fire exit staircase between the terraces on each side, completely enclosed, so someone standing on one terrace couldn't see anyone standing on the one next door.

The bodyguard standing in front of the open door to Eric's suite must have been at least six feet six and weighed over three hundred pounds of solid muscle. He was wearing black pants and one of those tight black T-shirts with *Grande Dames of New Orleans* written across his gigantic pecs in gold glitter. His shaved scalp gleamed in the light. Dark sunglasses hid his eyes. A wire ran from his ear down his back. I held up the keycard. He didn't say anything, just waved us inside with a big meaty hand.

I handed my coat to a young woman in a maid's uniform. The big living room was filled with people, clustered into groups. The enormous windows running along the terrace were covered in condensation. It was stuffy inside, from the crush of people and the hot air coming through the vents. Already feeling a little claustrophobic, I smiled and nodded at people I vaguely recognized as I walked through the crowd to where a full bar had been set up. I recognized the young bartender from somewhere. He was pouring martinis into chilled glasses, garnishing them with olives. Despite my decision to stay sober, a dirty vodka martini with extra olives sounded good to me. As Paige moved off to find Ryan, I looked around for Taylor while I waited for my turn with the bartender.

Well, just one wouldn't hurt.

"Yes, please, a dirty vodka martini with extra olives?" I asked the bartender when he turned his attention to me. He tossed a cocktail napkin down and went to work. I glanced around the room, looking for Taylor. I finally spotted him near the terrace windows. He was laughing, but I couldn't see who he was talking to from where I was standing. Which was fine. I didn't need to hover over him all night. He was twenty-one years old, and Goddess knows, I was doing all kinds of things with very little supervision when I was that age. He was a good kid with a good head on his shoulders and never gave any of his uncles a reason to worry. He was so damned responsible that I wished sometimes he'd sow some wild oats—*give us a reason to worry.*

An extremely good-looking young man in his late twenties or early thirties walked up to the bar and also ordered a martini. He was taller than me, and handsome. His brown hair was cut short, and he wore tight black jeans and one of those ubiquitous *Grande Dames of New Orleans* T-shirts. His shoulders were broad, the T-shirt sleeves clung tightly to his big biceps, and his stomach was flat. He had an enormous smile with a mouth full of glowing straight white teeth.

Ah, youth.

His ass was also impressive.

"I gather you're with the show?" I said, nodding at his shirt as I took my martini from the bartender. "And yes, I have a keen grasp of the obvious."

He laughed as the bartender shook the martini shaker. He had a great laugh, and gorgeous green eyes. "Brandon Bernard." He held out a big strong hand for me to shake. His grip was strong and firm, and I felt a slight electrical charge as our skin touched.

Did I mention that he was very good looking?

"Yes, I'm on the production team for the show, assistant producer," he replied, with a roll of those green eyes. "Which means I'm Eric's bitch, twenty-four seven. Thank God he's got his eye on some young twink right now, so I can relax and have some fun." He took a swig of his martini and pulled the olive out with the little sword, popping it into his mouth. He shifted slightly, standing close enough to me that we were almost touching, so I could smell him.

He smelled good.

And was he—yes, he was flirting with me!

I know it probably sounds a little pathetic that being flirted with by a young man was a little exciting for me. I don't think of myself as being over forty. I always think of myself as being still twenty-nine, I think because that's how old I was when I first met Colin and Frank. It always catches me off guard that they're aren't thirty-three and forty-four anymore, either.

And then one night in a bar some kid called me *Daddy*, and it hit me, right between the eyes: I wasn't the hot young thing in the bars anymore.

But you know what? I'm fine with it.

I still get hit on, guys still flirt with me—but I've noticed that I'm becoming more and more invisible to younger guys. I don't care. I like myself, I like my age…although I wouldn't mind having some of my old energy back.

Or the ability to bounce back from a night of partying, or from working hard at the gym.

Or getting up on a cold morning without feeling my joints aching.

Okay, maybe I do mind a little.

And having Taylor around also has changed my perspective some. The thought of having sex with anyone in his peer group kind of creeps me out. I know there are older guys who are into younger ones, and vice versa. That's great, to each their own. But for me, having sex with someone Taylor's age just doesn't seem right. I can think they're cute, maybe sexy, but I don't see them in a sexual way.

So, being flirted with by this gorgeous younger guy was kind of fun. It wasn't going anywhere, but it was nice.

"Eric likes twinks?" I sipped my martini. I knew the answer was *yes*. I'd seen any number of pictures of Eric at clubs or parties or beaches, his arm draped around some kid less than half his age. They also ran shots of him shirtless from weekends—one had even anointed him "hottest guy over fifty." Eric was good looking enough, I suppose, but he didn't do anything for me. There was an element of him trying too hard for me to find him sexy. I'm sure when he was younger, he was cute and got away with a lot. Unfortunately, he clearly *still* thought he was young and cute. He was good looking for a guy in his fifties, and he didn't look like a guy in his fifties. But he *was* in his fifties, and he still acted like he was the cutest twink in town on his talk show. He got on my nerves so much I was never able to watch more than five minutes or so.

Brandon rolled his pretty eyes. "Does Eric like twinks? Does blood excite sharks?" He shook his head. "And always talking about wanting a relationship. Bitch, *please*. The stories I could tell…"

"It must be interesting working for him," I said, frowning. I'd lost sight of Taylor and was trying to find him again without making it obvious. There's nothing ruder than looking over someone's shoulder while you're talking to find someone better to talk to.

And then I saw him. His cheeks were flushed, and he was laughing.

He's an adult, I chided myself. *Stop acting like he's a child.*

Brandon rolled his eyes. "Did you see the movie *The Devil Wears Prada?*"

"*The details of your incompetence don't interest me,*" I quoted, and we both laughed.

"I wish I were kidding," he sighed. "I started years ago as his personal assistant, got promoted to assistant producer...but he still sometimes treats me like I'm his gofer." He snapped his fingers and scowled. "*Brandon, where's my coffee? Brandon, have you seen my phone?*"

"That's got to suck," I commiserated. Frank and Colin sometimes still treat me like the goofy stripper I was when we met. "How long have you been working for him?"

"I interned for him when I was in grad school, just when the shows were getting started." He shook his head. "It used to be worse. At least now he..." He hesitated, then tossed back his martini and held the glass out to the bartender for a refill. "I probably shouldn't tell you this"—*then don't*, I thought, but people always do—"but he used to get kind of handsy and inappropriate with me. I put a stop to it, though." His face was grim. "I was worried, you know, it might hurt my career with the network, but with all of the Weinstein stuff and everything else...I just jokingly called him Mr. Weinstein once and he stopped pretty damned quick."

So, Eric was even *worse* than I'd thought. "I'm glad it didn't, you know, affect your career."

"Thanks. You know, I have the night off..." He rolled his eyes. "The first time in weeks I've had a night off. And he's finally in a good mood. He's been a real bitch to work for the last few weeks."

"Since the Valences threatened to sue?"

His eyes goggled at me. "You know about that?"

"New Orleans is a very small town, Brandon. It's about a block long and we're all on a party line."

"What?"

Sigh. He was too young to get the reference. "Never mind. Everyone knows everyone, is what I meant, and everyone talks." I shrugged. "Everyone in town is talking about the Valence lawsuit." A slight exaggeration—I'd only just heard about it—but I was curious to hear his response.

"Can you believe he actually wanted me to try to seduce Remy Valence?" He took his glass back from the bartender. "And set up hidden cameras!" The alcohol was clearly loosening his lips. "I mean, I want to get ahead in this business but I'm not going to whore myself out for the network." He laughed. "At least without a guaranteed promotion. In writing. You can't trust Eric. You always have to get everything in writing."

"I imagine the cease-and-desist will be a pain to get around?"

He made a face. "No, Chloe and Remy signed a contract pretty much waiving all their privacy rights. The network lawyers made sure of that after the *Malibu* problem a few years back. It's a nuisance, you're right, but that's all it is. But we have plenty enough footage that if we need to switch storylines and re-edit the season, we can. There's always a lot of footage that's never used."

We chatted for a little while. It turned out he was originally from Birmingham, went to the University of Alabama like Taylor before going on to film and television school at Columbia. He seemed like a good guy, but I kept deflecting the flirty compliments and turning the conversation back around to him and his work. I saw Taylor walking through the crowd toward me.

"There's the twink du jour right now," Brandon said with an excessive eye roll.

I froze.

Taylor is the twink?

"Hey, Scotty," he said, grinning. His cheeks were a little flushed the way they always got when he'd had a few drinks, but he wasn't slurring and seemed fine. "Do you care if I go bar-hopping with some people after the party?"

"Who are some people?" I asked casually, noting out of the corner of my eye that Brandon's jaw had dropped.

"Eric Brewer and some other people from the show!" Taylor was clearly excited to be included.

I had reservations about him going off to clubs with Eric, especially after everything Brandon had just said. But I also didn't want to ruin his night. Maybe it wasn't the most responsible thing to do as an almost-parent/sort of role model, but Taylor was a good kid with a good head on his shoulders, and he always made the right decisions. I could trust him to behave and not get into any trouble.

No matter who he was with.

"Okay. Try not to be too late." I laughed. "And you know you don't need my permission." I touched his arm lightly. "Just be careful."

"You're the best!" He turned and disappeared back into the crowd.

"You're the twink's dad?" Brandon asked.

"More like an uncle, but—"

"You shouldn't let him go with Eric."

"Well, he's an adult...it's not like I can stop him." I shook my head and masked a yawn. "It's been lovely talking to you, Brandon, but I think I'm going to head home now. It's been a long night."

"I'll tell you what," he lowered his voice, "I'll go along with them, make sure nothing happens to your nephew."

"That's very nice of you, but you don't—"

"I want to." His voice was grim as he pressed a business card into my hand. "I'll make sure nothing happens to your nephew." His dimples deepened as he flashed me that *I wanna fuck you now* smile that was hard to resist. "Give me a call sometime."

I put the card in my coat pocket. "I may do that."

The rain had stopped, but it was even colder when I went back out the front doors of the hotel. I put in my ear buds and cued up *A Partridge Family Christmas Card* on my phone. I turned up the collar of my trench coat and started walking quickly down Royal Street. The wind was brutal, but the magical voices of David Cassidy and Shirley Jones and some unnamed backup singers in my ears made it slightly bearable. I dodged tourists obviously from colder climates gawking at the lights and decorations. The Quarter was done up for the holiday—everyone in New Orleans loves the chance to decorate.

The only thing missing to complete the picture of a Christmas wonderland was snow—and the air felt cold and damp enough for that to not be entirely out of the question. I thought about stopping at Mom and Dad's. Their lights were on and their shutters were closed, but there was no telling who was there—their place was a kind of salon at night, and I was kind of tired. I hadn't made that up.

I kept trudging along in the cold.

My nice warm bed was sounding delicious.

To distract myself, I started thinking about whose Christmas presents I had yet to buy, and what might be the perfect gift.

It worked. Before I knew it, I was rounding the corner at Decatur.

I unlocked the gate and walked down the dark passageway to the courtyard. It was quiet back there as I started climbing the stairs, thinking, *One thing I am definitely doing if we renovate is enclosing these stairs from the weather*.

When I reached the third-floor landing I was surprised to see the door slightly ajar.

I distinctly remembered closing and locking it.

I took my phone out, cued up 9-1-1, and walked inside. At the end of the hallway I could see the lights in the living room were on and a pool of dark liquid—what looked like *blood*—was spreading across the hardwood floor just beyond the couch.

What the hell?

I crept down the hallway, and a body lying on the living room floor came into view.

Colin was standing beside it, his gun in his hand, his face grave.

He looked up when I cleared my throat.

"Hi, honey," he said with a rueful grin as he relaxed and dropped his gun arm. "I'm home?"

CHAPTER FOUR

THE MOON

Change and deception

In all fairness, it *had* been a while since Colin brought his work home with him.

Still, something you never get used to is seeing a dead body— or at least, I hoped not.

I've certainly had my fair share of experience with them, and it's still unsettling.

Thank God Taylor went bar-hopping was my first coherent thought after the reality began sinking in.

I could feel myself starting to go into shock, so I bent at the waist, looked down at the floor, and took some deep breaths. It didn't take long for the weird buzzing in my ears and the grayness on the edge of my vision to go away.

I took another deep breath, straightened up, and took an assessing look around.

Our living room was trashed. The television had been knocked off the entertainment center, connector cables ripped out of its back. The entertainment center itself looked like it had been kicked or something; the side panel was smashed and the whole thing was tilting dangerously. The cable box was blinking all red zeroes. The coffee table was also lying on its side, the glass top shattered, shards and glittering beads of broken glass scattered around on the faded and worn Oriental rug. The couch had been shoved out of line and the end table was in pieces. One of the easy chairs was on its back; the other had been knocked aside and was splattered with blood. The hideous, tacky cuckoo clock Storm bought me in Switzerland had been knocked off the wall and lay in the debris from the coffee table, smashed, the door open and the little yellow cuckoo bird dangling on its wire.

Everything that had been hanging on the walls in the living room was now on the floor, frames bent out of shape and the glass cracked. I couldn't tell if any of the art itself was ruined—but that could wait.

And there was the blood...

There was a huge puddle of it spreading out from under the dead man's head. He was on his side, his back to me. The way his head rested against the floor made it look like it had been smashed in on that side, and his neck looked broken. His thick bluish-black hair was soaked with blood. His head was turned away from me, so I couldn't see the face. He was wearing what Colin called "cat burglar garb"—black pants, a black turtleneck, black sneakers.

"Glad I waited to put up the Christmas decorations," I heard myself saying. I shook my head and took my first good look at Colin. I immediately switched over to caregiver mode. "Jesus, Colin, are you okay?"

Under normal circumstances, Colin was probably one of the best-looking guys I've ever seen—certainly in the top ten, at any rate. He is so handsome it's almost absurd. He's shorter than most people think or remember, because he's so charismatic he *seems* taller. But he's only five seven on a good day, with about 210 pounds of pure, defined, thick muscle packed on his frame. If he weren't one of the top undercover operatives in the world, he could make a living as a fitness model. His olive skin tans easily, making his emerald-green eyes pop, and when his thick bluish-black isn't cut buzz short, it cascades in Apollonian curls around his face. He has dimples in his cheeks, a strong square jaw, and perfectly straight white teeth beneath sensual thick lips. He can move not only quickly, but silently. He is ridiculously flexible and agile.

Once he'd rescued me when some bad guys had drugged and kidnapped me, and to make our escape he strapped me to his back and rappelled down the side of Jax Brewery.

It's a long story.

Right now, there was a nasty-looking bruise on his right cheek and a huge discolored lump on his left forehead. His right eye was blackened and swelling shut. His big strong hands were covered in blood. His upper lip was also getting fatter as I watched, and there was some blood leaking out from both nostrils. His tight black T-shirt was ripped, the fabric hanging loose from his left shoulder. Angry red scratches, bleeding in places, ran down his chest, and his left nipple was also bloody. His dark jeans were soaked with blood.

"Um, I can explain," he said. He put his hands on his knees and bent forward, trying to catch his breath. He straightened back up with a sheepish look on his face. "I'm sorry about the mess, but..." His voice trailed off.

I took off my coat and hung it on the coat tree. "Yeah, well, I'd been thinking about redecorating."

I walked into the kitchen and got the heavy-duty first-aid kit I kept under the sink. I shook my head. Part of the cost of being in love with someone who does the kind of work Colin does is you have to patch him back together from time to time. "I assume this has something to do with whatever case you're working on right now and you can't tell me anything or you'll have to kill me," I said, walking back into the living room.

That's another part of the cost.

You can't ask questions, you can't know anything, you just have to have blind faith.

Like right now. There's a dead body in our living room and I may never know why.

Sometimes I lose sleep worrying about where Colin is or what he's doing. That usually happens when Frank is off wrestling somewhere and I'm home by myself...and have probably smoked too much weed. I'll lie there in bed, missing them both and imagining the worst.

Having a vivid imagination can be a curse.

But the sad reality is worrying doesn't change anything. So, I just push those fears into a dark corner of my mind and forget about them. Life doesn't give you anything you can't handle, and should my worst fears come true someday, I'd deal with it then.

As Mom says, "Worrying is just borrowing trouble."

"You're dressed up," Colin said, taking a step toward the couch.

He winced and put a hand up to his ribs. "Where are Frank and Taylor?"

"Taylor and I went to the premiere party for the *Grande Dames*," I replied, opening the first aid kit. "Frank's wrestling in Pensacola and Taylor went out with some people from the party. Thank the Goddess for small favors."

Colin gritted his teeth and made it to the couch, sitting down with a groan. "He was a really bad guy, Scotty." He gestured with his head toward the corpse. "Believe me, the world's a better place without him. If I hadn't killed him, he would have killed me...and then you would have walked in here..." He closed his eyes and winced again. "I was terrified you or Frank or Taylor were here, or would come home, or..."

"Are you sure you're okay?" I sat down next to him on the couch and started dabbing at the bloody slashes on his chest. "Do I need to get you to a hospital? You don't look so good, Colin. Seriously." His face was pale beneath the tan. "I'll get you a painkiller." I had some leftover from an abscessed tooth situation I'd suffered through during the summer.

Rule number one: never discard medication, because you never know when it'll come in handy.

"No, I'll be all right." He yanked down on his T-shirt, finishing the job of ripping it from his muscular torso. He wadded it up and tossed it on the floor. There was an even more hideous bruise running from the hip bone to the bottom of his rib cage. "He got some good licks in, though." He started pressing on his ribs. "You know what? I think a painkiller would be terrific, thanks."

Shaking my head, I carefully stepped around the broken glass and the debris on the floor and walked down to the bathroom. I found the bottle of pain pills, shook one out, and filled a Dixie cup with water.

"Thanks," he said as he took them from me. I flipped the coffee table back up onto its legs. The cigar box holding my deck of tarot cards had been knocked across the room, spilling out cards in front of the wrecked television. I gathered up as many of them as I could—I'd check to see if any were missing later.

"I suppose calling the police isn't an option?" I sat down on the edge of the coffee table, retrieved some antiseptic wipes from the medicine kit, and touched them to the scratches on Colin's chest. His chest flexed as I wiped the scratches clean. His nipple didn't appear to be torn, just scratched. "Let me get some ice. That eye and your lip..."

He smiled at me. "Am I still pretty?"

I kissed the top of his head. "You'll always be pretty."

He'd managed to get his jeans off when I came back with the ice pack. There were bruises on his legs, too. He was wearing black Calvin Klein low-rise briefs. His leg muscles rippled as he bent his knees, checking for any breaks or fractures. He took one of the ice packs and placed it over his swollen eye.

"Brace yourself," I said, putting a little pressure on Colin's ribs with the other ice pack. "This doesn't hurt?"

"Nothing's broken, I was just a little winded." He smiled. "I've taken much worse in the field when I didn't have a sexy nurse to take care of me."

I wiped the blood from under his nose, checking to make sure the bleeding stopped. I glanced back over at the body and felt another wave of nausea. *Get over it, you can't get sick*, I told myself sternly.

I take great pride in being good in a crisis.

"But how did he get in?" After the last time someone broke in trying to kill Colin, we'd made the building more secure. We replaced the wooden door on the street level to the passageway with a steel door and had the frame reinforced. Razor wire was strung across the top. The vacant space on the first floor also had a reinforced and padlocked steel door into the courtyard. The shed at the back of the courtyard had a door to the parking lot, but it was also reinforced steel.

The parking lot was a vulnerable spot. If someone managed to get past the big steel garage-style door without a pass card or the entry code, they'd need a ladder to climb up to the roof of the shed and over into the courtyard. And the top of that wall had broken bottles embedded in concrete to discourage climbers.

Of course, international assassins could still climb onto the roofs of the buildings on either side of ours, but since the shutters were still closed and latched, he couldn't have gotten in that way.

"He was already here waiting for me, sitting in the dark with his gun trained on the door." Colin shook his head.

A cold chill crept up my spine. What if Taylor had come home first?

Colin saw the look on my face. "I'm sorry, Scotty. I don't even know how he could have gotten in. But he was here, waiting to kill me." He gestured with his head. "I think his gun wound up over by the desk." He shrugged. "Thank God I got home before you two."

"Yeah." I took a deep breath. "We're going to have to get rid of the body, aren't we?" I was about to become an accessory after the fact.

It's not the first time, a voice reminded me.

He shook his head. "I'm sorry, Scotty. No police. You have to trust me."

"It is what it is." I stood up. Okay, crisis mode was kicking in. "We're going to have to get rid of this rug, there's no way we'll ever get the blood out of it." It was an old Oriental rug I'd been meaning to replace for years anyway. I just hadn't taken the time to look for a new one. "We can roll him up in it. But the blood on that recliner—"

"I'm pretty sure that's mine." Colin stood up, wincing. "Just use some spot remover on it. I'll get bleach and rags."

I stood up and walked around the couch opposite the body. I'd left the back door open and a cold draft blew down the hall. It had started raining, and it was really coming down now. I looked at Colin. He seemed okay. I felt a crazy laugh rising and forced it down. I needed to stay calm—I could have a breakdown later if necessary.

I walked over and picked up the feet. He was heavy, but I bent my knees and pulled backward. It took a few tries, but I finally got him onto the carpet as Colin returned with a bucket and rags. I could smell the bleach as he started wiping up the blood.

"I'm sorry, Scotty." Colin's voice was grim as he carefully wiped the floor. "I can tell you this much: my cover was blown. Angela told me to get out of...where I was and come back here to wait for further instructions." He dipped the rags in the bleachy water and started wiping again. "I covered my tracks, believe me. Different flights, different airports, different passports. You can imagine my shock when I turned on the light and he was sitting there." He pointed to where one of the dining room table chairs had been splintered and smashed. "He shot twice."

I followed his pointing finger with my eyes. Yes, there were two bullet holes in the plaster wall. Shit, shit, shit. "He had a gun and the drop on you? Damn, you're good." I looked back at the chair. "He was a fool. He should have shot you before you turned on the lights."

"Bestuzhev was always an arrogant prick." He stood up. "I told him before it would bite him in the ass one day."

I decided not to think about the fact Colin knew the guy. "But why here? Why kill you?" I was starting to feel dizzy again and sat down on the couch, hard.

"I've no idea. There was no way—my private life, my cover, has always been incredibly protected. Or so I thought."

"Do you think—" My voice broke. *Oh God.* "You don't think other—"

"I don't know. I hope not. You guys aren't the target...I am. If I'm not here, you should be safe."

Assuming they—whoever they are—won't want to use us to get to you. He somehow knew you were coming here today. He didn't care if we were here or not.

And just how *did he know to come here to wait for Colin?*

I felt queasy.

"You have to believe me, Scotty, I had no idea this was going to follow me here. There are so many firewalls between me and Blackledge..." His voice was grim. "Nobody could have known I was coming here. But I used my Blackledge credit card...which means either the credit card company or Blackledge has been compromised."

"But he knew where to find you." This was bad. Really bad. "Would they have known that from tracking your Blackledge Amex?"

Colin shook his head. "No."

My heart was beating fast. I needed to stay calm. But if Blackledge had been compromised...I swallowed and said what I was thinking.

"There's no chance...no chance Angela might have sent him?"

Angela Blackledge ran the agency Colin had been working for since he'd left the Mossad in his late twenties. "I know you can't tell me about your latest mission—any of your missions—but you haven't done anything that would make her want to, um, you know…" I gestured toward the body. I couldn't say it. I didn't even want to think it. "Have you?"

"No. This last mission—it was a total shit show right from the start," he replied, nudging the corpse with his foot. "I suspected we'd been compromised. The mission blew up in our faces too fast for it not to have been. But it never occurred to me to think that the agency had been…shit, agents all over the world could be in jeopardy. I need to call Angela." He got up and walked over to where his duffel bag was sitting in the hallway. I hadn't noticed it there. He pulled out his secure satellite phone and pressed a few buttons. After a few moments he said, "Angela, it's Colin. Call me the moment you get this." He slipped the phone back into his bag. He started pacing. "Well, yes, we were compromised, certainly. I can't tell you much, but I can tell you that our 'surprise' mission to rescue a hostage wasn't a surprise to the hostage takers. We lost a couple of men, good men. Angela told me to abort, get out of there as fast as I could, and just come back home to New Orleans." He stared at me.

I knew him well enough to know he was thinking the same thing I was.

If Blackledge was compromised, maybe they'd gotten to Angela already.

"Take a hot shower and get dressed," I said. "I take it you're going to have to skip town?"

He didn't answer, just gave me a sad smile as he walked past on his way to the bathroom. I wanted to hug him, kiss him, do something to let him know I loved him, but let the moment pass.

Once I heard the shower come on, I checked out the front door. It hadn't been forced, and there were no signs the lock had been tampered with. The deadbolt was sturdy but had been sticking lately. I'd been meaning to spray some WD-40 into it, just hadn't gotten around to it yet.

It was still pouring down rain. Lightning flashed close by, and the thunder that followed shook the house. I shivered.

The assassin—what had Colin called him? Bestuzhev? He'd either had a key or picked the lock.

But how did he get past the gate? Rain or no rain, you can't pick a lock on Decatur Street, even at night, without being seen, questioned.

I bit my lower lip. *Is Colin telling me the truth?*

He'd lied to me before.

We'd separated from him for a couple of years back when we first became a throuple (I hate that word. Taylor was the first person to use it to describe our three-way relationship, but I'm getting used to it the more I hear it), because his job—a case he was working on—required him to let us believe he'd murdered two of my uncles (that's a *really* long story). But he hadn't killed them, and we'd all welcomed him back into the family once we knew the truth.

I also knew if it was necessary for his job, he'd lie to us all over again.

But with Taylor part of our family…we hadn't been completely honest with him about Colin's job.

Such a fucking mess.

I glanced up at the ceiling.

What if another assassin is upstairs?

My blood ran cold. That hadn't even occurred to me.

I was walking back to the kitchen to get my gun when there was a crash from the bathroom.

I ran back down the hall and opened the bathroom door. Colin sat on the floor, naked. The room was filling with steam from the shower. He looked dazed, woozy.

"Are you sure you're all right?" I knelt down beside him.

He winced. "I slipped getting into the shower like an idiot. I'm really sorry about all of this, Scotty." He pushed himself back up to his feet and gave me a sad smile. "You know the last thing in the world I want is put any of you in danger. And the living room—"

"Frank wanted a new television anyway, and I've been meaning to redecorate," I replied breezily, holding his arm as he climbed into the shower. "Just get cleaned up, I'll lay out some clothes for you. Are you sure you don't want to go to the emergency room?"

"Too many questions." Colin stepped into the spray. "I love you."

"I love you, too." I picked up his underwear off the floor and went into the spare bedroom. Since Colin wasn't home as much, we kept his clothes in the spare bedroom. I found him some clean underwear, a T-shirt, and clean jeans, walked back into the living room, and got his bloody pants and the torn scraps of his T-shirt. I put the T-shirt in the trash and tossed the pants into the empty laundry basket in the bedroom.

Shit, DNA, I thought. *Oh, well, I'll just wash everything with bleach.*

I placed the clean clothes on the toilet and shut the bathroom door.

I'd finished cleaning up most of the mess in the living room when Colin joined me. His hair was still damp. "I'm so sorry about this."

I shook my head. "I don't know how I'm going to explain how everything got wrecked to Taylor, though." I shrugged. "Let's get the body rolled up in the carpet."

"Okay." Colin checked his satellite phone. "Hang on, Angela left a message." He pressed some buttons and held the phone up to his ear. After a few minutes he turned the phone off and tossed it back in his bag. "She's just as shocked as I am. I'm going to head out of town once we're done here—there's a six a.m. flight out of New Orleans to Houston." He glanced at his watch. "That should give me just enough time to get rid of this mess and get to the airport. You mind if I take the CR-V?"

"As long as you don't leave any evidence in it."

"Get some twine and some garbage bags. You're going to have to help me carry him out of here."

I got the twine and Colin tied the carpet securely once we finished rolling him up in it. He then tied garbage bags around the ends and the center.

"What do you think? The Rigolets?"

The Rigolets was the narrow mouth connecting Lake Pontchartrain to Lake Borgne, which wasn't really a lake but a narrow-mouthed bay that opened out to the gulf.

"The tide should be going out now," I said, looking at my watch. "With any luck the tide will take him right out of Lake Borgne and into the gulf."

"Perfect. Let's get him up." On the count of three we lifted the rug and started carrying him down the hallway. He was incredibly heavy, and my back and shoulders were screaming as we made our way out the door and to the staircase.

There was about an inch of cold water in the courtyard, but the rain had lightened up some. Still, I was sweating and out of breath by the time we got the body out to the parking garage. Once we'd lifted him into the hatch of the car, we kissed and I held on to him. "Be careful," I whispered into his ear.

He kissed me and whispered back. "I'll call as soon as I can." He stepped away from me and touched the side of my face before slamming the hatch shut. "All right. I'll leave the car at Park'n'Fly lot at the airport. I'll text you the spot number when I'm in the terminal. Wait and pick up the car later in the afternoon or wait until Sunday morning. And don't worry, I'll clean the back out once I get rid of the body." He climbed into the driver's seat. "I love you. I'll get in touch as soon as I can."

"Love you, too." I paused. "I have to tell Frank about this."

He winced. "It's better if he knows so you can both be on guard. But do you have to tell Taylor?"

"I won't." It was bad enough I was an accessory after the fact and was going to make Frank one, too. I wasn't putting Taylor at risk.

Maybe…maybe he could stay with Mom and Dad for a while.

I watched Colin drive out of our parking garage.

This might be the last time I ever see him.

My eyes filled with tears, but I wiped them away.

Exhausted and drained, I went back up to the apartment. I finished sweeping up the broken glass and splintered wood, carried the wreckage down to the garbage cans in the courtyard, and tried to get the living room as back to normal as I possibly could.

It was about two thirty in the morning when I finally got undressed and got into bed. I was worried I would be too stressed out to sleep, but exhaustion trumped worry and I fell asleep almost as soon as I closed my eyes.

I woke to the sound of my cell phone ringing on the nightstand. Thinking it was Colin, I opened my eyes and reached for it.

Taylor's face was looking at me from the screen and it was 8:17 in the morning. I unlocked my phone. "Taylor?"

"Scotty?" He sounded weird, his voice kind of slurring. "I—I need help. Can you come?"

I swung my legs out of the bed and was walking into the bathroom as I said, "Where are you? What's wrong?"

"I—I don't feel so hot. I feel really strange." He gulped. "I'm at Eric's suite in the hotel. And—and he's dead."

"What?" I put him on speaker and splashed water on my face. "Did you say he's dead?"

"Dead." He muffled a sob. "And I'm naked and I don't know what happened and I'm scared and I don't feel good. Can you come?"

"Stay where you are and don't touch anything. I'm on my way."

CHAPTER FIVE
TEN OF CUPS, REVERSED
Chance of betrayal

It is amazing how motivating absolute terror can be.

Exhausted, sleepy, and bleary-eyed one moment, about three seconds later I was wide awake and operating in crisis mode for the second time in less than twelve hours. Adrenaline had my heart thumping as my body operated on automatic pilot while my mind focused on remaining calm. Pair of jeans and sweatshirt to wear, grab socks and shoes. Run into bathroom, turn on hot water, wash face and brush teeth. My fingers shook as I tied my shoelaces.

Deep breaths, Scotty. You need to be calm. Focus.

Horrible guilty thoughts raced through my mind.

You shouldn't have let him go off with that prick, I thought as I pulled my Saints hoodie over my head, *you knew better, you had a bad feeling, and since when do you not listen to your instincts? All you had to do was make him come home with you.*

"Right. Because helping me and Colin dispose of a body would have been better," I said aloud.

All right, Scotty, think. Phone, keys, wallet.

I shoved my wallet into my back pocket and grabbed my trench coat, pulling it on and fumbling with my keys. They flew out of my fingers and bounced underneath the bed. "Damn it!" I shouted, dropping to my knees and looking. I shoved my right arm the darkness, feeling around with my still-shaking fingers. I felt dust and dust bunnies, a paper clip, a pen...and finally the damned keys.

I need to clean under there, I thought as I stood back up.

I shook my head. "Get a grip, Scotty, you can have a nervous breakdown later," I said. "He needs you to be strong. Focus on taking care of Taylor."

Yes, that's the key. I felt myself calming down already.

Besides, why borrow trouble?

Stay calm until you get there, hear what Taylor has to say.

One good thing about having activist parents who frequently got arrested during protests was learning at a young age how the criminal justice system works.

No matter what, I was glad Taylor hadn't come home with me last night.

Whatever happened at the Aquitaine last night, I wasn't sorry he wasn't complicit in helping Colin cover up a murder.

And there was no way I was going to tell Taylor what happened.

The three of us had decided to not tell Taylor the whole truth about what Colin actually does after Taylor came to live with us. I still worry about lying to him—as Mom always says, "it's stupid to lie because the truth will always come out"—but both Frank and Colin thought Taylor would be living with us only while he was finishing college at Tulane, and after that it wouldn't be an issue.

We'd moved the cache of weaponry we used to keep in the spare bedroom on the fourth floor to the closet in the bedroom Colin used on the third floor.

Taylor had only asked once why that closet door was padlocked, and I just said, "It's where the guns are."

I guess we could thank his small-town rural Alabama upbringing for him not questioning us having a gun closet.

But how the hell was I going to explain the living room to him?

Well, Taylor, I've been meaning to redecorate for a while. So when I got home from the party last night I was bored and thought I'd get started.

Yeah, *great* idea.

And what if more assassins showed up looking for Colin?

Worry about that later. Right now, you need to get to Taylor and figure out what to do to fix this situation. The rest can be dealt with later.

I made sure I locked the deadbolt on the back door as I went out into the cold, glancing up the stairs. *Should I go check on Taylor's apartment?*

Scooter.

He hadn't been fed and who knew how long I'd be gone?

I dashed upstairs. He was sleeping on Taylor's bed and didn't even look up as I filled his food and water bowls.

I resisted the temptation to run down the back stairs but was still taking them too fast. I could almost feel time slipping through my fingers.

Taylor is alone and terrified with a dead body.

I shivered. It was cold and damp outside, not nearly as cold as the night before, but at least it wasn't raining. *You're not going to be any help to Taylor if you break your neck on the stairs and if you can't think clearly. Get a grip.*

When I got to the bottom of the stairs my phone chimed. I pulled it out, thinking, *What if it's Frank? What am I going to tell him?*

I couldn't deal with Frank right now.

He's coming home today, you're going to have to deal with him eventually.

But it wasn't Frank. It was a text from Colin: *Park n Fly, N47.*

And I was relieved—relieved that it was just my accomplice, telling me where to pick up my car, which he'd used to dispose of a body.

This is what my life has come to now.

For fuck's sake, Scotty, get a goddamned grip.

I slipped my phone back into my pocket, compartmentalizing. Colin was fine, he was an adult and could take care of himself. I didn't need to worry about him.

I needed to worry about Taylor.

And what I was going to find in the penthouse at the Royal Aquitaine Hotel.

I headed down the passageway to Decatur Street, putting up the collar of my coat against the cold. Nobody would believe me if I told them about the last twelve hours of my life. I closed the steel door behind me and listened for the bolt to catch. There weren't many people out—it was still early on a cold December Saturday morning. I scanned in every direction to see if anyone was watching our gate.

So far, so good.

I chose not to think about most professionals being too good for me to spot.

I started walking as fast as I could to the corner and turned right. The wind coming from the river was icy cold, and the air felt damp, like it was going to rain again at any minute. I shoved my hands down into the pockets of my coat, cursing myself for forgetting to wear gloves. I reached the corner at Royal and turned left again.

The sun was trying to break through the gloomy dark clouds as I hurried up Royal Street. A heavily bundled-up woman was walking her dog, who wagged his tail and barked a hello at me. I smiled and nodded at her, saying "good morning" while dodging around the dog. She gave me a startled look.

I probably looked like hell but didn't care.

Every instinct inside me was screaming at me to break into a run.

But I didn't want to attract any attention, so I resisted the impulse.

Maybe Taylor's wrong and Eric's just unconscious, what does he mean he doesn't feel good he said he was naked oh my God what if he killed Eric I knew I shouldn't have let him go with Eric but then he would have come home with me and—

When I reached the corner at St. Philip Street, I stopped walking, closed my eyes, and took another deep breath.

O Goddess, help me get through this whatever it may be, I know I have the strength to handle this, just guide me to do the right thing.

Scotty, you know what to do, I heard her voice whisper. *One of your greatest strengths has been your family.*

Family.

Of course.

Of course.

Feeling calmer, I pulled out my phone. I pulled up my contacts and touched Storm's name on the screen. Having an older brother can be a pain in my ass sometimes—he's a horrible tease—but he's also a damned good lawyer.

Good lawyer trumps tease, every time. Believe me.

"Scotty! What are you doing up so early on a Saturday morning?" He sounded out of breath. He'd started exercising lately—his cholesterol was high, and so was his blood pressure—and I'd helped design a workout program for him. "I was just doing some planks."

"I need your help," I replied.

"Why else would you be calling me? You only call me when you're in trouble," he teased.

"Storm, not now—please. Not a good time."

He flipped a mental switch and went from pain-in-the-ass older brother to cutthroat lawyer instantly. "What's going on? Are you in trouble, and how bad is it?"

While it would have been a relief to tell him everything, I couldn't involve him in the Colin mess—especially since I didn't even know what it was.

"It's not me this time, believe it or not." I was amazed at how calm I sounded. I started walking again. "I'm on my way to the Royal Aquitaine Hotel. Taylor just called me. He's there and he's in trouble." I filled Storm in on everything else from last night, from me and Taylor going to the Sazerac Bar to Taylor's call this morning. I just skipped coming home to a wrecked apartment and a dead body. "I told him to stay there and not do anything, not touch anything, and wait for me to get there. Please tell me that wasn't the wrong thing to do?"

"We'll have to call the police, but that can wait until I get there. I've got you on speaker now, I'm getting dressed." I heard my sister-in-law Marguerite say something unintelligible in the background. "Do *not* call the police before I get there, is that clear? Do not do a damned thing until I get there, are you listening? You wait in the lobby for me and we'll go up together. I am not joking, Scotty. If you go up there without me, you can be charged with tampering with evidence or contaminating a crime scene. That won't look good for Taylor. Taylor's all right, though?"

"He didn't say he was hurt. He sounded funny, though."

"I've got an Uber on the way and I cannot emphasize enough that you are not to go up there without me, is that clear?"

"Got it." I put the phone back into my pocket, feeling better.

I put my other hand in my coat pocket. The keycard for the elevator was still there. It was kind of strange that they hadn't collected them back, wasn't it, especially since those cards could be used to access the private penthouse floor? Kind of a huge security lapse, particularly from the hotel's point of view.

They couldn't have been too thrilled to pass out all those key cards giving people access to a secured floor.

That might be important. If everyone at that party had kept their cards...

I still didn't know what I was going to find when I got there, but knowing Storm was on his way was a load off my mind.

The cavalry was coming to the rescue.

I walked faster, my mind racing with every step.

So, this must be what it feels like to be a parent, I thought as I went around the corner of the Royal Aquitaine, wincing as the cold wind blasted me in the face, almost knocking me back a step. I nodded at the liveried doorman with a smile as he held the door open for me, feeling warm air washing over me as I stepped into the opulent lobby.

There were two people in uniforms at the front desk, but no one at the concierge stand. The big lobby was quiet and empty. It was still too early for checkouts and far too early for check-ins. I sat down in a wingback chair near the elevator banks.

I couldn't get the thought of a terrified Taylor up there in that penthouse, alone with a dead body, out of my head.

But maybe Eric Brewer *wasn't* dead? Maybe he was just unconscious, and Taylor was too scared to realize it.

I would want me up there, if I were him. He called me, didn't he? Wouldn't he be wondering where I was, if I was coming?

No, fuck this. I wasn't going to wait.

Sorry, Storm, I thought as I pushed the up button. The right elevator door opened, and I stepped in, using the keycard to activate the PH button. The doors closed, and the elevator started going up. I watched the numbers light up as the elevator passed each floor. It seemed to take forever, but finally the elevator jolted to a stop. The doors opened.

The hallway of the penthouse floor was empty and silent. I walked over to the door to Eric Brewer's penthouse. I didn't hesitate. I held the card over the sensor and the light turned green. The lock clicked open.

I used the tip of my index finger on the outermost edge of the handle to push it down.

I stepped inside and let the door close behind me. I pulled out my phone and started taking photos as I walked down the little entry hallway into the main room of the penthouse.

No one had cleaned up after the party. Both bars were still set up and the curtains were still open, exposing that stunning view of downtown and the river. There were trash cans full of empty bottles and plastic cups next to both bars. There were plastic cups everywhere, with varying amounts of liquid inside of them. The place smelled like sour alcohol and sweat.

"Scotty?" I heard Taylor call from the right side of the suite. I barely had time to turn before Taylor almost tackled me. He was wearing his clothes from last night but was barefoot and shivering. He's almost eight inches taller than I am but somehow buried his head in my right shoulder and started sobbing.

My heart broke and yet I was filled with rage at the same time.

"Shh, there, there, it's okay, I'm here now," I whispered, stroking his back. "Come on, let's sit down and take a minute, okay? Where are your shoes?"

He let me lead him over to one of the couches. He was ugly crying and his red nose was running. I sat him down and knelt in front of him. He looked terrible. His skin had a greenish pallor, his eyes were red, and his breath reeked of stale alcohol and vomit. "Storm's on his way, shh. It'll be okay, Taylor. I'm here now. Where are your shoes and socks?"

"In-in-in-in th-thuh-thuh-there." He gestured over his shoulder with his head. His hair was matted and sweaty.

If Eric Brewer wasn't already dead, I might just kill him myself.

"You just stay here and I'm going to go take a look around and grab your shoes and socks, okay? I'll be right back, okay?"

He nodded, wiping his nose on his sleeve. He looked about twelve years old.

I crept over to the bedroom door and bit my lip.

For the second time in less than twelve hours, I was looking at a dead body.

There was no question about it. Eric Brewer was dead, all right. His glassy eyes were staring up at the ceiling.

He was wearing a white fluffy hotel robe with *Aquitaine*

embroidered in gold script over the right chest. The robe had fallen open, exposing his hairy chest and legs and a pair of red bikini underwear. He wasn't wearing anything else. The right side of his head was just...well, gore. Someone had hit him very hard with something very hard on the right side of his head. His mouth was open, like he'd been surprised, and there was a puddle of blood coagulating under his head. The huge bed itself was rumpled, used, and the sour smell of vomit came from the bathroom. There were a couple of glasses on one of the nightstand with purplish red liquid in them. Right next to them was a bottle of red wine, about half full. There was also a package of condoms, and a condom wrapper tossed onto the floor on that side.

You're lucky you're already dead, I thought, resisting the urge to kick the body.

Taylor's shoes, the socks carefully tucked inside them, sat next to the bathroom door. I took a picture of Taylor's shoes before picking them up and bringing them to him.

I wanted nothing more than to tell him to put them on and get us both out of there.

But that would make things look worse than they already did.

He was reclining on the sofa, his hand over his eyes. He'd stopped crying, but he still looked green.

"Honey, are you okay?"

"Scotty, I don't feel so good." He swallowed. "It's not a hangover, I swear. I don't understand what happened last night. I had two glasses of wine here at the party, and then Eric wanted me to take him around to some of the bars. I just had water everywhere we went. And then...when we were at the Brass Rail I started to feel, I don't know, woozy and dizzy." He sat up and moaned. "And Eric got us a cab, said he'd take me home. I don't remember anything else, Scotty, until I woke up this morning and called you." He swallowed. "And...when I woke up, Scotty, he was...he was just lying there on the floor and I didn't have any clothes on..." His eyes filled with tears. "I don't know what happened, Scotty." His voice broke. *"I don't know if he did something to me."*

Stay calm stay calm stay calm.

"We're going to have to take you to the hospital," I heard

myself saying. "What else happened this morning when you…woke up?"

"I went into the bathroom and…" He started crying all over again.

"As soon as Storm gets here, we're going to get you to the hospital, okay?" I pulled him into a hug and kissed the top of his head. "Everything's going to be okay, Taylor, believe me. We're going to take care of you."

My phone vibrated. It was Storm. *You'd better not be upstairs.*

"I have to go get Storm," I whispered. "Stay right here. Don't move or touch anything."

Taylor nodded.

I cried all the way down to the lobby. There's no worse feeling in the world than when someone you love is hurting, suffering, and there's nothing you can do to make them better.

I wanted to curl up in a ball and sob. I also wanted to put my fist through a wall.

This is your fault, that insidious voice in my head whispered. *You knew better than to let him go off with that pig.*

Storm was pacing in the lobby when I got out of the elevator. "Are you—" He stopped short when he got a look at my face. "Jesus, Scotty, how bad is it?" he whispered.

"I'll—I'll tell you in the elevator."

By the time the elevator doors opened on the penthouse floor Storm's face was as thunderous as I felt. "You shouldn't have come up here in the first place," he said, in a frighteningly calm voice as we walked into the penthouse. "They're going to accuse you of tampering with evidence."

"I don't fucking care."

He turned to me. "I want you to go back out into the hall and call Venus while I talk to Taylor."

"But—"

"Scotty, from this moment on Taylor is my client. You cannot talk to him about this case, you cannot talk to him about anything because you could be called to testify against him." He held up his hand when I started to splutter. "Shut up. You coming in here—that could be really bad, Scotty. I know why you did even though I told you not to, I get it. Believe me, I do." He lowered his voice. "If that son of a bitch wasn't already dead I'd kill him myself with my bare hands. Death is too good for him. I may be able to retain you and Frank as investigators, which may muddy the line of client-attorney privilege, but until then…" He shook his head. "I know, we've done that before but there have some rulings lately I need to study in greater detail, just in case. Now, go in the hall and call Venus. We need to get him to a hospital, have a rape kit done, and get him on that drug that," his voice broke, but he pulled it together, "that will keep him from getting HIV. Ask Venus if you can go to the emergency room or if she wants you to wait."

It felt like the floor had dropped out from under me. I'd not even thought about HIV or other STIs.

This just kept getting worse.

I walked out into the hall and called Venus.

Venus Casanova is a New Orleans police detective. Our paths have crossed many times over the years, almost always over a dead body, and while I used to annoy her, I think she now has a grudging respect for me.

What can I say? I grow on people.

She answered on the first ring. "Casanova."

"Hey, Venus, this is Scotty Bradley." I swallowed.

"Please tell me you haven't found another dead body."

"I really wish I could."

She sighed. "Where are you?"

"The Aquitaine, on the penthouse floor." *Never answer any police question with more information than asked for*, I could hear my mother and Storm's voices both say in my head.

"And the name of the deceased?"

"Eric Brewer."

She inhaled sharply. "As in the producer of *Grande Dames of New Orleans*?"

"Are you a fan?" It was amazing who all watched these shows—Academy Award–winning A-list stars were willing to show up on Eric's horrible talk show just to talk about them.

"Well, no," she replied. "I'm actually on my way there."

"You are? Why?"

She sighed. She obviously didn't want to tell me, because it took her another few moments to say, "Because Chloe Valence was murdered last night. Her husband said we should talk to Eric. There was apparently some bad blood there."

I sat down hard on one of the chairs in the hallway. Chloe was dead? Someone had killed her?

But—and I knew it was awful to think it—this was actually good news for Taylor.

"And just how did you happen to stumble over Eric Brewer's body?" Venus asked.

"He had an after-party here last night after the premiere of the show at the Joy Theater," I said carefully, my mind racing. "You've met Frank's nephew Taylor? Well, he took Eric on a tour of the Quarter bars last night, and this morning," I hated to say it, "Taylor woke up naked in Eric's bed. He doesn't remember anything. I think Eric roofied him and he also may have raped him. And someone killed Eric last night."

Silence on the other end of the phone.

"Venus?"

"I'm going to call the lab and get uniforms and techs over there," she said slowly. "I'm also going to get an ambulance over there for Taylor, okay? You can ride with him to the hospital, but Blaine's going with you. And I'm going to need a statement from you."

"I'm here waiting. Storm's here, too."

She whistled. "Calling him was smart, Scotty, but I never said that. See you in a few minutes." She paused. "I'm sorry about Taylor."

"Me, too," I replied, turning off my phone and slipping it back into my pocket.

I buried my face in my hands.

Chapter Six

Two of Cups, Reversed

A too violent passion

Time behaves very strangely when you're under stress.

The rest of that morning is lost in a vague fog, and there are gaps in my memory. I wasn't allowed back into the penthouse, so I sat out in the hallway in one of those ornate decorative chairs placed discreetly away from the suite doors. Venus questioned me herself, while her partner, Blaine Tujague, interviewed Taylor—with Storm present. At some point that seemed like hours later, the crime lab technicians arrived, with their sheets and evidence bags and cameras. I knew Taylor was in good hands—Storm is a shark of a lawyer—but I couldn't stop worrying. Yes, I knew intellectually that a crime had been committed and the cops needed to talk with him while his memories were still fresh.

But he couldn't remember even coming back to the hotel, so he wasn't going to be much help to them.

So, when Venus said, "So, you can't think of a reason why Taylor might want to kill Eric Brewer?"

I guess what I was thinking reflected on my face. Venus held up a hand. "I've got to cover all bases, Scotty."

"Taylor," I said coldly, my voice dripping with contempt as I sat up straighter and crossed my legs, "would never kill anyone or anything. He's the victim here, Venus."

She nodded. "I know, Scotty, and I'm sorry but I have to ask these questions. You don't know how sorry I am this happened to him. I'm not trying to upset you."

I nodded. I knew she was right but couldn't wrap my head around it. Taylor couldn't have killed Eric. He was drugged and out of it, for one thing, and he wasn't that kind of person. He never got angry—not even when talking about his horrible parents who'd disowned him for being gay.

You've just never seen him get angry. And he might be making up the whole thing about being drugged, as a cover.

I pushed that hateful voice out of my head. "Go ahead."

I answered the rest of her questions. No, Taylor had just met Eric last night. No, they'd never been involved before, and as far as I knew, they met at the after-party for the first time. I was with Taylor all evening before we came to the penthouse. Taylor didn't hate Eric, if anything, he was a fan—which was why he went out drinking with him after the party started to break up. No, I don't know where they went or if anyone saw them who could back up Taylor's story. I didn't hear from Taylor until this morning when he called me.

On and on and on, answering the same questions over and over again, only asked in a different way. I knew she was just doing her job but...

"There's an ambulance waiting," she said finally, closing her notepad and slipping it back into her purse. "We're going to have a rape kit done."

A rape kit.

I wanted to throw up.

But Eric was wearing his underwear under his robe. I remembered seeing his underwear on.

Would he have put his underwear back on after raping Taylor?

"Blaine will drive you to the hospital." Venus stood up.

"Can't I ride in the ambulance with Taylor?"

She shook her head, and her face was sad. "Storm and I will ride in the ambulance."

Terrific.

It was raining again as I rode over to Touro Infirmary with Blaine in Venus's black SUV. Blaine's a good guy, really good looking, but I don't trust him completely. He tried to bond with me once by pretending like we'd slept together or made out on the dance floor at Oz or something like that.

I suppose it says something about me that I didn't remember but couldn't be certain it hadn't happened. Like I said, good looking and totally my type—deep blue eyes, square jaw, olive skin, muscular, a little taller than me, and bluish-black thick hair.

He's a nice enough guy for a cop, but it's always been hard for me to get past him trying to pull that on me in order to get me to spill dirt about my family. He's got a much older partner who owns a gallery in the Arts District, and they live in a gorgeous house on Coliseum Square in the lower Garden District.

We made small talk on the way, him mouthing the empty platitudes everyone coughs up when something bad has happened.

Over and over that judgmental voice kept saying, *You knew Eric Brewer was a dirtbag and you should have stopped him from going with him.*

I knew there was no point in feeling guilty. There wasn't anything I could have done to prevent this. But that's part of being a parent, even a pseudo-parent like me: you can't help blaming yourself when something bad happens because emotionally you feel like it's your job to always protect your child from all the horrible things in the world.

Even though you can't.

Because it's impossible.

But knowing that doesn't make the feeling go away.

The ride seemed to take hours, but it couldn't have been more than twenty minutes. Blaine parked illegally and put some kind of police plate in the window, but I was already out of the car and hurrying up the sidewalk to the emergency room entrance.

Then came the fun part of doing the paperwork and handing over insurance information and a credit card, just in case. The woman asking me all the questions was trying to be kind, but I was monosyllabic and impatient. I finally signed the credit card slip.

She gestured to the waiting area. "The doctor will be with you as soon as she can."

I started to protest, demand to be allowed to see Taylor—but none of this was her fault. So I got up, walked numbly into the waiting area, and took a seat next to Blaine, who was scrolling through his phone.

"He'll be okay," Blaine said, not looking up from his phone. "It's going to be okay."

I didn't answer him because I wasn't sure I wouldn't start crying.

And I'd be damned if I'd cry in front of Blaine Tujague.

Waiting there, drinking hellishly bad coffee that gave me heartburn, paging through worn magazines without seeing what was on the well-thumbed pages, was an entirely different kind of hell. I kept taking my phone out of my pocket, thinking I needed to text or call Frank...but would put it back in my pocket because I couldn't think of what to say. Maybe I was being a coward, but wouldn't it be better to tell him in person? Telling him on the phone would just stress him out, and there wasn't anything he'd be able to do until he got home, anyway. But every few minutes I'd finish paging through *Good Housekeeping* or *People* and would pull out my phone...only to put it back and reach for another magazine.

"Scotty Bradley?" a lightly accented voice said.

"Yes?" I scrambled to my feet. The doctor was a woman of indeterminate age, wearing green scrubs, her dark hair pulled back into a braid. She was slight, barely over five feet tall, and looked wispy inside the baggy scrubs.

"I'm Dr. Desai," she said, holding out her hand. "Please come with me." After shaking her hand, I followed her into an empty examination room. "Please, sit." She gestured at a chair.

I sat. "How is he?"

"As good as can be expected," she replied. "There doesn't appear to be any tearing, and I found no traces of lubricant or semen in his rectum." My eyes filled with tears at the thought of the exam Taylor had undergone—how humiliating it must have been. But I wiped at my eyes as she continued, "I have prescribed him something to help him sleep, and something for depression. I have also prescribed a regimen of PEP. Are you familiar with PEP?"

"Vaguely."

"It's a post-exposure prophylaxis to prevent HIV infection taking hold. I know I said I don't believe there was any penetration, but it's a precaution that should be taken. It will have some side effects." She ran through a list. "Some people experience none, some experience more. It depends on the person." She shrugged her small shoulders. "I have given him a precautionary treatment for other STIs, but I would recommend that he get tested again in three months—a full panel of everything."

"Of course." I nodded. Numbness was spreading through me and I could hear that roaring in my ears again.

"I strongly urge you to have him see a therapist. Even though I saw no evidence of penetration, your nephew has been through a trauma, and this is not something he can work through on his own or with the help of family and friends." She handed me a folded slip of paper. "These are some local therapists who primarily work with sexual assault victims."

"But if he wasn't actually assaulted…"

She touched my arm sadly. "He was drugged, Mr. Bradley, and would have been assaulted had circumstance not intervened. He doesn't remember anything that happened after a certain point in the evening last night. He may not have been legally assaulted, but he is still the victim of a sexual predator. Now, I will take you back to see him."

I wiped my eyes and followed her back into the emergency ward to an area closed off behind curtains. Taylor still looked green, his eyes red and watery. He was sitting up on the bed and wearing a hospital gown. "They took my clothes," he said in a very small voice. The light that was usually in his eyes wasn't there, and my heart broke more than just a little bit. "Scotty, I'm so sorry."

My heart broke. "You have nothing to be sorry for. You didn't do a damned thing wrong, understood?"

He wiped at his eyes and nodded. He looked like a child.

Storm put his arm around me. "I called Mom to go over to your place and pick up some clothes for him. The police needed his clothes."

I just nodded. I hadn't thought of that. I wasn't thinking clearly.

"He gave a statement to the police," Storm went on. "Although I think it's pretty clear what happened. He was drugged and doesn't remember anything."

"I'm so sorry," Taylor said in a voice that broke my heart, tears in his eyes. "I'm so sorry."

"Stop that, okay?" I replied, sitting on the side of the bed and taking his hand—it was so cold—in mine and squeezing it. "You didn't do anything wrong, and I won't hear anything else, okay?"

He nodded as another tear fell down his cheek.

Eric Brewer was so lucky he was already dead.

Someone outside the curtains cleared his throat. "Um, Scotty," Blaine said, staying outside the curtain, "would you mind if I asked you some questions now?"

"I already talked to Venus." I looked at Storm, who just nodded. I'd been taught since I learned how to speak to never talk to the cops without a lawyer present, but in this case, I guess it didn't matter. "I'll be right back to take you home, okay?" I kissed the top of Taylor's head and walked back outside.

"The, um, nurse said we could sit in here." Blaine gestured toward a door. I walked through it. There were some chairs, a table, and shelves of bed linens. "I think they use it for quick breaks," Blaine said, shutting the door behind him. "I'm sorry we have to do this now, but we need to know more about what happened last night. I know Venus asked you some basics…"

"It's okay, Blaine, I know the drill." I waved my hand tiredly. I was so tired. "Let's get this over with."

"How did Taylor wind up with Eric Brewer last night?"

"We went to the premiere party for *Grande Dames of New Orleans* last night, Serena Castlemaine is a friend and she got us the invitations," I replied. "And there was an after-party at Eric's suite at the Royal Aquitaine. She got us invited to that as well." I explained how we were all given keys that worked the elevators. "And at the party, Eric took a liking to Taylor and asked him to take him clubbing, show him the real gay French Quarter." I shook my head. "I wasn't really comfortable with it, to be honest—Eric is older than me, and Taylor's just a kid, but I also figured…" I exhaled. "I figured Taylor was an adult and could handle himself. I didn't know I was letting him leave with a predator."

But that Brandon guy tried to warn you, didn't he? a voice whispered in my head. *And you let him go anyway.*

"A guy named Brandon went with them," I said slowly. "What happened to Brandon?"

Blaine bit his lower lip. "Apparently he left Taylor and Eric alone at the Brass Rail. And what did you do? After the party?"

"I was tired, so I went home."

"By yourself?"

"Frank and Colin—" I couldn't tell him when I got home Colin was there with the dead body of a foreign agent. "They're both out of town." Grief overwhelmed me again. "And left me in charge of Taylor. That was a big mistake, wasn't it?"

"Scotty. Listen to me. *Listen. To. Me.* You are dealing with something most people never have to deal with, and there's no way to prepare for it, and there's no right way to deal with it, okay? Do you understand me? You couldn't have known what would happen. And if you did know, you would have prevented it. I know you well enough to know that."

I wiped at my eyes and nodded. "Sorry. Go ahead." I took a deep breath.

Seriously, Scotty, hold it together.

"So, you went home alone?"

"Yes. I didn't go back out again, I went to bed, and was sleeping when—when Taylor called me this morning and told me that he needed help."

"And then?"

I took a deep breath. None of it seemed real. It was hard to believe it had been only a few hours. It wasn't even noon yet. "I got dressed and I went to the Royal Aquitaine. I called Storm to meet me there. He—he told me not to go upstairs, but I didn't wait for him. Once Storm arrived, we called the police."

"How did you get up to the penthouse level? Didn't you need a key card?"

I fished it out of my coat pocket and waved it. "I still have mine from last night's party. No one asked for it back."

Blaine stared at me. "Are you telling me no one collected the cards back after the party?"

I stared back at him. "Really weird. It didn't occur to me last night but yeah, once I used my card to get the elevator to go up to the penthouse floor, I just put it back in my pocket. When I was walking to the hotel this morning, I realized I still had it." I shook my head. "I mean, the whole point of a penthouse floor is security, right? Why did the hotel let Eric Brewer give these out in the first place? And then he didn't collect them?"

"I imagine the hotel had the numbers logged and could deactivate them." Blaine took the card from me and put it inside an evidence bag, writing on the outside label. "But yours still worked?"

"It did this morning. I imagine everyone who was at the party still has theirs, and if mine still works, doesn't it stand to reason everyone else's keys still work?" I exhaled. "Someone at the hotel is getting fired over this."

"Probably." Blaine shook his head. "So, anyone who was at the party could have gone back up there and killed Eric."

That wasn't such good news for the cops, but it was great news for Taylor. But there was probably security video.

Taylor was lucky to be alive.

I started shaking as I realized that the killer easily could have killed them both.

"Are you okay? Do you need me to get a nurse?"

I shook my head, my teeth chattering. "No, no, I'm okay."

Blaine slipped his notebook into his pocket. "If I think of any other questions, I'll give you a call. And if you think of anything—"

I nodded. "I got your numbers."

Blaine slipped out of the linen closet and the door clicked as it shut again. I sat there, trying to get my head together. I couldn't let Taylor see me losing it. I had to be strong for him. I could always have my own breakdown later, when I was by myself in my room with the door closed.

Be strong. Be strong.

I wiped my eyes and exhaled. I got to my feet and walked back outside.

Mom, Dad, and Storm were all standing outside Taylor's cubicle. I've never been so glad to see my parents in my life. They looked a little worse for wear, but were holding it together. Mom and Dad enveloped me in a group hug, my mom patting my head and my dad rubbing my back as they both murmured "it's going to be okay" over and over like a mantra.

"Taylor's getting dressed," Mom said, "and Dad's going to drive you home while I run get his prescriptions filled. Do you want to just come back home, or do you want to go to your place?"

Fuck.

My apartment was a disaster area. Sure, I'd cleaned up most of the mess, but the rug was gone, and the television was destroyed and who knew what I'd missed in the process?

And it might not be safe there for any of us.

Fuck.

Too many questions to answer.

"Do you mind if Taylor stays with you tonight?" I asked.

"Of course not," Mom replied, putting her arms around me. "I was hoping you'd let us take care of him. Not that you aren't great with him," she added hastily, "but I think he needs a mom right now, too."

So, Taylor and I rode back to the Quarter with Dad and Storm, while Mom ran to CVS to get his prescriptions filled. Taylor didn't say anything the whole way. I kept looking over at him, but all he did was stare out the car window. His color was getting better, but the bags under his eyes... Dad dropped us off at the back gate to their place and went to park the car. I took Taylor upstairs and set him up in my old bedroom. "Can I get you anything?" I asked, once he got under the covers.

He shook his head. "I just want to sleep for about a week." He rolled over onto his side, facing the wall, with his back to me. Not knowing what else to do, I turned off the light and shut the door.

Was he blaming me for letting him leave with Eric?

Dad was loading the big glass dragon-shaped bong when I got back to the living room. "How's he doing?"

I shook my head, willing myself not to cry. "Not well."

"And you?"

"Not well."

He held the bong out to me. "Being a parent is rough, Scotty."

I debated not taking it from him, but then figured at best it would make me feel better, at worst it would make me fall asleep. I took a hit, letting the weed work its magic. I blew out the smoke. "I'm a terrible parent."

"No, you aren't." Dad shook his head, his long loose hair swinging. I'd never noticed how gray his hair was before, and it hit me with a shock how old Mom and Dad were getting. I was in my forties. That meant they were in their seventies. And their parents...

No, I didn't want to think about that.

"And you were totally unprepared for it," Dad was saying. "I mean, we had months to prepare for babies, and we learned as we went, you know? You just do the best you can. You had a nineteen-year-old dropped on you, fully grown and fully formed, and you love him and take care of him the best you can. All he needed from you—all he needed from any of us, was love, Scotty. And you've given him that."

I remembered the first time I saw Taylor, after Frank had dropped the bomb that his nephew was coming to live with us because he had nowhere else to go. *Of course* we were going to take him in. That was never in question. My heart broke for this poor kid whose parents had thrown him out, cut off all financial support, disowned him, for the crime of being gay. Frank and his sister weren't close, and he'd never come out to his own parents, who pretty much felt the same way about homosexuality as his sister. He always brushed it off, never talked about his family, changed the subject over the years when I'd bring it up, but it had to be hard on him. And I felt like taking Taylor in had helped heal some of those wounds for Frank...

Frank.

I hadn't told Frank.

I fumbled for my phone. "Oh, God, I have to tell Frank—"

Dad reached over and took my phone away from me. "No, you don't. He's on his way home. He'll be here soon, in fact. Your mom and I called him as soon as we heard from Storm." He smiled at me. "We knew you'd be too worried about Taylor to think of anything else."

I really have the best family.

"How did he—how did he take it?"

"As well as can be expected." Dad smiled, taking the bong from me and taking a hit. "Eric Brewer is lucky he's dead. I can't imagine what Frank would do to him. If there was anything left to do anything with after your mother and I were done with him."

I heard feet pounding up the back steps, and the kitchen door opened. I got up and ran into Frank's arms. For the first time all day, I felt like everything might wind up being all right. "How is he?" Frank whispered.

"He's sleeping. I don't know. I'm worried."

"Everything will be okay." Frank sounded like he was convincing himself. "Everything will be okay."

We spent the afternoon there, talking and smoking pot and waiting for Taylor to need anything, to wake up. He was glad to see

Frank, and I let them have some time alone together while I tried to think pleasant thoughts. When Frank came back out his eyes were red. Mom and Dad wanted us to stay for dinner, but Taylor had gone back to sleep and we decided we'd head home, making them promise to call us if anything changed or if Taylor needed anything.

As we walked, hand in hand, back home down the cold streets of the Quarter, Frank said, "I love you, Scotty."

"I was so afraid you'd blame me—"

"You couldn't have done anything to prevent this from happening," Frank said as we walked across Ursulines. "You need to let that go, babe. We're going to get through this, and we need to be strong for Taylor."

"I know." I hesitated, then blurted out, "Just to prepare you, the apartment is kind of a mess."

"That's fine, we can clean it up before we head back over to Mom and Dad's."

"Well, it's a little bit more than that." I filled him in on everything that happened with Colin last night.

He listened, his face expressionless. "So, we need to get a new television and replace some frames and glass, and the rug."

"Yes. Oh, and the car's at the airport. We'll need to pick it up."

He nodded. "Okay, the first thing we need to do is clean the apartment, make sure you got everything. You used bleach where the blood was, of course, but we'll have to run over to the West Bank to Target and get everything replaced before we can bring Taylor back home. Did you check the upstairs to make sure everything was fine up there?"

"I looked around a bit when I fed Scooter, but I was in a rush to get to the Aquitaine," I admitted. "But it may not be safe there for us. Should we bring Taylor home?"

His face looked grim. "Once we have this Taylor situation under control, we need to talk about the Colin situation. I love him, too—but this? We're accessories after the fact, Scotty, Christ. I love him, but not enough to go to jail for him. I don't blame you—what else could you do?" He bent down and kissed my cheek. "What a shitty twenty-four hours you've had."

"Yeah, I agree with you about Colin," I replied. "And I appreciate the sentiment, but Taylor had it a lot worse than I did."

CHAPTER SEVEN
ACE OF PENTACLES, REVERSED
Great plans may come to naught

Since we had to pick up the car from the airport, we decided it made more sense for Frank to go to the Target on Clearview Parkway in Metairie to look for a rug and replacement frames.

We rode out to the airport in comparative silence. I was exhausted, and all I wanted to do was go to bed and sleep for a week. I leaned my head against the cold passenger window of the car. It was getting darker, and the temperature was dropping. The hot air blowing from the car vents just wasn't enough to warm me up. I was thinking I might not ever be warm again.

We took the off-ramp for the airport service road.

"Where are you going?" I asked Frank as he bypassed the exit to Airline Highway, where the Park 'n' Fly was located, and headed for the terminal.

"It will look funny if I drop you off at the Park 'n' Fly," Frank replied. "I'm going to drop you at baggage claim so you can take the shuttle. Grab my overnight bag from the back seat and you'll look like just another passenger. No one will notice you."

One of the reasons I love him so much is because he's so smart.

I'd prefer to think I hadn't thought of it because I was tired, and my brain fried.

He pulled the car to a stop alongside the concrete island across from the Southwest baggage claim. He leaned over and kissed me. "I'll see you at home. Be careful driving. I love you."

"I love you, too," I said, grabbing his overnight bag from the back seat. I slung the strap over my shoulder and watched as he drove off, disappearing around the turn at the end of the terminal along with the other cars and taxis. I shivered and crossed the three lanes to the parking garage. There was a Park 'n' Fly van idling at the curb on the ground floor.

The driver, a heavyset woman in her early fifties, smiled at me as I climbed into the van. "Do you have your ticket?"

The van drivers always give you a slip of paper with the spot number where you parked written down so you didn't have to remember. I made a face. "I don't remember what I did with it," I smiled at her, "but I'm pretty sure it's N-47." I pulled out my phone. "Yes, here it is in my Notes. N-47."

"No worries," she said, making a note on a pad by the steering wheel.

I sat down in the back. There were three other people in the van—two men and a woman—and they were all staring at their phones. The van door closed, and the driver pulled away from the curb. I pulled out my own phone and checked for text messages or emails or something, *anything*, from Colin.

Of course, there was nothing.

What a *fucking* day.

I'd spent the day so worried about Taylor I hadn't given much thought to the Colin situation. But at least Frank was home now, and I didn't have to deal with it alone.

It started raining again as I tipped the driver three dollars and climbed down out of the van. I clicked the fob to unlock the car and got into the driver's seat. Once the van pulled away, I grabbed an umbrella from the back seat and unlocked the hatch door. As the rain pelted the umbrella, I used my phone flashlight to check the back. No visible blood, no carpet fibers—at least nothing I could see.

Colin said he'd clean it out. I should've known he'd be thorough.

It was why he was still alive.

I started the car, turning the heater up and shivering while I waited for hot air to start blowing through the vents. The rain was making it hard to see, but in the distance, I could make out the headlights of the van moving down a row in the back. Once heat started coming out of the vents, I turned on the windshield wipers. The parking ticket was right where Colin said it would be—tucked into the visor.

My hands shaking, I backed out and drove to the exit. Cars were zooming past on Airline Highway, and only one of the exit lanes was open. I pulled up behind a big black Lexus SUV and waited my turn. My hands were still shaking a little, so I gripped the steering wheel more tightly.

It's just a natural reaction to all the shit that's gone down since last night, I told myself.

I was also bone tired. I'd been running on adrenaline since getting out of bed and now was crashing, hard. I'd need to stop and get a bottle of Coke somewhere.

Hell, if there was a Starbucks with a drive-through anywhere nearby, I could get a double-shot-of-espresso-latte.

Which sounded so heavenly I almost moaned aloud.

I started searching for a Starbucks on my phone when the SUV moved through the gate. I put my phone down, pulled up to the booth, and handed the young black man working the booth the ticket stub.

He put it into the machine and remarked, "Well, you weren't here for very long."

I handed him a twenty and smiled. "I just had to fly over to Houston for a meeting." The lie rolled off my lips easily. I started fiddling with my phone again. There *was* a Starbucks on Veterans before it crossed under I-10. I could make a detour there and get right back on the highway.

Perfect.

The booth attendant nodded, handing me my receipt and change. "Have a great day, and thanks for parking with us."

"You, too." I drove the Honda out onto Airline Highway and turned right, heading for Williams Boulevard. Williams bisected Veterans right before the on-ramp. I turned right there and kept an eye out for the Starbucks sign. I was disappointed to see there wasn't a drive-through, but I had to stop—if I didn't get a boost of caffeine, there wasn't any way I could drive all the way home. My eyes were drooping by the time I pulled into the parking lot. The cold rain was bracing as I ran inside. I was the only person there and took a seat to wait for them to make my drink after ordering.

I couldn't remember the last time I was so tired. I just wanted to get home, crawl back into my bed, and sleep. They called my name. The hot cup felt terrific in my hands and I took a sip. Hot, caffeinated, perfect. I carried it back out to the car. It was still raining, and the wind just seemed to go straight to my bones. I put my latte in the cup holder and started the engine again. The rain was coming down hard, big fat wet drops pelting the windshield and the car so hard I worried about dings. Lighting flashed close by and thunder shook the car.

Great. There's nothing more fun than driving on I-10 during a thunderstorm.

I took another healthy drink of my latte. My body was starting to warm up, and I could feel energy starting to flow through my blood again.

I turned on the satellite radio and tuned into the local NPR station, WWNO. Some cool jazz would be perfect.

Instead, it was a news broadcast, already in progress.

"...found in Bayou Le Saire out along Chef Menteur Highway this morning by a party of fisherman."

Fuck.

Fuck, fuck, *fuck*.

I turned up the sound.

"The male, so far unidentified, was beaten badly and his neck was apparently broken, according to the New Orleans Police Department. He was a Caucasian male, between the ages of thirty and forty years of age, about six feet tall and weighing around two hundred pounds. He was wearing black jeans, black sweater, and black coat. If anyone has any information that could help the police either identify him, or help find his killers, please call the tip line at..."

I turned off the radio.

Fuckety-fuck fuck.

The cops had *already* found him.

How was that even possible? Bayou Le Saire was out in the middle of nowhere. Yes, the Chef Menteur Highway ran beside it, but at this time of year there shouldn't have been any fisherman or shrimpers out. Few people went that way, preferring I-10 to get to the North Shore.

So how was this even possible?

This day was just getting better and better. My hands shaking, I started to text Frank but deleted it before finishing. I couldn't have anything on my phone in case...well, if the police ever needed to look at my phone.

And given I'd turned up at a murder scene this morning *because* the person who found the body—and was a suspect in *that* murder— had called me, it wasn't far-fetched to assume the cops would at some point want to take a look at my phone.

It would be funny if it weren't so serious.

I had to be careful...because Taylor was a suspect in *one* murder while his uncles were busy covering up *another, completely different* one.

Then again, I'd heard Argentina was lovely this time of year.

Leaving the country sounded like a damned good idea.

I plugged my phone into the car and cued up a dance playlist I'd made for doing cardio. Maybe listening to dance music cranked up as loud as possible would put me into a better mind-set and let me forget all of this for a little while.

I *always* take my problems to the dance floor.

With Deborah Cox wailing through my speakers I got back on Veterans and headed for the highway. The rain was still coming down in buckets. In places, the highway was covered in water. But I just kept listening to my music and tapping my hand on the steering wheel to the beat.

Seriously, there's nothing better than a gay dance mix for picking up your mood.

I took the 610 bypass and later, the Elysian Fields exit. I finished my latte as I went through the intersection at Claiborne, slowing every time the car went through a deep puddle, sending a spray of water into the air on the right side of the car. By the time I got to our parking garage on Barracks Street, the water had risen so high out of the gutter it was covering the sidewalk. I waited for the garage door to go up and drove inside. Frank's parking spot was empty, and I turned off the car as the garage door came back down.

I could hear the rain pounding a tattoo on the roof, glad again the lot owners decided to enclose it a few years ago instead of leaving it open. I took the back way in, using the shed door to the garage, and listened to the rain on the shed's tin roof.

I opened the door to the back courtyard and looked through the downpour at the back stairs. The courtyard was underwater, and water was spilling over the sides of the fountain.

Is it safe? I wondered.

Another flash of lightning sent me dashing through the water, soaking my shoes and socks. I went up the stairs carefully and checked Taylor's door—still locked. Scooter must have heard me, because I could hear his plaintive cries on the other side of the door.

Of course he was crying. He'd been alone since last night, and it was time for dinner.

I unlocked the door and Scooter starting twining around my legs as I tried to walk down the hallway without tripping over him. I cooed at him, pulled his tail, and stroked his back while I got the big plastic jar we keep his expensive cat food in down from the top of the refrigerator.

Once he heard the food hitting his bowl, of course, I ceased to exist.

"I'll come get you later," I said as I hurried back down the hallway. I locked the door behind me and went down the stairs to our apartment.

I tried the door. It was still locked. Hadn't Colin said the Russian guy had already been inside with the door locked?

That didn't make sense. *How* did he get in?

Maybe Colin wasn't telling you the whole truth. He's done that before, remember? To protect you?

I turned the heat up as I walked down the hallway. I did a quick survey of the living room. I didn't see anything incriminating. Maybe UV lights would show bloodstains on the floor. But the couch looked fine. It just looked weird to see the prints stacked up against the wall, no television on the entertainment center, and the rug gone.

There wasn't any reason for the police to search the apartment, was there?

No, Eric Brewer had been killed at the Aquitaine, and Taylor had been there when the police arrived. They'd only need to search the apartment if they had reason to believe he'd come home at some point during the night—which wouldn't make sense. Why would he go back?

I rolled a joint and grabbed my cards. Smoking some pot and reading the cards, communing with the Goddess and the spirit world, always helped me calm down, and my mind was racing. I was going to need to stay calm and cool, especially when Taylor came home.

I lit the joint and took a couple of hits before pinching it out. I sat on the floor and shuffled the cards. The pot was working already, I could feel myself relaxing. I took some cleansing breaths and cleared my mind.

I spread the cards with my eyes closed, murmured a short prayer, and looked at the cards.

Danger for you or for someone close to you.
A calm head is needed.
A deceptive woman who cannot be trusted.

Great. Which Grande Dame did She mean?

As I was picking up the cards, I heard footsteps on the stairs. I finished putting the cards away just as Frank came walking in carrying the enormous box containing our new television. "I got some more stuff down in the car," he said, tossing me the keys. "Do you mind getting the bags while I hook up the television? It's stopped raining."

"Great." I caught the keys out of the air. "Were you able to get a rug?"

He bit his lower lip and shook his head as he tore open one end of the box. "No. It's going to be harder replacing that rug than we thought," he said as he slid the television expertly out of the box. "They didn't have anything even remotely close. We're going to have to look at some secondhand places, I think." He shook his head. "We're not going to be able to get an exact match."

"Well, if anyone asks, I'll just say I spilled bleach on it," I replied.
Lies, lies, and more lies.

There were more bags in the car than I was expecting. *This,*

I thought as I grabbed them all, and slamming the hatch of the Forester shut, *is why I never let Frank go shopping. He always gets too much stuff.* I lugged the bags across the courtyard, shivering. It felt ten degrees colder now than it did when I got home. I could smell pot as I kicked the door shut behind me. I dumped the bags in the kitchen and peeked into the living room. The television was mounted on the wall where the old one had been, just above the old entertainment center. Frank was holding the joint I'd rolled in one hand while fiddling with the remote control with the other.

"It's bigger than the old one," I said, getting the frames out of the bags.

"Yeah." He held out the joint to me as I set the frames down on the couch. "I figured we might as well upgrade. If anyone asks—"

"By anyone you mean Taylor?" I popped the glass out of one of the frames and put one of the pictures inside, replacing the glass. "What are we going to tell him?"

"I don't know. I hate lying to him." Frank finished with the remote, and the Amazon Prime screen popped up. He punched in our account name and the password, and our watch list came up. "Everything's all set now." He placed the remote on the coffee table and sat down on the couch to help me.

"I don't want to lie to him either," I replied, working on another frame. "But with this Eric Brewer mess—"

"Murder." Frank interrupted me. "We have to say it, Scotty. Eric Brewer was murdered, and Taylor was there. We can't pretend." The muscle in his jaw that always jumps when he's angry started twitching. "Brewer's lucky he's already dead."

"Yeah." I reframed another picture. "Although I imagine once Venus and Blaine are finished watching the security camera footage, Taylor will be in the clear, and we'll know who killed him. Chloe, on the other hand…"

"Don't you think it makes the most sense for Remy Valence to be the killer?" Frank took the pictures I'd finished framing and started hanging them on the walls again. "He had a reason to kill Brewer, and I'm sure he had plenty of reasons to kill his wife."

"Yeah." I slid the glass back into the last frame and held it out to him. "We also have to consider…" I hesitated. "We have to consider that Taylor may have killed him."

Once the words were out of my mouth, I wished I could take them back. I couldn't imagine any world where Taylor—sweet, sweet Taylor—would, or could, actually kill someone. But he'd been drugged, and he'd had a sazerac at the bar and some wine at the Joy Theater before we even got to that stupid party.

That stupid fucking party—I'd never be able to forgive myself for agreeing to go.

"I know." Frank's voice was grim as he sat down next to me on the couch. He put his arm around my shoulders, and I leaned into him. "Much as I don't want to think it, we *have* to think about it. We don't know what went on up there after they got back from wherever they were."

I could hear his heart beating. He was so warm. "Taylor said the last place he remembered being at was the Brass Rail." I glanced at my watch. "Whoever was working there last night is probably working tonight. Maybe we should head over there and ask some questions before it gets busy."

He tensed. I knew he hated the Brass Rail, would never go in there in again if he could avoid it. I hadn't been there in a while myself.

The Brass Rail was a sleazy gay strip club in the upper Quarter, near where the straight strip clubs were on Bourbon. The Brass Rail wasn't on Bourbon Street but stood on a corner on a side street. It was just two big rooms. The rectangular bar was in the front room, and in the back room there was a pool table and video poker machines. It was like any number of other neighborhood bars in the city except, of course, for the strippers. Don't get me wrong, I don't judge anyone for stripping. *I* used to be a stripper when I was younger and prettier, and I enjoyed every minute of it.

But the Brass Rail was *different*.

The guys…well, the guys who stripped there were an eclectic mix. Every possible type you could imagine, from muscle boys to twinks. Some of the guys who worked there were straight. Some of them stripped to pay for drug habits. Some of them were for hire, would do a lap dance for you in the back room, would let you stroke their dick or stick a finger in their ass for a twenty. Frank hated the place the first time I ever took him there, thought the dancers were being exploited and felt bad for them. I'd never really thought about it that way before, but he had a point. I always thought it was just kind of a campy, fun place to go and have a few beers, look at some skin, maybe see a naked penis. I'd never thought of the guys' lives outside of the place, and Frank kind of made me see that…so I never even thought about going in there myself anymore.

"It's work, Frank, not for fun," I reminded him. "If someone there remembers Taylor being there, and the condition he was in when he left…"

"I know. I just hate going there."

"I can go by myself if you'd rather not," I replied. "That might be better, really. You're not really good at hiding how you feel, and—"

"You don't mind?"

"Of course not." I looked at my watch. "I'll go around nine. There won't be many people there then."

My phone started ringing. It was Storm. "Hey, Storm, I'm putting you on speaker so Frank can hear. What's up?"

I could tell he was in his car. "I just got off the phone with Venus and Blaine. I've got good news and I've got bad news."

I glanced at Frank. "Bad news first."

He whistled. "The bad news is there's no security camera footage from last night. The Aquitaine's system crashed last night around seven o'clock, and it's still not back online right now. So… yeah."

"Fuck fuck fuckety fuck." We'd all been counting on the footage not only to back up Taylor's story but to see who else had gone into the penthouse. "What's the good news?"

"The good news is that there are records of the times key cards were used to open Eric's penthouse door. Venus is going to send me electronic copies, I'll send them over to you once I get them. But she did tell me key cards were used three times to open the door between three thirty and four fifteen in the morning. We have to assume Eric only used his card once, so at least one other person used a card to open that door twice more. So that right there is enough reasonable doubt to keep them from filing any charges against Taylor."

"Thank God," Frank said.

"Also, the murder weapon was not recovered at the scene."

Storm exhaled. "That also works in our favor. It's possible Taylor might have left to get rid of the murder weapon and let himself back in, but it doesn't make much sense…plus it doesn't account for all of the unlocking. So, yeah. It also looks like Chloe Valence was killed with a similar type weapon. Has Loren McKeithen gotten in touch with you yet?"

"No."

"He might be over at Mom and Dad's. He was heading down there to talk to Taylor. You two need to make yourselves available to him and listen to what he has to say. And whatever you do, do not ask Taylor any questions that aren't cleared by Loren. I cannot emphasize this enough, guys. Listen to Loren, and remember—he works for Taylor, not for us. Taylor is his client no matter who's paying the bills. Do not do anything he tells you not to do."

I looked over at Frank. He nodded. "We got it, Storm, and thank you."

"He's my nephew, too. Catch ya later." He disconnected the call.

I leaned back against Frank's chest, and he stretched out along the sofa, with me curled up alongside him. "The police are going to be looking long and hard at Remy," Frank said as I felt myself drifting off to sleep. "I wouldn't want to be Remy Valence right now."

CHAPTER EIGHT
THREE OF CUPS, REVERSED
Beware of gossip from an old friend

It was raining again when I left the house at quarter till nine.

I paused at the bottom of the stairs and wrapped my muffler around my neck more tightly. There was about an inch of water in the courtyard, and water was still spilling over the side of the fountain. Loren McKeithen hadn't called yet, but I was tired of waiting around. I wanted—needed—to do something other than sitting around smoking pot. If asking questions at the Brass Rail could help back up Taylor's story, well, I'd probably have better luck with their clientele than the cops.

Taylor was still staying at Mom and Dad's.

Much as I hated him not being home with us, it was the best option we had right now. He'd have too many questions about the apartment, for one thing—there's no way he wouldn't notice the missing rug or the new television or the new frames for the art—and telling him the truth wasn't an option. I'd napped for a couple of hours and when I'd gotten up, Frank and I both agreed it was best to keep Taylor out of the Colin mess as much as possible.

The longer we had before we had to come up with a cover story for the changes in the apartment, the better.

Sure, eventually we'd have to deal with it, but *later* was better.

And there was also the little matter of it not being safe. I didn't want Taylor to be around in case another Russian operative showed up looking to kill Colin.

So, when Mom called around seven to let us know Taylor was doing as well as could be expected but she thought it was a better idea for him to stay there overnight, we didn't argue with her. Mom and Dad's TLC and spoiling was exactly what he needed right now—and no matter how much I tried, I couldn't spoil anyone the way Mom could.

It also broke my heart that his own mother wasn't there for him.

I hoped I'd get the chance to slap the snot out of Teresa Sobieski Wheeler at some future date—even if it meant driving up to Corinth, Alabama, myself to make it happen.

When I went out the front gate I checked to see if anyone was watching the place. I didn't spot anyone who looked out of place or suspicious. I locked the gate behind me and walked to the corner. There weren't many people out on the street. The cold must have everyone bundled up warm inside. All the doors to Café Envie were closed, and most of their tables were empty. I thought about getting a hot chocolate with some brandy to warm me as I walked the ten blocks or so to the Rail but decided not to.

If it got too cold and wet for me, I could always flag a cab or summon a Lyft.

I kept my head down as I walked up Chartres Street. The Rail wasn't near the other gay bars or the Fruit Loop, as we locals called the stretch from the 700 Club to Café Lafitte in Exile at Dumaine and Bourbon. It was actually right up the street from the Royal Aquitaine—the longest walk from my apartment for any of the Quarter gay bars. I cut over to Dauphine at Dumaine. The lights were on at Mom and Dad's, and I decided I'd stop by on my way back home to make sure Taylor was fine. Mom and Dad were usually up all night anyway, their apartment was about halfway between the Brass Rail and my place, and I could warm up there. I hated leaving Frank alone at home by himself, but he said it was okay—he wanted to do some online research and was also going to keep trying to reach Angela Blackledge.

I felt better than I had. Spending some time napping and cuddling Frank was just what I'd needed. I still needed more sleep, but I wasn't tired as I'd been, and my mind was functional.

I couldn't stop wondering how the Russian could have gotten into our apartment. If he'd been waiting for Colin—*how did he get in?* Neither the front gate nor the door to the garage had been tampered with. There were no signs of forced entry on my apartment door. The shutters had been latched from the inside and the windows locked.

Could Colin have been lying?

It wouldn't be the first time Colin had lied to me, to us, but this was the first time I'd wound up as an accessory after the fact.

If I'd come home twenty minutes earlier…

I pushed that thought out of my head.

I was feeling pretty frozen all the way through when I finally got to the Brass Rail. It was too early for anyone to be working the front door charging cover and checking IDs, but a couple of guys were standing around outside shivering and smoking cigarettes. Dancers, most likely. Eric was into younger guys, so of course he'd want to go to the Rail.

But the guys who danced at the Rail? Some of them danced there to pay for their drug habits, others had a wife and a baby at home and this was the best way for them to make some money, and some of them could be had for as little as twenty bucks. Rail dancers rarely made the transition to the other gay clubs where they could make more money…but then, who knows? Maybe they made more money than I had dancing at the Pub.

Stop being such an elitist snob, I told myself as I pulled the front door open, a blast of warm air washing over me.

Oh, yeah, I was definitely taking a cab home.

An old Donna Summer song was playing softly in the background. The televisions were all tuned in to a showing of *It's a Wonderful Life* on some cable channel—George and Mary were walking home from the dance where they'd fallen into the swimming pool. The lights above the bar were on, and it was brighter inside than I ever remembered seeing it. There was a Christmas tree in the back room, past the pool table, where a couple of shirtless tattooed young men were playing. Their sweatpants hung down low enough to show their underwear. Dancers, most likely. Christmas lights twinkled along the bar. The guy behind the bar was pouring a vodka tonic for one of the two men sitting near the cash register. They were the only non-employees in the place. Both appeared to be older men, late fifties, maybe early sixties, and were sitting at the bar as far from the door as they could get. I shivered again as I took a seat at the other side of the bar.

"Scotty! Long time no see! How you doing?" the bartender asked as he put a napkin down in front of me. "What can I get you?"

"Something hot," I replied, casting around in the darkest recesses of my brain to try to conjure up the bartender's name without luck. He looked familiar, and I'm pretty sure at one time I'd known his name. I was surprised to see him still working there. I met him back when my old workout partner David and I would come down here after a few drinks at the Pub or Good Friends to kill some time and slip some dollars to the dancers…but whoa, that was over fourteen years ago. This same bartender had worked here then. He was short, maybe five feet five on a good day, and I'd always thought he was cute back then. He had a compact little body and had always been in good shape. He looked the same, only now there was some gray in his dark hair and lines on his face I didn't remember.

It really pissed me off I couldn't remember his name.

Oh, well, I figured. At least I hadn't slept with him. That would have been worse.

Or had I?

Stupid aging memory.

"You really don't want our coffee," he replied with a grin. "It's terrible even when it's fresh. How about a hot buttered rum?"

"That'll work," I replied. I wasn't a fan of rum, but something warm sounded good, and butter is never the wrong choice. "Were you working last night, by chance?"

"Every night except Monday and Tuesday," he replied, pouring some rum and a dollop of butter into a coffee mug.

I pulled out my phone and scrolled through the photos till I found a good one of Taylor. "Do you remember seeing this guy last night?"

He finished making my drink and placed the steaming cup on the counter. I wrapped my cold hands around it, the warmth tingling through my hands and making me tingle a little bit. I took a sip. It was perfect. The rum and the hot water warmed me up from the inside as he looked at my phone, and the butter made the rum somehow taste richer and sweeter.

He frowned. "I've seen him around, yes. But I—" He gave me

a *wish-I-could-help-but* look. "I work five nights a week, people look familiar. I couldn't swear to it he was here last night. You care if I ask Leonard and Sam?" He gestured over his shoulder to the two older guys sitting at the other side of the bar.

"By all means." I took another sip. It was warming me up, and the glow was starting to spread down my arms and legs. I'd have to get some rum for the house and learn how to make these, I thought. Who knew hot buttered rum was the perfect antidote for being cold?

The bartender carried my phone over to the other men, and I could barely hear what he asked them. One of the men looked over the top of his glasses at my phone and then looked around the bartender at me. "Your young man was here last night," he called over to me. "I saw him. But he wasn't alone."

I picked up my mug and walked around the bar. I took my phone from the bartender and slipped it back into my pocket. "So, you saw him?"

He nodded, nudging the other man with his elbow. "Right, Sam? This is that tall kid you thought was so cute." He gave me a look. "Better looking than most of the guys dancing last night."

Sam tilted his head back and looked at my phone, squinting. "Yeah, that's the kid who was with that television asshole. The *Grande Dames* guy." He snorted. "Never liked that guy on television, either. And he drugged that boy, if you ask me."

That got my attention. "What do you mean? Did you see him do something?"

"And what's it to you, anyway?" Sam asked me, a suspicious look on his face. "What business is it of yours?"

There were several ways I could play this: I could whip out one of my business cards and present this as a case I was investigating—which was true. Or I could play the concerned uncle card, which was also true.

Or I could do both.

I exhaled. "The tall kid is my nephew." I pulled out my wallet and slapped one of my business cards down on the bar, along with a ten for my hot buttered rum. "He was out with this Eric Brewer last night, and the last thing he remembers is being here. He swears he wasn't drinking, but he doesn't remember anything after getting here." I shrugged. "It sounds to me like this Eric Brewer dude might have slipped him something."

Leonard snapped his fingers. "Eric Brewer. That's his name. Yeah, they were here last night. Remember, Marty?" he said to the bartender, who was putting my change down on the bar along with a receipt. "Brewer was making a big deal out of being a TV star, tipping the dancers with fives and tens, buying people drinks." He turned back to me. "Your nephew is right, he wasn't drinking."

"Only ordered water." Marty the bartender nodded. "I remember now. He was here last night, with Mr. Big Shot. I didn't know who the guy was, I don't watch much television—I'm always here at night. But my barback last night, Felipe, knew him from TV." Marty shook his head. "I didn't pay much attention. But he was drinking Bombay Sapphire martinis. Extra olives, and dirty. He bitched because we didn't have glasses." He rolled his eyes.

"How long were they here?" I left a couple of ones on the bar as a tip.

"A couple of hours." Leonard thought for a minute. "It was about two when they got here, I think. Yes, because I noticed them right after I looked at my watch. I only stay here until three," he explained. "The dog needs to be let out around then, so I leave here and walk home. I was checking my watch to make sure I hadn't stayed too long."

"Every fifteen minutes." Sam interrupted. "You could set a clock by it. After one thirty, every fifteen goddamned minutes he checks his watch instead of just setting his phone alarm."

"Fuck off, Sam," Leonard replied casually. "Anyway, they stood over there by the ATM machine," he pointed to where the ATM sat, just inside the fire exit door, "and Mr. Big Shot, who wasn't even five nine if you ask me, got them some drinks. He started getting the dancers to come over. I think he even got Rocky—was it Rocky, Sam? The lap dance?"

"Yup, Rocky was the one," Sam agreed.

Please, please, tell me the lap dance was for Eric.

"The kid clearly didn't want the lap dance."

"I felt sorry for him, all right," Sam went on. "He was so embarrassed. And then Mr. Big Shot got him another drink. It was after that the kid started acting funny, like he was wasted." He clucked his tongue. "I thought it was funny he got drunk so fast. You can't trust them television people."

"I don't understand why people do that kind of thing," Leonard said. "Shoot, why drug someone when—no offense, Marty, pretend you don't hear me—some of the dancer boys are more than happy to do you right if you've got some money?"

Marty started whistling and walked away, lifting up a panel in the bar to walk through and heading back to the stockroom with a bucket for ice.

"I thought for sure he was going to buy Rocky for the night when he got the lap dance," Leonard sniffed, taking a sip of his drink. "I mean, I didn't see him actually put anything into your nephew's drink. All I know is he was back there getting a lap dance and Mr. Big Shot came back to the bar and ordered a couple of drinks, took them back there. And the next time I see him, Rocky's back up on the bar and your nephew looked wasted, was weaving, Mr. Big Shot was holding him up, you know? If the kid wasn't drinking, then what the hell else happened back there? He slipped him a Mickey, all right, or whatever it is they do nowadays."

"This isn't the 1950s, Leonard." Sam snorted. "A Mickey. This isn't a Frank Sinatra movie. He slipped him a roofie. And they left after that, right? He helped him out the front door, at almost three?"

"Almost three. I left about ten minutes or so later," Leonard confirmed. "I didn't see them on the street, either, but I wasn't looking for them, either."

"Thank you." I got out my pen. "Do you mind if I get contact information from you?"

They both gaped at me. "Why?"

"I may need you to talk to the police, to confirm my nephew's story."

"Oh, I don't know about that." Sam shook his head. "I don't know about talking to the police. I mean, I didn't really see anything."

"Me, either." Leonard chimed in.

I took a deep breath. "Look, you both seem like nice guys. My nephew? The one you saw last night? The guy he was with, Eric Brewer, well, he was murdered last night. My nephew was in the suite with him, but he was unconscious. He says he was drugged, wasn't awake, didn't know what was going on, doesn't remember anything after he got here. I may need you two to back up his story."

"I don't know." Sam looked down at his drink.

"Coward," Leonard snapped. He took my business card and wrote his name and phone number on the back of it. "I'll be happy to help your nephew. I can't imagine how terrible it would be to be *falsely accused*"—he practically shouted the words at Sam—"and have no one believe you. How about you, Sam?"

Sam turned red but mumbled, "I'm not talking to the police."

Leonard rolled his eyes. "I'm glad to help you, Scotty." He gestured with his head at Sam, and whispered, "He had a bad experience with the cops. You leave him to me."

"Thanks." I gave him another one of my business cards. "You call me if you think of anything else." I started to turn away, then gave him another one of my cards. "Can you give that to Rocky and ask him to call me? The more people we have who can confirm my nephew's story, the better."

"If he's dancing tonight, you can count on me." Leonard winked and dropped both cards into his shirt pocket. He looked at me again. "Didn't you used to be a dancer?"

"Not here," I replied, grabbing a plastic cup and pouring my cooling drink into it. "But yeah, I did."

"You used to dance at the Pub!" Leonard smiled, delighted. He winked at me. "I never forget a pretty face."

"Thank you." I felt oddly flattered.

"You remember him, don't you, Sam?" Leonard elbowed him again. "You used to have a thing for him, remember?"

I flushed, but Sam wouldn't look up. "Thanks, guys." I waved goodbye to Marty as he came out of the stockroom carrying the buckets of ice. I went out the front door and into the bitter, strong wind. I gulped down the rest of my drink and tossed the cup into a garbage can as I hurried down Toulouse Street to Royal, tucking my hands deep into my pockets. I crossed the zoo that was Bourbon Street on a Saturday night—which was a lot more crowded and happening than I would have thought, given how cold and wet it was, but people love to have a good time no matter the weather. I turned left onto Royal Street. The Royal Aquitaine was right there across the street, the enormous gray building looming in the darkness.

If only we hadn't gone to that stupid party.

I hurried down Royal Street. Sure enough, when I reached my parents' tobacco shop, the Devil's Weed, all the windows in their apartment upstairs were ablaze with light. The hot buttered rum had worn off and I was cold.

I wanted to see Taylor, just to make sure he was okay.

My phone vibrated as I made it to the iron gate to the back staircase. I checked it as I fumbled with my keys. The text was from Serena: *Darling, I just heard about darling Taylor. Such nonsense! That boy wouldn't hurt a fly. Can you make it to brunch tomorrow? I may be able to help.*

Any port in a storm, I thought, unlocking the gate and stepping inside, slamming it shut behind me. Being out of the wind was a lot better, but it was still cold. I pulled off a glove and typed, *Any help would be greatly appreciated, What time?*

One? came back almost instantly.

Perfect, see you then.

I dropped my phone back into my pocket and climbed the steps to the kitchen door. I didn't bother knocking. I unlocked it and stepped into the warmth. "Mom? Dad?" I called. There was jazz music coming from the living room, and the thick green smell of burning marijuana. I walked across the kitchen. Mom was taking a big hit off an enormous glass dragon bong, and Dad was sitting in an easy chair. He smiled at me. "Come in, son!" he beckoned. "Have a hit."

Mom expelled an enormous cloud of smoke. It never ceased to amaze me how a woman in her early seventies could inhale so much smoke. She held out the bong to me. I took off my jacket, gloves, and hat before taking it from her and sitting down in the empty easy chair. "Where's Taylor?"

"He got up for a while but went back to sleep," Mom said as I took a big hit of my own off the dragon. The bong was enormous and required a lot of lung power to suck up enough smoke to get a hit. I thought my lungs were going to explode before I could feel the smoke settling into my lungs. I put the bong down, held it for a moment, and let it go.

Almost instant relaxation. Mom and Dad *always* have the best weed.

"How's he doing?" My voice sounded raspy, and I started coughing. Mom handed me a bottle of water.

"As well as can be expected," Dad said. He shook his head. "As much as I've seen, I am still shocked by the evil that people are capable of. How's Frank handling everything?"

I was tempted to tell them everything—but couldn't. I couldn't place the burden of what Colin had done—what Frank and I were in the process of covering up—on them. No sense making the situation worse.

"As well as can be expected." I waved off the bong when Dad offered it to me again. "No thanks, I'm good. I shouldn't even be here. But I found some guys at the Brass Rail who can back up Taylor's story—they saw them arrive and Taylor was fine. The bartender only served Taylor water, but somehow he was wasted and barely able to stand on his own when they left."

"It's like that show is cursed," Mom said. "Both that bastard rapist producer and Chloe Valence murdered on the same night." She shook her head. She hated the shows, talked all the time about how much they demeaned women and dehumanized the cast—but she never missed a minute of any of them, had an opinion on every feud, and followed some of her favorites on social media. "That's got to be a nightmare for the network. I wonder what they'll do about the show."

"Well, obviously Eric can't host the reunion show, that's for sure."

"I like that lawyer Storm got for Taylor, that Loren McKeithen," Mom went on. "I've met him before at fundraisers. He's a shark, and that's what we need. The police aren't going to hang this on our Taylor."

I grinned at her. I was pleasantly stoned, and I was feeling the glow from the hot buttered rum. I got to my feet. "Well, tell him I stopped by and I love him. He wasn't upset we had him stay here?"

"He wasn't upset—I told you, the boy needs a mom right now." Mom was putting a couple of buds into a baggie for me. "Here, take this. This is better than the stuff we got you last week." She kissed me on the cheek. "You tell Frank there's nothing to worry about. We've got you all covered."

As I went out the back door, I thanked the Goddess again for my family.

I was the luckiest gay man alive.

CHAPTER NINE

THE HERMIT

A meeting with one who will guide the Seeker to his goals

I pulled up in front of Serena's house in the Garden District the following afternoon. I was a few minutes early according to the clock on the video screen in my dashboard, so I could sit for a moment and strategize. Plus, it was warm in the car and I didn't want to get back out into the cold.

The hard freeze threatening for several days had happened overnight. It was in the low forties now, and probably wasn't going to get much warmer. There'd been ice in the courtyard fountain when I walked through to get the car. It wasn't much—just a thin layer over the water basin that looked like icing on a glazed donut—but it was ice. The sun was hiding behind a carpet of gray clouds, the wind whipping and howling around the car.

Frank stayed home with Taylor. He'd called, early that morning, waking us both up and wanting us to pick him up. He wanted to come home—which led to a heated discussion between Frank and me. We couldn't very well tell him he *couldn't* come home without explaining why, so we decided we'd just not leave him there alone until we knew no Russians would be coming to our door with murder on their minds. As for the living room, Frank decided to take the blame. "I'll just tell him I kind of went crazy angry and started smashing things," he said.

I hated the lying, but we didn't have much choice.

And seeing Taylor shattered my heart. He seemed like a completely different kid from the one I'd grown to love, whom I'd gone to that stupid party with on Friday night. He'd always slouched—it was something I constantly nagged him about—but now he seemed even more slumped, like he was trying to compact his frame and make himself as small as possible. His eyes were red, and he kept wiping at his nose. He wouldn't look either Frank or me in the eye.

If he noticed the changes to our living room, he didn't mention it. He just lay down on the couch and covered himself with a blanket. Frank went upstairs and got Scooter. When Scooter jumped on his chest, kneading it with his paws and head-butting Taylor, it was the first time I'd seen the light in his eyes come back on since it happened.

"I'm sorry to be so much trouble," he mumbled, rearranging Scooter so he was tucked between Taylor's left arm and torso. Scooter sighed, curled up, and closed his eyes.

"You've done nothing wrong," Frank replied, glancing over at me.

"I'm sorry to be such a bother," Taylor said, turning his head into the couch.

"You aren't a bother," I said, sitting on the arm of the couch. "I thank the universe every day that you've come into our lives, become a part of our family, Taylor."

I started to say more, but Frank gave me a warning look.

As tempting as it was to bash Taylor's wretched parents, Frank was right. It wouldn't make Taylor feel better.

I waited to cry until I was in the car.

Then I wiped my eyes and took a deep breath.

We'll get through this. We've been through worse things.

Life doesn't give you anything you can't handle. It's how you handle it that matters.

"Okay," I said aloud. "It's not going to get warmer if I wait longer." I turned off the ignition and opened the car door just as my cell phone dinged. I disconnected it from the car and looked at the screen. It was from Frank:

Loren McKeithen is coming by to talk to us at 4. Try to be home by then.

Will do.

I walked to the front gate to Serena's mansion.

The house had been the site of one of New Orleans's most notorious murders when I was a kid and had stood empty for years until Serena had bought it. She'd relished the house's history rather than been turned off by it. It was a gorgeous Victorian, with a spacious yard enclosed by an enormous leaning brick fence.

I'd originally met Serena when she'd had her housewarming party a year ago this past August. She'd just moved in from her condo at 1 River Place, and she hadn't finished furnishing the place yet. My sister had worked on a charity with Serena and scored me the invitation. I'd liked Serena immediately. She was larger than life and loved it. She was beautiful, with minimal work done on her face—she liked to say "just enough to keep it fresh, darling"—and swore her enormous breasts were hers and not enhanced. She was tall and curvy, probably a little heavy for a *Grande Dame* but said she didn't care. "I can be a role model for full-figured women," she said with that booming laugh of hers, "and it's past time those skinny little bitches had a real woman to deal with." We'd bonded over our love of trashy reality television. She'd already been cast in the New Orleans franchise, but filming hadn't yet begun when she had the party. She also admitted she'd campaigned to get cast. Her money came from oil—she was one of the Crown Oil Castlemaines—and she had been through numerous husbands, including a football player, a ballet dancer, and a rodeo cowboy.

The longest of her marriages lasted just under three years.

"I'm not meant to be a wife," she always said with a slow wink, "I'm much better as a mistress."

I was sure she'd be a fan favorite.

Serena, being still a relative newcomer to New Orleans—it would be years before she'd be considered a local—had done her research on her cast members, asking everyone she knew questions about the other women.

She'd even quizzed me a few times. I helped her…to a point.

I mean, this whole town runs on gossip. But it's one thing to tell friends stories over drinks or at the dinner table and something else entirely when the gossip you share could wind up on national television and in tabloids. New Orleans has always been clannish, closing ranks against outsiders. I wasn't comfortable with seeding a storyline for the show.

I haven't watched hours of these shows for nothing.

I was relieved to see there were no production trucks around as I walked up to the front door. A maid answered my ring and took my coat, saying, "Ms. Castlemaine is in the drawing room," nodding to an open doorway just past the foyer.

"Fidelis Vandiver is a *bitch*," Serena Castlemaine was saying grandly in her thick Texas accent, the diamonds on her fingers flashing fire, as I walked in. She was probably the most animated person I knew.

"Hello, Serena!" I said, bracing myself as she leapt to her feet and crushed me to her enormous bosom in one fluid movement. She managed to hold on to not only her champagne glass but the electric cigarette in her other hand.

"Darling!" She air-kissed me on both cheeks. "It's been too long, my dear. You remember Sloane Gaylord, my production assistant? She's been such a help to me."

Sloane was seated across the coffee table on the love seat. She smiled and held out a tiny hand for me to shake. "It's lovely to see you again, Scotty. I'm just sorry it's under such terrible circumstances." She shivered. "I still can't believe someone killed Eric. And Chloe." She shook her head, the ponytail swinging. "This—I mean, I..."

"How's the network going to handle this?" I asked, sitting down in a wingback chair with my back to the front windows. Serena leaned forward and poured me a mimosa from the pitcher on the coffee table.

"No decisions have been made yet," Sloane replied, hugging herself with her thin arms. "Eric isn't *really* our producer, he's the executive producer, so he just oversees the shows. But his talk show—I don't know. I'm glad it's not my problem. And as for Chloe...I don't know. I mean, this is a whole new situation." She took a deep breath. "They may just cancel the show. The premiere will definitely be postponed, at the very least."

"You know, they could always reshoot, do some editing, and just cut Chloe out of the show." Serena drained her champagne glass. "It really wouldn't be much of a loss, other than I suppose it would be expensive. And it would eliminate the entire lawsuit problem. They can't just *cancel* the show, can they? I'd think the murders would be great publicity—people would watch out of gruesome curiosity. I know I would."

"There *is* a lot of money tied up in the show," Sloane agreed.

Serena saw the look on my face and laughed. "What a bitch you must think I am, Scotty." Diamonds flashed as she waved her hand. "It's not like I knew Eric that well, and Chloe...I'm sorry she's dead, I wouldn't wish that on anyone, but...anyway, we're bound to be more entertaining than the other shows—especially *Marin County*. Those women are such bores." She rolled her enormous blue eyes. "It's a wonder anyone watches."

I bit my lip. Two people were dead, and *the show* was their biggest concern?

Then again...a certain degree of narcissism was necessary for people to get cast.

"I doubt the network will just cancel the show." Sloane demurred. "They'd take a pretty big loss if they did. And—awful as this sounds—the murders will push up the ratings."

She was right. It did sound awful.

But she was probably right, which was even more awful.

People *would* watch.

"How is Taylor doing?" Serena asked, turning back to me. "How's the poor dear holding up? I would never believe that darling boy could ever kill Eric. Or anyone, for that matter."

"The two murders have to be related, don't you think?" Sloane chimed in. "And from what I understand, there's no way he could have killed Chloe."

"I suppose hoping Fidelis is the killer would be too much to ask for." Serena sighed, ringing a bell. "I hope you don't mind, but it's just muffins and fruit salad."

"Not at all." I sipped my mimosa. It was delicious. "Taylor is doing as well as can be expected. He's shaken up, obviously."

"Did Eric really drug him?" Serena was about to add something, but the maid showed up with a tray full of food. *Just muffins* apparently meant two dozen freshly made, steaming hot muffins of various kinds—blueberry, cranberry, corn, and chocolate. And the fruit salad was an enormous Baccarat crystal bowl filled with melon balls, watermelon chunks, strawberries, blueberries, blackberries, and sliced kiwi. As soon as the drawing room doors closed behind the maid, she went on, "But he didn't sexually assault him?" She grabbed a small plate and grabbed two muffins, smeared butter on them, and spooned fruit salad into a bowl. "Help yourselves, both of you."

"I don't suppose we'll ever know for sure what happened." I waited for Sloane to help herself. She neatly sliced a corn muffin in half and put it on her plate. She added a small spoonful of fruit to it. "The doctors didn't think so, but," my voice started to crack, "we're taking all the necessary precautions. You know. Just in case."

"Poor darling. If there's anything we can do..." Serena gestured dramatically with the muffin she was holding.

"Whoever killed Eric did us a favor," I replied. "Sexual assault cases are hard enough for women to pursue...and seriously, if he were still alive..." I shook my head. "I could kill him myself. So could my mother, and Frank. I've heard he had a history of this?" I looked at Sloane. As someone who'd worked for him, she'd be more likely to know anything.

"I've heard...stories about Eric before." Sloane nibbled at the half muffin, took another sip from her glass. "I didn't want to believe them, of course, but...there's so much of this in the industry, you know? You never know what's true and what's not."

"A gay man with power is still a man with power," Serena replied. "Why wouldn't he take advantage of his position to get hot young men to have sex with him? Had you heard about him drugging people?"

"If we could establish a pattern of behavior, that would be great." I bit into my blueberry muffin. "I don't think the police seriously consider Taylor as a suspect—or at least they won't once the toxicology report comes back—but it can't hurt. Frank and I are trying to see what we can find out. Just in case."

"I hadn't heard about him drugging people, no," Sloane replied. "Just the casting couch thing. I worked on the *Spring Break* show before the company moved me to *Grande Dames*." *Spring Break* followed the antics of a group of rich kids spending a week in a gorgeous house in Cancun. It had proved popular, so the same group of kids rented a house together for the summer in South Beach, *Summer Rental*. "A couple of the guys on that show told me that Eric had, um, you know, made certain demands in order to cast them."

All the guys on the show were incredibly hot. I have to admit I watched because they spent most of their time shirtless. And for the occasional bare ass shot, which happened more than one might think. "Which ones?"

"Dean and Timothy," she replied. "I bet if I ask around, I can come up with some more names. Do you want me to?"

She works for the network—it's not in her best interest to expose wrongdoing by Eric, is it? Maybe she had a grudge against Eric or Diva Network. "Would you mind? Anything will help." I took another sip of the mimosa. I was already feeling a bit loopy from the alcohol, so I finished my muffin and took another. "And were you serious about Fidelis, Serena?"

Fidelis Vandiver was already a familiar face to longtime New Orleanians before she'd joined the cast of *Grande Dames*. She'd landed a gig as the weather girl on one of our local news broadcasts right out of LSU. She was tall and pretty with incredible bone structure. She had a penchant for enormous statement necklaces, low-cut tops designed to show off her breasts, and showing off her long lean legs. When she left the news show—the rumor was she'd been sleeping with the station manager, and his wife insisted Fidelis had to go—she managed to get her own fitness program on a rival station. *Fitness with Fidelis* wasn't a huge ratings success but did well enough to stay on the air for a ridiculously long time and enabled her to open a chain of health clubs in the New Orleans area, Fid's Gyms. I never worked for her, but I knew people who did.

What I did know was that she ripped me off.

I'd only met her in passing, at parties. She was always pleasant, and even though it was hard, I always managed to put on a happy face and be nice right back to her. It was kind of irritating, in a way.

She didn't even have the decency to remember who I was.

She'd stolen a workout program from me.

After I flunked out of Vanderbilt, I worked as a dancer with the Southern Knights booking agency, flying all over the country to dance in underwear or a thong or a Speedo or whatever would make me the most tips at gay bars and circuit parties. I also worked as a personal trainer at Riverview Fitness and taught aerobics classes. I really hated aerobics, but every cent mattered back in those days before my grandfathers relented and let me have access to my trust funds. So, I came up with my own aerobics style class—a mix between floor movement, using the step, and using small hand weights to build muscle while toning at the same time. It was popular, and it worked. I taught five or six of those classes per week.

And then one day, Fidelis Vandiver showed up to take my class. She came in right before we started and dashed out again as soon as we were finished.

The next week, on her show, she premiered a workout program she called "Fidfit," which was the workout I had come up with.

She also trademarked the name and copyrighted the idea.

And I could no longer teach the class unless Riverview Fitness paid her a fee.

I was furious, but as Storm told me at the time, "There's really not anything you can do about it. You should have copyrighted it before you taught your first class."

I thought about reinventing the class with Storm's help, but finally decided to let it go and just teach regular step aerobics.

It was annoying, though, whenever I'd flip through the channels and see her show, or a commercial for her gyms.

But I believe in the rule of three—whatever you put out in the universe comes back to you threefold—and one day karma was going to kick her right in her toned, tight ass.

"No, nothing other than she's a bitch," Serena replied cheerfully. "Rain told me you had an issue with her?"

"She's not my favorite person," I replied carefully. "I suppose I'll have to watch the show to see why you think she's a bitch?"

Serena grinned wickedly at me. "Confidentiality agreement," she replied. "I'm not really allowed to talk about what happened during filming, you know. Although I suppose that doesn't apply to *murder*, does it, Sloane?"

Sloane put her plate down. She'd only eaten two bites of her muffin and one melon ball. "I'm not one of the network lawyers. I don't know." She pushed her glasses up and rubbed her eyes. "This is such a mess."

"Besides, it had to be Remy, right? Who else had a reason to want to kill both Eric and Chloe?" Serena said. "I wonder..." She glanced over at me. "I wonder if Eric and Remy were lovers?"

Sloan shook her head. "Eric had a thing for younger guys. Remy was too old for him."

"What about the other women?" I asked. "Do you think anyone else in the cast might have a grudge against Eric and Chloe?"

Serena frowned. "Margery, I suppose...but Chloe wasn't suing her."

"She wasn't suing anyone," Sloan interrupted. "It was just a cease-and-desist letter, asking Margery not to say Remy was gay in front of the cameras and asking the network not to air her saying it."

"I can't imagine Margery killing anyone," I replied. I only knew Margery Lautenschlaeger in passing, but everyone in New Orleans knew who she was. She and my grandmother were involved in the same charities, and sometimes I ran into Margery at parties at my grandmother's or charity events when someone in my family was involved. "She'd hire someone to do it." She was filthy rich. "Who else did Chloe clash with on the show?"

Sloane mimed zipping her lips and locking them.

"I've probably already told you too much about the show as it is," Serena replied regretfully. She moved to refill my glass again, but I waved her off.

"I'm driving, I can't have any more."

"Just call an Uber, and get your car later," Serena coaxed.

"No, I really can't. I'm meeting with a lawyer later, so I need to have a clear head. Some other time, though—when all of this is cleared up—I'd love to come over and drink mimosas all afternoon with you." I checked my watch. "I probably should get going."

"Oh, damn." Serena pouted. She rose and gave me one of her intense hugs, burying me in her massive cleavage. "If there's anything I can do, please don't hesitate to call me, okay? And Sloane and I will check with the lawyers, see, you know, how binding that confidentiality agreement is...I just don't want to get sued."

Or kicked off the show, I thought, hugging her back.

I shut the front door behind me and shivered. It was starting to rain as I ran down the walk and through the front gate. I started the car and checked my phone.

Nothing from Frank.

Maybe that was a good thing.

I sat there with my eyes closed, waiting for the car to start blowing hot air, thinking, letting the champagne cobwebs clear a bit.

Eric had a history of using his casting power to get men he found attractive to sleep with him. That had to be a plus. That information alone was worth the trip over, even if it didn't show a history of drugging guys and assaulting them. It would, as Storm would say, lay the groundwork for showing Eric was a scumbag. And once the story got out, maybe more guys would come forward, other guys he'd victimized like he'd tried to do to Taylor.

As I put the car into drive, I realized I actually wasn't very far from the Valence house.

Maybe I was tipsier than I thought, but it couldn't *hurt* to stop by and talk to Remy, would it?

I drove the car around the block, trying to remember exactly where the Valence house was. I made a wrong turn and had to double back, but finally pulled up in front of it.

The Valence house was also in the Greek Revival style, a mansion with side porches and balconies hanging off the upper floors. It was a huge place, built in a time when you had to have living space for a passel of children, relatives, and guests. There was also a huge separate building that was now called a "dower house" but had been slave quarters before the Civil War. An enormous live oak stood directly in front of the house, between the sidewalk and the curb, and its roots had upended and cracked not only the sidewalk and the curb but the tall wrought iron fence that ran the length of the property. On the side bordered by Coliseum Street, the house sat right on the sidewalk and went back for what seemed like forever. All the downstairs windows were lit up, as were the gallery lights. I'd never been inside the Valence house.

The Valence family was considered "old money" in New Orleans, and their mansion in the Garden District had been their "home in town" when they still had the indigo plantation in St. John the Baptist Parish. The plantation was long gone, of course, and the big Greek Revival mansion on Third Street had been their primary residence since before the Spanish-American War. I knew the Valences had made money importing coffee and bananas, and I think they'd even found oil on one of their properties somewhere in the early twentieth century. But the Valence family businesses were long gone, and the family had lived for decades off the pile of money their more ambitious ancestors had earned.

I pushed through the gate and walked up to the front porch.

I hope this isn't a mistake, I thought as I rang the doorbell.

CHAPTER TEN
TWO OF PENTACLES, REVERSED
The seeker is having trouble achieving his goals

As I shivered in the cold waiting for someone to answer the door, I looked off to the right.

The pool, hidden from street view by a line of hedges, was visible from where I was standing. Wisps of steam rose from the water. Crime scene tape stretched from the hedges to a series of deck chairs placed to enclose the pool, reaching back to the hedges from another chair on the far side of the pool. It flapped and fluttered and snapped in the wind. The pool looked grayish-blue, but on the far side, away from the hedges, there was a rusty stain in the water. There was also a dark puddle of water, with a thin coat of ice covering it, on the tile near the stained water.

That must be where Chloe was killed, I thought, the muffins I'd had at Serena's turning to burning acid in my stomach. *What in the hell was she doing in the pool area at that hour of the night? On a cold night like Friday?*

It didn't make sense.

Unless it was a burglar? She'd heard something, and come outside to check?

A woman in the house alone would go outside? No, she'd call the cops—or at least Garden District security.

During the late 1990s, when crime was on the rise in the city and splashed all over the front page of the newspaper every day, the Garden District Association decided that the New Orleans Police Department wasn't enough to protect them against the criminal element. The Garden District Security District was created to protect the privileged and the wealthy—an officer would, for example, come escort you from your car to the front door of your palatial home if you were one of those who didn't have off-street parking—and so forth.

If Chloe had heard a noise or a prowler, she would have called security, not gone outside.

She only would have gone outside if she knew her killer.

But why didn't she invite the killer inside?

I shivered as a sudden blast of cold wind blew rain onto me. I was reaching for the doorbell to ring it again when I heard footsteps approaching over groaning floorboards on the other side of the door. I noted that the porch had been painted probably within the last year, and its floorboards felt solid under my weight, meaning it had been renovated. The shutters on the windows also looked like they'd gotten some fresh paint recently. The newer paint made the paint on the house itself look older and more weather-beaten.

It was also peeling in places.

My guess was they'd had the porch and shutters painted for the show but didn't have enough money to have the house painted.

I tried to remember if I'd heard any gossip about the Valences' financial situation.

I'd assumed Chloe had gone on the show to promote her writing career, but maybe they'd needed the money.

Then again, maybe they'd just run out of time before filming started to have the entire house done. New Orleans contractors never deliver on time—a sad fact of life we've all become accustomed to.

The front door opened, and I found myself face-to-face with Remy Valence.

He hadn't aged well since I'd seen him last, but maybe that was unfair. His wife had just been murdered, which could explain why he was unshaven, looked unkempt, and stank of body odor and stale liquor. He'd put on weight, and his hair had been dyed to hide gray—which I could see at the roots in his disheveled part. He was wearing an old green velvet dressing gown over a dirty white T-shirt and jeans. His slippers were stained and battered looking.

He didn't seem to recognize me. "Yes?" he asked, and his breath was about forty proof.

I took a step back but kept my smile plastered on my face. "Hello, Remy. I'm Scotty Bradley, do you remember me?"

He blinked a few times before recognition dawned on his face. "Sure," he slurred, and I realized he was still drinking.

"I heard about Chloe. I'm so sorry."

His bloodshot eyes filled with water, and he wiped at them angrily. "Yes, well, thank you. I suppose you think I killed her, too?" His voice rose until he was shouting the last few words at me.

"Well, no, of course not." I took another step back. His breath was truly foul. "Is that what the police think? That's ridiculous." I hoped I sounded convincing.

"The New Orleans police aren't known for their brains." He ran a hand through his hair and smiled a terrible smile at me. "Corruption, yes, brains, no."

"How are you holding up?"

"Well as can be expected." He hiccoughed. "It's fucking freezing out here. Come inside." He stood aside and gestured.

As I walked past him his hand brushed against my ass. *God, his wife's body is barely cold and he's still a fucking pig.*

He closed the door and walked around me, signaling to follow. For a brief moment I worried he was going to lead me to a bedroom.

As I followed him along the hallway the cloying, stuffy, stale heat made me start sweating. I took off my hat and gloves, shoving them into my pockets, and undid the coat buttons.

Even over the stale air coming through the heating vents, the house smelled musty and damp. That generally meant somewhere in the house old wood was rotting. Many of the old houses in New Orleans have that smell, which makes a homeowner's heart—and bank account—shrink. It means thousands of dollars in renovations, walls and ceilings and floors being ripped out and replaced. And it can't be put off, else toxic black mold will form where it can't be seen—a silent but deadly killer. Wet wood also attracts termites, which thrive in our hot damp climate and are a constant threat. Most houses in New Orleans—like the Valence place—were built up off the ground for protection from flooding. But that only protects the house from water damage from *below*. The constantly shifting ground can crack foundations and walls, and water gets in through the cracks. Between the humidity, the damp, and the daily rain all spring and summer, water damage from above is a greater risk than flooding from below, depending on your neighborhood.

Hadn't I heard somewhere that the Valences had more house than money?

I had a vague memory of someone telling me that all the money from Chloe's book had gone into house repair, and that the old mansion was crumbling faster than they could throw money they didn't have at it. I was also certain someone had said the Valences could only afford repairs on the first floor of the house—the part people could see—and had let the upper floors go to ruin. As I walked past a hanging staircase I glanced up, but the lights were out upstairs so I couldn't get a glimpse of anything.

But...if Remy and Chloe had picked out the green and gold flocked wallpaper in the hallway, their inability to afford renovating the upper floors was the house's good luck.

"Come on into the parlor." He stepped into a room just off the front hallway. The parlor had French doors that opened out onto the pool. The heavy brocade green and gold curtains were pulled back. Fortunately, the glass was covered in condensation so I couldn't see the crime scene tape or that hideous stain on the pool water.

There was an open bottle of Scotch on a table next to a faded old wingback chair, and a glass with melting ice. "Sit." Remy pointed to another chair and walked over to the doors, pulling the drapes shut. "I'm not at my best, Scotty. You're looking good, though." He gave me a crooked grin that turned my stomach.

He is hitting on me.

"I'm sorry about your wife," I replied, slipping off my coat and draping it over an overstuffed wingback chair. "I didn't know her, but I can't imagine what you must be going through."

"Sit." He pointed at the chair again as he sat down in the matching chair. "My wife was murdered." He shook his head and wiped at his eyes again. "Friday night, after that stupid show's premiere party. If I'd known...I would have stayed in town."

"And you might be dead, too."

He gave me that leering smile again. It made me feel slimy. "And on that very same night your nephew"—he made air quotes as he said *nephew*—"was killing that rat bastard Eric Brewer." He picked up the bottle of Scotch. "I'm going to have to have the pool drained and cleaned," he said glumly, staring at the melting ice in the empty glass. "That's going to cost a fortune."

Such an inconvenience. I sat down on the other side of the little table. The fabric of the chair felt coarse against my arm. "My nephew didn't kill Eric Brewer."

He made a face and filled his glass without offering me any.

"The police surely don't think *you* had anything to do with Chloe's—"

"Of course not," he snapped. "Well, they did, but I have an alibi." He narrowed his eyes to slits and took another big drink of the Scotch. "I wasn't even in New Orleans."

"You didn't go to the party on Friday night?"

"Why would I go celebrate that—that *show?*" He glowered at me. "It was a disgrace that Chloe went on that show in the first place. Thank God Mama is dead. She would have never allowed it. Never."

If it's not the first rule of being a detective, *talking to a witness when he's drunk* should be in the top five.

"You didn't like Chloe being on the show?" I asked.

"Hell no! The last thing I want is cameras following us around, prying into our lives." He glowered at me. "I didn't see anyone in your damned family being on the show, nor any woman who is actually a part of *real* New Orleans society, on it."

"Margery Lautenschlaeger—"

"That miserable old bitch isn't society." He laughed.

I waited for him to make some anti-Semitic remark, but that was as far as he was willing to go. "I heard you had some problems with her."

"The old bitch said I was gay in front of the cameras." He took another swig of the Scotch and turned his glassy, bloodshot eyes to me. "Can you believe that shit?"

Maybe he *didn't* remember we'd slept together all those years ago, and inwardly I breathed a sigh of relief. "Yeah, that's terrible. I guess that's why the cops thought you might have killed Eric Brewer Friday night?"

"Yeah, they were going to try to hang killing them both on me." His eyes got watery, and he wiped at them. "Damn it, I still can't believe she's dead, that someone killed her. I keep expecting her to walk in the room and say something that doesn't make sense the way she always did and then laugh at herself, you know? Why would someone kill Chloe? She was amazing, and so sweet and kind and loving…" He choked off his sentence with a sob.

"Can you think of anyone who would have wanted to hurt Chloe?" I prodded, feeling like an asshole. "I mean, besides the people on the show."

"Thash what's sho weird," he slurred. "That shtupid fucking show. I told her not to do it, but she thought it would be good for her career. I told her no one would take her seriously as a writer if she was doing a reality television show. I mean, can you see Curtis Sattlefield or Claire Messud doing a reality show? Please." He shook his head. "She really hated Eric Brewer, though. He was a real dick to her…" His voice trailed off and he stared off into space. "Look, I probably shouldn't tell you this…"

"You can trust me," I replied, feeling like an even bigger asshole.

"Chloe and I have had an open marriage for a while now." He tried to straighten himself up but couldn't. He slurped some more Scotch from the glass, spilling some onto his shirt. I reached over and took the glass from him.

"I don't think you should have any more, Remy," I said. "Let me get you some water."

"Ish fine." He waved his hands. "Yeah, maybe no more booze. Whatever. Anyway. Chloe and me, it was our business and nobody else's, you know? As long as we were safe, and discreet, we had a deal we could do whatever we wanted as long as we didn't endanger each other. No babies, no VD…nothing like that." He tried to focus on me, but his eyes looked a little too bleary for that. "She was seeing someone lately. We never told each other who we were fucking, that was part of the deal, but she was fucking someone. And she was happy, you know? So happy I wondered if maybe she was going to finally say she didn't want to stay married to me anymore." He waved his arms sloppily. "I mean, what did she need me for? We hadn't had sex in years, and we didn't even sleep in the same bed anymore."

"You don't know who she was having an affair with?"

"No." Remy slumped over on the chaise, some drool coming

out of the corner of his mouth. "She never told me. But I know it was someone who had something to do with the show."

How had I ever found this man attractive enough to have sex with? Granted, it was a long time ago, but...I've always felt you have an obligation to people you sleep with to remain reasonably attractive the rest of your life, so they aren't mortified when they see you. But to be fair, he was still in decent shape, and despite the redness and slight alcohol bloat to his face, he was still handsome. A few weeks of exercise and eating right would shape him up.

"Not—Eric Brewer?" Maybe he was bisexual.

Remy started laughing, until he choked. "Eric Brewer? The only Valence who was fucking Eric Brewer was *me*."

Wait—what?

"You were sleeping with Eric Brewer?" So much for Eric only being into younger men.

Remy nodded. "It was only a couple of times. Before filming started. And he swore—he swore to me—nothing about it would ever show up on the show." His eyes narrowed to slits. "And then the Lautenschlaeger bitch said something on camera."

"And you threatened to sue them, right?"

"How did you—Jesus H. Christ, I always forget what a small fucking town this is." Remy reached for the bottle, but I got to it before he did it and placed it on the floor on the other side of my chair. He glared at me for a moment, and then sighed. "It was a cease-and-desist letter, but I wasn't going to sue anybody. Besides, it wasn't *real*."

"What do you mean, it wasn't real?"

"It was for the *show*." He threw his hands up in the air. "Chloe was upset Margery said it in front of the camera, sure." He shook his head. "*She* was the one who cared, not me. She wanted everyone to think we had this terrific, perfect, normal marriage and she was New Orleans society and that would be ruined if people knew about my men. The cease-and-desist letter was something she dreamed up with Eric."

"I don't understand." I scratched my head. "It wasn't real?"

"Nothing about these shows is real, Scotty, haven't you noticed?" He took another swig from his glass. "Eric thought it would be good for the ratings. Everything was about the ratings, and what kind of shit-show the gossip rags would make out of it. I didn't fucking care. Everyone knows I fuck men, okay? Everyone. Chloe liked to think no one knew, but we would have been *laughed* out of court if we tried any real legal action." He looked at me. "*You* could testify I'd had sex with men."

Great. He does remember. Perfect.

But I was also trying to wrap my mind around the cease-and-desist letter not being real. "Did Margery or the others know the legal stuff wasn't for real?"

"I doubt it." He was staring into his glass. "You know, that way they'd be convincing. These aren't professional actors, Scotty." He waved his hand. "Eric and his production team set the women up in all kinds of ways and situations, to create drama. None of it's for real."

"So, you said you have an alibi, though, for the murders?"

His cheeks were wet, and a tear was dangling from the side of his chin. "I found her when I got home. I was at our place in Destin for a few days. She wasn't around when I got home, and so I came in here for a drink. When I opened the curtains—" He shuddered and started sobbing again.

My head was starting to hurt. "So, you were out of town?"

"I had breakfast with my friends in Destin before I drove back Saturday morning. It was when I got home...that I found her," he said brokenly. "Friday night I had dinner with some other friends, was with them until midnight or so."

You still could have driven to New Orleans, killed them both, and then driven back to Destin in time for breakfast, I thought, doing the math in my head. It was pushing it, but it wasn't impossible.

And if you're trying to alibi yourself...the point is to make it seem impossible that you could have done it.

"And you have no idea who the guy she was involved with was."

"I told you, no. We didn't talk about our...other people."

"And you can't think of any reason anyone else would have for wanting to kill her?" I looked at Remy.

"I don't know. Maybe one of those other bitches on that stupid show." Remy slammed his hand down on the coffee table. "I told her not to do the fucking show!" He buried his face in his hands again. "I told her not to do this show. I begged her, but she really thought it would be a big help to her writing career, and I wanted to be supportive. I thought it was an incredibly stupid idea, like I said a thousand goddamned times."

"There wasn't anyone she had made angry? Is it possible the guy was married?"

If the guy was married…and it was going to somehow wind up on the show, and the guy didn't want his wife to know—*there* was a motive for both murders.

Killing Eric to stop the show from airing was stupid.

His death didn't guarantee the show would be canceled.

But if the murders were connected, then Taylor was off the hook. He couldn't have killed Chloe, even if he had killed Eric.

But if the murders *weren't* connected…

My head was really starting to hurt.

"Those vulgar, nasty, vicious bitches!" He dropped his hands and his face twisted. "They were all so jealous of Chloe, you know. Especially that Fidelis Vandiver bitch." He spat the words out. "West Bank trash is all she was. I don't care who she slept with to get that stupid fitness show, or who her sugar daddies were—the way she always went after Chloe! And me!"

Okay, he was the second person to bring up Fidelis. I knew from personal experience she wasn't a good person.

So, maybe she did bear looking into.

If you have something to hide, the last thing you should do is go on a reality show, I thought, *even if it is mostly scripted in some ways. Things have a way of coming out on camera.*

"You're a detective, aren't you?"

Startled, I looked at him. "What? Yes, yes, I am. I already told you that."

"I want you to find who did this to Chloe. I owe her that."

"It's a conflict of interest, Remy. I already have a client."

"I'll double what they're paying you."

I stood up. "I can't, Remy. I wish I could help you, but I can't."

He somehow managed to get to his own feet and leered at me. "You want me to sleep with you?"

He lunged toward me, throwing his arms around me but going limp at the same time, so his dead weight dragged me down to the floor with him half on top of me and half off. Repulsed, I shoved him off me, and he rolled over on his back, eyes closed, drool running out of the side of his mouth.

He'd passed out.

I got back to my feet, shaking my head.

I said, "Thanks, I can see myself out."

I walked down the dark hallway back to the front door, shutting it behind me with a sigh of relief. I felt like I needed a long, hot shower.

How had I ever slept with him in the first place? It was a long time ago, but *still*.

It was pouring rain now, lightning lighting up the sky with thunder shaking the house almost immediately after. I sat down on one of the iron chairs on the porch. I didn't have an umbrella, and the rain was coming down so strong and hard that I was going to get soaked just running to the car. I checked my watch. I still had some time before Loren was supposed to show up at the house. I could wait a few minutes before braving the rain and running to the car.

Chloe had a lover and Remy claimed to not know who it was.

Remy also claimed to have slept with Eric Brewer.

He was also drunk. Drunks generally don't have the wherewithal to lie, so I had no reason to think he wasn't telling me the truth. I made a mental note to talk to Storm about the cease-and-desist letter. If we could prove it was just manipulation for the show…

What if *Margery* had found out that it wasn't real? That Eric was setting her up for some drama for the sake of the cameras?

Wouldn't that give *her* a motive for killing Eric? And Chloe, too?

But I couldn't see the glamorous liquor heiress killing two people in anger.

She's rich enough to pay someone to do it for her, though.

I pressed my thumbs against my temples. I was getting a bad headache, and the rain was getting worse rather than letting up.

I was going to have to brave it, much as I didn't want to.

Just as I was getting up my nerve, a black Chevy Suburban pulled up to the curb on the other side of the street from the Valence house. I watched Venus and Blaine get out and open umbrellas before dashing across the street.

"I might have known you'd be here," Venus said expressionlessly as she climbed the steps to the porch. She closed her umbrella and shook it to dry. Blaine was doing the same.

"If you're here to talk to the widower Valence, you're out of luck," I replied. "He's passed out drunk."

"He was in pretty bad shape yesterday, but it's not every day you find your wife's body floating in the pool," Blaine replied.

"I know you can't talk about the case, but don't you think the murders—Chloe and Eric—have to be connected in some way?"

"It's too early in the investigation to make assumptions," Venus said. "But I will tell you this: both were killed with a very similar weapon, if not the same one." She reached out to ring the doorbell. "A baseball bat, to be exact—or something similarly shaped."

"A baseball bat?"

She nodded as she pressed the doorbell.

Yeah, you'll be waiting a long time for the lord of the manor to answer.

I ran through the rain to my car, unlocking it as soon as I reached the bottom of the front steps. I waited for the heater to start blowing hot air, shivering as I noticed that some of the rain was actually sleet. I turned the wipers on and pulled away from the curb, I turned right on Prytania and started driving back downtown.

The last thing I remember was seeing a car coming up, very quickly, out of the corner of my eye as I entered the intersection at Sixth Street.

There was a crash, and everything went dark.

CHAPTER ELEVEN
THE HANGED MAN
Self-surrender to higher wisdom

I returned to awareness wrapped in a warm, comforting fog.
Drifting, as always.
Love. Peace. Harmony.
It had been a while since the Goddess chose to speak with me. Usually, this happens when I lose consciousness in some way. I've chosen to never wonder if She arranges things so that I will go into this state so She can speak with me when She wants.
She doesn't like being questioned. I've found that out the hard way.
Floating downward, I can see the blue-black night sky above me, stars winking into existence as I stare at that velvety darkness. Not too hot, not too cold, everything perfect, everything just right as I float downward. My body shifts in the air, the air seems to change, which means I am close to the ground. My feet settle on earth. Not dry, not soggy with wet, but dark dirt, the kind that will grow anything. I smell honeysuckle, jasmine, rose, and lilac. I can hear voices murmuring somewhere out there in the velvet darkness, words that are just sounds no matter how hard I try to listen, to shape them into the familiarity of words. The warm gentle breeze wraps itself around me, and I see her, taking shape, materializing, becoming real a few feet in front of where I am standing. This time she is taking the form of Artemis, the huntress; Selene, the twin of Apollo, goddess of the night and the moon to his glory as god of the sun. She has a quiver on her back, a leather strap over her right shoulder. Her tunic is white, shimmering, baring shapely legs and tied tightly at the waist. Her right breast is exposed, the fabric of the tunic tied at her left shoulder. I cannot make out her face—I can never see her face—but her hair is lustrous silver, hanging in plaits down her back and wrapped like a crown around

the top of her head.

Artemis. Selene. Diana. The huntress. Why this form?

I search my mind and my memories for what I know of this form of the Divine Feminine. She was a virgin. She protects virgins and mothers in childbirth. The stag was sacred to her. She was protector of forests and hills.

Why? Why this form?

"You and those you love are in great danger," She said, the sound of her voice music in my ears. "You must be brave."

"Is Taylor going to be all right?"

She quivered, and her body began to glow a brilliant white. "Taylor will survive this test, as he will survive many other tests. But there are lies—so many lies, so many deceits. You must be strong, you must be brave, you must be fearless in order to sift the truth from the lies."

"As long as Taylor will be all right, I can face anything."

"Can you?" She began to fade away in front of me, those final words echoing in my ears as everything began to get lighter, brighter, as the sun seemed to suddenly rise as she faded. "Can you?"

I opened my eyes, aware of the blaring of a car horn.

I winced.

I'm not sure how long I was unconscious, how long I was with the Goddess, but the airbag was almost finished deflating. I blinked a few times, still trying to process what had just happened. My ears were ringing, my eyes watering, and my chest was aching. My head hurt, and there was still gray around the edges of my vision. I started coughing, and stars danced in front of my eyes. There was a chemical taste in the back of my throat, and it tasted horrible, awful, disgusting. I hacked again, trying to cough up whatever it was I'd somehow swallowed—something from the airbag, I suspected— but there was nothing to come up and that scratchy feeling, like you get from bad coke you buy in a club at four in the morning, was still there. As my vision began clearing slowly and I could start focusing my mind again, I saw that my car was sitting in the middle of Prytania Street, well over the broken white line, facing toward St. Charles.

The impact of the accident had not only spun the car a quarter turn but had moved it. That was kind of scary.

How fast was he going? How hard did he hit me? I managed to think through that terrible ringing in my ears. I could see, through a windshield now road-mapped with cracks, that the front hood was not only crumpled but had come open. There was steam coming out from the engine. I blinked a few more times, shook my aching head a little bit, and tried taking inventory of myself. I could move my arms, and my legs seems to be okay, too. As I shifted and moved a little bit in the driver's seat, I realized I was covered in sparkling little diamonds of greenish glass from the shattered window on the passenger side of the car. I started brushing the fragments off my body. I reached up and looked at my reflection in the rearview mirror, turning it so I could get a good look.

No cuts, nothing bleeding, no cuts or abrasions on my face... at least none I could see.

The miracle of the airbag, no doubt, had protected my face.

And out of the corner of my eye, I could see serious damage to the passenger side door. I winced as I turned my head—my neck was sore—and sure enough, that must have been where the other driver's car had hit mine. The door was buckled inward, and all that was left of the window were some jagged edges jutting up from inside the door.

Someone was pounding on my window. With the airbag deflated I could see the dummy lights on the dashboard were all lit up. The engine was stalled, and I couldn't hear what the woman was saying over the ringing in my ears. I pressed the button to roll the window down but of course nothing happened.

I carefully unbuckled my seat belt with shaking hands and opened the car door.

"No, no, don't get up!" I could barely hear her over the ringing. There was also pressure in my eardrums, like I was on a plane descending toward the runway. I held my nose and tried to blow through it. Both eardrums popped and cleared, and I could hear what she was saying better. "You might be injured—you never know! You could have whiplash or have hurt your back. Stay there until the paramedics come. Can you tell if anything is broken?"

"I think I'm fine." My voice sounded hollow and far away. "My head—"

"I called 9-1-1," she said.

I turned my head—slowly, because my neck did hurt, bad—and got a good look at her. She was possibly somewhere in her forties, but it was hard to tell exactly because her face had been pulled tighter than a snare drum. She was also wearing a lot of very carefully applied makeup. Her reddish-gold hair was pulled back into a tight ponytail, which smoothed out her forehead and made her blue eyes appear to bug out a bit. (Some people called that kind of tight ponytail an "Uptown face-lift.") She was wearing a Saints jersey and black yoga pants. She was fairly small—maybe five one, five two, and if she weighed more than one hundred pounds, it was due to her significantly augmented breasts.

"I used to be a nurse," she went on. "You really shouldn't move until the paramedics get here." She looked up as a car passed us on the right. "I mean, seriously, you could fuck yourself up big time."

I turned and looked out where the passenger window used to be. I could see the other car—dark, black, two-door, vaguely sedan-ish. Its hood was also crumpled up, the windshield cracked, steam coming out of its radiator, other fluids leaking out under the engine. "Is the other driver okay?"

She shook her head. "He's gone."

I gasped in horror. "Oh no!"

"Not dead, *gone*." She waved down Sixth Street, toward the river. "I was coming home from the gym—my house is over there," she gestured to the other side of Prytania, "and I had just pulled into my driveway when I saw him coming up the street really fast and I saw you coming up Prytania and I realized he wasn't going to stop...if anything, he *sped up*." She stopped, inhaled for a moment, and went on, "And I saw the whole thing." She shivered, wrapping her arms around herself as she remembered. "I called 9-1-1 immediately and came running. He got out of his car and took off running back that way. I yelled for him to stop, but you weren't moving and I figured I needed to check on you to make sure you're okay but I filmed him." She held up her phone. "Video, film, whatever you call it now. I recorded him. I don't know if the police can identify him, but I mean, why would he run?"

I gaped at her. The ringing in my ears was getting softer, I could hear better, but my eardrums still felt like they needed to be popped, like there was too much pressure in there again somehow. I popped them again and they felt better.

I could hear sirens approaching now. If what she said was true—and why would she lie—it sounded like someone had *deliberately* hit me.

Why?

It didn't make sense, unless it was some kind of insurance scam my mind was too scrambled to figure out. An ambulance, lights flashing and siren blaring, braked in front of my car. The back door opened and a pair of EMTs—a man and a woman—popped out and came running to where I was still sitting.

A penlight beamed into my eyes, while one of them—the man—started firing questions at me. *Can you see? Is anything broken? How's your hearing? Can you turn your head?*

A blood pressure cuff went onto my left arm, while the woman took my pulse. "I'm fine, I think," I said, but my voice sounded hollow and far away, which meant my ears were still messed up.

A uniformed cop took the lady in yoga pants aside and started asking her questions and nodding at her answers, scribbling down notes. The EMTs helped me to my feet, checked my arms and legs, and then helped me over to the ambulance, securing my neck first in one of those collar things you always see on television shows about whiplash scam lawsuits. I kept answering questions as they hooked me up to machines.

"Deep breaths," the woman urged me, as she listened to my lungs through a stethoscope.

"I'm fine, really," I kept insisting.

"We should take you in, get some x-rays," the man said, checking my eyes again. "You could have a concussion, and whiplash isn't always apparent right away."

"My neck is sore," I agreed, turning my head from side to side, wincing. It hurt, but I could do it. "I don't want to go to the hospital. I just want to go home."

She looked dubious. "You really should—"

"I'm just sore," I insisted. "And I don't live alone. If anything goes wrong after I get home, I'll go to an emergency room immediately."

It took me a few more minutes, but they finally agreed to let me go—as long as I signed something absolving them of responsibility if something should actually be wrong with me from the accident.

Ah, our litigious society.

"Here are your keys." A uniform was standing in front of me. I looked up into the cop's face. "We've pushed your car over to the side of the road. It's not drivable. If you're not going to the emergency room, is there anyone you can call to give you a ride home?"

I looked over at where my car was sitting. I hadn't even had it for a full year yet. I was going to have to deal with the insurance company. My heart sank. I didn't have the slightest idea of what to do in this situation. It was going to have to be towed. But where?

"We can give you a lift."

I looked up to see Venus and Blaine standing next to the uniform, their faces expressionless. *Any port in a storm*, I thought. "Sure, okay. Thanks, I appreciate it."

I signed a release form from the EMTs and got a copy of the accident report from the cop in charge of the scene. He warned me I was going to have to get the car towed away at some point. I nodded and followed Venus and Blaine over to Venus's black SUV. I got into the back seat. The pressure was starting to build up in my ears again and I could still hear that faint ringing. My chest ached and I still had that chemical taste in my mouth. I coughed a few times, spat up something into a tissue.

"You know your car is totaled, right?" Blaine said, looking over the seat at me in the back.

"Yeah, they told me." I leaned my head against the cold window. "It's not even a year old. I guess the insurance company will know what to do with it, right?"

"Yes," Venus replied. "They're going to want to look at it, of course, but call them when you get home and let them know. They'll walk you through it. Have you never had an accident before?"

"Not in a car I owned."

"Why would someone want to kill you, Scotty?" Blaine asked, his eyes still on the road, his tone still conversational.

"What?" I couldn't have heard that correctly. "No one is trying to kill me. At least not that I know of. What are you talking about?"

"Come on, Scotty, tell me the truth. What's really going on?" Blaine went on, glancing back at me in the rearview mirror. "That car deliberately hit you, Scotty."

I didn't know how to answer that, but my stomach started churning. "No, it was an accident."

"So, what are you up to? What are you doing that would make someone want to kill you?"

"Nothing." My mind was spinning. "I mean, you know about the Eric Brewer/*Grande Dames* murders." I closed my eyes and thought, *Colin and the Russian*. The headache was worsening. "Seriously. No one wants to kill me. It was an accident, that's all. Why are you trying to scare me?"

Venus looked at me in the rearview mirror. "Scotty, that car never braked. There's a stop sign at the corner, and there are no skid marks, nothing to indicate the car even tried to stop. If anything, it *accelerated*. The witness confirms it." She shook her head. "And the driver ran away. You don't need to worry about having the car towed," she went on. "Just have your insurance company contact me. Your car—both cars—are being taken in custody of the police, to be examined. You're sure you're not into something that would make someone want to kill you?" She swallowed. "There's nothing going on with Colin?"

Colin.

My car was being taken into police custody, to be examined.

There was a dead body in the hatch less than twenty-four hours ago.

But they wouldn't be looking for anything like that, would they?

Unless someone tipped them off about that agent Colin killed?

This was just getting worse and worse.

"You know, I don't think so, I can't think of anything." I closed my eyes and tried to keep my breathing normal. *Focus, focus, focus.* "My mind is kind of scrambled, and I'm still in a shock, I think? But I'll let you know if I think of anything. What's going on with Taylor and the Eric Brewer murder? Have you figured out anything about Chloe Valence's murder?"

"You know we can't talk about an open investigation," Blaine replied.

"Did Remy's alibi check out?"

Venus looked at me in the rearview mirror again when she stopped at the light at Jackson Avenue. "How did you know about Remy's alibi?" She narrowed her eyes. "Scotty, you and Frank are *not* getting involved in this, are you? How many times have I told you not to get involved in a police investigation? Are you ever going to listen?"

"It's *Taylor*, Venus." I looked out the window. "How can we *not?*"

"How is he doing?" Blaine asked.

"Not good." I took a deep breath. "But you know, he'll get through this. Life doesn't give you anything you can't handle. It's how you handle it that matters."

"I'm really sorry that happened to him, I want you to know that," Blaine went on. "We both are."

"At least he wasn't sexually assaulted." I caught myself, choking off a sob. "It seems weird to be grateful to a murderer, but..."

"Yeah," Blaine replied.

We rode the rest of the way in silence.

"We'll let you know when we release the car," Venus called as I climbed down out of the back of her SUV to the curb.

"Thanks." I shut the door, waving as they drove off. My legs were a lot wobblier than I would have liked. I somehow made it to the gate, got it unlocked, and walked down the entryway, one hand lightly against the wall in case my wobbly legs gave out. I probably should have called Frank to help me, but I didn't want to freak him out. He was already going to freak out when I told him about the car, and added to all this stuff with Taylor—yeah, he didn't need to be worried about me on top of everything else. I used the rail to help myself up the stairs and have never been happier to get to my apartment.

I could hear voices from the living room.

I glanced at my watch. It was almost four; Loren McKeithen must have arrived.

Why hadn't Frank called me? I pulled my phone out of my pocket and found the answer. My phone was broken. The screen was shattered, and no matter how many times I pressed the home button it just stayed black.

Damn it.

"Oh my God." Frank stood up when I walked into the living room, his face draining of color. "What happened? Are you okay?"

"I'm fine." I made my way to an easy chair, plopped down, and closed my eyes for a minute. "Car accident. We can talk about it later. Thanks for coming, Loren."

Loren looked at Frank and back to me, concerned. "We can do this another time—"

"Seriously, I'm fine. Where's Taylor?"

"Upstairs." Frank looked up. "Loren wants us to look into the murder, you know, help find things to—"

"The police aren't taking Taylor seriously as a suspect," Loren said, gesturing with his hands. "If anything, he's a victim who was very lucky. But the police investigation isn't closed yet, either. We don't know what *they* are going to find, or what the district attorney's office is going to want to do. I'm sure the city and the mayor are going to want this case closed fast." He shook his head. "I mean, if show business people are going to be getting murdered here…" He shrugged. "They're trying to bring all that Hollywood South stuff back, you know, and this doesn't make New Orleans look good to production companies and networks." He stood up. "See what you can find—particularly focus on a pattern of behavior. As I said, I'm not worried about Taylor being charged, but it's always best to be prepared." He shook my hand, and Frank walked him down to the gate.

When Frank returned, I got him up to speed on both the car accident and Remy.

"The police impounded the car?"

I nodded. "And it worries me that Venus asked about Colin. I mean, I cleaned the back of the car pretty thoroughly, but there's no telling what they might find if they're looking for something. What if they connect the car to the body?"

"Before Loren came over I looked around online to see if there was anything more about that body," he replied. "Nothing. There's not even enough information out there to know whether or not it's the *same* body."

"What are the odds?" I replied. My headache was getting worse and my muscles were starting to tighten up. "It has to be Bestuzhev that they found. And if the accident wasn't an accident..." I didn't finish the sentence. I stood up and stretched, aching muscles screaming in agony. "You're sure Taylor's all right?"

"As good as can be expected." Frank put his arms around me and hugged me. "I'm so glad you're all right."

I hugged him back. "It's good that Loren has hired us. What did I miss?"

"We aren't allowed to discuss anything with Taylor," Frank shook his head, "or even ask him questions. The news about the witnesses at the bar was good, he thought, and of course Chloe's murder with a similar weapon is also a plus. God, listen to me. You'd think I'm happy that woman was murdered."

"I'm going to take a long, hot shower," I said. "Why don't you do some digging online, see what you can find out about Brewer and his past?"

Frank nodded, and I walked down the hall. I turned the shower on to get the water nice and hot and walked back into the bedroom, peeling off my clothes. There were still small splinters of glass in my hair and some seriously hideous bruises on my torso that I examined carefully. I brushed my teeth and gargled, hoping to get that chemical taste out of my mouth and the back of my throat, before climbing into the hot water. I stayed until the water turned lukewarm, climbing out into the foggy bathroom. I toweled myself dry, ran a brush through my short hair to make sure there weren't any more glass splinters in it. I put on my robe and stepped into my house shoes. The bedroom was freezing, as I figured it would be, and I could hear the pelting of rain on the stairs outside. That meant it was going to get even colder. I pulled on a pair of tights, then sweatpants and a T-shirt under a sweatshirt before heading back into the living room.

"Anything?" I asked Frank, who was sitting at the desk and staring at the computer screen.

He shook his head. "I found some rumors on gossip sites, but nothing concrete, and no names." He sighed. "If the network or the company had to pay hush money—"

"Brandon." I snapped my fingers. "Brandon would know. He told me the night of the party that Eric liked twinks, was into younger men, had even harassed him at first when he was hired."

But of course, Brandon's number was in my cell phone. Which was broken.

"I called the insurance company," Frank said as I sat down in the living room. "They're getting in touch with Venus, and I gave them the accident report number."

"Thanks," I replied. I reached for my cards and shuffled. I spread the cards out on the table and looked at them.

The way forward is not clear.
A scheming woman who will do what she needs to get her way.
Danger.
Pray for a brave heart.

I sighed and swept them all up, absently shuffling them before wrapping them back in their blue silk and putting them back inside the cigar box.

A scheming woman.

That was no help at all.

I mean, which one?

Chapter Twelve
Knight of Cups, Reversed
Beware of trickery or fraud

I woke up on Monday morning sore in some places and stiff in others. Some careful stretches seemed to do the trick. My neck was the worst. As I showered and got dressed, I noticed some bruises had formed in places while I slept that I didn't remember hurting. The good news was I hadn't thrown up and didn't have any double vision, so no concussion. I didn't even have a headache.

I could handle being stiff and sore for a few days.

Taylor was eating cereal at the kitchen counter when I walked in. I reached up and ruffled his still-damp hair. "How you doing this morning?"

He shrugged. "As well as can be expected, I guess." He wasn't mumbling, so I took that as a good sign.

"I'm driving him to school this morning," Frank called from the desk in the living room.

"You don't have to do that." Taylor's voice was a monotone. "I can take the streetcar or get an Uber."

"You can stay home if you want." I lowered my voice. "You don't have to go if you're not ready."

The exasperated eye roll I got in response made my heart leap a bit—that was a normal response. He must be doing better.

"Finals are next week," Taylor said, dumping his milk in the sink and letting out the long-suffering sigh I hadn't realized I'd missed, "and just because something shitty happened to me doesn't mean the world stopped turning." He kissed the top of my head. "I'll be fine, Scotty. I was luckier than most people who wind up in that situation." He picked his backpack up from the floor. "Come on, if you're driving me, Frank. I'm going to be late."

"Take the Jaguar," I said as Frank reached for the keys. "I have an appointment at the Apple Store to replace my phone." I hated driving Colin's specialty Jaguar. I'm not a great driver—I wouldn't drive at all if I could get away with it—and that Jaguar was souped up, custom made to order, and the dashboard looked like the control panel for a fighter jet. I always fear I am going to press some button by mistake and launch a missile or something.

The only Apple Store in the New Orleans metropolitan area is at Lakeside Mall in Metairie. Going to Lakeside Mall at any time is a nightmare for me—it's located right where Veterans Boulevard crosses Causeway Boulevard, so the traffic is always terrible at the best of times, and this was Christmas season. I didn't have high hopes as I set out for the suburbs, but traffic was actually light, and while I waited for the nice young man to set up my new phone, I walked down to Macy's and bought some presents for Frank and Taylor.

Since I was at the mall already…

My phone was ready when I returned to the Apple Store, and I called Frank as I walked my packages out to the car. "How's he doing?"

Frank sighed. "He's dealing with it, I suppose. I think we should get him to see a therapist or a grief counselor or something. He's really young and this is a lot to handle…I'd hate for us to screw him up for the rest of his life."

I started to reply, *We can't screw up him up any worse than his parents did,* but checked myself. Frank can be weird when it comes to his sister—there was obviously more story there than he'd shared with me. I'd never pressed. I figured he'd tell me when he felt comfortable enough to talk about it. He'd never talked much about his family in all the years we'd been together. I'd known his parents were already dead when we started seeing each other, and there was a sister he wasn't close to, but I hadn't known Taylor existed until he wound up practically on our doorstop and joined our family. Taylor was just as close-mouthed as his uncle, but I knew he was the youngest. He'd let slip once he had two older brothers who were both married. I'd been tempted to do some online research more than once, but never did.

What kind of relationship did we have if I didn't recognize boundaries?

"It's a lot for him to process," I agreed. "It's a lot for *us* to process."

"Work has always been the best thing for me," Frank replied. "So, let's dive in when we get home, come up with a plan of attack on the case. If we can't figure out who killed Eric…"

"Terrific. See you soon, love you."

"Love you, too." He hung up as I was getting on I-10 to head back into the city. The great thing about having a partner who was ex-FBI—well, besides the great sex, of course—was that he was a great planner and organizer and was really detail-oriented. Those qualities also served him well in his professional wrestling career; the guy who ran the promotion he worked for told me on more than one occasion that Frank had a flair for keeping things running smoothly and a gift for match choreography.

I suspect that whenever Frank finally decides to retire from the ring once and for all, he'll probably work behind the scenes for the promotion. He absolutely loves it.

I took the 610 so I could bypass the CBD traffic and drove along the backside of City Park, thinking. There was never much traffic on the bypass, so I could let my mind wander as I drove on autopilot.

This couldn't have been the first time Eric had drugged someone in order to rape them—oh, how I hated using that word because it reminded me of what a close call poor Taylor had had, but it was the right word—so there had to be records somewhere. One doesn't suddenly just decide *oh I'll drug this pretty boy so I can fuck him* out of the blue without some kind of a history existing. Accusations, hush money payoffs, or both—it was just a matter of digging until something turned up.

Harvey Weinstein had finally been brought down, hadn't he?

Brandon.

If anyone knew where the Diva Network bodies were buried, it was Brandon.

If you want, I can go along and keep an eye on him.

I was so startled I swerved onto the shoulder for a moment before righting the steering wheel again.

With everything that had happened since, I'd forgotten.

Brandon went with them. The guys at the Brass Rail didn't mention a third guy—but I also didn't ask.

Taylor hadn't mentioned Brandon to me as being there at the Brass Rail.

I took the Elysian Fields exit and pulled over. I pulled out my new phone and touched the contacts app. I scrolled through to Venus Casanova and touched Call. It went to voice mail immediately. "Venus, this is Scotty Bradley. I just remembered—Brandon Bernard was with Eric and Taylor Friday night...if Taylor didn't mention that, you might want to talk to Brandon..."

Of course she talked to Brandon. Brandon worked with Eric...

His business card was in my trench coat pocket...and my trench coat was hanging in my closet.

I disconnected my call to Venus and texted Taylor: *What happened to Brandon Friday night?*

He was in class, though, and wouldn't answer until later.

I pulled away from the curb.

Would Brandon be willing to talk to me? At the party, with a few drinks under his belt and feeling flirty, he'd been a little more open about talking than he might be without a martini in his hand. What all had he said? I hadn't paid as much attention as I should have...he was young and attractive and seemed good at his job. Someone had to take over for Eric. I'm sure Brandon would love to be the new Eric Brewer at Diva Network.

So he would be more interested in protecting the network than helping clear Taylor.

Maybe he'd wanted Eric out of the way, so he *could* take his job.

No—no one would kill anyone over a job. Especially since there was no guarantee they'd get the job.

But show business *could* be cutthroat.

It was a motive to consider.

And Chloe. It was just too big a coincidence that they were both murdered in the same way during the same time period—the murders had to be connected in some way. Based on what I knew, Remy was the only person with a motive to kill them both.

But someone else out there could have wanted them both dead.

Remy said the lawsuit was faked, for the show.

I made a mental note to check with either Brandon or Sloane about that. If Remy was lying...

But Remy had to know that the cops would zero in on him... how convenient that he had an ironclad alibi. It's almost *always* the husband.

My mind was still racing as I pulled into my parking space. The Jaguar was already there, so I knew Frank was home. I winced getting out of the car. My neck and my lower back had stiffened up again. Taylor wasn't the only one who might have PTSD. I'd flinched every time I saw an approaching car...and I was relieved Frank was home because the last time I came home to a supposedly empty apartment there'd been a corpse in the living room.

So many secrets and lies! We were keeping things from Taylor, and now he had to keep things from us.

Climbing the back stairs in the cold wind, I wished for this all to come to an end and our lives to go back to normal.

Or what passed for normal around here, at any rate.

The apartment was blissfully warm when I walked in. I heard voices coming from the living room. My stomach flipped, and my heart jumped into my throat. Frank called, "Scotty? Is that you?"

"Yes." I slipped my jacket off and tossed it on the bed in our bedroom before walking down the hallway to the living room. "Who's here? Oh, hello."

Rebecca Barron was sitting in the living room, a Starbucks cup in her hand. "You must be Scotty?" She stood up and smiled, holding out her right hand.

She was exceptionally tiny. The ridiculous red leather stiletto heels she was wearing gave her at least another four to five inches in height, and her head was still barely chest level with Frank. Her waist was so small I could have put a hand on either side and my fingers would meet at her navel. Her legs were muscular but slender, undoubtedly toned from yoga and aerobics classes. Her silk wrap dress showed off her incongruously large breast implants.

Steve Barron had loved his women to get implants.

I'd never met Rebecca, but it was impossible to live in New Orleans and not know of her late husband, Steve. He loved the spotlight, and his motto was clearly *No publicity is bad publicity.* People used to joke that the most dangerous place in New Orleans was between Steve Barron and a camera. I'd met him a couple of times. He owned numerous not-good restaurants around town that catered to tourists. He'd originally made his fortune by founding a fast food chain specializing in "New Orleans–style" po-boys. Steve Barron was one of those people you either loved or hated. He spoke his mind and worked hard, although I was pretty sure the story about him dropping out of school and working on fishing boats as a teenager was a fairy tale invented by his corporate publicity department. But it was true that he came from nothing and was a self-made millionaire.

Unfortunately for Steve, he was one of those men whose ego wouldn't permit him to age gracefully. He wanted to remain young and virile, so kept having work done to his face. By the time I met him it barely moved and was shiny as polished plastic. His hair was the jet black that comes from a bottle, and he grew it long, slicking it back into a ponytail. He worked out every day and jogged, so was in great shape—as evidenced by the tight black shirts he always wore at least one size too small. He favored black pleated slacks, and black patent-leather loafers, and there was always a gold medallion hanging around his neck on a thick gold chain. He was a loud, abrasive, and borderline offensive man, always dancing close to the line of saying something sexist or racist or homophobic but never quite crossing it. He feuded with other people publicly—and loved to pay for full-page ads in the newspaper explaining his side of the story.

He was a character, and New Orleanians love our local characters.

Rebecca was either his fourth or fifth wife—I'd never been sure how many times he'd been married.

Rumors were flying all around town about a looming court battle between the widow and her stepsons. The story was Steve had an enormous fight with his sons over the restaurant empire and cut them out of the will—but had intended to reinstate them when his marriage got into trouble.

Unfortunately, he'd had a massive coronary before he could change his will, and everything had gone to the widow.

"Nice to meet you," I said, glancing over at Frank with my *what the hell is going on* look on my face.

"You probably don't remember me," Rebecca said. She took my cold hand in both of hers, which were warm and dry. "We met at a fundraiser for Children's Hospital a few years ago, right after I married Steve."

"Of course, I remember," I lied. Her enormous, wide-set eyes were bloodshot and her hands were trembling slightly. Her makeup wasn't quite perfect—I could see mascara clumps on her lengthy eyelashes, and her pinkish lipstick was slightly smeared at the corners of her mouth. Her thick platinum blond hair was pulled into a side ponytail.

"You're probably wondering what I'm doing here, right?" Rebecca sat back down and sipped her coffee. I couldn't get over how tiny her waist was. She smiled at Frank. "I was just explaining to your partner—I think we can help each other out."

What the hell, I thought, sitting down on the couch. "Okay."

"Yes, you both want to clear your nephew of any involvement in Eric's murder, and I think I can help you with that." She crossed her slender legs. "As you might know, my husband left his entire estate to me when he died." Rebecca took a deep breath. "Steve had two sons from previous marriages, and three ex-wives. None of them were happy about the will. Steve's sons had worked for him since they got out of college, and he wasn't happy about the direction they were trying to take the company." She made a face. "He also wasn't happy about Billy's messy divorce. Billy is his older son." Her face darkened. "Steve was furious about the divorce, he said Billy had made a laughingstock out of the entire family, and Billy wasn't smart enough to have her sign a pre-nup."

I frowned. "Why would that matter to Steve? It didn't affect his money, did it?"

She shook her head. "No, but he thought it showed a lack of business sense. He said if he couldn't trust Billy to have the sense to protect himself from losing everything in a divorce, how could he trust Billy's business sense when it came to the future direction of the company?"

"What direction was that?" I was puzzled. Steve Barron, despite his enormous success, wasn't popular or respected in a city that prized food. His original chain of fast food joints had been sold at a huge profit, and he'd tried to break into the higher-end restaurant market. The problem was Steve wasn't a chef, he was a businessman, and his success with the fast food chain had convinced him that was the way to run a restaurant. His first Barron's had opened on St. Charles Avenue, taking over a building that had been empty for decades and turning it into a hideous display of multicolored pastel neons and art deco atrocities that had pretty much appalled the entire city. The place was enormously successful—the food wasn't bad and the servings were large enough to give great value for the price. But his not being a chef showed. Rather than hiring a great chef and giving him free rein to design the menu, Steve chose to hedge every bet. The menu at Barron's was as varied and as thick as one at Applebee's or Chili's—the kind of place that did everything, but nothing extremely well. The hamburgers were a half-pound and came with enough French fries to feed a small Southeast Asian village. Locals tended to avoid Barron's, but tourists loved it. After a year he'd opened another one in Metairie, and within five years there was a Barron's in Houston, Dallas, Jacksonville, Tampa, Salt Lake City, and Birmingham. Soon they were as ubiquitous as the Hard Rock Café.

"The boys wanted to..." She hesitated. "Well, they wanted to sell all the Barron's restaurants and open a local five-star restaurant, trying to compete with the Brennans. Steve wouldn't have any part of it, and he knew once he was gone that's exactly what they would do. So that's why he left everything to me. Oh, he always intended to change the will back—he changed it, really, just to show them he could and to let them know whose money and company it was, but then he had his heart attack and was gone." She gave a slight little shrug. "It's not my fault he died before he could do it."

That's cold, I thought but said nothing.

"You think I'm a bitch, don't you?" Rebecca gave me a sardonic glance, a corner of her mouth twitching. She gave a little shrug. "I won't bore you with the stories of how the two of them—and their mothers—did everything they could to make my life miserable." She barked out a laugh. "Bleach your hair and get some implants and everyone thinks you're an idiot. For the record, I have an MBA from Duke University." She leaned back in her chair. "I've been running the company since Steve died, and profits are up."

"But—" I was impressed. "Why did you agree to do a reality show?"

Rebecca cleared her throat. "I joined the show because I wanted to—my stepsons are contesting the will and fighting me for control of the company." She blew out a breath. "Now I realize it was a mistake—but my thinking was if I went on this show and could show everyone in America what a good businesswoman I actually am…" Her mouth twisted. "After seeing the way they edited the first episode, I'd swear Eric Brewer was on my stepsons' payroll."

I had to agree with her. The woman sitting across the room from me today was nothing like the woman I'd seen on the screen Friday night. The show had clearly been edited to make her look and sound like someone who could barely read, rather than the cool, competent professional head of a major restaurant company.

"And that Fidelis Vandiver." Her face twisted into a sneer. "That fucking bitch needs to be slapped."

"There's some history there?"

"Fidelis was involved with Steve briefly—before he met me. She apparently thought *she* was going to be the next Mrs. Barron. Steve thought she was an idiot—he never would have married her. But she resents me, has said some pretty terrible things about me around town…and she's working with my stepsons, I know it." Her eyes narrowed. "She's probably sleeping with Billy." She rolled her eyes. "Women always seem to fall for him. I don't get it. He's so transparent."

"But I really don't understand. Why did you agree to do a show with her if…"

"I didn't know she was a member of the cast." Rebecca angrily played with her ponytail. "I didn't know until Margery's cocktail party who the other women were, other than Margery, of course. I've known Margery for years—obviously, we use Black Mountain Liquor for the local restaurants. I was horrified when I saw Fidelis there." Her jaw set. "And to hear the things she said about me! Things that are *going to air on national television!*"

I couldn't really remember anything specific that Fidelis might have said that deserved such ire.

Then again, I wasn't in the middle of an ugly legal battle for control of a multi-million-dollar food empire.

"The point being," Rebecca went on when I didn't say anything, "when I heard about Chloe—well, I couldn't go to the police with what I know."

I glanced over at Frank again, raising my eyebrows. "And what do you know, Mrs. Barron?"

"Rebecca—please, call me Rebecca." She spread her hands out expressively. "Part of the issue my late husband had with my stepson Billy is—well, for want of a better phrase, he can't keep it in his pants." She leaned forward. "You see, Billy was having an affair with Chloe Valence."

"Wait—what?"

She nodded, the side pony bouncing vigorously. "Oh, yes, it's been going on for quite some time. They were very discreet—I don't think any of it got on camera, of course, Billy is many things but he's not an utter fool—and now?" She sat back with a smile. "I mean, can it be a coincidence that both she and Eric are murdered on the same night?"

I didn't quite follow, and was about to say so when Frank said, "Rebecca doesn't want to take this to the police, Scotty."

"They wouldn't take me seriously. I may look like a dumb blonde, but I'm not one." She shook her head. "Everyone knows Billy is trying to break the will, and the police, well, they'll think I'm just trying to make Billy look bad so I can win the suit." She laughed. "But the police need to know about Billy and Chloe. And I know he argued with Eric Friday night at the premiere." She licked her lower lip. "I saw them. I stepped out to have a cigarette and there they were, yelling at each other on the sidewalk. Billy had grabbed the front of Eric's shirt, like he was about to hit him."

"You can tell the police that, though," I said.

"I was the only witness. How credible am I?"

She had a point. "What do you think they were arguing about?"

"I don't know." Her eyes narrowed. "Eric—Eric wasn't exactly a nice guy, as you well know. Look at what he tried to do to your nephew! Maybe he did have something on tape with Billy and Chloe. I don't know." She batted her eyes at me and looked over at Frank. "Can I trust you to look into this?"

"We'll definitely follow any lead," Frank replied.

She stood up and slid her arms through the sleeves of her mink coat. "Lovely." She held out her hands to Frank, kissed him on the cheek. She did the same with me, pressing a business card into my hand. "That's my private cell number. Call me any time if you have any questions."

"Thanks for coming by."

We both followed her down the hallway to the back door. When she reached it, she turned back to us with an enormous smile. "Oh, yes, one thing I forgot to mention. Weren't they both killed with a blunt instrument?"

"Yes."

"You both know that Billy was a baseball star at LSU, don't you?" Her eyes sparkled with malice. "He even played in the minor leagues for a few years. He's kept all his bats from back then, of course. Someone might want to check his bat collection."

CHAPTER THIRTEEN
KING OF CUPS, REVERSED
A powerful man who might be double-dealing

"She's playing us," I said once Frank returned from walking her to the gate.

"Totally." Frank shivered as he sat down at the computer. "Man, it's cold. But yeah, Lady Barron is trying to get us to do her dirty work. But on the other hand...if there's something to the stuff about Billy Barron, we've got to look into it."

"Well, he *was* a baseball star," I replied, trying to remember. "He went to Ben Franklin? Maybe it was Newman, I don't remember exactly. It was around the same time I was at Jesuit. I mean, he was a pretty big deal...everyone in town knew about Billy, like we knew about the Mannings and Leonard Fournette. It didn't hurt, either, that his dad used to take out full-page ads in the paper congratulating him on his successes..."

"That must have been mortifying for him," Frank replied as he started typing on the computer keyboard.

"You'd think." I shook my head. "But Steve Barron used to do that all the time—take out ads, I mean. Usually to let everyone know his side of his latest feud or something." I scratched my head. "Billy was also a big-time player at LSU, played on a couple of national championship teams—Steve bought at least three full-page ads both times, I think, and of course he had his restaurants all done up in LSU colors, hosted viewing parties for the College World Series...I think he donated a lot of money to the LSU baseball team, too."

Frank frowned at the computer screen. He leaned back in the

desk chair and put his hands behind his head. "Didn't he have a big fight with his neighborhood association?"

"Wow! I'd forgotten all about the Christmas decorations thing." I laughed. Steve Barron built one of those hideous McMansions on the north shore of Lake Pontchartrain. It was a gated community, just outside of Mandeville, and his mansion was on lakefront property, with a mini-marina for his boats.

When Steve was alive, his mansion's Christmas decorations were legendary. People came from all over the state just to see them. The lights could be seen by passengers on airplanes both landing or taking off from Armstrong International. His neighborhood association insisted they be either removed or toned down, and the annual battle over the Barron Christmas decorations was breathlessly reported on by local news outlets.

"He feuded with the Garden District Association, too, when he put in that Barron's on St. Charles Avenue, between Felicity and Jackson. They thought the original plan for the place was too tacky for the Garden District. They wound up in court, they settled. He agreed to tone down the outside décor of the place." I tried to remember. "It wasn't a Barron's, though, I think he was trying to launch another brand? It was only open a couple of years."

"Sounds like he was quite a character," Frank commented.

"Yeah, he was. But he wasn't so interested in getting his name in the papers after Katrina. And then, of course, he died last year." I walked up behind him. "Hey—is that Billy Barron?" An image search was up on his screen.

"Yeah. Why?"

"He was at the party Friday night. I saw him there. He was with a woman—I didn't see her face, but I saw him. He talked to Ryan, and then the woman pulled him away." I frowned. "Now why would he go to the premiere party for a show with his stepmother?" I crossed my arms. "Rebecca certainly didn't get him on the guest list. Maybe Chloe? Since Remy didn't go?"

"But you said he was with another woman."

"Yeah." I looked at the computer screen. Billy Barron was a good-looking man, I'd thought so when I saw him at the party.

"Interesting." Frank pulled up an address directory and typed in *William Barron*. "He lives in English Turn. Shall we head over there and see if he's home, maybe have a chat, see if he knows anything?" He glanced at his watch. "We should have time before Taylor gets back."

"Let's go."

English Turn was a gated community on the West Bank, which meant taking the Crescent City Connection to cross the river. It was across the river from Chalmette, below the battlefield where Andrew Jackson commanded a ragtag group of Americans that turned back the British army, winning the Battle of New Orleans after the War of 1812 had ended. But that wasn't how English Turn got its name. The story we learn as children in Louisiana History was that the original French explorers had made camp at the site that is now the French Quarter. Bienville, the city founder, was traveling back down the river to the gulf when he and his men encountered an English frigate sailing up the river. Bienville somehow convinced the English that the river and the territory had already been claimed for France and convinced them to turn back. Some say that he also warned the English that there were incredibly hostile native tribes farther up the river. Whatever the reason, the English turned around and sailed back to the Gulf. That bend in the river where they turned around has been called English Turn ever since. This gated community for recently wealthy people who didn't necessarily want to deal with living in historic homes or neighborhoods (with all the rules that come with them, and the sky-high Orleans Parish taxes) had sprung up around the time New Orleans got a reputation for being "dangerous"—as a cover for white flight from the newly segregated public schools in the city.

It's true that crime in the city began to rise in the 1980s, but white flight had already started.

Based on what I'd seen on the show Friday night, Fidelis also lived in English Turn—yet another grande dame of New Orleans who didn't live in New Orleans.

"New Orleans adjacent," as the locals sneered.

"The Barron civil war would be an interesting storyline for the show," I commented as Frank took the Charles de Gaulle exit once we crossed the bridge. "Props to Rebecca for going on the show. If she could manipulate the narrative..."

"But can she actually control the narrative?" Frank asked. "Only Eric had the final say on what storylines they used and how the women appeared on the show, right?"

One of the things I'd always found interesting about the *Grande Dames* shows was how manipulative they were. Scenes *could* be edited to eliminate context; something sounding completely innocuous in a casual conversation might sound horrifically damning when removed from its original context. Eric's eyes were fixed firmly on the bottom line: it was interesting how women who became enormously popular and developed huge social media followings—and therefore might want more money or more control over their image—wound up getting the so-called bitch edit. As their popularity and social media following plummeted, the sufficiently humbled Dame would either leave the show or bow down to Eric Brewer.

Everyone had to kiss his ring, which could lead to resentment... and possibly murder.

I pulled up a search engine on my phone and googled *grande dames of new orleans reviews*.

A lot of articles about Eric's murder popped up—some mentioned Chloe's as well, but apparently Eric was much bigger news outside New Orleans—but there was also a review on Nola.com, the *Times-Picayune*'s website.

The headline was amazing: "The Grande Dames Are Here, and It's Everything We Feared."

Ouch.

It was from this morning but had been filed before the murders.

> *The latest iteration of the enormously popular Grande Dames shows, a New Orleans franchise, premiered on Friday night to a packed house at the Joy Theater on Canal Street.* *

I scrolled down to the footnote, which read, as I suspected, *This review of the show was filed before the news broke about the murders of producer Eric Brewer and cast member Chloe Valence. For our coverage of those events, please click here.*

I didn't want to click there. I didn't want to see what the news said about Taylor. I didn't want to even think about Taylor's name being on sites like TMZ or E! I was kind of surprised that tabloids hadn't descended on our apartment the way they had when we were involved in the Metoyer investigation—an experience I'd rather not ever live through again, thank you very much.

Especially with the Colin thing going on.

The Colin thing.

I glanced over at Frank. His jaw was set, his teeth clenched, and that muscle in his lower cheek was twitching the way it always did when he was angry.

Probably not the best time to talk about the Colin situation.

I scrolled back up on the screen.

> *One can't help but wonder what these shows could have been. Producer Eric Brewer often talks about how he initially intended the first show—the Marin County edition, the so-called "OG" of the Grande Dames—to be a documentary about modern day women trying to have it all. Most of the women in the original cast of the show were all successful women running their own small businesses or companies, trying to maintain the work-home-family-career juggle, trying to have it all, and how difficult that was. But as the shows aired, the personalities of the women became more central to the show, their personal foibles and interactions with the other women, and the breakout star was Kristi Domanico, a woman with a volcanic personality, her own high-end real estate business, a failing marriage and an inflated sense of her own importance in the lives of everyone she knew, including children, employees and the other women on the show. It was a formula that drew ratings, and that became the formula for the first spin-off franchise, the enormously popular Manhattan show, and with Marin County about to enter its twelfth season of filming, Kristi is the sole remaining member of the original cast.*
>
> *The news that after one failed attempt to launch a New Orleans franchise, the network had managed to succeed the second time around was not greeted with much joy in the city. Television shows and movies have a bad history with New Orleans, emphasizing the stereotypes of "boobs, beads, and booze"—the Dennis Quaid film "The Big Easy" in particular*

held in derision in the city to this day—and when one of the Grande Dame of New Orleans says, within the first five minutes of the premiere episode, that the city is about "beads, booze and boobs"—you could almost hear the collective groan of New Orleanians all over the world.

The other great irony of the show is that several of the women are not actually residents of New Orleans. Two that are—Chloe Valence and Margery Lautenschlaeger—are the closest thing to reaching into the social stratosphere of New Orleans that the show has; the Valences are one of the oldest families in the Garden District, and of course, Lautenschlaeger is one of the wealthiest women in the city (one has to wonder what she is doing on this show? This reporter certainly did). But Chloe Valence is not to the city bred; she is originally from Mississippi and wasn't a debutante, despite the impressive Rex and Comus credentials the Valence name carries with it.

Serena Castlemaine, who also lives in the Garden District, is a recent transplant from Dallas. Megan Dreher lives in the lower Garden District.

The other women boast addresses that aren't necessarily New Orleans: Rebecca Barron lives on the North Shore, and Fidelis Vandiver lives in English Turn on the West Bank.

But all the ingredients are there for another successful Grande Dames franchise: conspicuous overconsumption, unashamed narcissism, and petty fights and arguments that basically have nothing in common with adult behavior and everything to do with junior high school mean-girl tactics. From most of what I've seen of these shows, it always comes down to a variation of the old "telephone" game; someone says something snarky about one of the women to another one of the women, who then tells the woman about whom it was said what was said, which leads to arguments and the other women being forced to either play peacemaker or choose sides between the two who are arguing. Lather, rinse, repeat, lather, rinse, repeat, over and over and over again. The viewers are encouraged to participate in this nonsense by reading the women's blogs on the Diva TV website, where you can also see deleted scenes and other videos of interest. Apparently, an entire cottage industry has sprung up around these shows; numerous websites and magazines publish recaps of each episode online and encourage comments from viewers; the dames themselves are encouraged to live tweet the episodes and engage with the viewers that way. Some of the women have used these shows quite successfully to promote themselves and their businesses; their personal brand.

The rest, apparently, just want to be on television, no matter how horrific it makes them appear to the casual viewer.

Props are certainly due to the production team and the editors who stitched the episode together. New Orleans looks stunningly beautiful in the shots used to provide local color, whether it's the streetcars going up St. Charles or a carriage ride in the Quarter or a barge moving up the river or the buskers in Jackson Square, the city looks lush and beautiful and inviting to tourists.

And ultimately, maybe that's the best we can hope for from this abominable show: that it will encourage people to come visit because it's beautiful—even if the show makes them wary of engaging with the people who actually live here.

"Ouch," I said, looking up from my phone as the car slowed. We were pulling up to the gated entrance to the English Turn development. "Good thing we brought the Jaguar," I said as we stopped outside the gatehouse. A uniformed security guard whistled as Frank put the window down.

"That is one beautiful car," the guard said. He was holding a clipboard. "Are you expected?"

"We're here to see Billy Barron," Frank replied. "And no, he's not expecting us."

"And your name?"

"Frank Sobieski," Frank replied, "We're with the production staff of the *Grande Dames*?" He said it as though he was used to having people bow and scrape to him.

The Jaguar was definitely a perfect prop for this performance.

"Oh. Let me just give him a call." He stepped back inside. We could see him through the window talking on a telephone.

"Well, it was worth a try," I said.

Just as I finished saying it, the gates swung open as he stepped back outside.

"Do you know how to find Mr. Barron's place?" When Frank said no, he gave us directions. Frank put the Jaguar back into gear and we drove into English Turn.

As far as new houses or McMansions go, it wasn't so terrible. I've certainly seen much worse (the Philadelphia cast all lived in a similar style development along the Delaware just north of the city, and their houses were tacky—the kind of place people who grew up with nothing or poor thought meant classy. And yes, I know that sounds snobbish, but you know what I mean), but there was a newness to the whole area that I didn't like. The houses on the left backed up to the lagoon that circled the golf course, and between houses we could see the water. Some of the houses had docks or gazebos out on the lagoon. Everything was perfectly manicured. I don't know, I guess I've been spoiled by the Quarter and the Garden District, but it all seemed a little prefabricated, a little too clean, a little too nice, a little too *perfect*. There were trees, but no massive live oaks with enormous roots to tear up the sidewalks and driveways and the streets. Some of the houses had fountains or statues in the front yards, bushes trimmed into topiary. The lawns were lush and so green they looked like AstroTurf.

The entire development had been built up around a golf course, so that was probably why the lawns looked like putting greens.

Billy's house was typical of *nouveau riche* Southerners with little to no taste: a two-story stone building, with two one-story wings extending on either side, an enormous front gallery with huge round stone columns. My mother sneeringly calls these houses "offensively racist *Gone with the Wind* wannabe clichés, and you'd think people would know better now." The driveway curved to a three-car garage attached to the wing on the left. Dormer windows broke the ceiling line above the porch. The lawn was that same lush dark emerald green, with perfectly trimmed bushes behind white stone gravel beds running along the front of the house. We parked in the carport and rang the doorbell.

It sounded like a bell tolling for the dead.

This, I reflected, was an awful lot of house for one person.

We didn't have to wait long before the front door opened.

"You're not with the show," Billy Barron said, a smile spreading across his handsome face. "But I knew the name. Great bluff, though."

I just stared at him, unable to speak.

Billy Barron was, without question, one of the best-looking straight men I'd ever seen. He had what some people call star quality, others charisma; whatever you wanted to call it, he had a lot of it. I couldn't stop looking at him. Standing in the doorway wearing only a pair of tan shorts, his stomach was flat with just a slight ripple of abdominal muscles. He wasn't ripped, but a focus on diet would get him there in no time. His chest was perfectly shaped and strong, with a patch of dark bluish-black hair directly in the center, a trail leading down over the flat stomach to the waistband of the shorts. His eyes were a sparkling violet-blue, his thick bluish-black hair pulled back into a ponytail. His chin was cleft, his cheekbones high, and there was a knot where the cartilage of his nose met the bone; it had been broken and set badly at some point in his life. His olive face was darkened by a bluish-black shadow from not shaving. His teeth were perfect and almost blindingly white.

"Come on in!" He waved us past him into the foyer of the big house. "Nice car!" He whistled as he shut the door behind us.

"You knew my name?" Frank was able to speak, which was a good thing. I'd apparently lost the ability. He led us into a big room with an enormous window, opening onto the backyard with a lovely view of the lagoon beyond. It was decorated in what a bitchy decorator would call *straight man cave testosterone*. The furniture was dark, bulky, and heavy looking. A gigantic flat screen television was mounted on the brick above the fireplace. The only thing missing was mounted animal head trophies. "Do you mind if I ask how?"

"Sure." He pulled an LSU baseball jersey on, the ripples in his stomach flexing as he yanked it down. "Your nephew—he's the one who was with Eric Brewer the night he was murdered." He flashed that mesmerizing smile at us again and held up his big hands. He grinned at me. "And you're Scotty Bradley, right?"

Dumbfounded, I nodded. "How—how did you know?"

He laughed. "Serena Castlemaine. I had drinks with her

yesterday. She told me all about you guys. You're trying to clear your nephew, which I can respect. You want to question me, right?"

Frank and I traded glances. This was going much easier than either of us had anticipated.

Maybe he has nothing to hide.

"Have a seat, make yourselves at home." We obliged by sitting down on the black leather sofa. "Can I get you something? Coffee? Water? Anything? Nothing? Okay." He sat down in an easy chair, his legs spread wide in that easy comfortable way of all good-looking straight men. "I'm going to be up front with you, okay? I think what Eric did to your nephew was terrible, absolutely terrible." His teeth gleamed again. "And I didn't kill anyone."

Telephone, telegram, tell Serena, I thought. Aloud I said, "Has anyone implied that you did?"

He waved his big right hand dismissively. He was wearing one of his College World Series championship rings. "You hear things. And I don't put anything past my stepmother." His face darkened into a scowl. "That gold-digging whore will do anything to keep me from overturning my father's will. You know she was just a hostess at Barron's on St. Charles when my father met her and decided to make her wife number five?" He crossed himself. "God rest my poor mother's soul that she didn't live to see this."

In for a penny, in for a pound, I thought, diving in. "But you were having an affair with Chloe Valence?"

"I don't know that I'd call it an *affair.* Do you mind if I have something to drink? You sure you don't want anything?" When we both demurred, he got up and grabbed a bottle of Pellegrino from the little refrigerator by the bar. "I slept with her. Probably not one of my better moments, but it was only twice, and we both agreed it would never happen again." He opened the bottle, filled a glass, and tossed a slice of lemon into it. He sat back down on the sofa, adopting the wide-legged spread from before.

And I became acutely aware that he wasn't wearing underwear.

He sighed. "This stupid *fucking* show. I went to one of the parties being filmed, at Margery Lautenschlaeger's. Chloe and I had a bit much to drink, and her husband was out of town"—he held up his hands in a kind of *what's a guy going to do* gesture—"and it just kind of happened."

"Weren't you—um—involved with another one of the grande dames? Fidelis Vandiver?" I asked.

"Fidelis and I have had an off-again, on-again thing for a number of years." He shrugged. "It's kind of a love-hate thing. We went to high school together." He grinned. "In fact, I went to high school not only with Fid but with Megan, too. And Margery's daughter, Amanda. And yes, Amanda and I had a thing in high school, but..." He sighed. "I know it's not gentlemanly to say this, but Amanda...well, she's not right in the head." He twirled an index finger around his right temple. "I know she's out of the hospital now, and back living with Margery...but..."

"Rebecca said that Fidelis was also involved with your father?" I asked. "Was that not true?"

He made a face. "Rebecca wouldn't know the truth if it punched her in the face. No, Fid was never involved with my dad. Like I said, we've had this off-and-on thing. It never works out for us, but we always seem to wind up back together if, you know, we're not involved with anyone else."

"You know that both Eric and Chloe were killed with blunt objects, that could have been baseball bats?" Frank asked. "And given your own history..."

"All of my bats are present and accounted for." Billy smiled, gesturing toward a door on the other side of the room. "My trophies and mementoes are all in that room, in cases." He smiled. "Well, I don't have all of my old bats, though. You know where the others are?" He leaned forward, his eyes gleaming. "My father's house. You know, where Rebecca lives?"

CHAPTER FOURTEEN
SEVEN OF WANDS
Victory depends on courage

"I guess Rebecca and Billy are pointing the finger at each other to try to get an upper hand in their fight over Steve's estate," I said, moaning a little as I bit into my cheeseburger. We'd both been hungry after leaving Billy's, so we detoured to Mid-city to stop at the Five Guys on Carrollton. I've always been a sucker for a good bacon cheeseburger with sautéed mushrooms. Taylor introduced us all to Five Guys—as a native New Orleanian I am a horrible snob about fast food and chain restaurants. I'll only stop at a chain when I am driving somewhere out of town. We'd all fallen in love with Five Guys, but chose to make it a special treat rather than somewhere we ate regularly.

The Carrollton corridor—a stretch from the highway to City Park—was nothing like it had been before Katrina. Mid-city was in the process of being completely gentrified. The houses were being redone (and the property values skyrocketing) while grocery stores and pharmacies, cafés and restaurants and coffee shops now lined the once-desolate stretch of Carrollton from Jesuit High School to City Park.

Back when I'd been a Jesuit High student, there was practically nothing out there.

All the changes to New Orleans were a little hard to grasp sometimes.

"Right, and that makes me tend to not believe either of them." Frank scowled, dipping a Cajun-seasoned fry into a little paper ketchup container. "The real truth is probably somewhere in the middle. I can't see Billy killing either Eric or Chloe, to tell you the truth. Why would he?"

"And yet we have a former baseball star smack-dab in the middle of a case where two people were murdered with baseball bats." I took another bite of my cheeseburger, dribbling some ketchup on my chin. "But...if *I* wanted to frame Billy Barron, my weapon of choice would be a baseball bat. Preferably one of his, but..." I shrugged.

"Do you have any idea how many baseball bats there probably are in the New Orleans metropolitan area? Probably thousands— tens of thousands. Think of all the teams there are—Little League, high schools, colleges, on and on." Frank shook his head. "You wouldn't need one of his. Using any bat would throw suspicion on him."

"But how did Eric's killer get the baseball bat up to the penthouse without being seen?" I picked up another French fry. "They're kind of hard to hide."

"Good point." Frank put the last bite of his burger in his mouth. "Christ, this food is good. Good thing it isn't more convenient, or I'd be the size of a house."

I just made a face. Frank was a hard gainer, meaning he'd fought hard for all the muscle he carried on his body, and it was ridiculously easy for him to get ripped. His body was a fat-burning machine; he could eat everything in sight and burn off every calorie without gaining a pound. I used to be the same way. I always ate whatever I wanted whenever I wanted and stayed lean and trim... and then I turned forty. My metabolism had slowed down, and one morning I was horrified to realize that I had a slight roll around my middle and love handles hanging over the side of my jeans. It had become a constant struggle keeping extra weight off. I was having to retrain myself to eat better...allowing myself a treat now and then, like Five Guys. I just had to do more cardio than I was used to doing. I looked down at the remains of my double cheeseburger and sighed inwardly.

At least we were splitting the order of fries.

"The problem is all of these people are probably—if not directly lying to us, then coloring the truth to make themselves look good and the others look bad, which is kind of like a *Grande Dames* episode…trying to control their narrative." I picked up another fry. "And we haven't even talked to Fidelis or Megan or Margery yet—and now Margery's daughter is also in the mix."

When we got home it was time to dig out our whiteboard. There were getting to be too many suspects to keep straight, and the crisscrossing stories were getting muddled.

We headed home down Esplanade Avenue. It was barely over forty degrees, the sky gray with threatening dark clouds, the air feeling heavy with water, like it does before one of those drenching, street-flooding rains. But the houses on Esplanade were all done up for Christmas, the fences and porches covered with lights and Santa imagery, nativity scenes on the front lawns, curtains pulled back to reveal gloriously sparkling and glittering Christmas trees. Many of the street lamps were festooned with candy stripes and big red velvety bows.

We needed to get all this cleared up soon so we could go back to enjoying the holidays. I still needed to decorate the apartment.

I pulled out my phone and typed *Eric Brewer murder* into the search engine. Obviously the first links to pop up were coverage of the murder. There was a link to the Diva website, TMZ, popular gossip blogs about the *Grande Dames* shows, and various other news sites. I started clicking and scrolling through quickly. Every one of them mentioned Eric had been with a "younger man" the night he was killed and that the younger man claimed to have been drugged. None of them mentioned Taylor's name. So far, Venus and Blaine had kept their word about not releasing his name to the media. But it wouldn't be hard for some enterprising journalist anxious for a scoop to figure out who the young man was. Hell, Paige had been there that night—she might have *seen* Taylor leave with Eric. Any one of the cast or crew members there that night could leak Taylor's name.

Our best hope was Paige would hold out for an exclusive—which she wouldn't get if she took his name public—and that Serena saw no advantage for herself in going public with Taylor's name.

I felt another headache forming between my eyes.

Plenty of people *did* know Taylor was the young man in question.

It was just a matter of time before Taylor's name was out there.

And all hell would break loose.

"So far Taylor's name has been kept out of it," I said, slipping my phone back into my coat pocket. "Frank, we're going to have to move fast if we want to keep it that way."

"I know." Frank glanced over at me. "I'm also worried about your car."

"Please don't bring that up," I replied. "I'm in a very lovely state of denial about that." I know it was childish to not think about it, but if the cops found blood or any other evidence in the back of the CR-V...yeah, better to deal with that when it happened.

"We're not going to be able to keep his name out of the media forever, Scotty." Frank sounded tired. "It's not ideal, but..."

"I just don't want him to always be *the twink that was there the night Eric Brewer was murdered,*" I replied. "This could ruin his life."

"We can only do what we can," Frank said as we stopped at the light at Claiborne. "He's a strong kid, Scotty. He can handle it. And it's out of our control."

"Maybe...maybe we should get ahead of the story." I rubbed my forehead. This headache was going to be a bitch. "Maybe we could talk to Paige. She was at the party, she knows Taylor was there—she might even know he left with Eric. She'd be fair, at least."

"We'd better ask Loren what he thinks. And Taylor. I mean, it's his decision."

"I just think it would be smart." I pinched the bridge of my nose. That worked, sometimes. "I mean, look how fast all of these people will sell each other out. I mean, what's to stop Serena from going to the tabloids?"

"You think Serena would do that?"

"I don't know what Serena would do." I didn't. I knew her, I liked her, but I didn't know her well enough to predict her behavior. "I'm going to call Loren." I pulled out my phone as Frank turned the corner from Decatur onto Barracks. The call went to voice mail. "Hey, Loren, Scotty Bradley here. Can you call me as soon as you can? I think maybe we need to get ahead of the story, you know, with the media. Call me." I hung up as Frank pulled into our parking garage. As we walked through the shed to the courtyard, my phone vibrated. I pulled it back out. I had a text message from

Venus: *hey we're on our way to the Quarter do you mind if we stop by and ask some follow up questions about your accident?*

Sure, I typed with my thumbs, *although I don't know what else I can tell you. We just got home.*

"Venus and Blaine want to come by to talk about the accident," I said as we climbed the back stairs.

Frank stopped at our back door and looked back at me. "That's not good. What other questions could they have? It was an accident."

"I don't know. Maybe they want to see if I've remembered anything. She said she just had some follow-up questions."

Frank unlocked the door. "I'm sure the car is totaled. I wish they'd hurry up so we can file the insurance claim."

"We can just go ahead and get another car," I said, as Scooter weaved around my ankles, his tail up, purring and rubbing against me. Clearly, he was hungry. I didn't fool myself into thinking it was affection. He was a very sweet cat—he'd completely won us all over during his time with us and was now a member of the family—and he loved to sleep on us, cuddle with us.

"Taylor?" I called. He didn't answer. Of course, he could be upstairs. I checked the time. His class wouldn't get out for another hour. But he must have come home early—Scooter was in our apartment, wasn't he? The first thing Taylor did every day when he got home was get Scooter and bring him downstairs to our apartment.

If Scooter was down here, then where was Taylor?

"Frank," I managed to keep my voice calm, "can you go look and see if Taylor's upstairs?"

I had a really bad feeling about this.

I waited until the door closed behind Frank and tried not to run to the computer in the living room. I pulled up the app for our phone service and clicked on *find my phones*.

The New Orleans map came up. Two phone icons blinked at our location on Decatur Street, labeled SB (me) and FS (Frank).

The TR phone didn't show anywhere.

He may have just turned off his phone, I thought, trying not to panic as I typed in a specific search for his phone.

Nothing.

No dot. Just *phone not found.*

"He just turned off his phone," I said out loud, my voice shaking a little.

Taylor never turns off his phone.

My fingers starting to tremble, I clicked on *Location history* and then selected Taylor's name from the drop-down menu.

He'd come home forty-five minutes ago.

I pulled up his Uber history—yes, I have all kinds of ways of tracking him, yes, I know it's controlling and smothering, yes, I know I shouldn't do this, but I rarely ever use them and sometimes it comes in handy, LIKE RIGHT NOW—and I saw the Uber that picked him up on campus had dropped him off forty-five minutes ago and maybe he was stressed and upset and he turned off his phone once he got home but I couldn't get out of my mind that Friday night I came home and A RUSSIAN AGENT WAS DEAD IN MY LIVING ROOM AND HE'D GOTTEN IN SOMEHOW AND...

Breathe, Scotty. Breathe. He's upstairs and asleep.

I stood up and walked into the kitchen. Scooter was howling. I absentmindedly filled his food and water bowls and listened, my ear cocked to the upstairs. I didn't hear anything.

That was...odd.

I nearly jumped out of my skin when the gate buzzer rang. I pressed the speaker button. "Yes?"

"It's us, Scotty." It was Venus's voice.

"Hey, let me buzz you in. We're on the third floor." I pressed the unlock button and heard the gate buzz. I kept the speaker on until I heard the gate close behind them.

Where the hell was Frank?

What could be keeping him?

What's going on upstairs?

I was torn between running upstairs to make sure everything was okay and needing to wait for Venus and Blaine. The knock on the back door solved the problem for me.

If you wait long enough, sometimes your decisions get made for you.

"Hey." I opened the door and stood aside for them to enter. A blast of cold wind came in with them, and their coats were wet. "Y'all want some coffee?"

"That would be terrific," Blaine replied. I took their coats and shut the door, hung the coats on the coatrack, and followed Blaine and Venus down the hallway.

"Make yourselves at home," I said, detouring into the kitchen. I knew she took her coffee black, and he used a sweetener packet. I filled the coffeemaker with water and set it to brew before heading back into the living room. "What's going on?" I asked, sitting down in one of the wingback chairs.

"Scotty." Venus gave me a brittle smile. "Is there anything about your accident you want to share with us? Something you might have left out at the scene, maybe?"

"I...don't know what else there is to share?" I was confused. I looked from one to the other, but both looked serious. "What's going on?"

"Is there anything going on in your life that you'd maybe like to share with us but don't feel like you can, for some reason?" Blaine cleared his throat uncomfortably. "Any, I don't know, cases you might be working on, you know, things you should tell us about to clear up some things?"

"I honestly don't know what you're talking about," I replied. "The only thing Frank and I are doing is trying to clear Taylor." I frowned. "You know, the *Grande Dames* murders?"

Venus nodded. "You're sure?"

"Yes."

"So, you can't think of any reason why there would be a tracking device on your car?" Venus raised her eyebrows and blinked at me, her head tilted to one side, a not-friendly smile twitching the corners of her lips.

"A tracking device?" I gaped at her, hoping they couldn't hear how hard my heart was pounding. *Fuck.*

"A highly sophisticated one, at that." Blaine pulled out his phone, played with it for a few seconds, then passed it over to me. On the screen was an image of a very tiny square box, with a red light in the corner. "In fact, our tech guys say it's Russian in origin, often used by Russian spies."

"Russian," I repeated stupidly. *Fuck.*

The accident wasn't an accident.

"Yes," Venus went on. "Apparently it broadcasts to a satellite, and those broadcasts can be monitored by computers…or even a cell phone." She folded her arms and smiled. "Modern technology is pretty amazing. So, yes, *someone* was tracking your car. It stands to reason that your accident might not have been an accident at all. Still sure there's nothing we need to know about?"

"Someone—someone deliberately *hit* me?" I gripped the armrests of my chair, to keep my hands from shaking. "But why… why would someone want to hurt me?"

Russian. The device was Russian.

Colin had been followed by a Russian agent. The guy he'd killed in our apartment on Friday night had been Russian.

Fuck, fuck, fuck.

What the hell is going on?

I looked up at the ceiling, my terror growing.

"The car that hit you had been stolen," Blaine was saying. "The owner last used it Saturday evening and didn't know it was gone until we contacted him yesterday after the accident. So, there's no telling how long the car was gone. We also don't know when that device was put on your car, or how long someone's been tracking you. At some point, we'd like to check your other vehicles to see if they also have been bugged."

"Yes, of course."

Venus cleared her throat. "Naturally, after we found the bug on your car, we turned the vehicle over to the crime lab. Luminol found some traces of blood in the back hatch, but the DNA had been ruined…"

"I cut myself a few days ago." I replied. "I had a box cutter and I was opening some boxes in the car, you know, so I could just put the cardboard into recycling?"

"Did you know that a body that was found early Saturday morning in Bayou de LeSaire? Out on Chef Menteur Highway, close to the Rigolets?"

"I think I heard something about it on the news," I replied. "Why?"

Fuck fuck fuckety fuck.

"Yes, what are you implying, Venus?" This was Frank. I hadn't heard him come in. He was standing in the hallway, his arms crossed.

"I'm not implying anything," Venus said. "I know there are any number of ways for blood to wind up in the back of your car. But the fact that there is blood back there, with the DNA ruined, coupled with the bug..." She held up her hands. "And the fact that the body we found out in Bayou de LeSaire had dental work consistent with the kind someone would get in Russia...you see our dilemma here. And I know..." She paused, searched for the right words. "Look. Off the record, okay? We know that Colin works for Blackledge, remember? *We know.* We were the ones who investigated your uncle's murder twelve years ago, remember? And got pulled off the case by the Feds? Forced to close the books on it without ever really coming up with an answer?"

"And then Colin was gone, right?" Blaine crossed his legs and leaned back into the sofa. "And stayed gone for several years, and then without warning he turns up again. No questions asked, no problem." He made a face at me. "Your personal life is none of our business, of course..."

"But we aren't idiots." Venus finished for him. "Is there something going on you aren't sure you can tell us about?" She sighed. "I mean, seriously, guys. Any minute I'm waiting for the Feds to swoop in and tell us we can't investigate your car accident anymore and to close and seal the damned file, just like twelve years ago with your uncles." She ticked off the points on her fingers. "So, we've got a dead Russian. We got a Russian bug on your car. You got a boyfriend who works for Blackledge. It doesn't take a goddamned rocket scientist to do that math and come up with *Colin*." And then she pointed at the floor. "Did I mention that the Russian found in Bayou LeSaire was rolled up in a rug that I swear I've seen here before? A rug that doesn't happen to be here anymore?"

Blaine gestured around the apartment. "It doesn't take Sherlock Holmes to notice you've got a new TV, and those frames are new, too. There's also a bullet hole in that wall right there I'm pretty sure wasn't there the last time I was here. Now, I can't swear to that, of course, and it's been a while since I've been here..."

I looked from one to the other. "I—I don't know what you're talking about." I am a terrible liar. I always have been, and I could tell by the sour looks on their faces they weren't believing anything I was saying. "Colin hasn't been back—I haven't seen Colin in a while." It sounded like a lie, even to me.

"Level with us, Scotty." Venus leaned forward. "I know we don't always see eye to eye on things, but maybe, just maybe, we can help you."

"Let me get you your coffee. I'm sure it's ready now." I moved into the hallway and could see Frank's face was pale, his jaw clenched. I gestured him into the kitchen, making noise as I grabbed two mugs down from the cupboard. "Frank, I can tell by your face something is wrong," I whispered, then called, "You take it black, right, Venus?"

"Yes," she shouted back.

"Sweet'n Low if you have it," Blaine also called.

"He's not up there," Frank whispered back. "His phone is there—the battery's dead—and so is his backpack." He exhaled. "And his keys are there, too."

"He wouldn't go anywhere without his phone or his keys," I whispered back, my heart sinking.

"Nope." Frank shook his head. "I'm going to tell them everything."

Finding Taylor had to be a priority. If Russians had taken him...

"We can't tell them everything," I whispered back. "At the very least *I am an accessory after the fact*, Frank. At LEAST. We can't say anything to them until I've talked to Storm. But we can tell them Taylor's missing."

That muscle in his jaw was bouncing up and down again. "Fine."

I followed Frank into the living room and gave Venus and Blaine their respective cups.

"I don't know what you think is going on, or what you think Scotty and I know, but..." He swallowed. "But that can wait. Taylor's not here. And he should be."

"And so," I went on, improving madly, "given that my car was being tracked, and Taylor isn't here—and didn't take his keys or his phone with him, and his apartment was unlocked..."

"Maybe whatever case Colin's working on...I don't know, but maybe his cover was blown? And his life here was exposed to people who want to hurt him," Frank finished for me. "And someone—that someone or something, may have taken Taylor. I mean, if they bugged Scotty's car..." He exhaled.

"I used phone tracking to make sure he got home from school—he took an Uber and so we know what time he got back here," I went on, my voice quivering. I hugged myself and took a deep breath. "The first thing he does every day when he gets home from school is he brings Scooter downstairs." Scooter was curled up in Blaine's lap, sleeping. "I know we can't file a missing persons report..."

"Text me a good photo of him," Venus replied. "And I'll put out a BOLO. You know it's possible he just went for coffee—"

"Without his keys or his phone?" Frank replied with a raised eyebrow.

Venus held up her hands. "I know, I know. Millennials never go anywhere without their phones. Did the apartment upstairs seem disturbed in any way?"

We trooped upstairs, shivering in the cold, and the silence of the apartment was scary. It seemed somehow empty, abandoned. Taylor's backpack was sitting just inside the door, where he always dropped it when he came home. His phone was in the kitchen, plugged into the charger—but the charger wasn't plugged all the way into the wall. Taylor was always afraid his battery would die on him, so he always recharged the phone as often as he could—if he had access to an outlet, he'd plug it in.

It looked like he'd been interrupted as he plugged it in.

But even more disturbing? His jacket was tossed on the back of the sofa. He'd come in the way he always did, dropped his bag, tossed his coat over the sofa, and started to charge his phone.

But nothing seemed out of place. Nothing was tipped over, no sign of a struggle.

That was promising.

Maybe he had run to the coffee shop and had just forgotten his keys.

But his jacket, too?

I also appreciated the fact Venus and Blaine were ignoring the bong sitting on the coffee table.

"We'll find him," Blaine said, rubbing my arm.

CHAPTER FIFTEEN
TWO OF PENTACLES, REVERSED
Possibility of loss

"We've got to stay calm," I said for probably the thousandth time since Blaine and Venus left. "We don't know for sure he's been kidnapped."

Okay, maybe I was babbling a little bit. *Saying* we had to stay calm wasn't the same thing as, you know, *staying calm*. My mind was a gibberish of emotions, thoughts shooting through the gray fog encroaching on the edges of my consciousness. My heart felt like it was going to spring from my chest. I could hear blood thudding through my veins in my arms, my temples, in my throat. I couldn't sit still. I needed to do something, anything, keep myself occupied, to keep the worst thoughts of what might have happened—what might be happening—to my precious Taylor at bay. I couldn't bear the idea of him being afraid, being in the hands of people who wanted to hurt him for some reason.

I would have gladly killed them, torn them limb from limb, poured gasoline over what was left, and lit a match.

He's okay, he's okay, he's got to be okay, I kept repeating inside my head.

But thinking it wasn't the same as believing it, and no matter how many more times I said that rosary in my thoughts, I felt certain I wasn't ever going to make myself believe it.

I had a gut feeling deep inside that Taylor wasn't okay, wasn't safe, was terrified and needed us to come to his rescue.

He may not be my blood child, but that sixth sense parents supposedly have?

I have it in spades.

I knew in my soul he hadn't just run down to the coffee shop. *Someone* had taken him against his will.

Our home wasn't safe. It hadn't been since Colin killed that Russian here on Friday night.

We *never* should have let Taylor come back until we were sure he'd be safe here.

Hell, maybe *we* should move into Mom and Dad's for the time being.

"Stop pacing," Frank said, his lips a compressed thin line, his jaw clenched tightly, "you're just making me more nervous. And much as I hate to say this, Scotty, we have to consider the possibility that Taylor ran away on his own."

My jaw literally dropped. *"What?"* I didn't add *have you lost your mind?*

But I was thinking it.

"I know it sounds crazy," Frank's voice was low and controlled, "and not like him, but we also have to accept that what's been happening to him over the last few days isn't normal, either. We have no idea what's going on in his head right now, Scotty."

"Taylor would never run away! He'd never worry us like this!" I insisted. "That's not how he handles things." One of the things I loved the most about Taylor was his inability to dodge problems. He always ran right at them.

He'd known how his parents would react when he came out to them but did it anyway. It was more important to him to live his life openly and honestly, even if it meant losing his relationship with his parents and the rest of his family.

That was a kind of courage I didn't know if I had.

"But he's never been almost raped before," Frank replied. "We don't know how…" His voice trailed off. "Or suspected of being a murderer." He gave me a weak grin. "I know, I know, but we have to consider every option, honey."

"So, we have to—" I took a deep breath. "Do we also have to consider the possibility that he may have killed Eric, too? He wouldn't, Frank, you know it as well as I do."

"Well, he was drugged, wasn't he?" Frank replied, scratching his head. "Maybe he just doesn't remember doing it. Maybe it was self-defense."

"Where did he get a baseball bat from?" I took another deep breath and counted to ten in my head.

Frank did have a point. Thinking logically and rationally was smarter than reacting emotionally.

Logic could also help me get a grip on myself and get my emotions under control.

"The bat might have already been there," Frank went on, leaning back in the computer chair and folding his arms. "Maybe Eric got one of Billy's bats from someone. Maybe even Billy. Or Rebecca."

"But the bat is gone." I walked over and put my arms around his shoulders and neck. His warmth felt good in my arms, like always. There's something about feeling the heartbeat of someone you love that's calming. "He might have killed Eric while under the influence and not remember, but would he have thought to get rid of the bat? No, the killer took the murder weapon with him—and that means Taylor's not the killer."

"Remember the crime scene." Frank leaned his head against my right bicep. "You saw it. What do you remember?"

I laughed. "I don't remember much, to tell you the truth. I was so worried about Taylor...oh my God, I can do better than remember." I walked back into the living room and grabbed my cell phone from the table. "I took pictures." I found the connector cable and plugged my phone into the desktop. The photo program opened immediately, and I moved the mouse to click on *download photos now* and also the box *delete after download*.

Several hundred pictures started popping up in the program window. It had been a while since I'd downloaded and deleted pictures, obviously.

Once the download was finished, Frank scrolled through until we reached the appropriate ones. "This was a smart thing to do—I don't know that I'd have thought so clearly under the circumstances," he said as he started scrolling through the crime scene photos.

"I figured it might come in handy in case I needed to prove I didn't tamper with the scene," I replied. You stumble over dead bodies as I often as I do, you learn—even when you're in shock and aren't exactly sure what you're doing.

"So, the body was in the bedroom?"

"Yes." I felt a little queasy and looked away.

"So, it's unlikely he let his killer in, isn't it?" Frank stared at a photo of the body. "If someone knocked and Eric let him or her in, wouldn't they have killed him in the living room? Why would Eric lead them back into the bedroom?"

"Unless the person was someone...someone he wanted to..." I couldn't say it.

It was bad enough he'd drugged Taylor and intended to rape him, but to have *someone else join in on the fun?*

I felt nauseated.

Frank wrote some notes on the legal pad on the desktop and closed the photo program. "We need to see who, if anyone, Eric was involved with—and if he was involved with anyone locally."

"Remy Valence, for one." I disconnected my phone and slipped it back in my pants pocket. "Maybe someone they met that night?" But no, the guys at the Brass Rail didn't mention anyone else being with Eric and Taylor.

Brandon. Brandon was with them.

I pulled my phone out and retrieved the card he'd given me from my trench coat pocket. I dialed the number, which went straight to voice mail. I left a quick message—*hey Brandon, this is Scotty, we met at the party Friday and you gave me your number? Give me a call.*

If he thought I was calling for a date, so be it. Whatever it took to get him to call back.

And of course, there were the key cards. I still had mine. Anyone who'd been at the party and had gotten one could have accessed Eric's room without him knowing.

Billy Barron hadn't been at the party, so that ruled him out.

Maybe.

I walked back into the living room.

"We still can't rule out that he might have run away," Frank said again. "I called Mom and Dad—he's not there, but they'll call if he turns up. What about other friends?"

I tried to remember. "I've never met any of his friends."

"Maybe go through his phone?"

"I don't know his passwords." I shook my head. "But, Frank—he would have taken his wallet and his phone. How far could he get without either?"

"How far could he get with his phone on him?" Frank reminded me. "You just tried to find him by tracking his phone. He's not stupid. He knows his phone can be tracked and his credit card usage checked. If Taylor really did kill Eric—"

"I wish you'd stop saying that," I sighed.

I sat down on the couch, reached under the table for the cigar box of my tarot cards, and started shuffling.

Sometimes I've wondered if my "gift" isn't necessarily some kind of psychic connection to the Goddess and to another plane, but rather *how* my mind manifests my own psychic ability when I am able to focus it; like my conscious mind can't handle the level of concentration I can achieve, so instead my mind reads the cards or, in some instances, takes me into another plane where I can commune with the Goddess. I try not to question this gift of mine too much—you never question a *gift* of any kind—and there was a very long fallow period in the wake of Hurricane Katrina and the flood that followed. I was angry because I'd had no warning, no foreshadowing of what was to come for my hometown, my family, and my friends.

And just like that, it was gone, gone like I'd never had the damned thing in the first place. I could shuffle the cards and pray and light candles, spread the well-worn deck out in any number of different layouts—Tree of Life, the Sorcerer's Sign, the ones I usually did, and others that I found on the internet—and the cards just looked back at me, unblinking, with no meaning, no answers, no nothing. They were just pictures on stiff, glossy paper with no more meaning than a regular deck of cards.

And I didn't mind. I really didn't. What was the point of being a little bit psychic when you didn't get a warning about a looming major natural disaster?

But it started coming back slowly, and while it's not as strong as it used to be—the last year, after I met Frank and Colin and before Katrina, was when it was the most powerful it ever had been—it's still there.

It's also still as maddeningly obtuse as it ever was.

But shuffling the cards and focusing on them was keeping me from worrying about Taylor.

"I don't want to even think about it." Frank sat down next to me on the sofa, putting a shaking hand on my leg. "But we have to consider it."

"Yes, I get it, but I don't believe for one minute he'd ever do anything on purpose to make us worry—that's just not Taylor." The well-worn cards moved through my hands as I cut and shuffled and moved them around. "This is the kid who texts us and lets us know he's running late when it's only ten minutes, so we won't worry." I started spreading the cards out on the coffee table. I closed my eyes and focused my energy on the cards, sending a quiet prayer to the Goddess up from my mind, as I thought about Taylor, prayed for his safety, prayed for some insight into where he was and what he might be going through.

I opened my eyes. Reading the cards might not count as evidence, but whatever they said was good enough for me.

I started flipping over the cards as Frank stroked the inside of my thigh. When I was finished, I leaned back and glanced over the cards in order.

A brave young man with no fear.
Heading into danger, he must beware.
He cannot do it alone, he needs help.
A strong woman who cannot be trusted.
Someone will tell lies that will obstruct the seeker's journey.
Wisdom and the answers will come from within.

"Well?" Frank breathed after a moment.

"Not great, but not bad," I replied. "He wouldn't run away, Frank."

"I don't think so, either." He brushed his lips against my cheek as he stood up. "I'm just going to go for a little walk around, see if maybe he's at the coffee shop or somewhere around, he might have just, you know, gone for a little walk to maybe clear his mind a bit. He's dealing with a lot."

Yeah, thanks for that brilliant insight, I thought but was smart enough to not say aloud. Once I heard the front door shut behind him, I went back over to the desk and opened the address book on the computer. I picked up my cell phone and dialed the private number we had for Angela Blackledge...the number we were only supposed to call for emergencies.

But Taylor being missing certainly counted as an emergency. And I knew Colin would agree with me.

The phone rang three times and then the voice mail message began. It was simple; a woman with a British accent saying *You have reached the party at 058-932-98764. If this is not the number you intended to reach, hang up now. If you wish to leave a message, do so at the tone.*

"Angela, this is Scotty Bradley in New Orleans." I took a deep breath. "I don't know when the last time you spoke to Colin was, but I know you must know about what happened here on Friday night. Well, our nephew Taylor is missing right now. It may have nothing to do with your business, or Colin's business, but after the other night I can't help but wonder. A tracking device was found in my car; I was in an accident the other day that the police now think was deliberate, possibly attempted murder. And now Taylor is gone. The tracking device was apparently Russian technology. And apparently the police have found a body they've tentatively identified as Russian. I don't know anything about your business, or what's going on, but none of this can be coincidental and I am very worried about my nephew. Any insight you might have and would be willing to share would be gratefully appreciated. And if you can get a message to Colin, that would be terrific. I'm sure he'd want to know Taylor is missing."

I disconnected the call.

She rarely, if ever, called back. But I felt better having left the message.

Somehow, she'd let Colin know something may have happened to Taylor.

I rolled another joint and had just taken a hit when my phone rang. The screen read *Paige Tourneur*. "Hello?" I said, exhaling an enormous cloud of smoke at the same time.

"Hey, Scotty, what's up?" She sounded a bit stoned herself, which wasn't out of character. "I just got some interesting intel from a source in the police department. About Eric and Chloe. I thought you might like to know."

"At this point anything is good to know." I lay back down on the sofa, taking another hit. What if Frank was right? What if Taylor just decided he couldn't deal with any of this and ran away? He was drugged and almost raped, suspect in the murder of his would-be rapist. I didn't know enough about whatever drug had been used on him to know whether he could have killed Eric and forgotten he'd done it because of the drug.

Fuck, this sucked.

"Well, both were killed with what the coroner believes to have been an aluminum baseball bat…but not the same bat." She exhaled. "The bat used on Eric left flecks of blue aluminum in his scalp; the one used on Chloe, red. So definitely not the same bat. Both were hit only once and on the right side of the back of their heads. So, the killer was right-handed, most likely, or bats from the right side." She laughed. "It doesn't mean the same person didn't kill them both, of course, but…you know Billy Barron was a big baseball star at LSU?"

"Does the coroner think the killer had collegiate level batting experience?" My tone was a lot more sarcastic than I'd intended, but she laughed.

"They were hit hard, but Eric was hit harder, if that makes any sense. The amount of force used on Chloe wasn't as extreme. So, either the killer didn't hate Chloe as much as he hated Eric, or there were two killers and Chloe's killer was weaker, physically, than Eric's. How's Taylor holding up?"

I bit my lower lip. Paige was a friend, but she was also a journalist. "As well as can be expected," I replied, which technically wasn't a lie. She hadn't asked me where he was, after all. "Better than I would have at his age."

"Well, there's something coming down the wire," she went on. She interrupted herself with a coughing fit—she must have been smoking weed—and excused herself after gulping some water down. "Diva TV is postponing the premiere of the show indefinitely—the press release is all platitudes, really, wishing everyone the best in this difficult time, blah blah blah—but what I am actually hearing is a lot of…well, you're the detective. You tell me what you think."

"Okay." Paige had sources everywhere, it was kind of creepy. She'd gotten sources everywhere during all those years reporting on the *Times-Picayune*'s crime beat before leaving to run *Crescent City* magazine. I felt a little bad for not trusting her—she'd done me any number of favors since we'd met, and she could have easily already broadcast Taylor's name everywhere as the "young man" in the Eric Brewer murder. I thanked her again for that.

"It's coming out either today or tomorrow." She brushed aside my thanks. "Someone at the *Advocate* has his name, and editorial is holding it back for now…but my guess it's going to be in tomorrow's paper, which means it's going to be everywhere. I don't have to tell you to let him know to keep his head down and not to talk to anyone?"

"No, but thanks."

"Anyway, someone's coming forward. There's going to be a big shake-up at Diva," she went on like I hadn't said anything. "There have been a lot of blind items and talk on some of the gossip sites… someone is coming forward to say that Eric drugged him and had sex with him while he wasn't conscious. Which is excellent news—it establishes a pattern of behavior with him, and of course, once one comes forward, they'll start coming out of the woodwork."

"Any idea of who it might be?"

"The gossip sites—at least the commenters—all seem to think it's going to be Rob Ricker."

"Seriously?"

Rob Ricker's mother Catriona had been a member of the cast of the *Malibu* show. Primarily known as a starlet with a penchant for marrying well, she'd joined the cast in the middle of a bitter and nasty divorce from her fourth husband, a music mogul. Rob was one of her two sons from her second marriage—her only children. Catriona was as shallow and narcissistic as the rest of her fellow Dames, but there was a sly, knowing self-awareness about her that audiences responded to, and she quickly became one of the most popular cast members from any franchise, landing talk show appearances and magazine covers and a book deal. Her sons, in their late teens when she joined Season 3, were gorgeous—their father Nathan a successful football star who'd made the transition to broadcasting. The combination of Nathan and Catriona's stunning good looks had combined to produce gorgeous sons. The problem was they were spoiled princes of Malibu, who didn't have any ambition other than to work out, tan, party, and get laid. Catriona was pushing them into modeling, but without much success. During Season 5 something went seriously wrong with Rob—he started drinking too much, doing drugs, disappearing for days at a time. Catriona's decision to use Rob's issues—whatever they were—as her storyline for Season 5 was a fatal miscalculation, and the audience turned on her. She wasn't asked to return for Season 6.

The good news was Rob got his act together, came out of the closet, and enrolled at USC—and his younger brother David had also cleaned up his own act.

"The story I've heard is that Rob was one of Eric's victims," Paige was saying. "That's why he went off the deep end on the show, and Catriona didn't know anything about it...and it was all a little too close for comfort for Eric, so he made sure she got a bad edit and lost her audience, then fired her at the end of the season."

"Wow."

"She's apparently planning to file a suit against the show *and* the network, because they knew and covered it all up to protect Eric."

"Rob isn't in town, by any chance?"

"The funny thing is...he actually is." Paige practically purred the words into the phone. "Didn't you see him at the premiere party on Friday night? I talked to him briefly—he was just drinking sparkling water, by the way—but he wasn't at Eric's after-party later. I'm trying to track him down even as we speak."

"But if his mother is about to file suit, there's no reason for him to want to kill Eric," I replied. "In fact, he had every reason to want Eric to stay alive."

"I'll let you know if I find him. I should have gotten his phone number." As she often said, it was easy for her to get people's numbers. She could always claim to need their help with an article for the magazine, or to even profile them.

"We think the Grande Dames are excessive narcissists," she told me once, "but almost everyone is a narcissist to some degree. They just haven't gotten the chance to show it yet."

I heard the back door open, so I told her to call me if anything new turned up. I hung up and ran around the end of the couch hopefully…but it was Frank, not Taylor.

Taylor doesn't have his keys, he'd have to ring the buzzer.

Frank hung up his coat and rubbed his hands together. "No sign of him anywhere. I'm really worried, Scotty."

I put my arms around him and hugged him as tightly as I could. It took him a moment or two, but his arms eventually went around me and tightened. "He'll turn up, Frank, he'll be okay."

"I'm wondering if I—if I should call his mother."

I let go and stepped back away from him, not believing what I'd just heard. *"What?"*

He held up his big hands, reddened from cold. "I know, I know, but she is his mother…and she has a right to know what's going on with him."

"They gave up their right to know anything about Taylor when they threw him out two years ago." I could feel the tears rising in my eyes and wiped them away. *"They threw him out like garbage."*

"The news is going to break that Taylor was the guy with Eric Brewer the night of the murder." Frank had the decency not to look me in the eye. "Better to give them a heads-up, don't you think? Or would you rather them coming swooping down to New Orleans and get in our way *when we don't even know where he is?"*

I stared at him for a few moments more. "Fine." I grabbed my coat. "Go ahead and call your sister. You're probably right."

"Where are you going?" Frank called after me as I headed down the hallway.

"I'm going to Mom's for a little while."

"I'll come with you—"

"Call your sister," I interrupted him as I opened the back door. "And get it over with. I kind of want to be by myself for a few minutes anyway."

I closed the door harder than I should have—he probably thought I was angrier than I actually was—and headed down the back steps. When I reached the bottom, I took a deep breath and sat down on the cold wood. The sky was gray, and the air felt damp—it was going to rain again; did I really want to get caught in the cold rain?

But I could hardly go back upstairs and get an umbrella.

It was small of me, I know, but I *wanted* Frank to feel bad for calling his sister.

"You're such a child," I said, getting up and walking to the shed, to cut through to the parking lot. "You're more mature than this, Milton Scott Bradley. Making Frank feel bad for doing the right thing just because you don't want him to do it is hardly the adult thing, now is it?"

I was out on Barracks Street, almost to the corner at Chartres when it hit me.

Paige had said Megan, Fidelis, and Billy had all gone to Newman together. Billy had said the same.

Was that their only connection, pre-show?

I started walking faster.

I could use Mom and Dad's computer.

CHAPTER SIXTEEN
ACE OF PENTACLES, REVERSED
Great plans may come to naught

It's very hard to be a private eye when the case is personal.

And it's not like we're *conventional* private eyes in the first place. Me with my weird psychic gift, Frank and his past as an FBI agent, Colin…well, like I said, there's nothing conventional about any of us. Keeping a professional distance is difficult when someone you love is involved—and that's how mistakes are made, clues overlooked, important things not recognized for what they are—which is why cops aren't allowed to get involved with cases involving people they know.

As I walked, I put aside my fears about Taylor and thought about the case.

Billy, Fidelis, Megan, and Margery's daughter Amanda had all gone to Newman together. They'd had a prior history before being cast in the show. It wasn't unusual—according to things I'd read, the producers would find a woman to be the cast anchor and then use her to recruit other women to the show. So the women usually had some kind of connection before they started filming. And as the show ran, the women would compete to find their own friends to replace the Dames who either quit or were fired.

New Orleans was a small town, so it only stood to reason that the cast would be connected to each other beforehand.

So, who had been the cast anchor for New Orleans?

My phone started vibrating in my pocket. I pulled it out and saw Brandon's number lit up on the screen.

I ducked into a doorway and answered. "Brandon! Thanks for calling me back!"

"I didn't think you'd call," his voice purred in my ear. "But I'm glad you did."

I bit my lower lip. "How are you doing? Things must be really crazy for you since…" I let my voice trail off.

"Oh, God, you have no idea." He went into a long diatribe about the network, and the future of the show, and they had asked him to step in for Eric temporarily, and there was just *so much* going on, and trying to put out fires and save the show and—

When he paused to breathe, I said, "I thought you were going out clubbing with Taylor and Eric Friday night?"

He took so long to answer I wondered if he'd hung up. When he did, his tone was cool. "Yes, I did go with them to a couple of places. But once we got to the Brass Rail—well, I know I'd told you I'd watch out for your nephew, but that just wasn't my kind of place, so I left." Another pause. "I suppose you blame me. I wouldn't have left had I know what was going to happen."

"I don't blame you, Brandon. I was just curious, is all."

"Yes…well, I have another call. Let's have a drink or coffee sometime soon?" He hung up before I could answer.

I slid my phone back into my pocket and started walking again. *Nice job, Scotty. He probably won't take your next call.*

I smiled. I could, of course, text him to meet me for a drink.

He was definitely interested—I'd just have to be sneakier about pumping him for information.

I shivered as another cold blast of wind came from the direction of the river.

So, who *had* been the anchor for the New Orleans cast?

It had to have been either Fidelis or Megan. But why cast Margery instead of her daughter, who was someone they'd gone to high school with? But that was the key; those three were the seed they'd planted to grow the show from. Rebecca Barron was connected through them through Billy, but even so…why would they cast Rebecca?

Maybe Rebecca was right. Maybe she'd been recruited as an underhanded way to hand Billy some ammunition to win his lawsuit.

And how were Serena and Chloe connected to the others?

I tried to remember everything Serena had said about getting cast on the show. For someone who was very open to talking about anything from the size of her breasts to the shortcomings of men she'd slept with, she'd been kind of cagey about how she'd wound up on the show. Maybe she was connected to one of the other women through charity work or something. That was how she'd met my sister.

I made a mental note to follow up on the casting and to see if there were other connections beside Newman High.

I started walking. Lord, it was cold. I could see my breath as I walked. According to the weather app on my phone, the hard freeze alert was still in place for the south shore of the lake until Tuesday afternoon. I tried to focus on enjoying the Christmas decorations on the houses as I walked up Royal Street, pushing everything else out of my mind. Taylor would turn up, we'd find out who killed Eric and Chloe, and the Colin situation would turn out fine. It always had in the past, right, so there was no reason to think this would be any different. He'd have to keep us in the dark, like always, and so I'd never know why that Russian had wound up in our apartment dead.

The important thing to do was stay calm and think clearly.

And consider every possibility, no matter how outrageous it might seem.

I tried to remember any time I'd seen Taylor lose his temper. It didn't happen often—unlike his uncle Frank, Taylor was pretty even-keeled. He wasn't even too angry with his parents for throwing him out.

I couldn't imagine any scenario where Taylor would take a baseball bat and swing at someone's head.

And from the position of the body, whoever had killed Eric had swung at him from behind.

Taylor might kill someone if he was defending himself, but I couldn't see any way clear to where Taylor—drugged or not—would hit someone from behind.

You don't know that. You don't know what Taylor is capable of.

I pushed that nagging little voice out of my head.

I *hate* that voice.

It started raining again when I was still about a block or so from reaching Mom and Dad's. The temperature was still falling, and my face felt frozen. I started darting from balcony to balcony, trying to keep dry. The drops were big and wet and stung a little on bare skin. The sun had vanished, and it seemed dark as night—which made the twinkling of Christmas lights in store windows brighter and more festive. I ran across Dumaine Street, managing to avoid being hit by a speeding yellow cab who also had the nerve to honk at me, even though he'd run a stop sign, and by the time my trembling gloved fingers were fitting my key into Mom and Dad's back gate, water was running off my trench coat and stocking cap. Cold water was also dripping from my coat collar onto my neck.

I ran up the back stairs, letting the gate slam shut behind me, and reached the back door.

At least the gate blocked the wind, even if it didn't block the rain.

I took the steps two at a time, hoping against hope that Taylor would be here. It wouldn't explain why he left without his phone or his keys, but...

Hope springs eternal.

I was a little out of breath when I reached the landing, but there was an overhang that protected me from the rain. I banged with my first on the kitchen door to let them know I was coming in before unlocking it—Mom and Dad can be a little jumpy if you just let yourself into their apartment without warning.

They may be hippies, but they also take full advantage of their Second Amendment rights.

And safe is always better than sorry.

Mom and Dad are late risers, usually not getting out of bed before noon. They're nocturnal by choice—they love staying up all night drinking wine and smoking pot and talking about politics and the things that were wrong in the world, and what they might be able to do to correct those wrongs. I remember many a night growing up, falling asleep in my bed to the murmur of their voices in the living room. The hardest part of moving out of their home was getting used to falling asleep to silence.

When I opened the door, warm air escaping the apartment washed over me and my skin started tingling from the temperature change. I stepped inside and pulled the door shut. There was a small foyer—Mom used to call it a mud room when we were kids, even though we were rarely muddy when we came home. But there were hooks on the wall for coats, and mats for wiping off your shoes. I slipped my coat and hat off and hung them up before stepping into the kitchen.

Mom was standing at the stove adding wine to whatever she was sautéing on the stove in her big black cast iron skillet. Whatever it was, it smelled amazing.

"Scotty!" Mom smiled, looking up from the stove. "A pleasant surprise! Are you by yourself?"

My heart sank. "Just me. Taylor's not here, by any chance?"

"No." She picked up the joint burning in the black-and-gold Saints ashtray on the counter next to the range. She took a hit as she reached up to give me a big hug. Mom is a little shorter than I am. Physically, she's a bit on the tiny side. I don't think she's ever weighed more than 110 pounds, even when she was pregnant.

She seems much bigger than she is because her personality is so huge.

She touched my cheeks. "Oh, you're freezing, you poor thing." She pressed the joint into my mouth as she stepped away from me. "Take a couple of hits and have a seat. You want me to make you some tea? It'll warm you right up."

I obliged, taking a small hit before handing the joint back to her. "Some tea would be great." I sat down on one of the barstools in front of the other counter top.

She filled the kettle with water, reaching with her other hand into the cabinet above the sink. She grabbed the metal container she kept her tea bags in and took off the top, frowning at the contents. "Oh, dear, I need to restock, I'm almost out of everything. Is English breakfast okay? I think that's all I have. But I can run downstairs if you want something else?"

"English breakfast is fine. Lemon and honey, if you have it."

She laughed. "Have you ever known me to not have either?" She turned on another burner, blue flames making a ring beneath the black iron top. She placed the kettle over the flames, opened the tea bag, and placed it in a mug. In one fluid motion she retrieved a slice of lemon from the refrigerator. The little plastic bear containing organic local honey was sitting on the counter near me. "Are you hungry? I'm making risotto."

My stomach still felt uncomfortably full from my lunch at Five

Guys. That seemed like it had been weeks ago. "No, I'm not hungry. I had lunch a little while ago, but thanks. It smells terrific." I took another small hit from the joint and put it back in the ashtray. My brain and body were already starting to relax from the weed, tension and stress drifting away in a cloud of smoke.

"Go sit in the living room with your father and get comfortable." Her smile started to fade as she looked at my face. "Something's wrong. What's wrong, honey?"

"It can wait," I replied, slipping out of the kitchen and into the living room.

Dad was watching a Marvel superhero movie on the big screen television—I couldn't tell which one, but the lead actor was a stunningly beautiful blond man whose body was the stuff of erotic fantasy—and wore a Saints hooded sweatshirt and matching sweatpants. A wisp of smoke was rising out of the bowl of the golden-colored dragon-shaped bong on the coffee table. "Hey, son," he said, blowing smoke out through his nostrils. "Have a seat. I'm watching a special effects movie."

I couldn't help but smile in spite of everything. Just being around my parents always makes me feel better. They had good energy. My dad loved what he called *special effects movies*, watching them all the time—but never knew what their names were, who the stars were, or what the movie was about if he was asked later. He just enjoyed the visuals—which probably had something to do with him being such a huge stoner. Mom usually could name the movies and the casts, although she despised the celebrity culture the American entertainment industry fostered.

Don't *ever* get her started on the E! Network. "Making people famous for nothing besides being famous," she would sniff angrily. "Dumbing the whole country down, making women feel like they have to have their faces reshaped and remolded, implants here, shave this bone down there...and for what? The almighty dollar? Thanks for setting women back a thousand years."

It probably goes without saying that she hate-watched *Grande Dames*.

"Everything okay, son?" Dad asked.

I've never had much of a poker face, especially around my parents. I've never been able to lie to them, primarily because I've never really needed to—they weren't *those* parents. They always trusted us to use our best judgment, and we weren't ever punished for making bad decisions. They believed that *experience* was the best teacher, and we needed to make our own mistakes so we could learn and grow from them. We were also what they call now free-range kids, and we grew up in the French Quarter. Sure, when we did something wrong, we didn't get away scot-free—but they didn't believe in grounding and they certainly didn't believe in hitting. Usually, they'd just sit us down and we would have a long discussion about *why* what we did was wrong, how it affected other people, and as long as we could figure out what lesson we'd learned from making the mistake, we wouldn't have to clean the tobacco shop or scrub the kitchen floor or any of the other chores used for punishment.

Doing domestic work was what my parents considered a win-win punishment. We hated doing it and an odious chore got checked off the list—which made the overall effect a positive one.

Mom and Dad were all about positive experiences.

Mom and Dad had also taught us, from earliest childhood, to think for ourselves and to use logic in making arguments. They didn't believe in shielding us from anything, either.

And since we grew up in the Quarter, we were pretty jaded by the time we were teenagers.

"I was kind of hoping Taylor would be here," I said. "He hasn't been by, has he?"

Mom walked into the living room, wiping her hands on a dish towel. "No, not today. You don't know where he is? Did you try calling him?"

"He left the house without his phone—"

Mom turned white and sat down, hard, on the arm of the sofa. "He doesn't go anywhere without that phone. Have you called the police?"

"It's probably a bit early to be worried, but yeah. He wasn't there when we got home from interviewing a witness on the West Bank," I replied. Mom and Dad wouldn't ask questions about the case—they'd want to know everything but respected confidentiality. "He left his keys and his phone behind. I thought I'd check here, you know, just in case."

"What did the cops say?"

"Frank and I talked to Blaine and Venus," I said, "but it's too soon for them to be able to do anything about it. I suppose it's not too much to hope that he might have gone somewhere without his phone, is it?"

"Well, I'd like to believe that," Dad said, "but that kid suffers from separation anxiety if he's away from that phone for too long." He shook his head sadly, and I could almost hear him thinking *kids these days*. "You don't think—you don't think something's happened to him, do you?"

"Does it have something to do with that awful man who was murdered Friday night?" Mom asked. "Because he deserved it, and no one will ever convince me otherwise."

"I don't know, Mom." I buried my face in my hands. I knew I probably shouldn't tell them about Colin and the body in the apartment, but I had to tell someone. The fear that it had something to do with Taylor's disappearance was too strong, and it was eating me up inside.

And they were family. Mom and Dad would never rat me out. Mom would go to her grave before she would tell the cops anything.

I took a deep breath and looked at them both. "Something else kind of happened Friday night…"

The great thing about my parents is they don't judge. Ever. They raised us all to have a sense of morality, a strong idea of right and wrong, but Mom and Dad's moral teachings probably wouldn't have passed muster for most people. Their politics definitely shaped their morality, and their deep distrust of government at every level—city, parish, state, federal—colored their values. But they also encouraged us to be free thinkers, to make up our minds, to come up with our own moral codes—even if that conflicted with what they believed.

Colin is a perfect case in point. I loved Colin, and so did Frank, therefore so did they. They looked at both Frank and Colin as two more sons, welcomed them to the family without question. Years ago, we had all been led to believe that Colin had been responsible for the deaths of two of my uncles—my mother's half brothers (it's a *really* long story)—and then he disappeared from our lives for three years. It turned out in the end (it's an even longer story) that he wasn't responsible, but his job as a secret agent for hire required him to let us think that.

When he came back into our lives, Mom and Dad welcomed him back, not just to New Orleans but to our lives and our family, even before I was willing to listen to him.

That had been a lesson in the meaning of family I hadn't known I'd needed.

Whenever Colin tried to explain, they just told him he was family and that was all they needed to know.

"If Colin killed him, he must have been a very bad man," Mom said, reaching for Dad's bong and loading the bowl carefully. "And you were smart not to tell the cops anything about that. Keep your mouth shut. Police involvement could put his life at risk—and yours, and Frank's as well. Do you think these Russians might have taken Taylor?"

"It's something we have to consider." I leaned back in my chair and closed my eyes. "I called Angela and left a message. She hasn't called back, of course. I just don't know what to do."

"Sometimes nothing is the right thing to do," my mother said, lighting the bowl and taking a big hit. She blew out the smoke. "And you'll know the right thing when the time comes. I just hate the thought of anyone hurting him." Her eyes glinted. "If they hurt Taylor, there's no place on Earth where they'll be safe."

She does scare me a little sometimes. "It's not like it's the first time," I replied. It was ridiculous how many times we'd all been kidnapped or held as hostages. "But these people know where we live, Mom, and that worries me. Even if they don't have anything to do with Taylor being missing…when will we be safe in our home again?" *If Colin was telling me the truth. He's lied to me before.*

And that was the worst part of this whole thing. I didn't know what was true and what wasn't. Much as I wanted to believe Colin…

I didn't know my ass from my elbow, to quote Papa Diderot.

"Have you reached out to Taylor's mother yet?" Dad asked, taking the bong from my coughing mother and passing it to me.

"Why would we do that?" I shook my head. "His parents gave up all claim to him when they kicked him out."

"Scotty." Mom gave me what we all call *the look*. "No matter what else she may be, the woman is his mother. And when the news breaks—and you know it's just a matter of time before some vulture claiming to be a reporter is going to release that Taylor was the young man with Eric Brewer the night he was murdered, all hell is going to break loose. And if he's missing…" She shook her head. "I'm not a lawyer, but even I know that looks bad, like he ran away or something because he has something to hide about that night. You have to find him."

"What can we do to help?" Dad asked.

"Just keep an eye out for him." I took a hit from the bong just as my phone started beeping. I put the bong down and reached for my phone.

There was a text message from Serena: *Scotty can you come over to Margery's? She wants to talk to you.*

Margery Lautenschlaeger?

Wanted to talk to *me*?

I texted back, *Frank and I will head over there in a few minutes.*

Serena: *Terrific. Look forward to seeing you both.*

I stood up and the head rush from the weed almost caused me to sit back down. "Whoa, that's some potent stuff."

Dad nodded. "Yeah. It's the best batch we've had in a while—I should have warned you." He started shoving buds into a plastic Ziploc bag. "Here, take some with you. It'll help you stay calm." He sealed the bag and rolled it up.

I shoved it in my pocket as I stood up. "Thanks. I have to run now—a witness wants to talk."

"So, you want us to call you if we see or hear anything?"

I nodded. "Stay here, for home base, while Frank and I head over there."

"What if he comes back to your apartment?"

I hadn't thought about that.

Fuck.

"I'll come mind the fort while you're gone," Dad said, getting up and walking over to the hall closet.

"No, you don't need to do that," I replied. All I needed was for Dad to get kidnapped. I still had nightmares from the last time that happened. (It's a really long story.) "Love you both—will keep you posted."

I galloped down the back steps and out the gate onto Dumaine Street. It was still raining, and the wind was still blowing. The gutters were filling with water. I groaned, jumped over the gutter, and started running as quickly as I could in my trench coat. The streets of the Quarter were almost completely deserted as I made my way downtown on Royal, hurrying from balcony to balcony, cold water dripping from my soaked stocking cap down the back of my neck and down my back. I was almost ready to start sobbing from the cold by the time I made it back to Decatur Street and the welcome cover of the balconies on our block. I unlocked the gate and run down the tunnel to the courtyard before taking the stairs two at a time. "Frank?" I called as I entered the apartment, tossing the sopping wet cap into the laundry basket and heading down the hallway to the living room.

He wasn't there.

Fuck.

"Frank?" I checked out on the balcony, but he wasn't there, either. There wasn't a note on the little whiteboard on the refrigerator—our preferred method of communication—and I checked both bedrooms and the bathroom to be sure.

I went out the back door and climbed the steps to Taylor's apartment. The door was locked, and I opened it. "Frank?" I called out tentatively. "Taylor?"

There was no answer.

I pulled out my phone and texted Frank: *where are you?*

I checked everywhere—the bedrooms, the closet, the bathroom, everywhere—but there was no sign of either of them up there.

I ran back downstairs. This time, I checked for Frank's coat.

It was also gone.

What the hell, Frank?

I had a really bad feeling about this.

CHAPTER SEVENTEEN
QUEEN OF PENTACLES
An intelligent and thoughtful woman who is rich and charitable

What to do, what to do, I didn't know what I should do.

Should I go to Margery's, or should I wait for Frank?

What if—Goddess forbid—something had happened to *Frank*, too? And shouldn't I help look for Taylor, or at least hold down the fort in case he came home?

But…if I just sat around waiting and wondering, I'd probably lose my already tenuous grip on sanity.

I texted *where are you* again to Frank, but this time I heard his phone chime in the living room.

Great, so he's run off without his phone, too. What's the point of having a phone if you aren't going to carry it with you?

I refused to consider the notion he hadn't had a choice.

Best not to even think that way.

I scribbled on the dry erase board in the kitchen: *Off to interview a witness. Please text me when you read this* and signed my name to it.

I changed into dry socks and dry jeans before summoning an Uber. I found a dry stocking cap in a drawer to replace my sopping wet one and grabbed an umbrella from the closet.

While I waited for the Uber, shivering, I repeated to myself over and over, *Frank is probably doing exactly what you're doing now—a lead came up and he ran off to check it out and didn't think to take his phone with him. Worrying won't change anything. Worrying just makes things worse.*

I felt slightly better when I got into the Subaru that pulled up to the curb.

I checked my phone for messages again as the driver, a pretty young woman of color, pulled away from the curb. She turned up Barracks to avoid the traffic congestion of Decatur Street as we headed uptown. We chatted, mostly about the weather, nonsensical conversations to while away the time as we rode together. Talking to her helped keep me from worrying and freaking out.

I get the convenience of Uber, but I'm never sure what the proper etiquette is in the car. With a cab, you just get into the back seat, tell the driver where you're going, and that's the end of it. Sometimes you get a chatty cab driver, but most times you don't, and you just sit in the back seat with boundaries pretty much predetermined by decades of riding in cabs. Maybe Uber is the same, but without the glass window separating the front and back seats...yeah. I never know if I'm supposed to sit in the front or the back or what I'm supposed to do. Technically, an Uber driver is just a cab driver you summon and pay through a phone app, but...it's also *not* the same.

We used to be warned about getting into cars with strangers. Now we do it, without a second thought, every day.

The enormous gates were open when my driver turned into the driveway of the Schwartzberg mansion. The house was built in the decades after the Civil War and was an anomaly in New Orleans. There was no other house like it in the city—it had its own aesthetic and design, never duplicated.

Isaac Schwartzberg originally made his fortune as a jeweler to New Orleans society before the Civil War. He'd built the house as a kind of *fuck you* to his anti-Semitic clients, who were more than happy to buy his diamonds but wouldn't invite him and his wife to dine in their homes—or allow them to join the Boston Club or the more exclusive Mardi Gras krewes. His goal was to build the biggest, most spacious mansion in the city—a showplace impossible to forget once seen, completely different from any other building on St. Charles Avenue. He brought in an architect from New York known for the colossal "summer cottages" he'd built for the wealthy in Newport or the Hamptons, told him exactly what he wanted, and opened his wallet, ready to spend whatever was necessary to get it. He wound up buying several lots and tearing down the houses already there. Most people in town called the house "Isaac's Folly" behind his back.

As far as fuck yous went, it was impressive. He definitely got what he paid for.

It was intended to look like a castle/mansion hybrid on the outside, while the inside was designed along the lines of royal chateaus in the Loire Valley. He even had an artificial hill built for his house to rest on, so that it was higher than every other house on the Avenue. It was one of the few big mansions in the city made of stone—tan Arizona sandstone, imported at tremendous expense by railroad. It was built in a square, each side the same length, and at each corner of the house was a square tower with crenellated molding at the top. The windows were all huge, but the curtains were rarely, if ever, open. I didn't even want to think about how much the entire property might be valued at today. Once the house was finished, he and his wife went on a tour of Europe, buying paintings to adorn the walls and sculptures for the alcoves and the gardens behind it. The collection was one of the most famous in the South, and Margery was always loaning pieces to museums. The library was one of the largest private book collections in the South—there were rumors that a first edition *Huckleberry Finn*, autographed by Mark Twain, was its showpiece.

There were even stories that Twain himself had actually stayed in the house on a visit to New Orleans.

Margery was the last descendant of Isaac to bear the name Schwartzberg. The Buchmaier family were also direct descendants of Isaac—they lived in a much more traditional Victorian mansion farther downtown on the Avenue. When Isaac wisely diversified his business into alcohol, he'd handed the jewelry business over to his daughter Leah and her husband, Judah Buchmaier. The liquor business Isaac founded, Black Mountain Liquors, stopped producing their own liquor in the 1970s but were still the major liquor distributor in New Orleans—and you'll never go broke supplying this city with liquor.

Margery herself had married into another liquor dynasty. The Lautenschlaegers had gotten rich on beer, schnapps, and wine.

The Schwartzberg mansion was polarizing—people either loved it because it was unique and different, or hated it because it was unique and different.

I'm one of those who fall into the "love it" category. I've

always wanted to see the inside. Both sets of my grandparents knew Margery—my grandmothers worked on charity events with her on a fairly regularly basis—but I'd never actually met her or had the privilege to be invited inside the castle. I'd seen her at some events, but we'd never been introduced. She had never attended any parties at either set of grandparents' homes.

Which was kind of curious, now that I thought about it more—perhaps evidence of some anti-Semitism on the part of my grandparents?

It wouldn't hurt to talk to Maman Diderot about Margery. Maman Diderot was sharp as a tack and missed nothing—and was pretty shrewd when it came to character. She saw through a lot of bullshit.

It finally stopped raining as we drove up the man-made hill and parked in front of the house. As I thanked the driver and got out of the car, a liveried servant opened the front door and stood there, patiently waiting as I climbed the stone steps. When I reached the small porch, I realized he was huge—probably taller than even Taylor, which was rare.

"Mr. Bradley?" he asked, his voice deep yet somehow soft at the same time, with a slight bow of his bald head. There was a trace of a British accent in his voice. "Madame is waiting for you in the library. Just walk down the hallway, and it's the second door on the left."

"Thank you," I replied with a smile as I walked into the enormous foyer. The floor was pale pink marble, polished till it shone. The massive chandelier sparkled with thousands of teardrop crystals as my wet workout shoes made squishing sounds on the floor. Everything in the foyer and the wide hallway had to be an antique—it almost smelled of money. Everything was completely spotless, shining in the chandelier light.

I wished I'd taken the time to change into something more appropriate for an audience with Margery Lautenschlaeger at Schwartzberg Castle.

Seeing that the second door on the left was open, I rapped my knuckles on it before entering the room. The room was something out of *Architectural Digest*. Each wall was built-in bookshelves from floor to ceiling, and each shelf was neatly filled with books organized efficiently by size. Another gorgeous crystal chandelier hung from the ceiling in the direct center of the room, over a beautiful carved wood table. In the very back of the room was a glass case, with an open book inside resting on a red velvet pillow.

The priceless *Huckleberry Finn*, no doubt.

Margery rose from her chair and walked toward me, a wide smile on her face. I already knew she wasn't a tall woman, but wasn't prepared for how short she was up close. She was wearing white Keds on her feet, and a pair of black skinny jeans beneath a beautiful white cashmere sweater. She'd allowed her dark hair to fall naturally to her shoulders, but I could see enormous diamonds sparkling at her ears, matching the enormous teardrop diamond hanging on a gold link chain around her neck. Her hands were unadorned other than a plain gold wedding ring. She wore very little makeup—some eyeliner, pale lipstick, and perhaps some mascara. Her smile was warm, and I realized that despite her age there weren't many lines on her face, or any telltale skin hanging from her chin. Her skin, though, glowed naturally—no surgeon's knife had ever touched her face.

"Scotty Bradley, at long last," she said, her voice soft and musical. "Thank you for coming. I've wanted to meet you for quite some time. I so admire both of your grandmothers. They are both terrific women with big, generous hearts."

"Thank you," I managed to stammer out as she clasped my right hand in both of hers. Her small hands were soft and warm, the nails perfectly manicured. Her eyes were a velvety brown and almond-shaped, her eyebrows too perfectly shaped to be natural, and a faint whiff of Chanel No. 5 lingered in the air.

"Do come in," she said, her smile never wavering. "Would you care for something to drink?"

As she gently maneuvered me deeper into the room, I became aware that the two dark blue wingback chairs with their backs to the door weren't empty. "Um, some water?"

"Have a martini," Serena said, rising from her chair. She air-kissed both of my cheeks. "Thank you for coming, so delightful to see you." She turned to Margery and drawled, "I told you he was adorable. Don't you just want to eat him up?"

"Serena," I replied as she simply allowed her hand to lie limply in mine. Serena wore a gorgeous pair of Jimmy Choo pumps, covered in silver glitter and sequins, matching perfectly the sleeveless top she wore over black jeans. The tight jeans emphasized how strong and shapely her long legs were. Her big, firm breasts were straining at the top in a desperate attempt to break free, and her thick blond hair had been curled and ratted and teased and lacquered into an enormous frame for her face. She seemed to have been bathing in Hermès Perfume 24 Faubourg, the same scent Maman Diderot prefers.

"You know Amanda?" Serena asked.

"I'm afraid I don't," I replied, and the other woman rose from her chair to offer me her hand.

"I'm Margery's daughter, Amanda," she said, our hands barely touching. She gave me the phoniest smile I'd seen in years. She sat back down, smoothing out her black silk Phillip Lim skirt and crossing her long legs. She wore a peach silk Phillip Lim T-shirt, and her shoes were peach leather Jimmy Choos. Her legs were, frankly, extraordinary, and she was tall enough—and beautiful enough—to be a supermodel. Her skin was flawless, and she'd pulled her chestnut brown hair back from a widow's peak into a chignon. A perfectly round diamond hung from each ear on a two-inch gold chain. There was a golden squirrel pinned to her left shoulder, studded with diamonds. Her makeup was perfect, accentuating the strong cheekbones in her heart-shaped face, and her waist was so tiny that it almost didn't seem human. She pursed her lips as she took a sip from an enormous crystal martini glass with two speared olives sunken at the bottom of what must be highly expensive gin.

She was the woman I'd seen with Billy at the premiere party on Friday night.

Despite my request for water, Margery handed me a martini glass filled to the absolute brim with the same liquid. "You do drink gin, don't you?" she asked as she settled into her own chair, picking up her own glass and taking an enormous swig. "I do love a good gin, don't you?"

I took a sip. It was perfect—but then, why wouldn't it be? Margery Lautenschlaeger was probably one of the definitive experts on liquor in a city where practically everyone drank heavily every day. I took another sip and set the glass down carefully on a gold coaster with the Black Mountain Liquor logo on it.

"You were at the premiere Friday, weren't you?" Amanda asked, leaning forward in her chair. "I think I saw you there?"

I nodded. "Yes. I was with my nephew."

"The poor boy Eric drugged," Margery replied with a slight shake of her head. "I'm so sorry that happened. How is the poor boy doing?"

"That was the boy?" Amanda made a face. "The police don't think..." Her voice trailed off.

There was something about her that wasn't quite right. But I couldn't put my finger on what it was.

"He's still a suspect, of course, but the police pretty much have ruled him out as one...or so they say."

Anger flickered across Amanda's face. "You can't trust the police, Mr. Bradley."

"Call me Scotty, please." I took another sip of the martini, glad I'd decided to Uber rather than drive.

"Serena tells us you're a private investigator, Mr. Bradley," Margery said, glancing at her daughter with what looked like concern. "And you are looking into the murders? To try to clear your nephew?"

"Murder investigations are best left to the police," I replied carefully. "But yes, I'm doing some digging around, see what I can find out."

"Do *you* think the murders are connected?" This was from Amanda. I noticed out of the corner of my eye that Serena was watching her closely.

Interesting.

"It would make the most sense if they were." I turned to Margery. "Have the police talked to you?"

"Me?" Margery looked surprised. "Why would they talk to me? I wasn't even at that stupid after-party. I came directly home after the premiere."

"I mean regarding Chloe's murder, sorry."

"That *bitch*!" Amanda exploded. "No one is sorry to see her dead!"

"Amanda!" Margery snapped, giving her a dark look. Amanda

looked down and started playing with the hem of her skirt. "Forgive my daughter. She's very protective of me, and this frivolous and absurd lawsuit Chloe was threatening me with...well, it was all nonsense, of course. My attorneys—and the network's—assured me she and her husband wouldn't prevail in court." Her eyes glittered. "I wasn't worried about that. They were just trying to make a lot of noise. The network, of course, came up with an absolutely ridiculous compromise..." She waved a bejeweled hand. "I'm sorry I said it, I shouldn't have said it, but that woman." She shook her head. "I'm sorry she's dead, of course, and I feel terrible for her husband, but Chloe Valence had a very trying personality. She deliberately tried to provoke arguments with people and certainly never took any responsibility for her own actions."

She still doesn't know the lawsuit wasn't real. Probably best, I decided, not to be the one to tell her.

"You talked to Remy, didn't you?" Serena asked in the silence that followed.

I nodded. "Yes, and he's devastated. He has an alibi for the time she was killed, and for the time Eric was killed, as well. He was out of town."

Serena and Margery exchanged a glance. "But Remy was the only person who had a motive to want to kill them both." Margery leaned forward in her chair. "So, if Remy couldn't have done it, maybe he hired someone."

"Maybe it was that Vandiver creature," Serena finished her martini and popped one of the olives into her mouth. "They were both awful women, but they certainly hated each other far more than they enjoyed torturing us."

"The two women didn't get along?" I asked. "Was it real, or was it for the show?"

"Maybe someone is killing all the Grande Dames," Amanda said with an icy grin. Her eyes glinted. "If so, they certainly started in the right place."

Serena had gone almost completely pale. She got up and refilled her glass from the pitcher on the sideboard, plopping another two olives in to the glass and heading back to her chair. She took a healthy gulp once she was sitting down. "Jesus, Amanda. Don't say things like that out loud."

"You said Fidelis and Chloe hated each other?" I said again, looking at Margery. "Is that true, Mrs. Lautenschlaeger?"

"Margery," she said, emptying her own martini glass and setting it back down. "Call me Margery, Scotty. And yes, it's true. It went deeper than just a storyline for the show." She sighed. "Why I ever let you talk me into going on that horrible show, Amanda, I'll never know. If this stupid lawsuit wasn't bad enough, murder?" She rubbed her eyes. "I shall never leave this house again."

"Drama queen." Amanda shook her head. She gave me a not-pleasant smile. "Pay no attention to my mother."

"It was your idea for your mother to be a Grande Dame?"

Amanda nodded. "They originally asked me, but I thought Mother was better suited to it." She shrugged, her shoulders lifting slightly. "These shows all have a formula, you know, and when Eric Brewer told me who had already agreed to do the show, I knew that Mother was a better fit—they didn't have an older woman to be the voice of reason, to be a *mothering* influence on the rest of the cast, to, you know, pour oil on the troubled waters and smooth out differences and disagreements between the women."

I nodded. I knew exactly what she meant. The best example of "older voice of reason" on the *Grande Dames* shows was Alison Flax on the *Manhattan* franchise. Alison was a wealthy widow who mentored the younger women, always available for advice, mediation, and support. Alison Flax was the gold standard women on the other franchises patterned themselves on—and always came up short. She had parlayed her enormous popularity into a nationally syndicated call-in radio advice show and had published several best-selling books.

"Obviously, I was wrong," Amanda finished grimly. "Rather than calming things down, Mother jumped into the conflicts with both feet."

"That's a little unfair," Serena said. "Amanda, you weren't always around. You don't know how awful those two bitches were to your mother." Serena turned to me. "Almost from the very start, they both were gunning for Margery—and the rest of us, too, for that matter." She patted her lacquered hair. "And each other."

"I couldn't believe how rude they both were to me, in my own house," Margery continued. "I'm curious to see how much of that will actually be on the show, should they even bother to air the show now." She looked at her hands, folded in her lap. "Maybe that would be the best thing for everyone, really."

"Is that a possibility?" I asked.

"The network is considering that option," Serena replied. "It's kind of in poor taste to air a show where one of the women has been murdered, I suppose."

"The entire show is in poor taste," Margery snapped. "And yes, Scotty, they were horribly rude to me at my own party. If it had been one of my actual parties—not something being filmed for the show, I mean, I would have tossed them both out. But that's neither here nor there, I suppose." She rubbed her forehead. "And now murder. More than one murder. Anyway, I shouldn't have let either of them get under my skin the way they did." She shook her head. "But of course, we also have those awful production people trying to stir up animosities. I shouldn't have said what I did about Remy Valence, no matter how much his wife aggravated me, even if it is true. I was *mortified*."

"It's about time someone called Remy Valence out as a gay man," Amanda replied with a laugh, her eyes gleaming maliciously. "And on camera!"

"It was hilarious!" Serena laughed along with her. "You should have seen the look on Chloe's face—it was priceless. When the episode airs—*if* it airs, I suppose—you can bet I'll watch that scene over and over." Her smile widened. "It was *brilliant*."

"It wasn't my proudest moment," Margery admitted. "But I'm not sorry I did it. She needed to be put in her place. And then for her to act all wounded." Her face twisted. "Besides, it's not like everyone in New Orleans doesn't already know about Remy and his little apartment in the Quarter."

I hadn't known, but it didn't surprise me.

"If you have things you don't want the world to know, you don't go on a reality TV show," Margery went on. "I knew that's how it all worked, you know—if I had any deep dark secrets, I wouldn't have done the show. But Chloe—"

Amanda cut her mother off. "Chloe thought she could have her cake and eat it, too. You know she put herself through college as a stripper over in Biloxi, don't you?"

"I've heard that," I said, very carefully, "but I was never sure if it was true."

"Oh, it's true." This from Serena. "That's where she first met Billy Barron—and where she first started sleeping with him." She shook her head, and her earrings caught the light and flashed fire. "That's why she and Fidelis hated each other, you know. They were both sleeping with him, all these years—even when he was married." She waved her hand. "His wife had no idea what was going on—she took him to the cleaners in the divorce, you know—but if she'd known about the other women?"

I didn't want to let on I already knew this. "So, Fidelis and Chloe were both involved with Billy Barron?"

But before anyone could answer, Margery stood up. "I'm sorry, but I'm feeling terribly tired. My apologies, Scotty, it was delightful to meet you at last. Give my best to your grandmothers." She paused on her way out, examining a chair. She looked back at us. "That Fidelis Vandiver and her stupid tanning bronzer. She got it all over my furniture, ruined some of it. This chair..." She shook her head, then swept out of the room.

The woman knew how to make an exit.

"The bronzer is why I call Fidelis the human stain." Serena laughed.

"I knew she wouldn't go through with it," Amanda said with a sigh.

"That doesn't mean you can't," Serena replied.

"Let me ask you something." I leaned forward in my chair. "You seem pretty certain that Chloe was a stripper—"

Serena interrupted me. "She wasn't just a stripper, she was a whore." She nodded at Amanda. "Give it to him."

Amanda opened her purse and pulled out a manila envelope, which she passed over to me. "Go ahead, open it up. I paid good money for this stuff."

I opened the envelope, sliding out a stack of photographs. The one on top was Chloe—a much younger Chloe, to be sure, but it was easily recognizable as Chloe. She was stark naked, sitting on a bed with her legs spread wide.

"Talk about morally corrupt," Serena sneered. "The tramp."

CHAPTER EIGHTEEN
FIVE OF WANDS
The courage to fight for what's right

Frank and Colin love lecturing me about the rules of working as a private eye. And to be fair, Frank had over twenty years with the FBI, and Colin...he's kind of a gay James Bond for hire.

Me? I was a personal trainer and go-go boy.

"Everyone," Frank told me once, "is a suspect, no matter what you may think you know about them and their motivations."

But the killer is almost always a close family member.

As I waited for my Uber in the dimly lit foyer of Margery's castle, I felt ruling her out as a suspect was a pretty safe bet. She certainly wasn't tall enough to swing a baseball bat at Eric's head. Chloe had also been more on the tall side. Margery hadn't been at the party, either—although she could have gotten one of the key cards from someone else.

She was certainly rich enough to hire someone, though.

And maybe that was the solution to the time frame problem—she could have hired two killers.

But she didn't have a good enough motive. So she hadn't known the lawsuit was a phony storyline for the show...but even if it were real, how much could the Valences have gotten out of her? I didn't know how rich she was, but both liquor companies were printing money. She was considered one of the richest women in the South—not just in New Orleans. Hadn't she just donated several hundred thousand dollars to the New Orleans ballet?

The lawsuit was nothing more than an inconvenience, and people didn't commit murder over inconveniences.

Her daughter, though...

I pulled out my phone again as my Uber came through the front gates and started up the sloping driveway. I walked out on the front porch, waved, and glanced down at my phone.

No messages, no missed calls, no text messages.

Frank, where the hell are you?

I pulled up Brandon's contact information again and hit Dial as I walked down the front steps to the idling car, a black Honda Civic. This time the driver looked to be a college-age young man, with a bright smile and smattering of pimples spread over his very pale face.

I said hello as I got into the front seat. I hung up when Brandon's voice mail picked up again. No sense in leaving yet another message.

We were just passing the Superdome on Claiborne when my phone chimed. I fished it back out of my coat pocket to see there was a text from Frank: *Sorry, didn't mean to worry you. I went for a run to clear my head.*

I rested my head against the cold window. *Hallelujah.*

No worries, on my way home, I replied. I was still planning on ripping him a new one, but it could wait till I got home.

No sense in typing it all out with my thumbs.

I opened my social media apps, typed in Taylor's name, and looked through his home pages. Nothing had been posted since we left for the party on Friday night. His last update—*be jealous, bitches! Off to see the premiere of the Grande Dames of New Orleans! #ilovemylife*—choked me up a little.

Had I but known, we'd have stayed home and watched it when it aired, like everyone else.

Come home, Taylor, wherever you are.

The manila envelope Amanda Lautenschlaeger handed me was resting in my lap. I didn't know if the pictures were relevant, nor could I quite understand why Amanda had thought it was important that not only see them but have copies. So Chloe had a bit of a sordid past? Paige had hinted at the same thing Friday night.

I didn't see how the pictures were relevant, other than letting me know Amanda Lautenschlaeger hated Chloe.

There was something…not right about her.

I couldn't put my finger on what it was, but I hadn't imagined it.

The way her eyes kept flicking back and forth, the strange half-smile, the absolute hatred that dripped from her voice when she talked about Chloe...

Some background checking on that one was definitely in the cards.

And Megan, Fidelis, Amanda, and Billy had all gone to high school together. Diva approached Amanda first, but she'd turned them down, recommending Margery instead. That also didn't seem right.

Why wouldn't Brandon return my calls?

He wasn't flirting with you Friday night. You're way too old for him anyway.

Yeesh, how I hate that voice in my head! I sighed. The driver put in his ear buds and started talking on his phone. He turned right onto Esplanade.

I shifted the envelope in my lap. I guess my reaction to Chloe's nude photos wasn't quite what the ladies had been expecting. Naked pictures—in this day and age who *doesn't* have nude pictures floating around out there?

Sure, they were explicit—you couldn't pull the old *but it's art* argument with these. This was porn. But celebrities leak their own sex tapes all the time. Enterprising paparazzi could, if patient enough, get a nude shot of almost any star.

And that's not even taking sexting into consideration, or the myriad hookup apps. How many young athletes had nudes from hookup apps go public?

Quite a few.

And the websites catering to celebrity nudes were legion.

Almost every day I got a push notification my phone from some gay "news" website it seemed like some other singer or actor or celebrity or whoever's NUDE PICS HAD LEAKED!!!!

Yawn.

I don't care about Justin Bieber's dick pic or anyone else's.

I prefer the real thing instead of a picture any day of the week.

So why did they think it was pertinent for me to see—let alone have copies of—nude pictures of Chloe obviously from her college days?

If anything, it made me more sympathetic to her.

I don't think any of the Grande Dames from the other franchises had ever had nudes surface—but I also couldn't swear to it. Chloe's nudes would have made a great storyline for the second season—had she not been killed.

What terrific television that would have made! The ratings would have been through the roof.

But it probably would have ruined any chance of Chloe ever being taken seriously as a writer again. How crazy had she been, to think doing a *Grande Dames* show would help her career? Sure, some of the Dames were best-selling authors—but they didn't write *fiction*. Their specialties were cookbooks and memoirs and lifestyles guides—like how to please your husband or how to live elegantly or how to throw a party on a budget.

Again, I couldn't help but wonder why someone with so much to hide would go on a reality television show. She had to know the pictures were going to surface at some point.

Did she think the boost in her book sales was worth *this* kind of—well, *literal* exposure?

I've never understood the puritanical attitudes toward nudity and the human body. What's the big deal? I used to dance in a thong or underwear for dollars in gay bars. Even when I wasn't go-go boying, I used to go out dancing all the time, and I always took my shirt off on the dance floor. Rarely did I wear underwear when I went out dancing.

Frank wrestles in front of cheering crowds wearing little more than a bikini.

These pictures getting out would have finished Chloe in her social circles. The conservative, prudish ladies of the Garden District would have frozen her out—if she'd survived doing the show with her position intact.

But that gave *Chloe* more of a motive to kill someone, not made her more likely to be a victim.

Remy would have killed to keep the pictures from coming out. He would have shared the humiliation and social ostracizing with her.

When I'd asked how they got the pictures, Amanda had explained that once Margery got the cease-and-desist letter from the Valences' lawyer, the two of them took matters into their own hands. Like many wealthy women with a score to settle, they'd hired a private eye to dig up any and all dirt available on Chloe.

Their private eye had dug up these pictures of Chloe—and the equally sordid ones at the bottom of the stack, the ones of Remy in flagrante delicto with another man.

And then it hit me: Margery's plan had been to bring the pictures to the taping of the reunion show, *intending to expose the two of them on camera.*

I shivered involuntarily.

Margery was clearly not someone whose bad side you wanted to be on.

Damn, that was some cold shit.

Part of the shows' appeal was pretending it was reality—the fights, the feuds, the arguments, and the overall silliness of grown women behaving like tweens. We viewers liked to think camera crews just followed them around all day filming everything they did and it was later edited into a cohesive season of episodes, with storylines for each character and scenes plucked from filming that bolstered the stories without boring the viewer with all the mundane, everyday stuff.

But I wasn't dumb enough to think that none of it was staged. Sure, they may not have actual *scripts* and lines to learn, but that didn't mean producers and assistants didn't tweak the ladies somewhat. "You know what Chloe said?"

There wasn't any way the women could possibly know what was said in their talking head interviews unless they were told by someone involved with production. Some of the Dames tried to convince people that the drama was manufactured and manipulated out of them.

It wasn't too hard to believe.

After all, no one watched to see the women getting along.

It was all about the drama, with each women trying to be good television to ensure they'd return the following season. Each woman blogged for the Diva TV website after each episode aired, and viewers could post comments. The viewers were encouraged to take sides in the fights and feuds.

And of course, every celebrity "news" magazine had pretty

much abandoned film and television stars to focus on this new breed of celebrity—narcissists who liked to air their dirty laundry on national television. There was an entire industry based on all this manufactured drama. It was one reason my mother hated the shows so much—in her opinion, they made the women look bad, and by extension, made all women look bad.

"Catfights are typical patriarchy bullshit," she would rant. "Because women don't support and nurture each other. This is the image of women that men want to perpetuate...and the people who watch? The worst kinds of gossips, only they think it's okay because they don't actually know the people they're gossiping about...which is really sad."

She kind of had a point, but she still watched.

The other franchises of the show's storylines pretty much followed the classic tropes refined on the old soap operas—misunderstandings, back-stabbing, talking behind each other's backs.

But the New Orleans bitches weren't playing around—they'd raised the ante in ways I would have never dreamed of—and I was sure even Eric Brewer hadn't expected things to get so far out of hand—assuming his death had something to do with the show.

Threatening each other with lawyers and hiring private detectives to dig up dirt on the other cast members was raising the bar far higher than any of the other shows had ever dared to go.

Not to mention the struggle over the Barron restaurant empire.

What had Rebecca Barron said? *Fidelis thought Steve was going to marry her, and he married me instead. She's helping my stepsons try to take the company away from me.*

It was possible Fidelis had no qualms about sleeping with a father and son—but most people outside of a daytime soap would. Serena, Margery, and Amanda all three agreed there was some animosity between Chloe and Fidelis that predated filming—and Billy Barron was the only link that had turned up so far.

Billy Barron.

It always came back to Billy Barron, didn't it?

Billy had no reason to want Eric dead.

They'd argued the night of the premiere...but I also only had Rebecca's word for that. Billy had denied it.

Who would want both Eric and Chloe dead, though? And why? Those murders had to be connected, but how?

And how could someone have gotten up to the top floor of the Royal Aquitaine, killed Eric, and then gotten to the Garden District to kill Chloe so quickly?

Without being seen by anyone?

It was all making my head hurt.

New Orleans society is so insular—there are feuds between people and families that have been going on for so long even those directly involved don't remember what started them in the first place. So it had to have come up during the casting process that the four of them were connected from high school. They'd cast Margery instead of Amanda, and Billy turned out to also be sleeping with Chloe.

And his stepmother had been cast, too.

It was almost like...like the show had been cast this way *on purpose*.

Billy was the link between all of them—except Serena. She was the only one with no connection to him.

At least, no connection I knew about.

He was the key. I was sure he wasn't the killer, but all of this circled back to him somehow.

Eric couldn't have known all these connections beforehand.

Damn it, Brandon, call me back al-fucking-ready, okay?

The Uber pulled up in front of my house, and I thanked the driver as I got out, digging my keys out of my pocket. I had just put the key into the lock when a voice in a thick accent whispered from behind me, "You make such an easy target, Scotty."

My blood ran cold for a moment before I recognized the voice. I spun around in delight, a big grin on my face.

It was my two favorite lesbian Mossad agents in the world, Lindy and Rhoda, aka the Ninja Lesbians. They were old friends of Colin's from his own Mossad days; he had trained them both. We'd met when they came crashing through my living room windows when—well, it's a long story. Rhoda and Lindy had since become good friends of ours, coming to visit us in New Orleans or meeting us some fun place for a couple of weeks of R&R. They were lots of fun—both had great senses of humor, and both could put away booze like it was going out of style. Like Colin, they seemed to be able to do almost anything. They were also a couple. Rhoda was a little older than Lindy, but both were beautiful, strong women.

I'm always grateful they're on our side.

"It's so good to see you both!" I held out my arms and they came in for a hug.

"Any word on Taylor?" Lindy asked, after crushing me in a bear hug and planting a kiss on my cheek. Slight and pretty and petite, Lindy is deceptively strong.

"Did Frank call you?" I asked, turning the key and opening the gate. I stood aside to let them in first and shut the door behind me. "How did you get here so fast?"

"We were on our way here already," Rhoda said. "Who knew it got so cold in New Orleans? I thought this was supposed to be the tropics." Rhoda had a thick Eastern European accent, but her English was always perfect.

"Why?"

They exchanged a glance when they got to the courtyard.

"Oh, come on," I said, waving them to follow me up the stairs. "If you were already on your way here—"

"All right," Lindy replied. "We'll tell you, but let's wait till we are all together. That way we won't have to explain it all over again to Frank, too."

"Frank did text us about Taylor," Rhoda said as we went up the steps. "Still no word?"

"No," I replied. I felt so much better now that they were here to help.

If anyone could find him, it would be the Ninja Lesbians.

The warmth of the apartment felt so damned good I didn't ever want to go back outside. Frank was in the living room. There was a brief flurry of hugs and kisses. Frank gave me a big hug and kissed my cheek. He smelled fresh and clean, like he'd just showered. "I'm sorry, it was shitty of me to not let you know where I was," he whispered in my ear. "I just needed to let off some steam and didn't think."

"It's okay," I whispered back. "I'll punish you later."

He winked. "Counting on it." He walked over to the desk and picked up his MacBook Air. "Everyone, have a seat. I actually know what happened to Taylor," he said grimly. He turned the television on to the Apple TV setting and then plugged a flash drive into the USB port. The television screen went blue for just a moment, and then a time-stamped image of our sidewalk popped up on the screen. Pedestrians walking, cars driving past on Decatur Street.

"What is this?" I asked, sitting down next to Lindy and Rhoda on the couch.

"I remembered that the bar on the corner has a surveillance camera," Frank replied grimly. "The manager was willing to let me make a copy of their recording." He made a face. "For a hundred bucks, the asshole. But it was worth it."

"You need your own cameras," Rhoda replied. "That way you see who is at gate and can keep an eye on courtyard."

I made a mental note, kicking myself for not thinking of it myself.

We watched as Taylor got out of an Uber and let himself into the building. Another couple of minutes passed, and then a dark panel van drove up and parked in front of our building. Someone wearing a hoodie got out of the van and walked up to our intercom. He pressed the button, talked into the intercom for a few moments, and stepped back away from it. He was also wearing a peacoat and had what I sometimes call a redneck body—you know, where the guy has really thin, pencil-like legs and an oversized upper body? He was built like that. After a few more seconds passed, the gate opened. Taylor stepped out again, holding the gate open and gesturing for them to come inside. Instead, the man grabbed him and pulled him away from the gate. Taylor fought back, but two more men got out of the van. They also grabbed him, dragged him to the vehicle, and tossed him inside. During the struggle the first guy's hoodie was pulled away from his head.

He looked sort of familiar, like I'd seen him before, but I didn't know who he was.

Frank froze the frame. He walked over to the television and tapped the man's face with his index finger. His face was red, and that muscle in his jaw that always twitches when he is angry was working overtime. "That," he said quietly, "is my fucking brother-in-law."

"Taylor's father?" Rhoda sounded incredulous.

"The one and only."

My heart sank. "Oh my God," I whispered. That was why the guy looked familiar. Looking at the freeze frame, I could see Taylor's eyes, the crown of his forehead.

"We've got to move," Frank went on. "If this is what I think it was—I've tried calling my sister, but she's either not near her phone or not picking up because she knows what's going to happen when I get ahold of her."

"What do you think this is?" Rhoda asked.

"They're taking him to a gay conversion camp, aren't they?" My words sounded hollow and far away to me. They'd threatened Taylor with this when he came out to them, after his year studying in Paris, when he'd come back to Alabama and told them the truth. When he refused to go to the conversion therapy camp, they'd disowned him and thrown him out. That was when he called his uncle for help and stayed with friends from school in Tuscaloosa before Frank could get him a plane ticket to come to New Orleans and live with us.

It was hard to believe gay conversion therapy was still a thing, that people still believed you could cure homosexuality.

But ignorance sometimes just won't die.

The thought of what those people could do to Taylor in that camp was terrifying.

"Is simple," Rhoda said with a chilling smile. "We find out where camp is and we get him out by whatever means necessary."

Frank advanced the recording frame by frame, until the van pulled away from the curb. He froze the picture again and enlarged the license plate.

You can't live in New Orleans and not be able to recognize an Alabama license plate.

"Lindy, search the databases for that license plate," Rhoda instructed. Lindy nodded and pulled out her own MacBook Air from her shoulder bag, walking over to the dining room table and turning it on.

"Can't we take this to the police?" I asked. "Taylor's not a minor, and he obviously went along against his will. Doesn't this count as kidnapping? And the Alabama plates—they're going to go across state lines. This brings in the FBI, doesn't it?"

"The line can be a little blurry because it's his fucking dad, but yes, it's kidnapping," Frank said. "I've already called the local office. I'm waiting for them to call back."

"Email the video to Venus—"

"Already did," Frank replied. "I'm waiting to hear back from them. And what were you doing at Margery Lautenschlaeger's?"

I looked at the manila envelope in my lap. I made a face. "Well, I guess Margery and her daughter Amanda wanted to weigh in on the murders." I tapped the envelope. "Apparently Margery hired a private eye once Chloe served her with the cease-and-desist, and her private eye dug up some serious dirt on the Valences." I placed it on the coffee table. "The images are pretty...eye-opening."

Frank didn't move to pick them up. "Terrific."

"My guess is she was planning on springing them on Chloe at the reunion," I went on. "It would have been good television."

"Do you think Eric knew about the pictures?"

"Who is this Eric and Margery?" Rhoda asked.

We quickly explained everything that had been going on since Friday—had it only been a couple of days, really? We left out the part about Colin killing the Russian in the apartment in the early hours of Saturday morning—that was need-to-know information, and no one needed to know it. I knew we could trust them—but Frank gave me a look and so we said nothing.

Rhoda shook her head. "You boys. Never a dull moment in your lives, is there?"

"Got it," Lindy called from the dining table. "The van is registered to Pine Bluff, which is some kind of retreat run by the Church of Christ the Lord in Corinth County, Alabama."

"Which is where my sister and brother-in-law live, and that's the church they go to."

"So they're probably heading back up there—"

The buzzing of our intercom startled us all into silence. Frank walked over to the wall and pressed the intercom button. "Yes?"

A woman's voice came through. "Is this where Frank Sobieski lives?"

"I'll be right down." He turned and took a deep breath. "Perfect." The muscle in his jaw jumped again.

"What's wrong?" I asked.

His eyes met mine. "It's my sister."

CHAPTER NINETEEN
QUEEN OF WANDS, REVERSED
A woman who is strict to a fault and domineering

Whatever I was expecting, the reality of Taylor's mom came as a bit of a surprise.

I'd spent so much time judging her over the last two years that I'd come to think of her as not being human. It was impossible for me to imagine any mother so awful that she could toss her child away like garbage for the crime of being gay.

But she was human. She didn't have fangs, nor snakes for hair, nor claws for hands, nor scales instead of skin. She wasn't a Gorgon.

When I was young, Mom once told me the most horrifying aspect of human monsters was that they didn't *look* like monsters. "On the outside they look like nice, friendly, kind people," she said with a sad shake of her head, "but inside they are monsters. Their minds are closed, they embrace darkness instead of light and love… and their minds will do backflips to justify their dark feelings and beliefs. If we learned *anything* from Nazi Germany, it's that anyone can be a monster. Anyone."

But the truth of Taylor's mother was that she was just a small-town Southern woman like so many others who didn't know how to deal with a reality she wasn't prepared for nor considered possible.

It didn't make her likable, but it did make her understandable… and maybe a little pitiable.

Teresa Sobieski Wheeler was a rather short woman who bore no resemblance to her brother Frank. The only similarity was the same clear, almost round, heavy-lidded gray eyes. She couldn't have been much taller than five feet, and the fact she was roundish made her look shorter. She was carrying maybe an extra twenty pounds, which softened her chin and filled out her cheeks. She was wearing more makeup than necessary—blush and eye shadow and lipstick, powder and eyeliner and mascara. Her shoulder-length gray hair was tucked behind her ears, and small diamonds sparkled on both lobes. Her long gray winter coat had faux fur trim at the neck and wrists. If not for the extra weight, her chin would be as sharp as Frank and Taylor's, and she'd have the same cheekbones. Her eyebrows were plucked into thin lines, her nose long and crooked, her lips thin. She looked like that nice lady who lives next door and is always making cookies on every family sitcom aired since the dawn of television—the one who always wears a nice dress and pearls and pumps while she cooks and cleans and whose entire life revolves around her family, whose entire existence was built around her children.

So how could she have just turned her back on her youngest the way she had?

What kind of parent *does* that? What kind of human?

And somehow thinks they'll still go to heaven?

I may not be a Christian, but I went to Catholic school. My takeaway on Christianity—all religion, really—was you were supposed to love people no matter what, and always be kind.

Frank took her coat and hung it on the track in the hallway. She was wearing a fuzzy pink sweater, imitation angora, over loose-fitting mom jeans with a high waist. Her gray eyes twinkled when she smiled tentatively at me.

Since Taylor had come to live with us, I'd rehearsed in my head any number of things I wanted to say to her should I ever get the chance.

But seeing her in the flesh…no matter how much I thought she deserved it, I didn't want to be cutting and mean.

I took a deep breath. She held out her hand as Frank introduced us, and after a pause I took it, giving it a little shake, wanting to let go as quickly as possible. Her hand was warm, soft, and damp. But she wouldn't let go of my hand, clamping her other one over the top of mine. "Thank you for taking in my son," she said. "It's been a real load off my mind knowing that Taylor is here safe with you both."

You wouldn't have to worry if you were a better parent.

Frank gave me a warning look as I opened my mouth, and

instead of saying what I was thinking I replied, "Taylor's a great kid and we're lucky to have him staying with us." I smiled back at her. "If anything, we should be thanking you."

A gay can always say something that can be taken two ways, like it's somehow hard-wired in our DNA.

She had the decency to look embarrassed, dropping my hand like she'd been burned.

"And these are our friends Rhoda and Lindy," Frank said, gesturing at the dining room table. Neither had looked up from their computer screens, but both waved when he said their names.

"Is Taylor here?" Teresa asked, sitting down in one of my wingback chairs without being invited to sit.

Go ahead and make yourself at home. I bit my tongue, reminding myself, *She's Frank's sister, and no matter what, she's Taylor's mom, so you be polite and find out what she wants.*

It's not a coincidence that he's missing and she just shows up out of the blue.

I cleared my throat, but Frank gave me a warning look.

"No, Taylor isn't here," Frank replied, and when I saw the muscle in his cheek twitching, I realized he was just as furious as me, but controlling himself. "As you well know, Teresa. You didn't just suddenly decide, after almost twenty years, that you needed to see your brother. So why don't you tell us why you're really here?"

Twenty years?

She looked stricken, putting her hands to her face. "So, Ron did get here before me?" Her voice shook a little. "I'm so sorry, Frank, I really am. As soon as I..." Her voice trailed off. She looked at me. "I tried," she said finally in a very small voice. "I tried to talk him out of it. I told him it was wrong. You have to believe me."

"Where is he?" I heard myself asking. "What have you people done with him?"

"Taylor is over eighteen," Frank said. "You know Ron and his buddies can be charged with kidnapping. That's a minimum of fifteen to twenty in federal prison, Teresa. It doesn't matter if he's Taylor's father. You can't just fucking kidnap someone off the street."

"I know. I told him it was wrong, it was a mistake." She was wringing her hands. "I know you won't believe me but he's...Ron... well, he's doing this because he loves Taylor."

"Taylor," I said, "can do without that kind of love."

Frank licked his lips. "I have security footage from the bar on the corner, showing Ron and some other thugs grabbing Taylor and forcing him to get into a van. We were just about to call the police when you arrived." He folded his arms, biceps bulging. "I can't think of a single reason why I shouldn't go ahead and call them."

"Please, Frank, don't do that. Ron…it's wrong. What we did was wrong, I know that, I've always known that…I begged him not to do this." A single tear rolled down her cheek. "Frank, I don't know what to do here." She wiped at her eyes. "He's my son. I love him. But Ron's my husband…"

"And one should always choose one's spouse over one's child." Frank nodded. "It's the Christian thing to do, right?"

"I said I was wrong—"

"The license plate is registered to a Duncan Fairchild, from some small town in upstate Mississippi," Lindy interrupted without looking up from her computer. "And the van does have satellite service." Her tone got a little smug, a smile playing at her lips. "So, we should be able to track it down easily once we hack into the company's signal. Shouldn't be long now."

Teresa Wheeler looked confused. "What…what's going on here?"

"Do it, Lindy," Frank commanded before turning back to his sister. "Do you know Duncan Fairchild?"

She exhaled heavily, wiping at her eyes with a handkerchief she'd retrieved from her brown suede purse. "I told Ron this was a mistake and to leave it alone," she said, her voice shaking. "But you know what he's like, Frank. Once he gets an idea in his head… there's no changing it. He's always been that way."

"You mean like disowning your son?" I couldn't stop myself. "Throwing him out with just the clothes on his back?"

She opened and closed her mouth a couple of times. She swallowed. "I—" She paused, looked down at her hands. She took a deep breath and looked at me. "You probably think I'm a terrible person."

I didn't look at Frank. "You're right, I do."

"I'm sorry to have to meet you like this, under these

circumstances." She looked from me to Frank. "I'm happy you've found someone, Frank, I am. It's just—"

"You love me, but you can't approve of my sinful lifestyle," Frank said tonelessly. "I'm very aware of how you feel, Teresa. You've always made that clear."

"Frank, I'm so sorry. I never...I never should have said those things to you." Teresa started twisting her handkerchief into knots. "I know I was wrong, Frank. I was wrong," she said softly. "I love you and I want you back in my life, Frank. I've missed you so much."

"We can talk about that later." Frank dismissed her with a wave of his hand. He was being much nicer than I would've been. "Duncan Fairchild. You need to start talking."

"Duncan is a deacon of our church, he's only been in Corinth for a couple of years now. He's a good man, just misguided." She cleared her throat. "He...well, when Taylor left..."

"When you and Ron threw him out," Frank corrected her.

She nodded slowly. "When we threw him out, after...after he left, we weren't sure if we'd done the right thing or not." She looked around the room before continuing. "I didn't want to throw him out, Frank, you have to believe that. I...I couldn't agree with his sin, with his lifestyle choice—"

"The only choice is whether to live a lie to please people who should love you no matter what, or to be true to yourself and be happy," Frank snapped. "You'd rather he'd be miserable."

Her eyes flashed. "Do you want me to tell you about Duncan or not?"

"I will interrupt and correct you every time you say something insensitive, insulting, and offensive," Frank replied evenly. "I'm gay, your son is gay, my partner is gay, Rhoda and Lindy are lesbians and they're in love. You're outnumbered here, sis. You're not in your backwater church in your judgmental little town now, and you don't have to be here. *You* came *here*. Anytime you want to leave, the door is right there." He smiled. "We can find Taylor without your help."

"I'm sorry." She looked down at her hands. "After Ron blew up and Taylor left, I called Duncan to come over to our house, to counsel us and to pray with us. I was hoping Duncan would convince Ron he'd been wrong, that the right thing to do was bring him home and accept him and pray for him, but that—that wasn't what Duncan thought we should do." She took another deep breath. "Duncan told us he knew of a place...a place in Mississippi, a church camp he was part owner of, and that lots of kids like Taylor went there to get help, to turn their back on their sinful choices, and came out as good strong Christian men."

"A conversion therapy camp?" It took all my willpower not to jump across the room and strangle her. Just the thought of Taylor being in one of those torture chambers... "You were going to send him to conversion therapy?"

"I didn't think it was the right thing to do," she replied. She sounded miserable, and I almost felt sorry for her.

Almost.

"But I'd already called you, and Taylor was on his way down here," her voice shook a little bit, "and so I didn't think I'd have to worry about the camp anymore, you know? But Ron...I guess Ron and Duncan kept talking about it. Without me there."

To her credit, she was convincing. She sounded like a confused mother, torn between her religion and doing what was best for her son.

Which, of course, is how they fool you.

This was the woman who'd not only denied her brother but happily gone along with her husband when he threw out her youngest son. Now she was saying she didn't think conversion therapy camp in rural Mississippi was the best thing for Taylor.

I supposed I should give her some credit for coming around at last.

If we could trust her.

"Well, Ron started bringing it up again lately, you know, about how Taylor was living a life of sin down here and going against God, and Duncan was sure if we just had him spend a week or two at the camp, he'd see the light and—"

Enough with the crocodile tears, lady. Get to the point.

"And he kept saying that if we took Taylor to Camp Cedars of Lebanon, we'd get our son back. So, when that woman called us on Saturday to tell us about the trouble he was in—why didn't you call me, Frank?"

"You know damned well why I didn't call you," Frank replied. "And what woman called you?"

"She didn't tell me her name," Teresa went on. "She just told me to look up Eric Brewer's murder online, and when I saw that there was an unnamed young man in his hotel suite with him when he was murdered, it was Taylor." She started crying again.

I am a sympathetic person—sometimes maybe too much so for my own good. But her tears didn't move me at all.

I felt nothing listening to her cry. Nothing at all.

Who was I turning into? How could I listen to a woman cry and not feel anything?

"So, you know, there we were, worried and not knowing what to do. And then Ron got the bright idea that we needed to come down here, get Duncan to come down here with us, and convince Taylor to come home and spend some time at the camp, you know? None of this would have happened if he wasn't gay."

"None of this would have happened if you and your husband hadn't thrown him out for being gay, like a piece of garbage," Lindy said from the dining room table. She was still looking at the computer screen, her fingers flying over the keyboard. "So, it's actually kind of your fault, isn't it? He'd still be going to school in Tuscaloosa, wouldn't he?"

"I deserve that," Teresa said softly. "I deserve worse. Frank, you have to believe me, when I looked up what a conversion therapy camp really does, I knew I had to come down here and stop Ron and Duncan. If it means he's gay and goes to hell, then fine. Fine. I don't want them torturing my son."

"I've got them," Lindy said triumphantly. "Their vehicle is parked at a motel out on Airline Highway, past the airport. And I've run Ron Wheeler's credit...he has booked two rooms at the Kingfish Motor Lodge." She pushed her chair back and stood up. "Shall we go retrieve Taylor?"

"Maybe we should call the police," Frank said. "Let them handle it."

Rhoda gave him a terrifying smile. "Or we can handle it ourselves and then turn the video over to the police, let them handle it. Kidnapping is like twenty years minimum, isn't it?"

Teresa gasped as Frank nodded. "Something like that."

"Frank, please..."

"You want us to retrieve him?" Rhoda asked. "You and Scotty

can wait here, Frank. Plausible deniability." She cracked her knuckles. "Besides, I love nothing more than humiliating these kinds of men." Her smile curdled my blood. "Nothing like having their ass handed to them by two women to make these real men types understand they are *little* men."

"I'm coming with you," I replied. "Frank, you stay here with your sister and keep an eye on her. Take her phone."

Frank grabbed her purse from her and removed her phone.

"You don't have to—" Teresa started to say before Frank cut her off.

"I don't trust you, Teresa," Frank said. "And you're not going to warn your asshole husband or his asshole friends that we're coming."

She didn't reply.

I grabbed my coat and followed Rhoda and Lindy down the back stairs. They had rented a black SUV with tinted windows. I got into the back but leaned forward between the two front seats as Rhoda started the car. "I know you can handle yourself," Lindy said as she buckled her seat belt, "but let me and Rhoda do the heavy lifting, okay? We'll take out the kidnappers, you focus on getting Taylor out of there." She opened the glove box and removed a Glock with a silencer attached to the end. She made sure it was loaded, slipping it into her waistband. She then did the same thing with another Glock before handing it to Rhoda, who dropped it into her coat pocket as we headed out of the Quarter. We got on I-10 at the Orleans street on-ramp and were soon flying through traffic.

Which of course came to a complete stop right where we reached the I-10 and I-90 interchange.

"American traffic," Rhoda growled in her thick accent. "Your highways don't make sense anywhere, but the ones in New Orleans…" She shook her head.

"Have you two heard from Colin lately?" I asked, trying to make it sound as casual as I possibly could.

They looked at each other before Lindy turned to look at me. "Not for a few days. Why?"

"You wouldn't happen to know what he's working on, would you?" The traffic had started moving again at a glacial pace, but at least we weren't sitting still. "Have you heard any rumors or chatter?" Saying *chatter* made me feel silly. I wasn't an international agent, nor did I really know how any of that worked...which was kind of how I'd always liked it.

Until recently.

"What's going on, Scotty?" Rhoda asked as she changed lanes, cutting off an eighteen-wheeler who blew his horn at her. She flipped him off in the rearview mirror, shouting, "You wanna try me, dough boy?" She shook her head. "Sorry. Road rage. I know I should not let idiot drivers get to me."

Lindy patted her leg. "You're doing fine, honey." She turned back to me. "We've heard that he's—that Blackledge—is trying to infiltrate a part of the Russian mob that launders money for a terrorist gang causing some trouble in the Middle East, especially in Syria. Syria is such a mess." She shrugged her shoulders. "We hear these things, you know, because anything involving terror is of interest to our country. It almost always comes back to Israel, at some point."

"If we didn't treat the Palestinians so badly," Rhoda glanced in the rearview mirror and changed lanes again, "they might not be so open to terrorism."

"Yes, yes, but this has nothing to do with the occupation," Lindy said. "We assumed Colin would be working on that, as their top operative. Why do you ask?"

If I couldn't trust Lindy and Rhoda, I couldn't trust anyone. I quickly sketched out what I'd walked into when I got home from the party on Friday night.

"Bestuzhev?" Rhoda whistled. "He's a very bad man, Scotty. We shall all sleep better tonight knowing he's in the grave. Colin saved many lives by killing that monster."

"So, when Taylor disappeared..."

"Oh, God." Lindy went pale as we took the Williams Boulevard exit. "You must have thought some of Bestuzhev's cohorts had taken him!"

"How safe are we in the apartment?" I asked. "If his cover is blown and the Russians know where to find him—"

"Bestuzhev might have been the only one who knew," Rhoda pointed out. "You can't do covert ops if you're constantly reporting back in. It's always need-to-know, which is why these bastards are so hard to catch. He might have found out about Colin's private life, came to New Orleans to check it out, but Colin found him and took care of the problem."

It wasn't as reassuring as I would have liked, but it was still a relief.

"I'll check in to see if there's been any chatter," Lindy said, pulling out her satellite phone, her thumbs flying over the keyboard. "If anyone has compromised Blackledge, that news won't be kept quiet for long. I'm so sorry, Scotty."

I didn't answer. We turned onto Airline Highway, heading out past the airport to the seedier side of Airline, where the cheap motels were frequented by prostitutes and drug dealers. The Kingfish Motor Court was a relic from the 1950s, a U-shaped two-story building with a fenced swimming pool in the center of the parking lot. There weren't many cars parked there, but I recognized one. "There's the van."

"According to the motel computer, they are in rooms 15 and 16," Lindy said as Rhoda pulled into a spot next to the white van. The two doors were very close to each other, with cheap, dirty curtains hanging in the filthy picture windows. Lindy pulled out her heat-seeking goggles and trained them on room 15. "No one in there, but I've got three human shapes in room 16," she said. "One is seated in a chair, might even be tied up, the other two are moving around." She pulled out her gun. "Are we ready?"

Rhoda and Lindy moved so quickly they were almost to the door of Room 16 before I realized they'd gotten out of the SUV. Guns drawn, Rhoda kicked in the door and Lindy ran in, her gun at the ready as Rhoda came in behind her. I could hear shouts and thuds as I opened my own door and dashed to the room, looking around to see if the noise had attracted attention.

It hadn't. One of the appeals of places like the Kingfish was no one paid attention to anything that didn't concern them.

It was all over by the time I stepped inside. Two doughy-looking rednecks were lying unconscious on the floor, and Rhoda was using their belts to tie their wrists together behind their backs. Taylor was tied to a chair, his mouth gagged. I ran over to him and removed the gag.

"Scotty, thank God," Taylor said. He sounded exhausted.

Rhoda tossed me a Swiss Army knife and I cut the cords securing him to the chair.

"Come on, boo, we're going home." I helped him to his feet. "Are you okay?"

He nodded. "Just tired."

As I helped him out to the van, he told me what happened. Going to school had been a mistake. He couldn't pay attention in class and being around people—particularly when someone came up behind him unexpectedly—made him uncomfortable, so he'd left early. He'd been home just a few minutes when the buzzer went off. He'd been stunned to hear his father's voice and went down to talk to him at the gate. He hadn't taken his keys or phone with him because he thought they'd just talk, and if things were cool, he'd let his father inside. But when he opened the gate his father and another man grabbed him and dragged him to the van. "They said they were going to take me to conversion therapy." He shuddered as Rhoda and Lindy came back out, closing the door behind them.

"Your mom's back at home," I said, but before he could answer, Rhoda and Lindy were back inside, strapping their seat belts.

"Bound and gagged," Lindy said cheerfully as Rhoda backed out of the spot. "Housekeeping will find them in the morning."

My phone vibrated. I pulled it out to see a text message from Paige:

Fidelis Vandiver is dead, same way as Eric and Chloe. Shall we pool resources?

I texted back, *meet me at my apartment.*

CHAPTER TWENTY
TWO OF CUPS
Harmony and cooperation

Driving back into the city from Kenner is never a pleasant experience, and this time was no exception.

Traffic bogged down around the Clearview Parkway exchange, Rhoda slowing the car to little more than a crawl and completely stopping at times. New Orleanians tend to back-seat drive when riding with a driver Not From Here, but I resisted the urge. She was, after all, a highly trained professional—so who better to deal with the shitty I-10 eastbound traffic disaster?

I sat in the back seat with Taylor. He seemed okay, all things considered. He was pale, dark smudges beneath his bloodshot, glassy eyes. He just stared out the window. Every few moments he would take a deep breath and let it out slowly.

"I know it doesn't seem like it now, but everything will be okay," I whispered. "Trust me."

He looked at me, his pain and anguish written so clearly on his face my heart hurt and I resisted bursting into tears of my own.

Stay strong, Scotty, you have to stay strong for him, I kept repeating in my head. *Stay focused on him. Pray for a brave heart.*

"I'm okay," he mumbled, turning to look back out the window again.

Are you, though? I bit my tongue to not say it out loud.

I took his hand and squeezed it. He didn't try to pull his away, and after a few seconds squeezed mine back.

That had to be good, right?

He seemed *different.* The light in his eyes had dimmed, and the usual high, positive energy he radiated was muted. He was going to need therapy. I made a mental note to start asking around for recommendations.

Is there anything worse than watching someone you love suffer and being unable to do anything to make it better?

I looked back out my car window. We were passing underneath the parkway bridge, with the Causeway Boulevard interchange gauntlet yet to run.

"This traffic is ridiculous for such a small city," Rhoda said from the front seat, glancing back at us in the rearview mirror. "Everything okay back there? Awful quiet."

Lindy looked over her seat. "Taylor, do you need anything? Should we stop for food or something to drink?"

"I just want to go home," he said morosely. "I just want this to be all over." The second sentence was a whisper, one I barely heard.

My heart broke again.

What kind of parent could do such a thing to their child?

I squeezed his hand again.

This time, he didn't squeeze back.

The first time I was kidnapped—and yes, it has happened to me often enough that it's a running joke for Colin and Frank—it took me a while to get past it. I had nightmares, off and on, for about a month or so. Sudden noises made me flinch. People coming up to me from behind or just out of eyeshot made my heart race. When the animal activists had kidnapped me and Taylor last year (it's a long story), he'd bounced back from it pretty fast. He saw it as an adventure rather than the terrifying experience it actually had been.

But *this?* Being kidnapped by his father and almost dragged away to conversion therapy camp?

This was going to take him a good while to get over. I'm sure he never expected his dad to ever go that far to the dark side.

I thanked the Goddess again for blessing me with my parents.

Rhoda started picking up speed once we crossed the parish line back into Orleans. Taylor said, almost too quietly for me to hear, "I'm sorry." He cleared his throat. "I owe you and Frank and Colin and your family so much…I hate to be so much trouble." His voice broke, his eyes welling with tears. "I don't ever want to be trouble."

"Taylor." I pulled him into a bear hug. "You're never a bother, you're no trouble at all. Ever." I kissed the top of his head as his rigid body began to relax in my arms. "We're family, Taylor. Never ever forget that. I know my family is a lot to deal with, but every last one of them would walk barefoot through fire for you. Once you're a Bradley, you're always a Bradley."

He started crying then, his head down on my shoulder, sobbing. "I'm so…so suh-suh-sorry."

"Shh, it's okay." I held him tighter, stroking his back, petting his head. "Go ahead and cry, get it all out, Taylor. None of this is your fault, baby, don't blame yourself, okay? And we're never going to stop loving you. Ever. Understood?"

I could have gladly killed his bastard father right then.

"Everything okay back there?" Lindy smiled back at us.

"Thank you for rescuing me." Taylor pulled away from me, wiping his face with his sleeves.

"Our pleasure," Rhoda replied. "We love kicking the asses of homophobic rednecks who probably belittle women. Their balls may eventually drop down again but not soon."

Taylor laughed. It was the first time he'd laughed since Friday night at the party.

I almost started crying myself.

We went around the curve in the highway taking us past the Superdome, and I remembered. "Um, Taylor?"

"Yeah?"

Just rip the bandage right off. "Honey, I hate to tell you this, but your mother is waiting for us back at home. With Frank."

"I don't want to see or talk to her. Not now, maybe not ever." His voice was cold, emotionless. I texted Frank: *Taylor doesn't want to see Teresa. She needs to leave. We'll be there very soon, coming up on the French Quarter exit.*

Frank's response was immediate: *okay. I'll get rid of her.*

"Frank's going to get rid of her," I said.

Taylor didn't answer, just looked back out the window.

As we took the Esplanade exit and headed through Treme, I looked him over. There were scratches and bruises on his neck. A hideously angry long red scratch ran down the side of his face, almost exactly where Frank's scar was.

Life never gives you anything you can't handle, I thought, *it's how you handle it that matters.*

We'd get him professional help. We'd get him the best goddamned therapist money could buy. We'd give him all the emotional support and love he could handle. Whatever he needed.

And we'd find out who really killed Eric Brewer.

And Chloe.

But what about Bestuzhev? Colin? Is the apartment safe?

Yeah, thanks, brain.

I tried using some yoga techniques to clear my mind but it didn't work. I hadn't felt this cloudy-minded since…

Well, since the levees broke.

I pushed that thought right back out of my mind. That was the last place I needed to go now. I tried shutting those memories behind a locked door in my head, but *have you ever dealt with it* flashed through my head. Maybe I had. Maybe I hadn't. Maybe I'd been carrying trauma scars for over twelve years. Who knows? That was—well, it was so long ago, and I was happy. I have a great life. This was just another bump in the road of life, and we'd get past it.

We always did. What choice did we have?

Sure, when a storm came into the Gulf possibly heading our way, my stomach would clench, and I felt a surge of momentary panic—but it always passed, and I never lost my head.

I think everyone who lived through the levee failure after Katrina was the same way.

How could we not be?

And Taylor was strong, a good kid with a level head, a strong sense of responsibility, and a compassionate heart. He'd get through this. It would be tough, but he had Frank and me and Colin and the rest of our family to lean on. We'd get him through this. We might not have been his birth family, but we were family now. Everyone on my mother's side accepted him without question. The Bradleys were a bit more grudging, but my dad's side of the family has always been problematic.

They still didn't know how to wrap their heads around me being gay and having *two* partners instead of one.

But at least they try, you know? They've gotten better over the years.

And at least they'd never tried to put me into conversion therapy—never even suggested it.

But if they had, Mom would have killed them all, burned the big house on State Street to the ground, and sown the ground with salt so nothing would ever grow there again.

My mom is really the best.

All the parking spots on Decatur Street were taken when Rhoda went around the corner, so she just put on her hazard lights and pulled over next to the curb on the other side of the street to let us out.

It was dark and gray and cold, and felt like the rain was going to start again at any moment.

I was unlocking the gate when Paige called my name. "You guys go on up," I said, hugging Taylor. "Scooter wants to see you," I whispered. "And I'll just talk to Paige for a minute, okay?"

He nodded and slipped inside. Lindy closed the gate behind them as Paige gave me a hug. "How are you doing? You look like death."

"Thanks. It's been an interesting day." The understatement of the year. I felt bone-tired and emotionally drained. "And it's fucking freezing out here."

"I've got a table at Envie."

Café Envie sat on the uptown lakeside corner of Decatur and Barracks. It's a nice little place that serves food and cocktails as well as coffee-based drinks. They did a brisk business, and usually there were no tables to be had. As the door swung shut behind us, I could see several tables were empty, and the hipsters who usually hung out there, typing away at laptops or playing checkers or chess, were nowhere to be seen.

"I'm just going to order something," I said. I ordered my cappuccino and paid, gave my name, and saw Paige sitting in the back with Megan Dreher when I turned away from the counter.

The side doors, always open during pleasant weather, were shut. Even so, it was still cold inside. I joined them at their table, back by the condiment stand.

"Hi, Scotty," Megan said, offering me her tiny hand. "I'm Megan Dreher. Thanks for joining us."

"Nice to meet you," I replied, slipping off my jacket and sitting down across from her. I glanced at Paige. "Why didn't you tell me she'd be here?"

"I asked her not to," Megan replied. She looked nervous. She was petite, tiny, her bones small and delicate. Her long, dark hair had reddish highlights in it and was pulled back from her triangular face with a couple of barrettes. Her eyes were hazel, almond-shaped, and framed by extraordinarily dark thick lashes. She was beautiful, although swimming in a green Tulane sweatshirt far too big for her. "She suggested I talk to you before I leave town." She flinched at the sound of the door opening behind me.

She's terrified. "Why are you leaving town?"

"It's not safe here," she replied simply, picking up her coffee cup. She wore a wedding band with an engagement ring. The diamond was surprisingly small.

The barista called my name before I could reply. I excused myself and retrieved my cappuccino.

When I sat back down, Megan went on, "You need to look at this." She reached into her bag and pulled out a file folder, which she slid across the table to me.

I opened the folder and found printouts of newspaper articles, so old they'd yellowed and faded. The article on the top had a headline that read *Newman Senior Killed in Tragic Car Accident.* There was a picture of the girl, a pretty, long-haired blonde named Deborah Holt. It was clearly her senior picture, and the date of the article was from the spring. "Deborah Holt?" I asked. "Should that name mean something to me?"

"Just read it."

I scanned the article, and my eyebrows went up when I saw that Deborah hadn't been alone when she was hit by the car—the driver was a minor and the name wasn't released, as such, but Deborah was with her friend Megan Tortorice when it happened. Megan Tortorice received minor injuries and was treated for them at Touro before being released. According to Megan, "the car saw us, the driver had to have seen us, but then she sped up and came right for us!"

"So vehicular homicide?" I asked. "I still don't see the relevance."

Megan took another sip of coffee. "My maiden name was Tortorice."

Paige leaned back in her chair, sipping her coffee with a big smile on her face, one eyebrow raised. "Are you aware that Fidelis, Megan, Amanda Lautenschlaeger, *and* Billy Barron were all in the same graduating class at Newman?"

I already knew but decided to play along, see what the two of them could tell me. "Wait—what?"

She looked like she'd just swallowed a canary. "I'm sure Venus is going to turn up this information, if she hasn't already, but don't you find it interesting this connection hasn't come up already? In *any* of the publicity for the show?" She sipped from her drink. "It's almost like *someone* doesn't want anyone to know."

"I met Amanda earlier today," I replied slowly, "and there's something not right about her. But was she involved in casting the show? She was at the premiere Friday night with Billy Barron."

"Amanda was the one who set me up with the show," Megan said. "And Fidelis. We were all friends back when we were kids." She exhaled. "Amanda was obsessed with Billy. *Obsessed.*"

"How do you mean *obsessed?*"

"I was there when it happened, Scotty. She ran Deborah down like a dog in the street. It wasn't an accident. It was *deliberate.*" She shook her head. "Billy had broken up with her and asked Deborah out. She kept saying crazy things…but I never thought she'd actually do anything, you know?"

I looked down at the clippings. "But how did she get away with it?"

Megan rolled her eyes. "Her mother is one of the richest women in America. Do the math."

"A deal was worked out where Amanda went into a mental hospital for treatment," Paige said, "and the charges were dropped, scrubbed from her records." Paige's eyes glittered. "Greased, no doubt, by Lautenschlaeger money. The judge got hefty contributions to his reelection campaigns until he retired…from Black Mountain Liquor. I've found at least one more incident where Amanda was out of control and attacked someone, and got sent off to a mental hospital yet again." She tapped the original newspaper clipping.

"Margery bought us all off," Megan said bitterly. "She paid for my college, and when I married Dave, she loaned him the money to get his business started. Whenever we need anything, all we have to do is ask Margery."

"Wow."

"Amanda didn't graduate with everyone else that year," Paige went on. "She was pulled out of school and finished the year at a private boarding school in New England." She laughed. "You know, one of those ritzy schools where princesses who get in trouble get sent to instead of juvie. Money talks."

"So, you're saying she's mentally ill, and has been since she was a teenager?"

"Yes." Megan stood up, slipping on her coat. "I'm going away for a while." She pointed at the newspaper clipping. "Now all the people who know about Amanda's dirty little secret are getting killed." She buttoned her jacket, her fingers shaking. "Well, not me. I'm getting out while the getting's good."

"But Chloe—"

"Chloe was sleeping with Billy," Paige replied. "Amanda thinks Billy belongs to *her*."

But what about Eric Brewer's murder?

"Paige knows how to reach me," Megan said. "If you need me." She got up and walked out of the coffee shop.

"Oh, and it gets better." Paige flipped through the file and pulled out another printout, which she pushed across the table. This was a copy of an old police report. It was a criminal assault case— and the person being charged was Amanda Lautenschlaeger.

The victim was Jane Barron, and the date on the report was twenty years ago.

"Jane Barron was Billy's first wife." Paige said.

I read the incident report.

Mrs. Barron was returning from an evening out with some of her coworkers (they work at a real estate management company). According to Mrs. Barron, Ms. Lautenschlaeger was hiding in the bushes at the Barron home, waiting for her to come home. She attacked her with a baseball bat, but Mrs. Barron was able to get away, running over to a neighbor's and taking refuge in their home while Ms. Lautenschlaeger screamed incoherently outside. Suspect was still screaming on the front lawn when squad cars arrived, and armed with the bat. Suspect surrendered bat without incident and didn't resist arrest.

A baseball bat.

Just like Eric and Chloe.

"Are you okay?" Paige asked. "Seriously, dude. You look terrible. Is it because Taylor was there when Eric was killed?"

I exhaled. "Taylor's father tried to kidnap him and haul him off to a gay conversion therapy camp run by someone from his church." I ran my hand over my head. It sounded crazier when said out loud.

She looked horrified. "That's still a *thing?* What the fuck is wrong with people?"

I nodded. "Well, it's in Mississippi," I said, with the typical Louisiana contempt for our neighbor state. "We were lucky to get him back without having to get the police involved." I shrugged. "We still might press charges. If Taylor wants to, I mean. He's already had a hell of a weekend."

"It's going to get worse," she replied grimly. "His name is starting to get out there as the guy who was with Eric the night he was killed." She lowered her voice, checking around to see if anyone was within hearing range. "I mean, it was already out there, but it's starting to pick up steam. I saw him mentioned on one of the Diva gossip blogs a little while ago, and someone found his Facebook page and his Instagram..." Her voice trailed off as I pulled out my phone and texted Frank: *Taylor needs to lock down his social media. Paige says his name is getting out there.*

Frank: *Will do.*

"If there's anything I can do..."

"Thanks," I replied. "If I think of anything, I'll let you know."

She shuffled through the pages again and pulled out another. There was a grainy, poorly reproduced picture, but the caption was clear: *Newman High School Homecoming King Billy Barron and Queen Amanda Lautenschlaeger were crowned last night in the school auditorium. Billy is on the football and baseball teams, and Amanda is a Newman cheerleader.*

The look on Amanda's face as she glanced adoringly at Billy was...at first glance, it looked like any other picture of this type:

two happy, excited teenagers enjoying a highlight moment of their high school experience. But a closer look—the look on Amanda's face was both sly and possessive at the same time; she didn't look…

She didn't look sane.

It was a bad reproduction, of course, and it might have just been something else, just a weird moment captured based on the timing of the picture being snapped; who hasn't ever had a picture taken where they look completely insane, one step away from being put in straitjacket? God knows there are plenty of those of me in existence, most of them preserved forever in my Jesuit High School yearbooks.

"Do you think Amanda killed Chloe and Fidelis?" I said.

"I think she's obsessive about Billy Barron," Paige replied. "And they were killed with what were probably baseball bats. And both women were currently involved with Billy Barron…and Fidelis knew about Deborah." She folded her arms. "Wouldn't hold up in court, but it's a good theory, don't you think?"

I touched the article about the assault on Jane Barron. "Is she still around?"

Paige grinned. "Remarried, lives Uptown with her second husband and family. You think maybe we should drop in for a visit?"

I looked at my watch. "Tell you what, let me run home and check on Taylor, see how he is…and if he's okay, you're on."

"Excellent." She stood up. "Let me get another cappuccino."

I braved the cold, hurrying and almost bumping into several other pedestrians who also weren't paying any attention, their heads bent against the cold. The air was frosty cold, and damp. It felt like it was getting colder as I hurried down the passage from the gate to the courtyard. As I climbed the steps to my apartment, taking them two at a time, I couldn't stop wondering about Paige's theory, and the biggest hole in it.

Why would Amanda Lautenschlaeger kill Eric Brewer?

It didn't make sense.

Maybe there was a problem stemming from her helping cast the show? I made a mental note to try Brandon again.

The heat from my apartment felt fantastic when I opened the door and headed down the hallway. I could hear Rhoda talking. When I reached the living room, Rhoda and Lindy were back on their computers, both looking up and smiling at me. Frank was sitting in one of the wingback chairs. There was no sign of Taylor or his mother.

"Where's Taylor?"

"I gave him a Xanax and sent him to bed," Frank replied. He looked utterly exhausted, and I couldn't say I blamed him in the least. "My sister…" He sighed. "I sent her back to her hotel room."

"Did Taylor talk to her?"

Frank shook his head. He looked like he'd aged ten years since I'd seen him last. "I sent her on her way before he got here. She had the decency to understand he might not be thrilled to see her."

"How did he seem to you?"

"Hanging on by a thread." Frank shook his head sadly. "I just hope he's not going to be scarred by this."

"By finding out that his parents are even worse than he already thought they were?" I said without thinking.

Frank flinched.

I sat down on his lap and kissed his neck. "I'm sorry," I whispered. "I know she's your sister."

He nodded.

"Are you going to be okay?" I filled him in on what Paige had found out. "We're going to go talk to Jane Barron, see if she can fill in some gaps about Amanda."

"Go. I'll stay here in case Taylor needs me."

I thanked the Ninjas again for rescuing Taylor, giving them each a hug and kiss. "I'm going to interview a potential background witness," I said, "What are you two doing?"

"Trying to see if we can find Colin," Lindy replied. She stood up and Rhoda slid into the chair, her fingers flying across the keyboard. Lindy stretched, her back cracking. "It's very weird…but until we know something for sure…"

My heart sank. "That doesn't sound good."

"It's not," she replied with a shrug. "There seems to be a blackout on Blackledge operations, and it's worldwide. No one's heard anything, no one's talking, and no one knows what's going on." She exhaled and looked over at Rhoda. "I'm worried about Colin, honestly."

I took a deep breath. "But he always lands on his feet."

She nodded, but she wouldn't look me in the eye. "Yes, he does. And we'll keep looking. Go." She added in a whisper, "And don't worry—we'll stay here to keep watch on Frank and Taylor."

"Thank you," I whispered back.

She grinned. "What is the point of knowing Ninja Lesbians if you can't put them to good use?"

CHAPTER TWENTY-ONE
THE SUN, REVERSED
Future plans clouded

"Yikes," Paige said, glancing up at me. She looked pale. "These are revolting, and I didn't think I could be shocked anymore." She started flipping through the photos of Chloe again, her eyes wide. Every so often she'd stop, swallow, and shake her head. "My God." She whispered finally, slipping them all back into the envelope and fastening it closed, "I think I need some brain bleach."

I sipped from my cappuccino. I probably didn't need more caffeine—my heart was beating a little too fast, and my mind was bouncing from one crazed thought to another.

What I needed was to take a Xanax and sleep for about three days, but that wasn't an option—not with the possibility of Russian assassins showing up at any minute as I was hoping that Colin was okay and alive wherever he was and would stay that way, worrying about Taylor's mental and emotional health, needing to figure out what to do about his mother...

On top of the murders. Because that's just how things go in my life.

At least I felt safer knowing Lindy and Rhoda were watching the apartment. You can't do better than Mossad agents when it comes to security.

A crazy laugh bubbled up. Taylor's awful father and his partner in homophobic crime sure didn't see the Ninja Lesbians coming.

I was only sorry I couldn't be there when housekeeping discovered them in the morning, bound and gagged in the wreckage of their room.

Go ahead and file a police report, assholes. See how that works out for you.

Frank was right. There was no way they could without implicating themselves in a kidnapping.

At least they had plenty of time to come up with a story for the maid when she showed up.

"I didn't like her when we worked together at the paper," Paige went on, pushing the envelope across the table to me, shuddering slightly.

"What was she like?" I asked, pushing everything else out of my mind and forcing myself to focus. "Remy loved her...but I've not heard anything positive about her from anyone." Which was kind of sad.

Paige made a face. "I feel like...well, like such a bitch now." She ran a hand through her mop of hair. "I'm not—have never been—patient with what I see as bullshit, and Chloe was just so full of shit." She pointed at the envelope. "Those pictures prove I was right, but it doesn't make me feel better. I can't imagine where she must have been in her life—what must have been going on with her—that resulted in those pictures being taken." She barked out a laugh. "Those aren't artistic nudes—I had friends who made money modeling nude for artists in college. You can't claim those pictures have any value other than..." She shuddered again. "Fueling masturbatory fantasies."

"Nudity doesn't shock me," I replied. "But those are...they need to be *burned*. I don't even want to turn them over to Venus and Blaine."

"The negatives aren't there anyway," Paige pointed out. "Destroying those won't get rid of them forever."

"Yeah."

"Poor Chloe." Paige stared into her coffee cup. "At the paper she was—I guess the right word is *prissy*." She rolled her eyes. "Very uptight, like there was a stick shoved so far up her ass you could see it when she opened her mouth. Maybe it was a reaction to her past."

"You mean like how someone can be a big partier and then find religion, and they're more hung up about it than people who've been religious their whole life?"

"Exactly like that. You know, she actually put up one of those swear jars—you know, so if you swore you had to put a dollar into it? In a fucking newspaper office!" She smiled faintly at the memory. "I made a big show of putting a twenty in it as a prepayment, and then just stood there and talked as loudly as I could about how fucking stupid a fucking swear jar was…and that was the last of that. God, I was such a *bitch*. I should have been more supportive of her…but she drove me nuts." She tapped her fingers on the table. "There's a special place in hell for women who don't support other women… but Chloe…she wasn't *good*, you know? She wasn't a good reporter. She flirted and played up to all the guys, and *she* didn't support other women, but that doesn't excuse my behavior." A flush began spreading up from her neck to her face.

"No sense in beating yourself up over it," I said, but clearly she needed to get it out of her system.

She went on like I hadn't spoken. "There were rumors around the paper, of course, that she'd been a stripper at one of the men's clubs in Biloxi, that she'd worked as an escort…and of course, when she was promoted to editor, people said she'd slept her way into that job, too." She exhaled. "Instead of shutting that shit down I listened to it—what does that say about *me*? It *was* typical misogynist bullshit…but the truth was she *wasn't* qualified for the job and she didn't deserve the promotion. Maybe she was just better at office politics than the rest of us."

"Did you read her book?"

"*Crazy White People*? Of course." She fiddled with the lid of her cup. "It was terrible, you know, typical white savior bullshit…but I was jealous." She looked at me. "I have three unpublished novels in a drawer in my apartment."

"Oh." I cleared my throat. "She quit working at the paper when she married Remy?"

Paige nodded. "That was when she wrote her book. She wasn't quitting because she got married but so she could write her book." She rolled her eyes. "I know she meant well with it, but…white people solve racism books are so 1950s, you know?"

"Apparently there's still a market for them."

"I think she was genuinely surprised when the backlash came, and of course they canceled the film version." Paige rubbed her temples with her thumbs. "I didn't like her, but now that she's dead

I'm kind of second-guessing that, I suppose. Maybe I could have been kinder to her while she was alive. Maybe…"

"Maybe your instincts were correct," I said, staring into the bottom of my now-empty cappuccino cup. "My mother always says how much she hates the hypocrisy of death; how an awful person dies and then everyone cries about how wonderful they were when they actually weren't." Mom's always pragmatic, if a little callous at times.

"Yeah, if someone hadn't killed her, I'd still loathe her." She laughed. "That, though"—she pointed at the envelope—"now I can't help feeling sorry for Chloe. Digging those pictures up was some serious dirty pool for Margery to pull, and especially for reality television. This franchise of the show…Lord." She waved her hand. "Oh, I know people have parlayed sex tapes into reality stardom and made entire brands and careers from it, but that wasn't what Chloe was doing. I don't know how she thought being on the show would improve her brand as an author…maybe some publicity for her next book, but…these pictures," she swallowed, "would have destroyed her in New Orleans. She was all about being a Garden District lady, even though she wasn't to the manor born."

It was one of the great reality show mysteries: why go on a reality show when you have skeletons in your closet?

Because they always wind up on camera.

"All right, enough about Chloe. Fill me in on Fidelis." I took the file folder from her and slipped it into my backpack.

"She was also killed sometime after the party on Friday night, maybe early Saturday morning," Paige replied with a shiver. "They didn't find her until today, when her cleaning service showed up— she didn't have someone in every day. According to the cops, there were no signs of a break-in, nothing was taken. She was in her nightgown and robe, on the floor of her living room. Just like Eric and Chloe, struck in the head with a blunt instrument with terrific force…a blunt instrument they think was most likely a baseball bat."

"What about the security guard?"

Paige looked at me like I'd lost my mind. "What security guard?"

"At the guard shack. No one gets into English Turn—"

She cut me off. "She doesn't live in English Turn anymore. She bought a house in old Metairie and moved a few months ago." She rolled her eyes. "Moving back to this side of the river was part of her storyline for the show."

As a fan of the *Grande Dames* shows, I shuddered inwardly. There was nothing more tedious than a Grande Dame building a story line out of finding a new place to live...but tired as those stories were, they popped up on every franchise almost every season.

"The cops are still canvassing the neighbors, but last I heard, no one had seen anything out of the ordinary." She shivered again as she finished her coffee. "Producer and two of the cast, all killed on the same night with the same kind of weapon."

"If it was the same killer, he had a busy night," I said idly. "From the Aquitaine to the Garden District to old Metairie."

"He or she," Paige said grimly.

"You're sure it was Amanda, aren't you?"

Paige nodded. "She killed someone when she was a teenager, Scotty. Deliberately. And her mother bought her out of it. She went after Billy's wife with a bat. That can't be a coincidence."

Or, I thought as we got up to go, *someone's doing a great job of framing Amanda.*

Paige's car was parked about two blocks away from Café Envie, and we walked as quickly as possible. As we shivered in her car while waiting for the heater to start blowing hot air, she commented, "Hard freeze again the next two nights, and it may snow tomorrow."

Snow in New Orleans is rare—so rare, in fact, that when it does happen no one knows what to do. The city literally comes to a screeching halt. City hall and city services shut down; they sometimes even close I-10 through the city. Most of our pipes aren't insulated, so hard freezes mean having to leave faucets running slightly so the pipes don't freeze and crack. Houses in New Orleans are built for comfort in our miserably hot and humid summers and are designed to be colder inside than outside. Heat rises, so when you turn on the heat it just rises up to those gorgeous eighteen-foot-high ceilings. The cold creeps in through the windows and the wind somehow finds every crack and crevice. Instead of running up the power bill in a futile attempt to heat up the apartment, it's just easier to put on layers and bury yourself under blankets.

Taylor's apartment, the top floor of our building, turns into a sauna if the lower three floors have their heat on. He's even had to turn the air-conditioning on when it's in the forties outside because his apartment is over ninety degrees.

That's life in New Orleans for you.

The former Jane Meakin Barron had remarried after divorcing Billy—I couldn't help but wonder if this was the divorce that upset his father so badly he'd cut Billy out of the will—and was now living in a huge house in Broadmoor, just off Napoleon Avenue, on Derbigny Street on the lake side of Claiborne Avenue. Paige took Claiborne just as it started raining. We were passing the Superdome when I started hearing this weird clicking sound and realized it was ice hitting the windshield.

Some of the rain's turning to ice.

Sleet? Hail? Madness.

I gasped when Paige pulled over in front of Jane Barron Bullard's house.

It was a three-story Caribbean plantation style house, with a wide, sweeping staircase leading up from the circular driveway to the second-floor gallery. It was painted dark green, with bright yellow shutters on the windows.

But I couldn't' stop gawking at the Christmas decorations.

Jane Barron Bullard's house was decorated like there would never be another Christmas in New Orleans. Her former father-in-law's decorations on his North Shore home purportedly could have been seen from space; her decorations would give his a run for his money. A colossal plastic statue of Santa Claus underneath a palm tree waved at passing cars. A sleigh and eight reindeer stretched across the roof. All the bushes and palm trees had white lights strung through the branches and up their sides, as did the round two-story-high columns on the gallery. Three gigantic red plastic bells took turns flashing on the front door. The windows were decorated with lights and fake candles. The lights of an enormous Christmas tree, just inside the window to the right of the front door, blinked in the gray late afternoon.

A black woman in her late fifties, wearing a hideous Christmas sweater and a pair of jeans, answered the door.

"Is Mrs. Bullard home?" Paige asked sweetly.

She looked at both of us suspiciously. There was a streak of flour on her cheek. "Who's asking?"

"I'm Paige Tourneur from *Crescent City* magazine and this is my assistant, Scott."

Assistant?

But it worked. "I don't think Mrs. Bullard is expecting company today," she said with a frown, standing aside to let us inside the overheated house. The hallway led to a back door. Holly and mistletoe were hanging from the ceiling, big red flashing bells were hung over the doorways, and tinsel was wrapped around the railing of the staircase. "Please wait in here," she gestured to a doorway, "while I go check on Mrs. Bullard. *Crescent City* magazine, you said?"

"Yes." Paige walked through the doorway. I hesitated a second before following her. This was the living room, which contained the Christmas tree visible through the windows. It was even larger than I'd imagined, and there was yet another tree on the other side of the room. The entire room smelled of pine and cinnamon. Candles were burning on the mantel and on the coffee table. Stockings hung from the fireplace, candy canes everywhere one could be hung.

It was much too warm, so I slipped off my coat just as Jane Bullard joined us. "Jesus CHRIST, it's hot in here," she said. She called out, "Toy, will you turn down the heat, please?" She gave us both a huge smile. "I may have to open some windows. My apologies, it was ice cold in here this morning, so I turned up the heat and wasn't paying attention to how hot it was getting! My bill is going to be insane." She rolled her eyes. "But you don't care about that. I'm Jane Bullard."

I know it's rude to stare, but I couldn't help myself. Jane Bullard and Rebecca Barron could have easily passed for sisters to anyone who didn't know them. Jane'd had some work done, obviously; her eyelids had that strange hollow look indicating they'd been lifted more than once, and her forehead was remarkably free of wrinkles. Her figure was slender, an almost impossibly small waist accentuated by a black cable-knit turtleneck sweater and the almost impossibly large breasts straining at the wool. She also wore slim-fit jeans that hugged her curves. She was maybe five three, five four at the most;

her equally impossibly blond hair pulled back into a tight ponytail made her seem more youthful.

Paige introduced us both, and Jane offered us drinks, which we declined. We sat down on the dark sofa, and she sat down across the coffee table from us, the Christmas tree behind her almost looking like it was growing out of her head.

"Your decorations are amazing," I said.

She laughed, pearl-white teeth flashing beneath her red lips. "I overdo it," she admitted, glancing around the room. "I can't help it, I love Christmas. I can't get enough of it."

"It reminds me of Steve Barron, on a much smaller scale," Paige replied.

Jane laughed again, sounding genuinely delighted. "Well, I kind of always felt responsible for that," she said as she crossed her legs. "He was my father-in-law and was very competitive, to say the least. When I was married to his son, I did up our first house like this for our first Christmas together." She waved around. "Steve stopped by, and the next thing I knew his place was lit up like a Roman candle. I always felt like I owed his neighbors an apology, and then it turned into an annual thing." She rolled her eyes. "What can I do for you? I don't remember being asked for an interview with *Crescent City*." She frowned. "I mean, I'd love to talk to you about the charity and the work we're doing, but I'm terribly unprepared. But we can certainly get started today!"

"Well, this actually had to do with something that happened to you when you were married to your first husband," Paige said carefully. "You were attacked by—"

"That crazy bitch Amanda Lautenschlaeger." Jane's lips compressed into a tight line. "I saw her the other day at Whole Foods, and I couldn't believe my eyes. How she is not in a straitjacket and locked up is...well, money talks." She shook her head angrily. "You know we all went to school together, right? To Newman? Yes, I was in the same class as Amanda and Billy." Her face was a taut mask. "Amanda was obsessed with Billy, for as long as I can remember. They started going steady when we were sophomores, I think? Oh, she was so awful and crazy and possessive, even then. If Billy so much as looked at another girl—" She closed her eyes and shivered, delicately. "And I don't care what anyone says, she murdered that girl senior year. No one will ever convince me that was an accident."

"It wasn't?" I asked, leaning forward.

"Billy had just broken up with Amanda and asked Deborah Holt to Homecoming." She leaned back in her chair and folded her arms. "I didn't see it happen, but less than three days later Deborah is dead, killed in an accident"—she made air quotes as she said *accident*—"and my friend Megan saw it happen. She was there wtih Deborah. She said Amanda sped up the car, didn't hit the brakes or anything, didn't try to stop."

"Megan? That would be Megan Dreher, wouldn't it?" Paige was making notes as she spoke.

"Why, yes, it would be. She was Megan Tortorice then, of course. And we never, you know, saw Amanda again." Her face twisted. "She had a *nervous breakdown*." More air quotes. "And was whisked away to a boarding school. No one will ever convince me Margery Lautenschlaeger didn't buy off the cops and the DA. Amanda murdered Deborah in cold blood. Megan and I both have always believed that." She barked out an unamused laugh. "And of course, she came after me with a baseball bat when I was married to Billy."

"How did that happen?" I was genuinely curious. I'd always known justice was sort of for sale in New Orleans—I suspect my parents have gotten away with things people who didn't have the Diderot or Bradley bloodline would have; the pot, for example— but I'd never had any real evidence of it.

We like to believe justice is blind and fair for everyone.

But it really isn't.

And it's not just a New Orleans thing, either.

"Billy and I started dating when we were both at LSU. He was on a baseball scholarship, of course, and I...well, I didn't want to go to school outside the state. We ran into each other at a fraternity party, I think he was a Beta Kappa? Long story short, we got involved and we got married after we graduated while Billy tried to make it as a pro." Her smile was sardonic. "He didn't, you know. And there's nothing worse than a failed jock who suddenly has to find something to do with his life. But Billy..." Her voice trailed off, and she looked off into the distance, a faint smile playing on her lips. "He's so charismatic, and charming. But he also can't keep it in his pants. I don't remember how long we'd been married before Amanda came back into our lives. But she did. I think we'd been married five years when he started up the affair with her again?" She sighed. "Yes, that was right, I was pregnant with Kyan, my second son." She pointed over at a framed photograph of a handsome young man in an LSU graduation cap and gown. "But she got it into her head that Billy wanted to marry her and that I was in the way and if I were gone..." She shrugged. "Somehow she got into the house when I was the only one home, me and my oldest. She came after me with one of Billy's bats from college. He kept them all, you know, including the one where he hit the home run that won the College World Series. He has a trophy room."

"How did you—how did you get away from her?"

"Stupid bitch didn't know I had a gun in the kitchen." She laughed. "I was in the kitchen, making dinner, slicing vegetables when she comes in with the baseball bat and takes a swing at me, telling me how I don't deserve Billy and she's going to get him back and all that nonsense." She ran a hand through her hair. "And me four months pregnant. I got to the drawer where I kept the gun and pulled it on her. I ran out the door and over to the neighbors' house and I called the cops. I wanted to press charges but Billy didn't want me to, said the scandal would be bad for the restaurants. But what he really meant was it would piss off his father. I think our marriage lasted like another five years before I was finished with him, once and for all."

"And what happened to Amanda?"

"Margery sent her off to another hospital." Again with the air quotes. She laughed. "I'm not ashamed to admit I made the old bitch pay me off, too. Fuck the restaurants, you know? I was *pregnant*. She belonged behind bars."

"Did you also know Fidelis Vandiver?"

"Of course. We were all in school together." Her eyes widened. "Oh my God, she was murdered the other night, wasn't she?" She stood up. "It was Amanda, I'm telling you. Oh my God, Amanda is killing people again, isn't she?"

"We don't know—"

"It said in the paper blunt force trauma to the head." Jane went on like Paige hadn't said a word. "Dollars to donuts it was a baseball bat. You should tell the police to check Billy's bats." She got up and started pacing. "Oh my God, someone told me the other day—maybe a week or two ago? That Fidelis was seeing Billy. Oh my God, oh my God, oh my God." She walked over to the Christmas tree, fidgeting with an ornament. "And Chloe Valence, too. Wasn't she killed recently? I'm so glad I refused to do that show."

"You were asked to be a Grande Dame?" I asked, startled.

She nodded. "Margery herself called me, to try to recruit me. Like I would do anything that horrible old witch wanted me to. She's just as crazy as her daughter." She rose. "I'm sorry, but I have a meeting I must get to."

She walked us to the door, and as we said our goodbyes, she snapped her fingers. "You know, if you're looking into Amanda, you need to talk to Ilana Holt."

"Ilana Holt?" I asked.

"Deborah's younger sister. She *worshiped* Deborah."

The door shut.

CHAPTER TWENTY-TWO
THE STAR, REVERSED
Chance of mental illness

Paige dropped me off in front of my building. "Call me if you find anything else out, and I'll keep you in the loop," she said as I unbuckled my seat belt.

"Thanks." I looked out the car window and shuddered inwardly. It was pouring rain again, and several massive streams of water poured down off the front of my building. The gutter was filling with swirling cold gray water.

"And if Taylor needs anything…" She bit her lower lip. "Keep me posted on how he's doing. He's a good kid."

Touched, I felt tears coming up in my eyes. *Get a grip, Scotty*, I reminded myself as I opened the car door. I stepped over the gutter and only got slightly soaked before I was safely under the cover of the balconies above. I fished my keys out of my jacket pocket as I walked to the gate, slipped the keys in the lock, and glanced down the street to the bar on the corner.

The Balcony Bar had gone through numerous changes of ownership and rebranding in the years since I'd moved out of Mom and Dad's to Decatur Street. Actor and magician Harry Anderson had owned it for several years. Two security cameras were mounted in the bottom of the balcony at the corner—one facing up Esplanade, the other facing up Decatur, facing me.

I hesitated.

You have no reason to doubt Colin's story, I reminded myself. *It's disloyal to question it. And besides, they probably tape over previous days' recordings.*

I unlocked the gate. I could feel the cold metal of the handle through my gloves. My teeth chattered as I made my way down the dark passageway to the courtyard.

We need our own security camera, and we need to light this damned passageway.

We also needed to make up our minds about how to renovate the building, and stop putting it off.

Once we're finished with this case. Once we know Taylor is okay. Once we catch this killer.

I shivered again as I reached the courtyard. The drainpipe that collects the water from the roof of the passageway was gushing water out into the courtyard. About an inch of water covered the flagstones. The fountain was almost full.

I dashed through the rain to the back steps. My teeth were chattering as I took the steps two at a time. It was definitely cold enough for the rain to turn to snow at some point.

Note to self: enclose the stairs when we renovate.

The apartment was quiet as I walked down the hallway. "Hello?" I called as I stripped off my wet hat and coat.

Frank was sitting at the computer desk, frowning at the screen. "Hey, honey," he said as I kissed his cheek and wrapped my arms around him in a hug. "Rhoda and Lindy took off for their hotel. They said they'd let us know if they heard back from any of their sources." He leaned back into my hug. "They said they were monitoring the house and not to worry."

"Did they bug us?"

"I thought it was better to not ask questions." He brought my left hand to his mouth and kissed it. "They did scan the place, and we're clear as far as that's concerned...I just wish we'd hear from Colin, you know?"

"I'm trying not to think about it." I kissed the top of his head, thinking again how lucky I was to have him in my life.

"At some point we're going to have to decide what we're going to do about him." Frank's voice was small. "I love him, but...what if someone had been home Friday night?"

"I'm just glad—" I paused. I wasn't sure how to say it. "I mean, I'm really glad it wasn't Russians or someone after Colin that took

Taylor. But on the other hand, it's almost worse that it was his dad. I mean, for him? Does that make sense? Sorry, my brain is fried." I walked over to the windows. *How did Bestuzhev get in?*

I'd turn this place into Fort Knox if I had to.

But there was still that niggling doubt in the back of my mind. *He was lying to you.*

Frank stood up and joined me at the window. The shutters were open, and I could see the Mint through the haze of the rain. "He seems to be doing okay, all things considered. He's still a little shaken up, but okay for the most part. The Xanax knocked him out. I went up to check on him a little while ago and he was sound asleep, poor thing." He sighed. "I'm torn. I know we should turn his father and his buddies over to the police, but at the same time, she's my sister."

"I can't imagine." I couldn't. My sister was awesome, and so was my brother. I couldn't imagine having to deal with what Frank and Taylor had to almost their entire lives. It did make me love them both even more for turning out so well in spite of everything awful. They could have easily gone to the dark side or been driven to suicide.

It was a chilling thought, but it still happened every day. Queer kids killed themselves at much higher rates than straight kids.

No wonder Frank never wanted to talk about his family or his life before we met. He was still sort of in the closet when we met all those years ago at Southern Decadence. I'd always thought it was because he was afraid of losing his job...but his family had probably fucked him up a bit about his sexuality.

"Anyway, everything we've been told about Amanda Lautenschlaeger is true." Frank yawned and stretched. "She did leave Newman during their senior year, and she was definitely driving the car that killed Deborah Holt." He sighed. "It's amazing how little there is about Amanda online. Not even a Facebook page. Seriously, who doesn't have a Facebook page these days?"

"You don't have one," I pointed out.

"I do have a fan page for Frank Savage." *Frank Savage* was his ring name. A smile played at his lips. He had over thirty thousand followers on his wrestler fan page. I always smiled when I read the adoring messages he got from female fans.

Some were pretty explicit about what they wanted to do to his body and what they wanted him to do to them...

Can't say as I blame them.

He looks smoking hot in his ring gear.

"Like I was saying, it's remarkable how little information there is about her online—unless, of course, you have access to private eye databases." He winked at me. "She transferred to a private school in upstate New York called St. Dymphna's—but did you know that the school is for 'troubled girls'?"

"Troubled girls? That sounds like one of those awful 50s B-movies."

He laughed. "It's basically a reform school for rich girls—you know, poor kids go to juvie, rich boys go to military school, and rich girls go to schools for 'troubled girls.' Anyway, St. Dymphna is considered one of the best in the country. According to the testimonials page on their website, St. Dymphna changes lives for the better. The gratitude of St. Dymphna graduates has resulted in a rather hefty endowment. The school has almost as much money as Tulane. But still—it must have been a big change from Newman."

"She ran down Deborah Holt in cold blood—she's lucky she wasn't sent to prison." I shook my head. "But rich people have been buying their kids out of trouble in New Orleans for centuries. I can't believe Margery sent her to a Catholic-run school. I mean, they're Jewish."

Frank shook his head. "It's an easy mistake, given the name, but it's not a Catholic school anymore. St. Dymphna was originally a home for pregnant girls, but about fifty years ago the church sold it off and it became what it is now—they just kept the name. It's completely nondenominational. But I can't find any court records, even sealed ones. I did some other checking—it's what I said, a reform school. You basically get sent there by a judge to avoid juvie, or if you have a drug and alcohol problem. Girls don't get sent there because they won't clean their rooms or listen to their mothers, you know what I mean? But her record has been scrubbed clean. I mean, her record would have been sealed because she was a minor but—" He shrugged. "And she's never been married, no tickets, no accidents, nothing like that. After St. Dymphna, she went to the University of Massachusetts, which isn't far from St. Dymphna.

She was a decent student, no dean's list or anything like that. She majored in American history, seemed to pretty much stay out of trouble the whole time she was there. She lived in the dorms as a freshman, shared an apartment the next three years with a girl named Erin Fleming, who seems to have vanished—I'm trying to trace her now, see what she has to say about Amanda." He scowled. "Anyway, she came back to New Orleans after she graduated, but there's no work history. She has her mother's address listed as her home address. She does some volunteer work, mostly fundraising. I couldn't find any record of any engagement announcements or anything, which is weird, don't you think? You'd think she'd have been engaged at least once. It's not like she's unattractive—I found some pictures from the social pages in the paper. It's remarkable what a low profile she keeps."

"I'm sure she's been involved with men. She's pretty and she's rich," I replied idly. Maybe it was time to talk to Billy again.

The weird loose ends always seemed to lead to either Billy Barron or Amanda.

"I also did some extraneous checking up on the Grande Dames."

Shows like Grande Dames usually cast women who knew each other slightly if they weren't actually friends off-camera. The problem with New Orleans, though, is that there really wasn't any way they could have cast women whose lives hadn't intersected many times over—and the producers couldn't have known about long-standing feuds when interviewing prospective cast members if the women themselves didn't bring it up. And would they, if it meant they might not make it onto the show? I certainly would have, but I didn't have the narcissism requisite to wanting to be on a reality television show.

No wonder my head ached.

And now two women were dead. And so was Eric Brewer, the man responsible for mixing up the ingredients into this toxic gumbo.

What a miserable little troll he was, I thought as Frank pulled up a document focusing on Megan Dreher. I'd always thought Eric was smarmy on his little talk show that aired after each episode, but I'd had no idea just how bad he really was.

Megan's husband had a bad reputation around town. A real

estate developer and building contractor before Katrina, he'd been sued so many times you'd think he'd have trouble staying in business or finding financing. He always managed to settle before going to trial. After Katrina, his reputation got even worse. He'd been one of the contractors for Poydras Tower—which had resulted in yet another settlement of a lawsuit. He'd built some houses in the lower Ninth Ward that failed inspections, and another contractor had been brought in to fix the problems.

Yes, Sam Dreher was bad news.

But Megan was another story entirely.

As I read the research Frank had done on her, I couldn't for the life of me figure out why she married a crook (well, an alleged crook) like Sam Dreher. She had been raised very upper middle class in New Orleans, gone to Newman, and after getting her degree in English from LSU, she worked as a teacher in the New Orleans public school system until she got married. That was it; she was squeaky clean other than marrying a con man. I looked through the rest of the file, and while there were pages and pages about the other Grande Dames, there were just a few short paragraphs about Megan.

"She was with Paige at Café Envie," I said, rubbing Frank's back. There were some serious knots between his shoulder blades. I started kneading them with my fingers.

"What was she doing there?" Frank moaned a little and leaned back into my back rub. "That feels so good, please don't stop."

"She told me she was there when Amanda ran over Deborah Holt—Margery bought them all off," I replied, digging my fingertips into a particularly nasty knot. "You know, it all comes back to Amanda Lautenschlaeger." I explained to him about all the lines drawing outward from Amanda Lautenschlaeger. "Her mother, two of her friends from high school, and Billy Barron's stepmother. They even tried to recruit Billy's ex-wife for the show. So Amanda is at the center of whatever it is that's going on here."

"Serena doesn't have a connection to her," Frank pointed out, moaning as the knot finally gave way to my digging fingers.

"That we know about," I replied. "Megan said she was leaving town—she's afraid of Amanda. Maybe we can catch her before she leaves and talk to her some more?"

"I don't know if I'm comfortable leaving Taylor here alone."

It was a good point. "Maybe we could get Mom to come over?" Frank stood up and stretched. "I'll call her."

Frank had dug up Megan's home address, and it was in the lower Garden District—the Drehers lived on Camp Place.

That figured. Camp Place was one of those New Orleans peculiarities, like how Magazine Street turned from a one-way street into a two-way street heading uptown at St. Andrew Street. Camp Place was a block-long street that ran alongside Camp Street for one block between Race and Orange Streets. It was separated from Camp Street by a neutral ground, and the large homes that lined the short street were incredibly expensive.

Mom and Dad both came over to stay with Taylor, and Mom was carrying a paper bag from Whole Foods. "I'll make you boys dinner," she said with a big smile as she started taking things out of the bag and placing them on the kitchen counter.

It would probably be some tofu atrocity, but you really can't say no to Mom.

The temperature had dropped even more. It had stopped raining, but the air was so wet and cold and heavy, this was probably just a break. I shivered as Frank turned off Melpomene onto Coliseum Street. Coliseum Square, usually filled with people and their dogs, was deserted. The fountain was going, and the live oaks were rustling in the wind. Megan's address was on Race Street, which bordered the park on its uptown side.

It was amazing how much Coliseum Square had changed over the years—the entire neighborhood, for that matter. When I was a kid, the neighborhood was sketchy. I could remember driving through here when the houses all looked derelict and blighted. Now they had all been renovated and the park area looked genteel.

We were almost to Race Street when I heard sirens approaching. A patrol car came screaming up Race from the direction of the river, and another shot past us on Coliseum. They both turned onto Camp Place.

"This doesn't bode well," Frank said, pulling over and parking in front of a big house on the corner at Race and Coliseum. We both headed down the sidewalk quickly, without running, to the corner at Camp Place. Both patrol cars had pulled up in front of a coral

Greek Revival house. Officers with weapons drawn were heading up the walk to the front door, while two others were going around the house to the back. We crossed Camp Place to the neutral ground and looked at the house number.

It was the Dreher house.

"Scotty? Frank?"

I turned to see Blaine frowning at us. He was wearing a pair of jeans and an LSU sweatshirt. He had his shoulder holster strapped on, the butt of his revolver clearly showing. He had both hands on his hips as he glanced over to the patrol cars before looking back at me, his thick eyebrows knit together.

"What are you doing?"

"We were actually coming over here when the police cars showed up," I replied. "That's the Dreher house, isn't it?"

He licked his lower lip. "Yeah."

"Is it Megan Dreher?"

He didn't answer for a moment. Finally, he said, "Sam Dreher called 9-1-1." He nodded. "It's Megan. He found her in the backyard." He shook his head. "At this rate, we're going to have to give the rest of the goddamned Grande Dames twenty-four seven police protection."

The crime lab van came around the corner. As he walked over to where it parked, Blaine said over his shoulder, "You guys get out of here, and be careful."

I watched as he talked with the crime scene techs before walking into the house with them. I almost suggesting waiting—Venus was bound to show up at some point, but—no, better to just head back home.

Frank scowled. "And now a third Grande Dame is dead." He sighed. "Come on, let's head over to Serena's, see what she has to say."

We started walking back to the car, lost in thought.

Maybe I was going about this whole thing the wrong way. Maybe it had nothing to do with the show, and everything to do with their private lives. Fidelis Vandiver had an ugly divorce and custody battle with her ex-husband—but that was years ago. What was the standard rule of thumb when someone was killed? It's almost always someone close to the victim, a spouse or a relative or a lover.

Billy Barron admitted he was having an affair with both Fidelis and Chloe and now they were both dead—and now Megan Dreher probably was, too. Was she having an affair with Billy Barron? Or was this about her knowing about Deborah Holt's murder all those years ago?

All roads led back to Amanda Lautenschlaeger.

My phone vibrated in my pocket, and I pulled it out. I didn't recognize the number. "Hello?"

"Scotty? Oh, thank God I got you. This is Margery Lautenschlaeger. I'm sorry to ask you this, but do you think you can come over right now? It's important."

"Well, yes, Margery, but what is it?"

"I'd rather not discuss it over the phone. Please hurry." She disconnected the call.

I stared at my phone for a minute, more than a little annoyed. I was getting sick and tired of these stupid Grande Dames. I was working myself up quite a state of irritation by the time we reached the car again when my phone vibrated again. "Yes?"

"Scotty?" It was a man's deep voice, one I didn't recognize. "It's Billy Barron. I was wondering if it would be possible to have a moment of your time?"

I put my hand on the door handle. *How weird that he's calling me right after Megan was murdered.* "What can I do for you, Billy?" Frank shot me a look as he started the car. I held up a finger as warm air started blowing through the vents.

"I've hired an attorney, but I don't really have anything to hide." His voice was calm and soothing. Even over the phone, that charisma was irresistible. "I think someone is trying to frame me for these killings." He sounded remarkably relaxed, if that was indeed true.

Murderers could often be charming.

"It certainly seems like all these murders could be traced back to you." Frank was looking at me, but I didn't want to put Billy on speaker, in case he could hear Frank with me and got spooked. "Doesn't this all have something to do with the death of Deborah Holt back when you were in high school?"

Silence for a moment. "You are a good detective." He exhaled into the phone. "And I think you're right. This has everything to do with Amanda Lautenschlaeger."

"You took her to the premiere party, didn't you?"

"Look, there hasn't been anything between me and Amanda since high school," Billy replied quickly—a little too quickly, in my opinion. "Yes, I've—we've—we're still friends."

"She killed that girl, didn't she?" I met Frank's gray eyes. His brow was furrowed. "In high school? It wasn't an accident."

"No, it wasn't. Megan and Fidelis and I—we've always known."

"And Margery—Margery pulled her out of Newman and sent her to St. Dymphna's." I closed my eyes and leaned back in my seat. "And she's pretty much been in and out of hospitals ever since, hasn't she?"

"She's not a bad person, or at least I didn't think so." He sighed. "She's obsessed with me, Scotty."

Yes, and I bet your ego just HATED that.

"She's got some kind of a chemical imbalance, bipolar, or something like that. When she takes her medications, she's fine. But when she gets better she doesn't think she needs to take the meds anymore and…" His voice trailed off. "She wanted me to take her to the premiere party. I didn't see the harm. But…"

"What happened that night?"

"She wanted me to bring her home with me. I already had made arrangements with Fidelis to come by later, after Eric's after-party, and I'm not interested in her that way anymore, you know? I haven't been since high school."

"She's killed for you before. You think she's doing it again?"

"Someone is setting me up. And no matter what Amanda…no matter what her illness makes her think, she wouldn't do this to me. She thinks we're meant to be together, so she wouldn't try to send me to prison."

"But if she can't have you…"

"I'm telling you, it's not Amanda doing this. This isn't her style."

"But you were sleeping with both Chloe and Fidelis, and she's killed a rival before."

"I would believe that if it wasn't being set up to make it look like I killed them." He took a deep breath. "Some of my bats are missing."

"You said you think you know who's setting you up?"

"It's complicated. I'll explain it all to you when I see you."

"Well—" I looked at my watch. It was getting late. "Not tonight, Billy. I'm on my way somewhere now, and it's just not possible. How about tomorrow morning?" I motioned to Frank to start driving, He put the car into gear and pulled away from the curb.

I didn't look at the Dreher house as we drove past it.

"Okay, but first thing?"

"I'll call when we're on our way." I disconnected the call and looked at Frank. "Why would he want to talk to us when he has a lawyer?"

Frank shook his head as he turned right on Magazine to head uptown. "None of this makes sense to me, to tell you the truth."

I resisted the urge to pound my head on the dashboard.

Billy and his brother were suing Rebecca for control of their father's company.

Amanda was the one who'd gotten Chloe and Fidelis and her mother and Megan on the show in the first place.

There was something there, but I couldn't get it all to come together in my head.

I was missing something, and it was driving me insane.

CHAPTER TWENTY-THREE
THE FOOL
A choice is offered

I couldn't help but feel it was staring me right in the face. It was like a having a loose tooth I couldn't stop worrying with my tongue.

I just couldn't fit the pieces together in a way that made any sense.

And this is why I hate jigsaw fucking puzzles.

Feeling like I was letting down Taylor only intensified the sense of utter failure.

If we ever close this case, I thought as I rested my head against the passenger window of the Jaguar, *I'm going to lock myself in the bathroom and cry for a week. Or sleep for a week. Maybe a weekend at a beach somewhere.*

I was so tired my synapses were barely firing. I looked over at Frank, behind the wheel. His leather driving gloves were clenched on the steering wheel, and that muscle in his jaw was jumping again. His eyes were bloodshot and the dark circles under his eyes looked angry. He wasn't sleeping well. He'd tossed and turned most of last night.

He didn't keep waking me up, either. I never fell asleep, other than maybe a few minutes here and there.

I reached over and put my hand on his right leg. He glanced over at me, smiled, and put his right hand down on top of mine. "I love you," he said as the light changed and he moved his hand to shift the car into first, "and I don't know what I'd do without you."

"Hopefully you'll never have to find out," I replied, leaving my hand on his leg, feeling the quad muscle fibers move and shift as he accelerated or slowed down Claiborne Avenue in the cold rain. An occasional click against the glass of the windshield reminded me that some of the rain was turning to ice.

I was teasing, but the Colin question hung over us like a dark cloud.

Is he okay? Did Bestuzhev's murder actually go down the way he said, or did he lie? Are we in danger?

And what if something happened to FRANK?

I guess some of those questions had always been there in the back of my mind, but I never acknowledged them until now.

"We do need to decide what to do about Colin," I said into the silence that had fallen as he turned onto Napoleon Avenue.

"We do." He clenched his jaw again. "But it's got to wait…"

"Unless Venus manages to trace Bestuzhev's body back to us somehow."

"Don't even think it."

Yeah, like it was *that* easy.

I rubbed my burning eyes and cleared my head again. I said a brief chant to the Goddess for strength and wisdom and started picking my way through the many pieces, seeing if there was another way to fit them all together in a way that made sense, would reveal who the killer was.

Amanda was mentally unstable and had been for most of her life. Everyone agreed she'd been fixated on Billy since they were teenagers. She'd spent most of her life in and out of institutions. I could certainly understand her fixation/obsession with Billy Barron—sex appeal and sensuality practically oozed out of his every pore. But we'd only been able to track down two instances where she'd been violent—running Deborah Holt over with her car and going after Jane Barron with a baseball bat. Both times Margery had bought her out of trouble.

But both of those crimes had been impulsive, spur-of-the-moment things, nothing premeditated. That didn't prove Amanda wasn't *capable* of coldly plotting out how to eliminate her rivals for Billy—maybe she learned from her failures. And yet…

She had a motive to kill all three of the dead Grand Dames.

But…again with the loose tooth.

Chloe and Fidelis were rivals for Billy, and she might *think* killing them got them out of her way to be with him again, and that *fit* with her past behavior. Everyone she'd harmed stood between her and a fantasy life as Mrs. Billy Barron that was never going to happen.

But *Megan* wasn't a rival. The only reason she had to kill Megan would be that Megan knew the truth about Deborah Holt.

The others could be crimes of passion, but killing Megan was cold-blooded and calculated.

But why *now?*

And trying to fit Eric's murder in with the other three? It just didn't belong. It was like a piece from another puzzle had gotten slipped accidentally into the wrong box.

The wrong box.

Two puzzles.

Maybe...*maybe* the crimes weren't related at all.

No, that wasn't possible. It was too big a coincidence that all four of them were killed over the course of the same weekend with the same kind of weapon.

It was irritating. I was almost there. I was so close to the answer I could *feel* it.

Think, Scotty, think. You're smarter than this.

You've met Amanda. What did you think?

Something had seemed off about her, sure. But not to this extreme—not to the point of being a borderline serial killer. Her sense of right and wrong could be skewed, and if given the *opportunity* to hurt someone she'd do it. I could see it.

I could see her behind the wheel of a car, her heart broken and seeing Deborah there, the stray thought *run her over and she can't be with Billy.*

Over a prom date, I reminded myself. *She killed someone over a fucking date to a high school dance. And then went after Billy's wife with a baseball bat years later.*

I could see her working herself up into a frenzy, grabbing a baseball bat, and going after Jane.

Not the behavior of the most mentally stable woman.

Yet none of these murders this weekend were crimes of opportunity, I was sure of it. This was a carefully crafted plan, and I'd eat my leather jacket if that didn't turn out to be the case.

These murders were designed to lead us all back to Amanda,

mentally unstable Amanda. And who would believe her? Margery would buy her way out of it again, if she could—never underestimate the power of wealth to affect both an investigation and a prosecution. She'd probably wind up back in a mental hospital and be released in a few years.

The killer used baseball bats to emphasize the connection to Billy and Amanda.

The stakes were high in the fight over the will, but I couldn't see Rebecca going to this much trouble to get Billy out of her way. Wouldn't it be easier just to have Billy killed?

I could see Amanda in a manic, obsessive phase driven to kill someone she felt was a threat to her or blocking her from getting what she wanted.

That tracked.

I did not believe that she could come up with a master plan and execute it so coldly, ruthlessly, efficiently.

It didn't fit.

Just like Eric's murder.

None of it made sense.

My head hurt.

And why the hell did Margery want to see me so badly?

I pressed my index fingers into my temples. Sometimes that worked to relieve headaches, but it didn't this time.

I needed sleep.

The gates to the Lautenschlaeger driveway were open as Frank slowed and took the turn. The driveway lights weren't on, and most of the house was in darkness.

The light beside the front door was lit.

Frank whistled. "Nice place. You'd think she'd have turned on some lights."

"It's gorgeous inside," I replied as we drove up the slope to the front steps. He turned off the engine when we stopped. We climbed the steps to the front door together, braced against the cold wind and freezing rain. He rang the buzzer and took my hand, giving it a squeeze. He gave me a weak smile while we waited what seemed like an eternity in the cold. There were no lights on in any of the windows lining the porch.

I was beginning to think no one was home when I heard the deadbolt sliding back.

"What took you so long?" Margery looked uncharacteristically sloppy and harried. Her hair was coming lose from the bun she'd tied it up into, and she wore little makeup, if any. She looked tired and worried. Her long red Chinese silk dressing gown was dusted with cigarette ash, and what appeared to be grease spots were scattered liberally over the top. Her eyes looked a little wild. She glanced around outside, and I couldn't help but notice her hands were shaking. "Get inside quickly, come on." She literally grabbed us both by our jacket sleeves and tugged.

Why the hell is Margery answering her own front door? I wondered as I followed her into the gloom of the entry foyer. I gave Frank a puzzled glance. The overhead chandelier wasn't on, but some of the smaller light sconces gave off a strange red light.

Margery slammed the door shut behind us.

The sound echoed through the house.

I squinted in the darkness and weird reddish light. "Can someone turn on a light?" I said, my eyes adjusting when I realized someone was standing on the other side of the foyer, in the shadow cast by the suit of armor.

It was Amanda.

She was holding a gun.

And it was pointing at us.

"Please, Amanda—" Margery started, but was cut off.

"Shut up, bitch." Amanda sneered. She waved with the gun. Margery finally flicked the switch on the wall, flooding the foyer with light. Amanda looked terrible. Her hair was greasy and unbrushed, and she was wearing garish makeup—blue eye shadow and dark lines drawn around her eyes, bright red lipstick, and two spots of red painted on her cheekbones. Beneath the clownish makeup her skin was greenish-white, with a slight sheen of greasy sweat on it. Her eyes were burning. She didn't look well. She licked her lips as her eyes darted back and forth between us. "Hands up, all of you."

The three of us slowly raised our hands.

While it wasn't the first time I've had a gun pointed at me, it's something you never get used to. I wasn't even aware I was holding my breath until I exhaled loudly enough to have her swing the gun toward me.

"I'm sorry," I heard Margery mutter. She'd moved until she was standing next to me. "She made me call you."

Yeah, thanks for that, we owe you one.

I heard a car door slam out front.

"Amanda." I kept my hands raised. "Put the gun down. You need help, it's okay. No one holds you responsible for—" Before I could finish, the door behind me opened. A cold wind blew in, and it shut again.

"What are you doing here?" Amanda's voice was shaky, and the gun swung in my direction again. "You're not supposed to be here. Go away, Billy. Go home. This doesn't concern you."

"Amanda, what are you doing?" Billy said softly, stepping around me. In spite of the situation, I was aware of his musk, his presence. Seriously, he was that charismatic. "What's wrong with you? You have to stop this, Amanda. You can't keep hurting people."

I took a step closer to him. Surely, she wouldn't shoot *him*, so standing close to him was the smartest place for me to be.

At least, I thought so, until Billy started walking across the foyer toward her. I glanced over at Margery, but her face was just an expressionless mask. Amanda looked pale and terrified.

"Stay away from me, Billy. You stay away from me!" Her voice rose, and her hands were shaking—which wasn't a good sign. "You—you don't love me! You never loved me! All I wanted was for you to LOVE ME!" She screamed the last words, spittle flying. "Was that so much to ask? WAS IT?"

Margery looked like she was going to start crying at any moment. "Amanda—"

"SHUT UP, Mother!" She swiveled the gun back and forth between Billy and her mother and me. She hissed, "I should have shot you years ago, Mother. And I'll do it right now if you don't STOP."

"Amanda, you aren't well again, it's okay, no one has to get hurt," Billy said gently. "Give me the gun, sweetheart, before you do something you don't really want to do, okay? Everything will be fine if you give me the gun."

"All I ever wanted was for you to love me, Billy." She turned the gun on him, her eyes wild. "Everything I've ever done was for you, Billy. All of it. Those women—those women, those *whores*, were wrong for you, weren't they? I told you. I'm the only one who could make you happy."

"But, Amanda." Billy's voice remained remarkably calm and I realized this wasn't the first time he'd talked Amanda down from a ledge.

Poor guy has been dealing with this for years.

And if this wasn't the first time—maybe he'd be able to talk her down.

"I'm sorry, Amanda, I'll always care for you. But I don't love you."

Out of the corner of my eye I could see Frank moving casually, cautiously, a little bit at a time, to the side. He met my eyes and gave a little headshake. He was going to try to flank her and didn't want me to draw attention to him.

"You have to love me!" Her voice was rising, getting more hysterical. "I don't have any other reason to live!"

"What happened to that girl in high school?" I asked. My voice sounded far away, and I knew I was being flooded with adrenaline. I could hear my own heartbeat. I was also sweating a little.

The gun swung toward me. "It was an ACCIDENT! No one believed me."

I took a step forward. "I believe you, Amanda."

"I didn't mean to do it! It was an accident. Everyone thought I did it on purpose!" Her voice came out in a choked sob. "Everyone turned on me! My own mother! My family! NO ONE BELIEVED ME!"

"That had to be rough." I took another step forward. "It's terrible when people you love, people you count on, don't believe you."

"You have no idea." Her lips tightened. "After everything I did for them! Everything I did for Billy, and you see how he treats me! He's been cheating on me for over thirty years!"

"I wasn't—Amanda, I wasn't cheating on you. We weren't together." Billy sounded tired, sad.

I glanced over at Margery. She was pale, and beads of perspiration dotted her forehead.

"Don't you lie to me, Billy Barron," Amanda went on. "You were *my* date at the premiere, but I saw you with her. I saw you talking, I saw you KISS her." Her face looked sad, and God help me, I actually started to feel sorry for her. "Why wasn't I ever enough for you, Billy? Why?"

"Amanda—"

"You know she was helping Rebecca. I heard them talking in the ladies' room...she was only sleeping with you to help get something on you for your bitch stepmother." She tilted her head to one side. "And that whore Chloe. She was fucking you to get even with my mother, because she knew it would hurt me. Neither one of them deserved to live for what they were doing...why can't you understand that, Billy? Why have you never been satisfied with just me? I would have made you happy, you know. More than any other woman, Billy, I would have done anything for you. I would do anything for you."

Margery let out a choked sob. "Amanda, please, put the gun down, we can get you help..."

"Like before?" Amanda swung around to her mother with the gun. "You're going to have me locked up again, Mother?"

Keep talking, I thought, *please, just keep talking.*

Frank was still moving, bit by bit. Soon he would be on her left. She couldn't keep the gun trained on all of us at the same time.

I took another slight step to my own left.

She was staring at her mother. There was a bit of foam at the side of her mouth.

I reached into my pocket and put my hands on my iPhone.

I took my eyes off Amanda for a moment to glance down at it. It was locked. Irritated, I swept a finger along the bar and unlocked it. I touched the contacts icon, all the while cursing Steve Jobs. *Goddamned fucking touchscreen phone!*

It's not easy to go through all that touch nonsense when you're trying to call the goddamned police while a maniac is holding you at gunpoint.

Once the contact screen was up, I touched a name and hit Call.

"As for that whore Chloe..." Amanda started giggling. She was pointing the gun directly at Billy, who was about halfway across the foyer now. "Chloe was all wrong for you and she was causing problems for my mother and then, you know, Megan, she wanted money, she called me and she wanted money, she's always wanted money from me and my mother...she said she'd tell about what happened in high school and she said it was all my fault, everything..."

What?

And then all the strange permits Stan Dreher had gotten to do construction in the city made sense.

Lautenschlaeger money had greased the wheels. That was how things worked in New Orleans.

"Is that why you killed Megan?" I asked, slipping my phone back into my pocket, hoping that Venus could hear everything.

"Megan?" The gun swung around to me. I'd moved far enough to the side so she couldn't see Frank moving now, as long as she was looking at me.

Billy was also looking at me. "Megan's dead?"

"She figured it all out, didn't she?" I said, taking a deep breath, needing to keep her distracted so Frank could come at her from behind. "Megan knew you'd killed them, she figured it all out, didn't she? Did she want more money? Was that why you decided—"

Margery started crying. "Baby, please."

"You had to kill her, too—you can never trust a blackmailer, can you? You killed Chloe and Fidelis to get them out of Billy's life, and then you killed Megan, too, to keep her quiet, right?"

"SHUT UP SHUT UP SHUT UP!" she screamed. "Stay back!" she screamed as Billy took another few steps forward. "I'll shoot you, you just watch and see!"

"Why did you want us here, Amanda?" I said.

Her head swung back around to me. She still hadn't noticed Frank creeping to her side.

Her eyes narrowed, but she looked a little confused. "I—I don't know why you're here," she said, "but I am not standing for this anymore! I WON'T HAVE IT AND I AM NOT GOING BACK TO THE HOSPITAL NO ONE CAN MAKE ME I'LL KILL YOU ALL BEFORE I LET THAT HAPPEN DO YOU UNDERSTAND ME?"

Frank moved ever closer to her while she was looking at me. But then Billy moved forward again, and if looks could kill, I would have vaporized him on the spot when Amanda turned back to him. Frank froze, but she still hadn't noticed he'd moved. A few more feet and he'd be close enough…

"Give me the gun, Amanda," Billy said softly. "You're not well, like you weren't when you hit Deborah with your car. We need to get you some help, now. And if you get help, we can be together. Isn't that what you want, Mandygirl? Give me the gun and everything will work out the way you want it to."

I could hear Venus's voice saying *hello* in my pocket. I glanced over at Amanda but she was completely focused on Billy.

"Do you mean that?" Her face looked so hopeful that my heart almost broke for her. "It's all I wanted, you know, Billy. All I ever wanted." She smiled so hopefully. He was almost close enough to grab the gun from her. Frank kept creeping along the wall. She couldn't see him now, not as focused as she was on Billy. Frank was so close now, but he couldn't move another step without drawing her attention. Margery looked over at me, her eyes pleading.

"What do you think you're doing!" Amanda screamed, turning the gun back to me. "Did I tell you you could move? I SHOULD SHOOT YOU RIGHT NOW."

I froze.

Amanda's eyes locked on mine.

Frank was close enough, and Billy was standing right in front of her.

What happened next all happened in slow motion, what I can remember of it.

The gun went off.

It took me a moment to realize that sudden burning feeling meant I'd been hit. I had a moment to think *that bitch just shot me* and my hands instinctively went to my side. There was numbness, and pain, and my vision began to narrow. My ears were ringing, and I could hear noise, but couldn't hear anything because the ringing was so loud, so *fucking* loud and I could see Frank's face across the room and everything was buzzing, and then the pain was so sudden and intense I dropped down to my knees.

I could feel my blood, hot and wet, on my hands.

I looked down, not able to believe it.

My mind couldn't grasp that I'd been shot.

Me, Milton Scott Bradley, he of the charmed life and the wacky but loving family. The ex-stripper and bar slut, who'd somehow managed to find love with two great guys.

I tried to say something, but when I opened my mouth nothing came out.

The ringing was so loud.

The buzzing, the numbness in my side was spreading and now it was burning.

Margery rushed to my side, pressed her scarf against my side.

There was another shot as I felt myself sliding, slipping, losing control of my balance and then my head hit the floor with a thud and it hurt and...

I was staring at the ceiling and I remember crazily wondering why Margery put up with such lazy maids. There were cobwebs in the ceiling corners.

Couldn't anyone else see them?

Someone was whimpering.

There was another shot and I heard Frank shout and everything on the edges of my vision was going gray and getting darker, and then I saw Frank's face, deadly, ghastly white, his eyes wider than I've ever seen them before and he was opening my coat and someone was shouting *CALL 9-1-1* and I was looking up into the deep gray pools of Frank's eyes.

I wanted to tell him I loved him, but nothing would come out of my mouth.

The numbness kept spreading, and my legs and arms felt cold, but my side still felt like it was on fire.

I was so cold.

Frank was tearing open my coat and I saw the tears on his cheeks and I wanted to tell him not to worry but nothing would come out, my mouth wasn't obeying the commands I sent it, and I sank down into a sea of gray darkness, shadows swimming around me and the last thing I remember thinking was, *is this what death feels like...*

CHAPTER TWENTY-FOUR
KNIGHT OF CUPS
A young man of rare intelligence

I wasn't cold anymore.

I was floating, adrift, light as a cloud moving in a warm gentle comforting breeze across the sky, but at the same time I was drifting downward. I could sense the ground somewhere below me, but I wasn't afraid of falling.

I was always safe whenever I was here—wherever here was.

I was drifting down through the air. My side didn't hurt anymore; the burning and the tingling and the numbness had magically disappeared, gone, like I hadn't been shot. I was wrapped in a cloud, it seemed like, drifting aimlessly ever downward through air that caressed my body like a blanket made of warm wool. I felt at peace, relaxed—all the stresses and worries were lifted from me and no longer weighed me down. I could feel knots in the muscles in my back, shoulders, and neck releasing as through pressed and massaged away by strong, firm fingers.

Everything was peace.

I sensed Her the way I always did; it was like She was suddenly there when She wasn't just a moment before. But over the years when I've gone to this place, summoned by the Goddess, I've learned that time has no meaning here, nor does space or weather or anything we measure reality by. The Goddess and her spiritual plane are different, a dimension that most people never have the chance to see or experience, and I am always grateful for the grace she has shown me over the years.

My body began to turn in the air as I continued my slow, soft descent, my feet reaching for the ground as the mists began to dissipate, and then my bare feet were on round pebbles, hard yet yielding to my weight, and in the distance as the mist cleared I could see the sea, green and sparkling and foaming as the gentle waves broke on their approach to the soft white sand of the beach, the sea farther beyond the dark blue of grapes, glittering in the soft light of a sun that was neither too bright nor too hot, but was just right, just perfect, the way things should be.

I've sometimes thought that where I go when the Goddess summons me might be what those who wrote the Bible might have called Eden, and maybe it was, maybe Eden was in another dimension and maybe Heaven was, too, which was why so many religions across the continents and history have so many legends and myths that are similar, because there was a commonality of experience, the tales changing slightly over the millennia as they were repeated, copied from copies, changing here and there as the words moved from one language to another.

I was standing on a cliff, I realized, and the woman who was standing there with me, the Goddess, was in Her guise of Aphrodite, I believed; I couldn't really get a glimpse of Her face or see it, but I could sense how beautiful She was in this incarnation of the Divine Feminine, the waves of love and peace and beauty radiating from her. She was wearing a flowing Grecian tunic of lavender, and there were flowers woven into the braids of Her glowing blond hair.

"You will not die," She said, without turning Her head to look at me. "It is not your time."

Which was, of course, good to know.

"They won't even keep you at the healing center," She went on. "They will simply treat your wound and send you home with medicines to dull the pain. But you must not allow your wits to be too dulled by these medicines. You have to remain aware; you and all you care about are still in grave danger."

"Is Colin safe?"

"His path is not clear." She waved one of Her hands, and I could see ripples in the air before Her, colors and lights swirling as they slowly began to take form, and I could see Colin. He was sleeping in a small room, his big chest rising and falling with every breath. I couldn't tell where he was, if he was safe, if he was free or if he had been captured. "But the danger to your world doesn't come from his. The man he killed was a monster, a demon, who often tortured women and children because he enjoyed it. No, Colin is not yet safe, but there will be no further danger to your world from his. He has made sure of it."

That was a relief. "And Taylor?"

"Taylor is a being of love and light," She replied, waving Her hand again to make the image of Colin swirl into color and light again before fading away to nothing. *"He will survive and continue to show everyone who comes into contact with him a better way."*

I felt myself starting to drift away from Her again, Her form dissolving into the rising mist, and I called out, *"But why are we still in danger?"*

"If you think, you will know the answer."

I began to surface from the gray darkness and the swirling fog. Color swirled, and sounds, all running together so I couldn't separate them in my head. The wailing of a siren. Electronic beeping. Tires on pavement. Voices talking, but the words were just sound. Someone was holding my hand in theirs, gripping mine strongly.

I willed my eyes open and was staring at a roof.

"He's awake!" a voice I didn't recognize said, and I turned my head slowly to my left. I saw a handsome scarred face and beautiful loving gray eyes.

Peace and love.

Frank.

I opened my mouth to say his name but couldn't say anything. There was something in my mouth.

"Shh," Frank whispered. "Don't try to talk. We're on our way to the emergency room. You've been shot, do you remember? How do you feel?"

I rolled my eyes. My body felt numb.

Memories came rushing back, images flashing through my head in slow motion. The foyer of the Schwartzberg Castle, Amanda with the gun, Frank trying to flank her, the gun going off.

And the pain, the shock, looking down at my hand and seeing it covered in blood.

My blood.

I opened my mouth again and made a frustrated noise.

"They gave you a painkiller," he went on, ignoring my attempt to speak. "You were very lucky, Scotty. The bullet went through you without hitting anything, but you still need to get checked out and stitched up and…all that stuff, but you're going to be okay." He gave me a big smile, dimples sinking deep into his cheeks. "You're not going to be going to the gym any time soon, and you're going to have to take it easy for a while, think you can do that?"

"Mmmm glurg mmm," I replied.

He swallowed and leaned in closer. "I love you."

My head was foggy from the painkiller, but I think I smiled back at him.

Then he whispered, "The bullet went through," he paused for effect, "your left love handle."

I got shot in the love handles?

"So maybe it's a good thing you put on some extra pounds," he went on. The gray eyes were twinkling. "Otherwise this could have been worse."

I closed my eyes and prayed for death.

I drifted back off to sleep.

It seemed like we were only there a few minutes, but we were actually at the hospital for just over three hours. The time flew past in a blur—primarily because of the painkillers, and I also kept falling back asleep. I stayed groggy and barely conscious as they kept giving me more painkillers and antibiotics and shining lights into my eyes and kneading my side and listening to my heart and lungs and taking blood pressure and monitoring the beeping machines next to the bed.

I just floated through it all on a euphoric cloud of pharmaceuticals. Sometimes I could feel the throbbing in my side, and at some point they also put me on a drip of some sort. Antibiotics, maybe. They'd tell me something and it would vaguely make sense but then whatever it was drifted away on the carefree cloud.

I kind of liked the fog, to be honest.

I lost track at some point of everything they were doing. I know at some point Mom and Dad showed up with Taylor, but I was too high from the medications and could only hope—when I cared—that Frank was making sure they were doing everything they needed to do. Finally, I had to sign some forms, and the doctor—I think it was the same woman who'd handled Taylor when we'd brought him in about a hundred years ago—handed Frank some prescriptions and made an appointment for me to come back in to have the stitches removed and be checked out again. "No showering," she said, "and get plenty of rest. Nothing strenuous until I see you again. You were very lucky," she went on as she signed my release papers. "Another half inch to the left and you'd be in surgery right now."

"I've always been lucky," I replied, giving her a sunny smile.

She laughed. "Well, don't push your luck. Everyone's luck runs out sooner or later."

Yeah, yeah, I muttered to myself as the nurse wheeled me out. Mom and Dad pulled up to the curb, and Taylor and Frank helped me into the back seat of their green Subaru. "We left our car at Margery Lautenschlaeger's," Frank said, and Dad turned the car around to head back uptown.

Frank filled me in on what he'd learned while I was with the doctors. The cops had taken Amanda in, and of course Margery was summoning the best lawyers in the 504 area code. "She's probably calling judges she knows," he said as the car stopped at the light at Napoleon. "Venus told me that they found two bloody baseball bats in the trunk of Amanda's car, so they think they have the murder weapons."

But why would she kill Eric? That still didn't make sense.

And why two bats? Why didn't she just reuse the same one?

I was too doped up to say anything aloud, though.

The police cars were still in the driveway of the Lautenschlaeger house when Dad pulled into the driveway. The Jaguar was still where Frank had parked it. The front door to the house was open despite the bitter cold, but at least it had stopped raining.

"I'll take the car home—y'all are in charge of getting him home safely." Frank leaned over and kissed my cheek. "I'll see you at the house, okay? Taylor, you're in charge till I get there, and don't let him do anything he shouldn't, okay?"

Taylor nodded. Frank got out and walked over to a group of police officers. I watched through the window as Dad reversed the car and headed back down the driveway.

Taylor patted my shoulder. "How ya doing, champ?"

My tongue felt like it had swollen, and so I had to talk slowly so he could understand me. "I've...had...better...days." My eyelids began to droop.

"Just sleep until we get home, okay?"

The next thing I knew a dull throb in my side woke me up. I opened my eyes as the car turned the corner at Rampart onto Esplanade. I moaned, and Mom's head popped up over the front seat. "Are you in pain?"

"Yes," I gasped out.

She shook a pill out of a bottle and handed it to me, along with a bottle of water. I choked it down with a glug of the water and leaned back into the seat.

It felt like someone was stabbing me in the side with a butter knife...and turning it.

I breathed shallowly as the car headed down Esplanade, my eyes closed.

I opened them again as the car stopped at the curb across Decatur Street from our apartment. Taylor got out and came around to open the door for me. Mom handed me two bottles of pills. "You just took another pain pill, so you can't take another for an hour," she said. "And the others are antibiotics, one every four hours so you won't get an infection. Your father and I will take the car home and then come back to take care of you. Are you sure you don't want to come home with us?"

Sweating from the effort and the pain, I turned to get out of the car. "I just want to be in my own place," I gasped out, amazed at the effort it took.

Would I—*could* I—make it up the stairs?

"We'll be back in about twenty minutes, then," she said.

I put my feet down on the pavement. The cold wind from the river felt good for once. "No need," I replied. "Frank and Taylor can take care of me. And I'll call if I need you." I kissed my hand and touched Mom's forehead. "Don't go all Mama Bear on me, Mom. I love you both, but I'll be okay."

I closed the car door and shuffled across the street. The cold wind was kind of bracing, and I looked back to wave at Mom and Dad while Taylor fiddled with the keys to the gate.

By the time I'd shuffled down the passageway into the courtyard, the pain was completely gone and my brain was feeling pleasantly fluffy again. *This*, I thought, *is why people get hooked on opioids*. I had to stop to catch my breath a few times on my way up the stairs, Taylor patiently waiting for me until I could focus on climbing the next step.

When I finally reached the landing outside our apartment door, Taylor got the door unlocked. I had a brief moment of anxiety—*what if there's a Russian here I am completely useless at this point*—but then remembered Lindy and Rhoda were watching things and stepped through the door into the apartment.

Taylor helped me into the bedroom and I sat down hard on the bed with a sigh of relief. He helped me get undressed and into my sweats, then into bed.

"You sure you don't need anything?" Taylor asked. "Let me get you some water for your nightstand, so you can take your pills."

I closed my eyes and rested my head against my pillow. My bed felt wonderful. It was cold inside the apartment, but even the wind rattling the window felt comforting now that I was home and in my own bed.

Taylor put the glass of water down next to my pill bottles on the nightstand.

"Are you okay?" I asked. "It's been a hell of a few days, hasn't it?"

He nodded. "It's a lot to process, but yeah, I think I'm going to be okay, really. I'm having lunch with my mom tomorrow. I know—you don't have to say it, I know how you feel about my parents, and my stupid father trying to send me to gay conversion therapy hasn't helped. But Mom says she's sorry. She should have stood up to my father before and has been sorry ever since that she didn't. This kidnapping and gay conversion thing was the last straw. She says she's going to divorce him if he doesn't straighten up."

"Mmmm-hmmmm."

"Are you being a dick, or can you not talk?"

"I can talk." My tongue felt like it was too big for my mouth, and the words came out slurred. "Just...want...you...to...be... happy."

"I know." He smiled at me, and it was almost like his pre–Eric Brewer smile, but there was a sadness to his eyes that broke my heart just a little bit. His smile still lit up his handsome, heartbreakingly young face, but not quite as brightly as it used to before Eric Brewer got him into his clutches.

I hoped that his light would shine again as bright as it had before, in time.

He is a creature of light and love, I heard the Goddess's voice in my head say again.

"I'm still not happy with either one of them," he went on. "And if we're going to have a relationship—well, they are my parents and I'd like to have some relationship with them. And it is Christmas season and all…and," he patted my leg, "I'd hate for something to happen to them before we had a chance to try to make up, you know?"

"You're such a good kid," I slurred. "They should be proud of you."

He nodded and grinned at me shyly. "Yes, they should. Mom thinks my dad is thinking a bit more clearly now—I guess the Ninjas put the fear of God into him." His face clouded over. "But if it's going to be conversion therapy or just telling me over and over that I'm going to hell, well…" And now the smile did completely light up his face, the way it used to, and I was so happy my eyes began to tear up. "I have my new family, and it's so awesome I don't need to have any other family, you know?" He leaned down and kissed my forehead. "Do you need anything?"

I shook my head. "I just want to sleep for a little while."

Taylor nodded. "The painkillers. Go ahead and fall asleep, Scotty. I'll just sit here and play games on my phone so I'm here if you need me."

Such a great kid, I thought, and drifted off to sleep.

I woke up in the early morning light. Frank was snoring next to me—I'd know that snore anywhere—and my wound was aching slightly. I took a deep breath and sat up in the bed, which made the throbbing only slightly worse. I managed to get to my feet and, with some deep breaths along the way, hobbled into the bathroom to wash my face and brush my teeth. I knew I couldn't get the bandage wet, so a shower was out of the question, but the hot water felt good on my face.

Shivering, I pulled on my robe and slipped on my house shoes and padded down to the kitchen to make myself some coffee. The throbbing wasn't great, I thought as the Keurig brewed my Starbucks Italian Roast, but it was something I could live with.

I didn't need any more of the painkillers, fun as they were. The last thing I needed was an opioid addiction. I'd stick to weed, thank you very much.

I sat down at the computer and checked my emails. Nothing but junk. There were, I noticed as I started doing a search for Amanda Lautenschlaeger online, several vases with roses spread out on every available surface in the living room. It took me another minute to realize people had probably sent them to me because I'd been shot.

There were plenty of write-ups about Amanda's arrest and my shooting, the discovery of the baseball bats in the back of her car, her past issues with mental illness—but there wasn't any mention of the girl she'd killed in high school; what was her name again? Oh, yes, Deborah Holt.

I did a search on her name, not expecting much to come up—after all, she'd died in the early days of the internet; the best I could hope for was maybe some archived things—and sure enough, her funeral announcement popped up as the first thing on the list. I clicked on it. It was from the *Times-Picayune*, complete with what had to be her junior class photograph.

It was odd, but...she looked familiar.

She'd been about Rain's age, but I don't think she'd been friends with my sister. I remembered most of Rain's friends from high school, and almost all of them went to McGehee with her. I would have remembered if she'd had any friends from Newman High School. I read the obituary quickly: grandparents and parents, a younger sister, Ilana.

I did a quick search on her parents—both were dead; one in the late 90s, the other in 2003.

Of Ilana Holt, there was nothing other than that funeral notice, and those of her parents.

How weird was that?

I got up and made another cup of coffee, dumping the grounds out of the reusable pod and refilling it.

Something just wasn't sitting right with me about any of this.

Sure, Amanda had confessed, but why would she have killed Eric? And why kill Megan? Megan was happily married, not involved with Billy Barron at all; and why would Amanda want to kill Megan now, after all these years, if the motive was to make sure no one was around who knew she'd killed Deborah? Megan and Fidelis had been around for years, so why now?

Amanda got in touch with me, wanted to see if I wanted to do the show. I wasn't sure why she thought of me, but I wasn't interested. I told her to get in touch with Rebecca.

That was what Jane Barron had said, wasn't it?

Even if Amanda was involved in the casting, why would she kill Eric?

It didn't make sense.

I'm sure the district attorney, the network, and the cops were thrilled to have the case solved and wrapped up in a nice little bow, with Amanda as the fall girl.

That didn't mean she'd done it.

I signed into Traceanyone.com. It's a website mostly for private eyes—you have to scan your license and submit it with your application to join, and it's like a hundred dollars a year—but it comes in handy when you're trying to trace someone. It follows Social Security numbers and tax returns around the country, so no matter whatever your name is, if you file your income taxes and pay bills from an address linked to your social, it's listed.

I typed in *Ilana Holt, New Orleans* and did some quick math to figure out year of birth.

Ilana had left New Orleans for New York, had had several addresses over the years in the city, varying from Manhattan to Queens to Brooklyn and back to Queens again.

But there was an asterisk next to her second New York address. An asterisk usually meant something like a name change, and if you clicked on it, it would take you to another page about the name change. Usually, it meant the person had gotten married.

I clicked.

I rolled backward in my chair.

September 14, 2004. Name legally changed from Ilana Holt to Sloane Gaylord.

Sloane Gaylord.

Sloane Gaylord.

CHAPTER TWENTY-FIVE
THE TOWER
Selfish ambition about to come to naught

Sloane Gaylord was behind everything.

My hands shaking slightly, I reached for my cell phone and scrolled through my past calls until I found Brandon's phone number.

But this time, he answered.

"Scotty?" He sounded pleased. "I'm sorry I haven't called you back. You can't imagine how insane things have been since Friday night."

Oh, I can imagine quite easily, actually. "Well, I'm glad you answered this time."

"I'm so happy you called. I wanted to call you once I heard about...what happened yesterday at Margery's, but I wasn't sure...I wasn't sure if I should." He swallowed. "Are you okay?"

"Yeah, I'm okay, doing better today." I shifted a bit in my chair and winced as pain from my side knifed through me. *Maybe I should take a pill.*

Deal with it, Scotty. That's how addictions get started. It's just a little throb. Tough it out.

"I'm so sorry, I mean, I've never known anyone who's been shot before, you know?" He hesitated. "I mean, I really liked you when we met and thought we'd made a connection—"

A connection? Are you fucking kidding me?

I lifted my sweatshirt and looked at the bandage. It was dry, so the wound hadn't opened. Another pain shot through me, so intense I clenched my teeth to keep from screaming.

"And maybe when you're better we could have dinner or

something?" He sounded breathless. "I mean, since it looks like the show is getting picked up for another season, and I'll be taking over for Eric." He sounded triumphant. "I just got the call from the network. It's temporary, of course, they have to do a search for a replacement, but if I'm already doing the job...and let's face it, I was already doing the job..." He continued babbling on in the background as another intense throb radiated out from the wound. I gripped the desk edge with both hands, breaking out into a cold sweat.

And it faded away like it never happened.

See, you didn't need a pill.

But what if it comes back? It's getting worse.

Take a pill, a voice whispered in the back of my brain.

"Well, congratulations." I said, breathing a little harder than I should have been. "We definitely should celebrate when I'm better."

He clicked his tongue. "That Amanda Lautenschlaeger, right? I knew there was something off about that woman. And to think, she killed Eric and three cast members! You wouldn't believe how crazy things have been with the network since Saturday...social media is exploding! It could be our highest rated franchise ever, but we've got to figure out now how to do a reunion and what the best way to recast for the second season would be and..."

I closed my eyes as he kept rambling on about the network and the decisions that would have to be made about the show, and when he finally paused to take a breath, I said, "How well do you know Sloane Gaylord? How long has she worked for Eric's production company?"

"What?" I could hear him inhale. "Why? What does Sloane have to do with anything?"

"Sloane Gaylord isn't really Sloane Gaylord," I said, my side starting to throb again. My racing heartbeat was probably making the wound hurt, so I needed to calm down. I took some deep cleansing breaths, focused on slowing my heart rate.

Focus, Scotty. This is important.

"What do you mean she isn't Sloane Gaylord? Look, don't you live in the lower Quarter?" he asked. "Why don't I stop by and we can talk?"

"I—" I almost screamed as the pain came back again. I tilted the phone away from my mouth and began breathing rapidly, little bursts of air to control the pain. I needed to just relax and breathe, not give into the temptation to take a pill. "Okay." I gave him the address. "Text me when you get here and I'll buzz you in."

I didn't want the buzzer to wake Frank.

"On my way!" Brandon hung up.

The pain was getting incredibly intense. I had to stop several times as I hobbled down the hallway to the bedroom, catching my breath, trying to take deep breaths, trying to focus on something, anything, other than the pain and the dull ache and the throbbing, but it wasn't helping, nothing was helping. I needed another pill. It seemed to take me forever, but I finally made it to the bedroom and there it was, sitting on my nightstand on my side of the bed, that magic brown bottle with the label on the side and I resisted the urge to get over there as fast as I could without reopening the wound and instead shuffled slowly. I opened the bottle, shook out one of the little white pills, and held it in my hand for a moment, looking at it.

Trying to decide whether I should take it or deal with the pain instead. Opioids were highly addictive, after all, and once the pills were gone…

There was a bottle of water on the nightstand. I washed the pill down with it and waited for the pain to go away.

Frank was still snoring, so I shut the door behind me while I waited for Brandon to show up. The entire time my mind was racing from thought to thought.

It couldn't be a coincidence all these years later that Deborah Holt's younger sister was involved in production of the show, and three people who'd been peripherally involved in Deborah's death had been murdered. I didn't have any evidence, but I knew I was right—call it intuition, my gift, whatever—I was positive Sloane was behind everything. Maybe she hadn't swung the baseball bats herself, but there was no doubt in my mind that Amanda had been manipulated by Sloane into killing the other women.

It all made sense. Sloane was involved with casting, worked with Eric, saw her chance to get even with everyone. Sloane must have been the one who approached Amanda, tried to get her on the show, get her help with casting. Amanda, of course, would have wanted her old friends from high school on the show, and hey, why not Billy's stepmother?

And his current mistress?

Sloane could have whispered poison into Amanda's ear, knowing she was mentally unstable. And if Amanda hadn't taken her bait, there was no reason why Sloane couldn't have done the murders herself and framed Amanda. Amanda would go to jail, and the people involved with the cover-up of Deborah Holt's death would all be dead.

But where did Eric fit into this? Had he figured it out, somehow?

Sloane certainly would have had a key card to Eric's room.

But could Sloane really be a criminal mastermind? A master manipulator? She was so bland and colorless, barely saying a word unless addressed directly.

It could have all been an act, of course.

No, it couldn't be. It had to be a crazy coincidence. If she wanted revenge on all these people because they'd killed her sister all those years ago, or helped cover it all up, what a weird plan to come up with: cast a reality show in New Orleans, get everyone involved in the murder all those years ago cast on the show, and then start killing them all.

And where did Eric's murder fit into all of this, if it fit at all?

But...if you took Eric's murder away from the equation, it all could fit together.

Eric's murder was the outlier.

Maybe...maybe Eric's murder wasn't connected? We all assumed it was because all the victims were connected through the show.

Or maybe I just wanted to believe they were connected because that moved any suspicion away from Taylor.

I felt a little nauseated. Wasn't that what they call confirmation bias? I so desperately wanted to believe Taylor hadn't killed Eric that I was making connections that weren't necessarily there...oh Goddess. That couldn't be the case, could it?

Didn't you overlook all the evidence pointing at Colin when it was patently obvious to everyone else he'd murdered my uncles?

"But he wasn't the killer," I whispered. Sure, years later, Colin had been cleared of any responsibility in those murders...but this might not be the first time I'd refused to see something that was right in front of my face.

I heard movement upstairs and glanced at the ceiling.

You're being completely ridiculous. And even if Taylor DID kill Eric, it was justifiable. The guy drugged him and was going to RAPE him.

The pain pill is fucking with your mind.

I walked over to one of the windows and pushed it open, unlatching the shutters and looking out.

It was gray outside, but it was also definitely snowing. Big, fat, wet flakes, like in every Christmas movie I'd ever seen.

Shivering, I pulled the shutters closed and slid the window back down. I just had time to make it back to the kitchen when my phone buzzed.

I'm downstairs.

I hit the intercom button. "Brandon?"

"Hey, Scotty, yeah, it's me."

"Follow the walk to the courtyard, and then come up the back steps to the third floor, and knock," I replied, pressing the unlock button. I heard it buzzing and kept holding the button down until I heard the big metal door slam back into place.

That was one of the rules Millie and Velma had insisted on— always listen until you hear the door slam shut.

The door was spring-loaded, so it would slam itself shut, but there was still always the possibility that someone could leave it slightly ajar, so the lock wouldn't catch.

And then anyone could come in.

Ordinarily, I rarely just buzzed someone in. I always went down and made sure it was someone I wanted to let in.

But I didn't want to wake up Frank, nor did I want to try the stairs with my injury and having just taken a pill that was making me feel a little loopy.

Besides, it was snowing outside. I might not go out of the house again until spring.

I did, however, put on my trench coat and walk back down to the end of the hall. I opened the back door while I waited for him to make it up the stairs. I couldn't believe what I could see from the doorway. The courtyard was a winter wonderland. The fountain had frozen, and the ice had a coating of snow. It was a big wet heavy snow, too. Usually snow in New Orleans is a very brief phenomenon—and it's usually just a light dusting that melts once the clouds clear and the sun comes out. The roof of the shed was covered with it, and so was the roof of the parking garage. I heard his footsteps before I saw him, and then he was there, his face red with the cold and his nose running slightly. I opened the door to let him in and he smiled at me as he wiped his nose. "I'd hug you, but I don't want to hurt you," he said as we walked down the hallway. He had a cup of steaming coffee in one hand. "I thought it didn't get cold here?"

"Well, not like up north, no, but it does. This is unusual." I showed him into the living room "Can I take your coat?"

"I'll keep it on for the moment, I'm really cold." He flashed that handsome smile at me again, and I couldn't help but smile back. He really was ridiculously good looking. "So you were saying something about Sloane?"

I sat down, wincing a little bit. "Sloane...it's a long story, but her real name is Ilana Holt, and she's from New Orleans originally." I rapidly explained how her older sister Deborah had been killed by Amanda for the crime of dating Billy Barron. "Megan and Fidelis helped Amanda get away with it—they were all friends," I went on. "They helped hush the whole thing up, made it seem like an accident. And now, all this time later, here's Sloane, working for the show, and the people who killed her sister are getting murdered."

"But how does Chloe fit in?"

"Chloe was seeing Billy, and Billy said it was getting serious," I said. "Billy thought she was ready to leave her husband, and he was ready to marry her."

"But wasn't he also sleeping with Fidelis?"

I took a deep breath and felt a bit of pain in my side again. "I think Sloane was either manipulating Amanda into killing everyone..." My voice trailed off. What had sounded so good in my head didn't sound so brilliant now that I was saying it out loud.

Brandon smiled at me. "Or maybe Sloane was killing the people who killed her sister, and Amanda took it upon herself to kill Chloe, since she was her main rival for Billy."

"But that doesn't explain—" I stopped, because for the second time in less than twenty-four hours I was looking down the barrel of a gun.

"You really are more than just a pretty face, aren't you?" Brandon said, shaking his head. He was still wearing his gloves—of course. And he'd left his coat on because the gun was in the pocket and he needed access to it.

Seriously, I can be incredibly stupid at times.

"Your nephew, of course, wasn't the first person Eric drugged." Brandon rolled his eyes. "You have any idea how humiliating that was for me? 'We can't tell anyone we're a couple because the network will make me fire you, Brandon. We can't tell, we have to be secret, we have to'…"

Brandon.

And Eric.

I felt sick.

"And the whole time he's drugging these people, having sex with them, paying them off or getting the network to pay them off. Oh, the bodies I've helped buried for that little prick! All the while waiting, waiting, because he promised to make me a producer of the next show. And then it wouldn't matter and we could be an open couple…and then came New Orleans and, 'oh, Brandon, we're not ready for you to produce just yet, the network won't go for it.'" His eyes narrowed. "Which was bullshit, because I had someone…well, Eric wasn't the only person who could use his body to get what he wanted."

"Sloane had nothing to do with any of it," I said slowly. "You did it all, you killed them all, to cover up that Eric was the real victim."

"I take it back. You're not that smart," Brandon said. "I knew Sloane, she'd worked for us for years. She's smart. Of course, Eric never took her seriously. She'd been trying to get us to do a New Orleans show for years. And when we did, she took a big part in the casting. It didn't take long for me to figure out she was up to something." He laughed. "Also not as smart as she thinks she is. Once I knew she was trying to use this season to get those bitches to admit they killed her sister and covered it up…well, she was like putty in my hands. Why count on them confessing on camera when you can just kill them all?" He waved the gun. "Sorry about your nephew; Eric wasn't supposed to go out that night. He was supposed to stay in. I was going to kill him that night. Sloane had stolen the bats from Billy's when we'd filmed there, and I had one of them. Sloane was going to kill Fidelis the next night, and then Megan, and we were going to plant the bats in Amanda's car."

"But Amanda was so jealous, she took one of the bats and killed Chloe."

"At first, I was concerned, but it really wasn't that big a deal. It actually helped." He smirked. "It confused everyone. And I realized if the police thought the show was being targeted, that would muddle everything up even more. So, we went on with our plan." He pointed the gun at me. "But you had to go get smart and figure out who Sloan was."

"You were there."

I turned. Taylor was standing there in the hallway, staring at Brandon, pointing at him. He was wearing his Tulane sweat outfit and his face was white, drained of color. "You were there," he said again, stepping into the big room, his voice shaking but his finger steady. "The night Eric was killed. I was in the bedroom, feeling woozy, and I heard voices. I got up and walked to the door and saw you. You hit him. With a baseball bat. You killed him."

"Aw, now, Taylor, why'd you have to go and say that?" Brandon turned the gun toward him. "Now I'm going to have to kill both of you."

"Taylor, get out of here," I said, wincing as I stood up. The gun turned back toward me.

"You move so much as a muscle," Brandon said, "and I'll shoot your uncle."

I've never hated anyone so much in my entire life.

I could feel it building inside me.

And before I knew what I was doing, I launched myself at Brandon while screaming at the top of my lungs. I felt the stitches in my side tear again and the pain, oh God, the pain, but Brandon didn't know what to do, how to react—maybe the Goddess was looking out for me, I don't know, but I hit him with my full body weight, driving him backward into the wingback chair, which flipped over. The gun went off and my ears, oh my ears hurt and my eyes watered and I could smell powder and he was hitting me, but I kept my head down and wrapped my arms around him and scissored his legs with mine.

I might not have wrestled in over twenty years, but I still had my instincts.

I shoved a hand into his Adam's apple and he wheezed, gasping for breath.

"Don't move," a voice said from behind us.

Wincing in agony, I rolled off Brandon to see Frank, looking hot as ever in just a pair of black underwear, pointing his gun at Brandon. "The cops are on their way," he said grimly. "Taylor, get an extension cord to tie him up with."

I stood up, wincing, feeling the hot blood running down my side. "You might," I said as I sank down onto the sofa, "want to call an ambulance, too."

EPILOGUE

My grandparents' house was ablaze with light as the Lyft driver pulled up to the front gate.

One of my favorite Christmas traditions was our annual reveillon feast after midnight mass on Christmas Eve. Reveillon meals were an old New Orleans tradition; you were supposed to fast all day before the midnight Christmas mass, and then afterward a late night feast.

Granted, you probably shouldn't eat so late at night before going to bed, but tradition is tradition.

Every year after attending a midnight mass the family headed over to Papa Diderot's in the Garden District for reveillon. Most of the family went to a different service uptown—Mom and Dad skip it entirely and just go straight to Papa and Maman's—but I always liked going to St. Louis Cathedral. Sure, it was always crowded and hot, but there was something about the ritual performed in the majesty of the beautiful old cathedral that touched my heart in ways Catholicism usually didn't.

And really, you can't beat the Catholics when it comes to mystic rituals.

The weather had warmed up some but was still colder than I prefer.

We hadn't heard anything more from Colin. The Ninjas were still out there, listening and trying to find out what they could about both Colin and Blackledge, but there was never anything other than radio silence to report back to us. And the more time passed without any word from Colin, the more worrying it was.

All we could do was go on with our lives, hope for the best, and wait.

The Ninjas had also designed and overseen the installation of a top-of-the-line security system for the house. Whether it made us safer, I don't know, but I certainly felt safer and had started sleeping better.

The bullet wound was almost completely healed, and I was barely aware of it anymore. I was going to have a lovely scar, though. When I was younger I would have been upset about it, but now…

Frank's scar certainly made him look sexier. Granted, mine was a round hole in the front and back of my left love handle…and I'd already vowed to make the love handles go away in the new year if it killed me.

Venus and Blaine were still sorting out the mess from all the murders. There still was no word from Diva whether they were going to air the season or not, and the hubbub was finally starting to die down on the gossip sites and in the tabloids. Amanda was locked up in a mental hospital and had already been declared unfit to stand trial; I'm sure Lautenschlaeger cash had gone a long way to greasing that particular wheel.

Neither Brandon nor Sloane were talking, but the way Venus and Blaine had explained it to us went something like this:

Sloane had always wanted to avenge her sister's murder and punish everyone who had any hand in either her death or the resulting cover-up: Amanda, her mother, Billy, Fidelis, and Megan. She knew Amanda was unstable and Margery's money would always bail her out of trouble. For many years her revenge fantasies were just that—fantasies. Her big break came when she got the job with Diva, and shortly after she started, the casting for the New Orleans franchise started.

Brandon's relationship with Eric had been deteriorating for years, and he also knew Sloane's back story; knowing she was originally from New Orleans and had changed her name was why he had originally moved her from the Manhattan franchise to the New Orleans one. When she started recommending cast members, he dug a little deeper into her past…and he was smart enough to figure out that Sloane was up to something; why else would she be casting people involved in her sister's homicide?

We may never know if Brandon and Sloane were actually working together or if he had just seen an opportunity to get rid of Eric once and for all, and took it. He was a good improviser, and there'd been enough filming at the Barron place on the North Shore for him to have access to one of Billy's old bats. We can also assume he knew that the security system at the Aquitaine was down…we may never know if Brandon planned to kill Eric that night or if Eric's interest in Taylor that night was what pushed him over the edge. But the cops found Rohypnol in his hotel room when they searched it; it's entirely possible that Brandon was the one who drugged Taylor rather than Eric. Why? Again, we may never know.

My theory is that he'd taken the bat he used from the Barron house just in case. Eric's interest in Taylor the night of the premiere pushed him over the edge. I think he drugged Taylor, not just to ruin Eric's chances with his twink du jour but to possibly even frame him for an assault or rape charge. Something happened to make him snap, and Brandon retrieved the bat and killed him with Taylor there in the suite.

And when both Chloe and Fidelis turned up dead the same night—with a similar murder weapon—well, the three murders were so entangled that the cops might not ever sort out the mess.

I also think Amanda killed Chloe; the bat in the trunk of her car was bloodstained and Chloe's DNA was on it.

Sloane killed Fidelis that same night. No one even suspected her, and the other two murders that night must have also made her feel pretty safe. What were the odds the cops would do a deep dive on her and find out she was Deborah Holt's sister? She must have felt pretty confident when she'd gone over to Megan's that day to kill her. She wasn't even being looked at as a suspect.

We were the last to arrive at Maman and Papa's. Everyone was already gathered in the massive living room, eating.

The enormous tree was lit up, and the entire room was decorated to within an inch of its life. Taylor made a beeline for the food table as I took our coats and hung them in the vestibule. Ice was tinkling in glasses, knives and forks were scraping on fine china as I joined Frank at the food table. We loaded up our plates and found seats at the dining room table.

I looked across the table at Taylor. The dark circles under his eyes were fading, and his color had come back. He'd blown through his finals easily, or so he claimed, and he was seeing a therapist twice a week. He was still sleeping in the spare room on our floor, but he was also sleeping through the night again.

He's going to be fine. It's just going to take some time.

His mother had filed for divorce and was looking for her own place. As we'd figured, neither his father nor the ex-gay minister reported anything to the police. We'd not heard from either since. Taylor and his mother were taking things slow, but she wanted to live in New Orleans to be close to him. I didn't like it but was biting my tongue and keeping a close eye on her.

She needs to earn my trust—and it's going to take a good long while.

Frank placed his hand on my leg as Papa Diderot launched into a story about Mom when she was a little girl. We'd all heard the story a million times, but it was one he loved to tell, so we always pretended to listen. I smiled at Frank and looked at the head of the table where my grandfather was gesticulating madly while he imitated my mother at age eleven. Maman was sitting next to him, her eyes adoringly on him. I looked around the table.

I was blessed, always had been.

I put my hand on Frank's and leaned in to whisper, "I wish Colin was here."

"Me, too."

We had never talked about the Colin situation. Maybe it was avoidance, I don't know. But I loved him still, and knew Frank did, too. Whenever one of us brought up the subject, the other dismissed it. We couldn't keep putting it off forever, but as more time passed it didn't quite seem so pressing.

Venus and Blaine never found the driver of the car that hit me. It made me nervous he was still out there...but it had something to do with Colin. I know it did.

I also knew more than I was letting Frank know...which was cowardly. I had already made up my mind to talk to him after the holidays. We seem to have tacitly agreed to table the Colin situation until the new year.

I closed my eyes.

It was the security cameras, you see, at the corner bar. We now had our own security cameras, thanks to the Ninjas, but I couldn't stop thinking about how Bestuzhev had gotten into our apartment and waited for Colin. I couldn't stop thinking about how Frank had bribed someone at the bar to get the recording of the afternoon Taylor's dad had kidnapped him right off the street.

So, one day while Taylor was taking finals and Frank was out Christmas shopping, I walked down there and talked to the manager.

Their system recorded digital files and uploaded them to the cloud, with dates and times.

Getting the computer file for the night Bestuzhev was murdered in our apartment cost me a couple of hundred bucks.

A couple of hundred dollars to find out Colin had lied to me, to us.

Again.

At a few minutes past eleven, Colin had come around the corner from Barracks Street, arm in arm, laughing, with Bestuzhev. He used his key and let them both into the front gate.

He'd lied to me. He hadn't come home and been surprised by Bestuzhev in our apartment.

He brought him there. Probably to kill him.

There was no way I was showing Frank that recording before Christmas.

My phone vibrated in my shirt pocket and I could hear Frank's doing the same. I pulled my phone out and there was a text message across the screen:

Merry Xmas, love you, hope to be home soon.—C

Frank and I looked at each other and smiled. Both of us had tears in our eyes.

"He's alive," Frank whispered to me.

I wiped at my eyes, hoping no one had noticed.

I had so many questions for Colin…and maybe I wouldn't like some of the answers.

Life doesn't give you anything you can't handle, after all—it's how you handle it that matters.

I looked around at my family again, from my parents to my grandparents to my siblings to their spouses to my uncles.

So incredibly blessed, I thought again.

He's coming home.

About the Author

Greg Herren is a New Orleans–based author and editor. He is a co-founder of the Saints and Sinners Literary Festival, which takes place in New Orleans every spring. He is the author of thirty-three novels, including the Lambda Literary Award–winning *Murder in the Rue Chartres*, called by the *New Orleans Times-Picayune* "the most honest depiction of life in post-Katrina New Orleans published thus far." He co-edited *Love, Bourbon Street: Reflections on New Orleans*, which also won the Lambda Literary Award. His young adult novel *Sleeping Angel* won the Moonbeam Gold Medal for Excellence in Young Adult Mystery/Horror, and *Lake Thirteen* won the silver. He co-edited *Night Shadows: Queer Horror*, which was shortlisted for the Shirley Jackson Award. He also won the Anthony Award for his anthology *Blood on the Bayou*.

He has published over fifty short stories in markets as varied as *Ellery Queen's Mystery Magazine* to the critically acclaimed anthology *New Orleans Noir* to various websites, literary magazines, and anthologies. His erotica anthology *FRATSEX* is the all-time best selling title for Insightout Books. He has worked as an editor for Bella Books, Harrington Park Press, and now Bold Strokes Books. His short stories have been nominated for both Anthony and Macavity Awards.

A longtime resident of New Orleans, Greg was a fitness columnist and book reviewer for Window Media for over four years, publishing in the LGBT newspapers *IMPACT News*, *Southern Voice*, and *Houston Voice*. He served a term on the Board of Directors for the National Stonewall Democrats and served on the founding committee of the Louisiana Stonewall Democrats. He is currently employed as a public health researcher for the NO/AIDS Task Force and served four years on the board of directors for the Mystery Writers of America.

Books Available From Bold Strokes Books

Royal Street Reveillon by Greg Herren. In this Scotty Bradley mystery, someone is killing the stars of a reality show, and it's up to Scotty Bradley and the boys to find out who. (978-1-63555-545-5)

Death Takes a Bow by David S. Pederson. Alan Keys takes part in a local stage production, but when the leading man is murdered, his partner Detective Heath Barrington is thrust into the limelight to find the killer. (978-1-63555-472-4)

Accidental Prophet by Bud Gundy. Days after his grandmother dies, Drew Morten learns his true identity and finds himself racing against time to save civilization from the apocalypse. (978-1-63555-452-6)

In Case You Forgot by Fredrick Smith and Chaz Lamar. Zaire and Kenny, two newly single, Black, queer, and socially aware men, start again—in love, career, and life—in the West Hollywood neighborhood of LA. (978-1-63555-493-9)

Counting for Thunder by Phillip Irwin Cooper. A struggling actor returns to the Deep South to manage a family crisis but finds love and ultimately his own voice as his mother is regaining hers for possibly the last time. (978-1-63555-450-2)

Survivor's Guilt and Other Stories by Greg Herren. Award-winning author Greg Herren's short stories are finally pulled together into a single collection, including the Macavity Award–nominated title story and the first-ever Chanse MacLeod short story. (978-1-63555-413-7)

Saints + Sinners Anthology 2019, edited by Tracy Cunningham and Paul Willis. An anthology of short fiction featuring the finalist selections from the 2019 Saints + Sinners Literary Festival. (978-1-63555-447-2)

The Shape of the Earth by Gary Garth McCann. After appearing in *Best Gay Love Stories*, *HarringtonGMFQ*, *Q Review*, and *Off the Rocks*, Lenny and his partner Dave return in a hotbed of manhood and jealousy. (978-1-63555-391-8)

Exit Plans for Teenage Freaks by 'Nathan Burgoine. Cole always has a plan—especially for escaping his small-town reputation as "that kid who was kidnapped when he was four"—but when he teleports to a museum, it's time to face facts: it's possible he's a total freak after all. (978-1-163555-098-6)

Death Checks In by David S. Pederson. Despite Heath's promises to Alan to not get involved, Heath can't resist investigating a shopkeeper's murder in Chicago, which dashes their plans for a romantic weekend getaway. (978-1-163555-329-1)

Of Echoes Born by 'Nathan Burgoine. A collection of queer fantasy short stories set in Canada from Lambda Literary Award finalist 'Nathan Burgoine. (978-1-63555-096-2)

The Lurid Sea by Tom Cardamone. Cursed to spend eternity on his knees, Nerites is having the time of his life. (978-1-62639-911-2)

Sinister Justice by Steve Pickens. When a vigilante targets citizens of Jake Finnigan's hometown, Jake and his partner Sam fall under suspicion themselves as they investigate the murders. (978-1-63555-094-8)

Club Arcana: Operation Janus by Jon Wilson. Wizards, demons, Elder Gods: Who knew the universe was so crowded, and that they'd all be out to get Angus McAslan? (978-1-62639-969-3)

Triad Soul by 'Nathan Burgoine. Luc, Anders, and Curtis—vampire, demon, and wizard—must use their powers of blood, soul, and magic to defeat a murderer determined to turn their city into a battlefield. (978-1-62639-863-4)

Gatecrasher by Stephen Graham King. Aided by a high-tech thief, the Maverick Heart crew race against time to prevent a cadre of savage corporate mercenaries from seizing control of a revolutionary wormhole technology. (978-1-62639-936-5)

Wicked Frat Boy Ways by Todd Gregory. Beta Kappa brothers Brandon Benson and Phil Connor play an increasingly dangerous game of love, seduction, and emotional manipulation. (978-1-62639-671-5)